THE EDGE OF ANOTHER WORLD

ALSO BY PEPITA SETH

The Spirit Land (1994)

Heaven on Earth: The Universe of Kerala's Guruvayur Temple (2009)

THE EDGE OF ANOTHER WORLD

Pepita Seth

SPEAKING TIGER

SPEAKING TIGER PUBLISHING PVT. LTD.
4381/4, Ansari Road, Daryaganj,
New Delhi–110002, India

First published by Speaking Tiger Publishing Pvt. Ltd. 2015

ISBN: 978-93-85288-37-1
eISBN: 978-93-85288-38-8

10 9 8 7 6 5 4 3 2 1

Typeset in Nebraska Regular by SÜRYA, New Delhi

For Ulisses Rolim

CONTENTS

For she is more beautiful than the sun, and above all the orders of stars; being compared with the light, she is found before it. She is the brightness of the everlasting light, the unspotted mirror of the power of God.

—*Wisdom 7.26*

Sarvam khalu idam evaham
Nanyadasti sanatanam.

Whatever is seen here is myself and myself alone.
There is nothing else that is imperishable.

—*Devibhagavatham*

PROLOGUE

Who am I?

Of course you think this is a simple question, and one I should have no difficulty in answering. Just tell me you think, just give me an answer, satisfy my curiosity, give me your name, age and sex, tell me where and how you live and who and what you are. This is the beginning and so we must get to know each other, we must be introduced. I understand your feelings, and am touched by them. Of course I am. And yet I hesitate, wondering how you will react if I tell you that your question is nowhere near as simple as you believe it to be, that it is easier to understand your curiosity than satisfy it and that all I can really do is ask questions of my own.

How indeed can I answer you? Will you really believe me if I say I am no more than a figment of the imagination, that the words you are now reading are not even mine, that I am a fiction, an invention, a deception? And even if I tell you this, and even if you believe me, will such an answer satisfy you? Will it stop you from wondering about me, from wanting to know how the stories that follow will unfold and what my role in them will be? Are you not, even now, thinking of skimming through these pages to see what clues you can find? If so be warned. Whatever snippets of information you glean will be meaningless. I am not so easily known. One of the many and unfathomable truths about me is that even when I seem to be present I am always elusive. Just as you think you are starting to know me I will slip away and disappear. Always. I am too shadowy, too indistinct, too veiled to be known so simply.

So who am I?

Again I am brought back to wondering how I can satisfy your curiosity. Should I risk telling you the truth—even though there is no single truth to tell? Shall I take the chance and tell you not to ask about me but about yourself? Shall I now, this early, and even before any real beginning has been made, tell you that if you really wish to find me you should first look into a mirror? Should I tell you that an answer will only be found—if at all one exists to be found—when you gaze into the depths of your own eyes, and then through and beyond them, into their reflection and then again beyond. If you are ever to find me you must first seek yourself.

I am because you are. I am manifest because of you. I am reflected in innumerable ways in more eyes than there are mirrors. I beat in more hearts than can be counted. There are songs, chants and hymns that endlessly describe me but they are only songs. They leave as much unsaid as said. I am like the nothingness left by burning camphor. I am and I am not. I exist in every living organism. I am formless and invisible though seen in everything. I am nameless but called by many names. I am ignored, denied, decried. I am accepted, honoured, revered. And yet I must repeat myself: I am merely a figment of the imagination. Here and not here, belonging nowhere, formlessly existing only in the hearts of those who search within themselves. Finding me as they desire me to be, as perhaps you too may find me, in the way you might one day desire me to be.

For this is how I am, have been and always will be. I am in the act of Creation and the breath of the dying. I am the breeze that shivers through trees. I am the flight of the solitary bird, the swimming of the fish, the bleating of the lamb, the howling of the jackal, the killing of the tiger. I am the wind's song, the river's flowing, the cloud's gathering, the rain's falling. I am like the waves with the sea and the flowers with the sun. The indivisible mystery. The absolute stillness. The breath and spirit of life. Standing before you in majesty. Or in simple humility. Or not at all.

Book One
SOPHIE

Mexico. The word jumped into my mind without warning. Immediately followed by: *now I'll never go to Mexico. Not now. Not ever.* Even though I'd never really thought of Mexico. One way or the other. Going or not going. It was as if the word had just appeared like a rabbit out of a hat. A word followed by the corrective thought that it was actually my *mother* who had wanted to go to Mexico. And now couldn't, wouldn't. Not now. Not ever. Which was about as certain as the fact that sometimes one has absolutely no control over one's thoughts. Especially when one's mother dies. Which was what mine had just done. So, the thought was clear now. I'd not said it but I had thought it. My mother had just died and she was the one who had always wanted to go to Mexico. Because Montezuma had lived there. But of course she never went. And now never would. And I knew that I wouldn't either, that Mexico had become as lost to me as my mother. And for the briefest moment it was the more tangible loss.

I'm uneasy with the idea of saying that everything began the day my mother died because I don't believe that life and the things that happen in it arrange themselves quite so neatly. No bell ever rings to announce the firing of a starter's gun and nothing ever really begins from a clearly defined point. Only later, when discussion is anyway pointless, does it become possible to look back and believe that certain events were triggered off by a particular incident and, though it wasn't immediately obvious, the real truth about my mother's death was that it was more of an ending—and not just of her life.

She had taken a long and painful year to die. A year which had begun with a sudden decline in her previously quite stable condition, a decline so marked that when her physical frailty finally forced her to London I could no longer sidestep the fact that she was never going to get any better. Earlier, when she first fell ill, we'd haltingly discussed the possibility of her coming to live with me but nothing was ever decided because nothing was ever quite brought out into the open. Instead we both hid behind discussing the difficulties of her leaving Phoeby Cottage and not quite knowing what to do about Bertie, her dog. No child ever knows how to talk about impending death to a parent—or anyone else for that matter—but, in the end, she made it easier for me when she called one late May evening to say she really couldn't cope, that Arthur and Mrs Boggis would take Bertie and that she wanted to be with me as much as possible. After that we both played a silly and futile game, hoping to deceive each other by pretending that as she was only coming for a short stay there wouldn't be any point in her bringing too many things. The irony of course was that she not only still brought far too much but went into hospital almost immediately, taking the few nightdresses that seemed increasingly to swamp her and were in any case immediately replaced by hospital gowns.

This charade finally ended late one evening when I got the call I had been both expecting and dreading. Somehow I still remember looking for the TV remote and lowering the volume before I picked up the receiver and heard the nurse's level and factual voice telling me to come as soon as possible. And I still remember how carefully I replaced the receiver before going into my bedroom and turning on all the lights before leaving. After that, though I remember the car stalling and how I swore, the drive to the hospital, parking and walking down the long corridors to my mother's ward are a complete blank. Of the endless night that followed I remember only odd moments. I remember shifting in the chair. I remember holding my mother's frail hand and feeling the occasional pressure of her fingers. I remember thinking it was like being connected to a shadow. And I remember thinking the awful thought *if only it was over.*

And all the while time cheated reality, shifting between the endless seconds when I held my breath and thought all signs of life had gone and the few too-short moments when a nurse came to check my mother's pulse as if everything was normal. In between I existed in a kind of limbo where my mind emptied and filled and often played, absurdly, with words. Vigil was one of them. Hope was another.

Then, just as the first streaks of daylight began filtering through the windows, she gave the faintest of sighs and it was over. And so too was all hope of Mexico.

♓

Throughout the day that followed I began measuring time in a new way. I calculated every hour and minute from a starting point that moved further and further away, going from *ten minutes ago she was still alive* to *an hour ago she was still alive* and gradually stretching, relentlessly, minute by minute to the falling of night and *this time yesterday she was still alive.* It was as if the fixed point of my mother's death had not only begun to define time in a different way but that her whole life had somehow been tidied up and placed neatly between two dates. Suddenly absolutely everything about her was in the past tense.

Yet even before that first day was over I was dealing with all the things I should have thought about earlier. Before it was forever too late. The things I should have talked to my mother about. First there was her funeral. Which I decided should be a cremation, and in London. Which led on to the doing of so much else that had to be done that I just followed instructions and moved like a sleepwalker through the demands of bureaucracy: filling in forms, making arrangements, answering questions, confirming facts and, finally, calling the people who had to be called and then handling their uncertain emotions. Whilst carefully avoiding my own.

In this way the days passed by and finally it was *this time last week she was still alive* and the evening before the funeral. An evening that drew to a close with me alone in my flat, having refused all offers of company. *Thank you, no really, I'm fine, but thanks... What? Oh yes, see you tomorrow.* And sitting there and thinking *this is it, this time last week I'd just got that phone call.* And then silence and the thought that this was really my mother's last night, that right now, just a few miles away from my warm flat she was lying still and cold. And waiting. Waiting until the morning when they would take her out, perhaps just as I was getting up. Somehow, so far, her death hadn't been marked, hadn't been real—despite the notices I'd put in the papers and the letters and visits and phone calls and flowers I'd received. Or maybe it was more that because of them she'd been noticed, talked about, in people's minds. Tomorrow though she would really start her last journey. The one that would take her, perhaps slowly, perhaps in fits and starts, into that void of absolute oblivion where the sound of her voice, her laugh, her mannerisms and the way she moved would all gradually be forgotten. Eventually she would become like a woman in an old portrait, someone with a name, a husband and children, perhaps even a lover, but whose identity somehow becomes uncertain and is eventually reduced to the anonymity of being called *An Unknown Woman.*

♓

The cremation ceremony was brief, its atmosphere sterile and almost coldly impersonal. The pallbearers arranged their faces in a mockery of grief. The lesson was read by a complete stranger who eulogized my mother as if he'd known her. The crematorium's staff sang the hymns with a gusto that drowned out not only my friends and the handful of relatives I hardly knew but the whispering voices of my mother's Suffolk friends, all looking vaguely ill at ease in their seldom worn Sunday best. I remained silent throughout, my eyes watching the coffin like an animal caught in headlights, transfixed by the small bunch of white anemones I'd placed on top. The worst moment came just as the service ended and the recorded music swelled up and the curtains behind the coffin parted to allow it to glide through the opening. I watched in horror as the coffin suddenly disappeared from view, vanishing completely as the curtains closed with a silent swish, taking my mother forever away from me. For a brief and insane moment I felt terrible rage and almost rushed forward to drag the coffin back. I wanted to shout, to scream out an angry NO, force open the lid, gather her body into my arms and carry it down to some wild sea and throw her to the elements. I felt sickened by the crematorium's sanitized denial of death and how it trivialized my mother.

But I remained still, stiff with pain and unable to move until the time came to leave the chapel. Then I stood outside with everyone else, watching them circle around like restless animals, no one quite knowing what to say. Although I'd arranged a lunch in a nearby restaurant, feeling I ought to gather everyone together and thank them for coming, all those who lived in London scurried away muttering that they had to get back whilst never quite specifying where *back* might be. The only people who remained were my mother's friends from Suffolk and I couldn't help noticing how their voices gradually rose as, quite unselfconsciously, they began to talk about her. Suddenly there was a naturalness around me that eased my tension and allowed me to listen as they reminisced about my mother, even making me laugh when a sly joke was told at her expense. Above all I realized how much the presence of Arthur and Mrs Boggis reassured me when they positioned themselves on either side of me in the restaurant, subtly acting as a barrier between my numbed mind and the people around me.

And I was grateful when they stayed back after everyone else had finally gone. Having them there softened the blow of being left alone and accepting that for everyone else it was over and that life, everyday life was going to continue. It also offered us the opportunity to discuss the practicalities of what had to be done next. Though I spoke first by raising the matter of Bertie's welfare the words were hardly out of my mouth before Mrs Boggis stopped me.

'You leave him be with us. He ain't a bit of trouble, so don't you worry, O'll see t' him,' she insisted. I smiled, imagining tiny Bertie being waited on hand and foot by the amply proportioned Mrs Boggis.

'It's the cottage though,' I continued, 'I'll have to decide...'

'Don't fuss yerself,' Arthur interrupted. 'Jes take it easy, don't rush things. We'll take care of it...'

'Oi look in regular anyway. Oi see that everything is kept clean,' said Mrs Boggis, getting in a few words before her husband spoke again.

'Yow're tired,' he pointed out, 'Its bin a long time. Now you should take some time for yerself. Go away, get a rest. We'll be here when yow want us. Don't go rushin' anything—and don't let anyone make yow.'

Arthur Boggis was right and later, after he and Mrs Boggis had left and I was alone in a suddenly unnaturally empty space, tiredness fell around me like a great blanket. It was a tiredness that came not so much from dealing with the cremation but the long, emotionally draining months that had preceded it. Yet the coming of night brought a strange combination of exhaustion and restless energy that seemed to not only possess me but make me drift aimlessly from room to room, looking for something to do. Finally I gave up and stood by the window, looking down at the darkened street, watching and waiting as if expecting an unknown someone to appear and tell me what to do. At one point I thought of going outside and walking but seeing the slight sheen of rain on the streets and sensing that it was sleep I needed I turned away from the window and went to bed. Although I unexpectedly fell asleep almost at once, I woke up with a start just after midnight. The room was quiet; all that could be heard was the faint clicking of the bedside clock and the sound of a passing car. And the thud of my heart beating. Too fast. For a moment, almost overwhelmed with panic, I wondered if something had happened to my mother before, with a sigh, I remembered that nothing would ever happen to her again. I lay down and eventually went back to a troubled sleep, waking up the next morning to a day that found me haunted by the constant feeling that I should be doing something else, that I should be somewhere else.

During the days that followed I devoted my time to dealing with whatever demanded my attention, moving in bouts of frenzied activity, making endless phone calls then hanging on and waiting for answers. I acted as relentlessly and unemotionally as someone overseeing troop movements. From time to time there were occasional, and very brief, pauses and it was in those sudden, unexpected moments that whole hosts of questions would gush towards me. It was also when, though I felt I knew why my hands were starting to shake, that nothing quite made sense. I would try saying 'My mother is dead'. I said it several times, as if hoping that the phrase, which seemed somehow to have wrapped itself in a secret code, would suddenly rearrange itself and I would be able to decipher its meaning. *My mother is dead, my mother is dead.* But it was useless. Nothing, no meaning ever seemed to emerge. I never absorbed the words or what they really meant. There was no emotion, no acceptance, no understanding. Just the bald and basic fact: *My mother is dead.* It was a fact that, with the coming of each new day and the mundane sounds of traffic, of the kettle boiling and whistling, of letters coming through the door and the telephone ringing somehow faded away into limbo, pushed aside by the things that had to be done simply because she was dead. Once, when I caught myself wondering how *long* she was going to be dead I became briefly conscious of my denial, of the fact that I hadn't quite grasped what had happened. I felt an ill-defined unease about how little her death seemed to mean to me and began to think that I was cruel and heartless. I *had* loved her hadn't I? Shouldn't I react, have some emotion, be affected? Occasionally I hoped it would all hit me when I went to bed but, except for that first restless night after the cremation, I was so exhausted by the amount I'd suddenly had to do that I tumbled into dreamless sleep as soon as my head hit the pillow.

It took just over a month for me to agree with Arthur Boggis and see that I had to take a break. I had to put a distance between the fact of my mother's death in order to deal with the dormant emotions I knew it must have generated. I had to accept that ever since she had fallen ill, and especially after she'd come to London, I'd pushed almost all my feelings aside in order to deal with her needs. And I had to understand that although she was dead, I was still on edge and constantly searching for a job that had to be done when no such need existed. And, most of all I had to realize that I was sidestepping mourning, blocking tears and denying grief.

And so it was that everything within me was perfectly aligned for a change when Leslie rang and said she was going to Portugal—on a freebie of course—and why didn't I come too? I didn't hesitate, I'd never been there before and the idea that Leslie, who has always made me laugh, was going to make all the arrangements made it easy to accept. Of course it's now glib to say I should have known better and admit that there are no decisions without repercussions. Most of all I should have known that when Leslie backed out a couple of weeks later, with the unlikely excuse of an extra work load when I knew in my bones that she'd once again found Mr Right, I should have done the same. Instead I went along with her assurances that she could fix things and that though I'd now have to pay it wouldn't be exorbitant. 'It'll do you good,' she said, 'you should go.' Perhaps too, in the same way that we often make plans, set the alarm clock and prepare ourselves for something we know we're never going to do, so it was that, though I decided I was going to cancel, I always knew I never would. My one reservation centred on the fact that I would have to go alone. Only now, with hindsight, do I think that even then I must have caught the whisper of an inner voice saying: 'Go on! Take a chance. Risk changing your life.'

♓

And so it was that, before I even knew how the time had passed, I was on an early morning flight to Lisbon. Up to that moment I'd managed to keep most of my fears and emotions in check but as the plane taxied down the runway a vague unease shivered through my body. I tried to pretend that I was merely disturbed by the suddenness with which the plane surged upwards and was instantly enveloped in a huge bank of dark clouds. I shifted in my seat, clutching at the tightness of the safety belt and fighting to dispel the idea that the endless closeness of the clouds was an omen of the unknown that awaited me. I huddled against the window, watching as we flew though an alien world, a world surrounded by an apparent nothingness, a vast greyness devoid of anything that marked progress or direction, a world without perspective or distance. Only when the man seated next to me asked if he could read the newspaper lying untouched on my lap did I manage to pull my mind back from the terrible blankness we were flying through and, for a brief moment, become part of my immediate surroundings.

Orphan.

The word popped up just like that. Unannounced. Uninvited. Like a word jumping onto a computer screen. Suddenly telling me that this is what I had become, that I was—and now always would be—an orphan. That is if The Bastard was dead. Well he was as good as dead, wasn't he? But can you be alive *and* as good as dead, I wondered? I suppose so, I wondered back, a question and answer conversation starting up in my head. After seven years anyway. They consider you legally dead after seven years. And it *has* been more than that since anyone has heard from him, the more solemn (and pedantic) of my selves observed. Don't be an idiot, I replied to myself. Stop pretending. The Bastard's been gone thirty-eight years. You never even met him. Or if you did you certainly don't remember the occasion since according to your mother's oft repeated phrase The Bastard never even bothered to say goodbye, he just pissed off without so much as a by-your-leave the week after you were born. I was born, that is.

The truth is that I hardly ever thought about The Bastard. My father The Bastard, that is. Why not? W-w-ell, I hesitated, surprised by this sudden turn of inquiry as my mind slipped casually back into its two-sided conversation. My mother I suppose. She didn't exactly encourage it. *Father* was not a word we had much use for. Or knew much about, I thought, as memories of Mary Cardy's sixth birthday party filled my mind and I remembered Mrs Cardy telling her daughter to 'Go and ask your father.' 'Who's he?' I had asked. Of course, even then, even at that age I hadn't been quite *that* naive. I'd immediately spotted my mistake. And caught the look that flashed between Mary's parents, a combination of pity and 'be careful'. Oh yes, I knew I was different and not like other children. Not that there weren't other children belonging to what are now called single parent families. There was Barbara Sweet. And Jill Byham. But though they lived with their mothers they still *saw* their fathers. They didn't really have only one parent, the other one's whereabouts unknown. The only exception had been Nina Little. Her father had died soon after the beginning of my second summer term at the high school and the whole class had gone to his funeral. I can still remember being confused—and transfixed—by the sight of Nina's weeping mother. I had wondered why she cried so much. Was that the first time I began to wonder what having a father really meant? All I had was The Bastard who'd pissed off—and I now wondered how old I had been when it finally dawned on me that this phrase of my mother's referred to my father?

All these years later I can understand why my mother had spoken like this, why she had concealed her pain under a mask of disdainful rage. Yet though I was now thirty-eight years old I was conscious that this was a forced and unnatural understanding, not an emotional one. It had been years before I had done anything more about my father than simply block out his existence. Up to then I had kept the very possibility of him at bay. If he cropped up at all it was always as The Bastard, a remote and unreal figure, a man, an entity I never thought of as having anything to do with me. I didn't even think of him as being 'out there'. At least not after the hysteria that followed me telling Judy Whymark that *my* father was in the French Foreign Legion. This was during the Beau Geste stage of my literary development and unfortunately I had not taken into consideration the possibility of there being other opinions as to where my father might actually be. As a result there had been a playground catfight and I had been sent to the dreaded inner sanctum of Miss Neame, the headmistress.

It was a meeting that brought me face to face with an unsuspected reality. A reality that, even now, makes me wonder why 'grownups' have, so often, to be so cruel. Why had Miss Neame needed to be unkind and tell me not to lie? And what had then made her add that 'everybody' knew my father had run off with that dreadful Mrs Baines?

Her statement had both devastated and enraged me. Devastated because I was totally confused and enraged since the term 'everybody' obviously didn't include me—and I had no idea who Mrs Baines was. But I was too overawed by the room and the woman in it to press for further details and as asking questions at home was an unthinkable option I soon buried, or thought I did, all that Miss Neame had said. Or until the following year anyway when—shades of Beau Geste—a girl whose family had just returned from Algeria joined our class, a girl called Gillian Baines.

I hated her. I hated her even before I saw her. I hated her with a passion I never bothered to examine. Or needed to hide since Gillian's condescending air of being a travelled and cosmopolitan sophisticate suddenly put down amongst bovine peasants meant that my hatred was shared—though for vastly different reasons—with the rest of the class. Instead I kept the true reason for my feelings to myself and waited, with apprehension and anticipation, for Sports Day when I could expect her parents to be present.

I hardly slept the night before. I was frightened that something terrible might happen and that my mother would be prevented from attending. I pestered her relentlessly for repeated assurances that she would come. And then refused to believe her when she said of course she would, she always did, didn't she? And even now I remember waking up with tension and anticipation knowing that, at last, it was Sports Day. And I can still hear the thumping of my heart when I caught sight of Gillian Baines walking between a rather ordinary middle-aged man and his overdressed wife. Was *this* my father? Was this, at last, The Bastard? With desperate urgency I dragged my mother away from her polite small talk with the science teacher and began frantically pushing and manoeuvring her around the playground in order to accidentally-on-purpose collide her with Mr Baines. And I can still see myself carefully studying their reactions when I bumped them together and they both started apologizing. But my efforts had been in vain. I had wasted my time. There wasn't even a flicker of recognition. And then, belatedly, the obvious dawned on me: The Bastard's surname, my father's name, wasn't Baines at all and even if he had married the mysteriously dreadful Mrs Baines she was now, of course, Mrs Neville.

For a moment a strange feeling of disappointment had engulfed me. Then I brightened. I hadn't, it was true, found my father but, because he was still the elusive Bastard, I could at least continue to think of him as being potentially a good deal more interesting than Gillian Baines' dull and obviously rather henpecked father.

After the Sports Day fiasco I erased my father from my mind. Up to a point at least for all I really managed to do was wall him up deep inside myself, denying his existence for nearly twenty-five years, never admitting to his being, or ever having been. Only now, with the death of my mother, did he seem to be slipping out of confinement and forcing me to readmit him to my conscious thoughts. As a result it looked as if, despite beginning to consider myself an orphan, I had to continue thinking of myself as only having one parent. Only a different one this time.

Meanwhile however it had to be said that, for all intents and purposes, my father did not exist. He *was* as good as dead.

♓

As I drove out of Lisbon, I realized how much I disliked the casual way air travel catapults people into different countries, cultures and time zones. Only a few hours earlier I'd been in a taxi, leaving the pre-dawn gloom of London, gliding along familiar roads, past comprehensible signs leading to known and expected destinations. Now I was driving in a city where every sign seemed to be a malicious distraction, a diversion designed to force me onto roads leading me to places where I would be eternally lost and out of my depth. Where an unknown fate awaited.

That was the core of my problem. I knew where I was going, even why I was going and what I was going for. But I still didn't *know*. And it was this thought, this fear that I tried to suppress as I negotiated my way out of Lisbon and onto the road to Évora. The car hire company had made it sound all too easy and their small map had colluded with their glib assurances of how simple my journey would be, that there was definitely no problem at all.

I drove as slowly as I dared, trying to deny the fluttery feeling in my stomach, all too aware of being pushed into going too fast as I kept my eyes open for the right road, worrying about not getting into the correct lane when the turn off came. But the gods were with me and I saw the sign in good time: To Évora—and onto a motorway that brought me, just over an hour later, to a well-marked turn off and a road that wound through a rolling landscape covered with olive trees and cork oaks. Forty minutes later, a few miles before Évora, I saw the first evidence of my destination, a sign directing me down a smaller, more rural road, pointing me not only to the Hotel Convento Nossa

Senhora da Boa Fé but somewhere called the Cromeleque dos Alemendres. Finally, a few miles further on, and after passing through a small cluster of brilliantly whitewashed houses, I arrived at another turning where a brand new sign pointed to the left and announced: *Hotel Convento Nossa Senhora da Boa Fé Only*. This last stretch was short, down little more than a dirt track that almost immediately took me under a great arched gateway and into the large, cobble-stoned courtyard of an old building, a building that had obviously only very recently been converted into a hotel.

♓

Most people who grow up in England have only vague and insubstantial preconceptions about convents, generally imagining them to be religious fortresses where cloistered nuns are forced to live lives of stern denial. In this I was no different to anyone else. As a result, and even allowing for the demands imposed on a fifteenth century building by a twenty-first century five star hotel, I was taken by surprise. The building was large and double-storeyed with great rows of windows along all sides. My urge was to stop and look, to abandon the car and explore. But before I had even come to a complete halt a beaming bellboy was rushing out through the great doors and somehow instantly shepherding me into the vastness of a flag-stoned lobby dominated by an enormous bowl of flowers placed in the middle of an old oak table.

The almost overwhelming impression of discreet luxury was enhanced by the bustling army of people who appeared to take my luggage, to welcome me, to help me register and, finally, to conduct me to the lift and up to the first floor. From there I was taken along a corridor overlooking the cloister, to a room on the far side of the building's enclosed inner space. Here the words *Cell 9* on a small hand-painted tile finally provided, along with the cloister, the first direct evidence of the building's religious origins, evidence enhanced when I stepped into the room and saw that it was considerably smaller than those in most luxury hotels. And yet despite the stark white walls, the austere lines of the wooden bed, the crisp simplicity of the linen bedcover, embroidered white on white with the name of the hotel, and an antique wooden chair underlining its monastic beginnings there was little to suggest penitential restraint. A small, elaborately framed painting of a young Madonna holding a laughing Christ Child completed the picture, though in doing so it made the telephone, the television set and all the other necessities of a hotel room seem incongruously out of place.

Suddenly, and for the first time, I was glad I had come alone.

I walked over to the window, curious to see the view, to see if the room would pass its last test. And it did. I found myself looking out over an extraordinary landscape, a kind of paradise. But a paradise that was untouched and natural, without any showiness, devoid of knowing it was paradise. The huge and obviously very old fig tree that came almost up to my window forced my eyes to gaze out and over it at a landscape dotted with cork trees, making me understand how the land gently undulated and rolled into the far distance. I leant out, wondering for a moment if any nun had once done the same, looking to see if anything manmade interrupted the view. And happy that it didn't.

I turned back into the room, seeing its qualities, sitting on the bed, thankful for the hard mattress and knowing the relief of the traveller who has reached journey's end and found peace and comfort. For now anyway.

♓

A small booklet placed beside the bed filled me in with enough about the hotel and its history to satisfy my initial curiosity.

The Cistercian convent of Nossa Senhora da Boa Fé was founded in 1298 by Rainha Beatriz de Castela, the second wife of Afonso III. The first Abadessa, Dona Uraca, belonged to the Portuguese royal family and the nuns were always women of noble birth.

In the early 16th century the convent, by then extensively remodelled and enlarged, was famous for the fine quality of its sweets which were ordered by local people as an offering to the convent. They were made by the nuns, often from the recipes of their families.

A few alterations were made in the early 15th century and in the 1540s an unknown artist painted the frescoes in the church. In the 18th century the blue and white azulejos depicting various religious scenes were added. The church also contains a fine ivory crucifix, carved in Goa and a Manueline font depicting Jesus being baptised by João Batista.

Each of the capitals on the cloister's columns is individually carved with Biblical stories, mostly depicting episodes in the life of Christ and His Mother. Though there are others—a moving depiction of S. Martim giving his cloak to a beggar is noteworthy—there are also several featuring demons and monsters. The cloister is lined with fine examples of 17th century tapete style tiles while the Capítulo Casa is well decorated with Arab-Hispanic azulejos of the 16th century, a testament to the region's Moorish past. While the original cozinha has been enlarged and adapted to the present needs of the hotel, guests may view the original 16th century oven and the pots once used for cooking.

The convent ceased to exist as a religious building in 1834 when all religious orders were suppressed. The last nun died in 1873 and a few years later it became a school which closed in 1989 after which it was unused for several years. Now, after almost 4 years of extensive renovation and refurbishment the Hotel Convento Nossa Senhora da Boa Fé welcomes its guests to enjoy the luxury of its comforts in the surroundings that reflect and retain the harmony of its religious and spiritual past.

To begin with my exploring was circumspect and kept, if not within the immediate confines of the hotel, at least within sight of the fixed point that it offered. I avoided other guests, taking my breakfast early since I had no desire to make human contact.

What continued—and grew—was the sensation of peace and security I experienced as I explored the hugeness of the building. I saw its qualities, its atmosphere of calm, of straight lines and arches, of shadows and coolness, a certainty that, despite renovation and change, the convent was still wrapped in its original purpose. My greatest sense of the past's presence was undoubtedly in the cloister where, despite it having been glassed in and filled, though sparsely, with comfortable chairs I could still believe it was where nuns once spent hours of quiet meditation. These sensations soon emboldened me to venture further afield, the positive answers to my enquiries calming any lingering doubts: Yes, I could wander where I pleased, the surrounding land was privately owned but no one, I was assured, would object to the presence of a considerate walker. Mysteriously it was within the courtyard that I found the only barrier: the comparatively small church attached to the main building was always fiercely locked, held fast by a rusty padlock that showed no sign of recent use, a condition underlined by a Portuguese notice I took as meaning it was permanently shut. A slight but further deterrent was that whenever I approached the church I saw a black mongrel curled up before the door. It was true that though he never snarled or made a threatening move when he raised his head to watch me examine the padlock, I subconsciously accepted that his purpose was to keep me away.

♓

Then one morning I had my breakfast early, having decided that the time had come to walk to the Cromeleque dos Alemendres, a site the hotel's booklet described as an ancient arrangement of prehistoric megaliths and which I had seen signposted as being nearby. As usual, I glanced towards the church, perhaps to see if it was open, perhaps to check and see if the dog was there, perhaps even nervous that he wouldn't be. But he was there and I smiled, calmed, as if his presence was an assurance that all was right with the world.

It is now no longer possible to know precisely what then happened. Did my imperceptible hesitation alert him or did he perhaps know where I was going? All I am sure about is that the unexpectedness of him getting up, stretching and walking slowly towards me stopped me in my tracks. It was an uncertainty that held when he stopped before me, looking up as I looked down. An uncertainty broken by my conviction that he would stand and watch me move away, that he wouldn't follow me. I shrugged and started walking, suddenly determined not to look back.

This determination was fading as I walked under the hotel's arched entrance and gone as I turned round and saw that he was right behind me—even as I caught the *of course* flitting through my mind.

In the end I was glad he was there, telling myself that his presence made the walk easier, allowing me to absorb the details of the land around me since I unconsciously assumed he knew where we were going. It took just over half an hour to reach our destination; a walk that took us in constant undulations like sailors on a gentle sea until we reached, and joined, a stony track that I instinctively knew had actually started at the convent, and which turned up a slight rise to a cluster of trees.

For an instant the trees hid everything and I wondered if I had been too trusting to simply assume that by following the dog I would reach the Cromeleque.

But then I saw it. Though the trees. On the crest of a slope. An assembly of prehistoric standing stones, rough-hewn, lichen-covered and, at first glance, scattered without order. Powerful. Still. Vibrating. Yet though this is what I *saw*, my first thought was gone so fast I never caught it until, surreptitiously, it decided to slip back and assert itself. *It is waiting*, I thought, understanding that though the megaliths were ancient beyond age they were sustained by such energy and power, that the passing of countless centuries had been irrelevant. *It can afford to wait* was my next thought; *it has the time it needs.* I carefully never asked *for what does it wait.*

Slowly I walked forwards, not even checking to see if the dog was with me. There was no threat, no malevolent unseen power, no reason to be afraid. The stones stood in a vast and silent circle, giving the space they occupied a sense of enclosure that time had tumbled into a less formal arrangement. The hotel's booklet had said there were ninety-five of them and at first glance they all appeared to be thick and rounded, standing straight and tall with just a few that tilted slightly, as if giants had leaned against them. Size was their only deception for though apparently of not much more than human height when I approached the first one I found myself dwarfed.

Dwarfed but not diminished.

Of the many reactions that danced through my senses, most, no doubt, are felt by all those who enter the Cromeleque's space. Such places stoke the embers of our primal past, reminding us of ancient, tribal ways, of powers and beliefs the modern world tends to dismiss with disdainful shrugs. So it wasn't in *that* way that the Cromeleque was different for me. What was different—though it was an understanding I took some time to grasp—was the sense of a particular and personal familiarity: that, though their ancient, eternally hidden eyes inspect all those who enter their realm, what I sensed, fanciful as it no doubt seems, was that they knew me. It was as if I might catch them whispering, that there was some connection between us, them, the place. A thought that took me, unbidden, to thinking that this was not my first visit, that there was a faint suggestion of déjà vu.

Was this an uncomfortable thought? No. Though even as I had it I began a slow retreat, conditioning pushing it away, telling me not to be so childish, so fanciful. It was a suggestion I failed to heed. The whispers around me were stronger than rational logic.

In the end I stayed about an hour, wandering from stone to stone, feeling their rough surfaces, touching the designs ancient hands had incised on some of them, seeing the shadows they cast, the wildflowers around them, the surrounding trees, the impression of vastness, the gritty earth and the sky-covered world that bound everything together. At one point I saw that the dog was sleeping, his head across his paws. He was, I understood, at peace and with this thought in mind I went and sat down beside him, drawing myself into the tilted shade of one of the more central stones, aware but attempting to ignore, the sense of peace I found there. Is there really a connection I asked myself?

And if so what could it be?

♓

My time at the Cromeleque was a turning point and the next morning as soon as I'd had breakfast I came out of the hotel and went straight up to the door of the church to see if, just this once, the door might actually be open. Nothing was as expected: the dog was nowhere to be seen and before I even had time to wonder where he was I noticed that the padlock was missing. The moment stretched until, like someone in a trance, I lifted my arm to push the door open. And found my hand hanging in empty space as it swung silently and effortlessly away from me. I hesitated, conscious of the lure now dangling before me but uncertain of quite how to proceed. Could I enter? Should I? Well, I thought, I'm not going to do any damage, I'm not going to touch anything. I just want to see what's there, for heaven's sake.

As soon as I walked in the contrast between the exterior sunlight and the interior darkness was too much and I instinctively closed my eyes. When I opened them again I gasped. I had entered another universe. Before me, and running all the way around the church's interior, was a luminous, glittering procession of painted medieval figures. Resplendent in reds and golds, blues and greens, yellows and purples these figures moved through a landscape of rolling hills dotted with walled towns. At first I was so amazed that I thought the images depicted one long, glorious procession. It was not until I slowed my eyes down and looked more carefully that I saw how each grouping was, though individual, linked to the next by a common goal. Every painted man, woman and child was making their way towards a single figure, a magnificent and regal Virgin seated in simple, painted majesty above the bare stone altar. And yet, though I saw how everything radiated towards Her, I also understood that She was the central figure in each separate group. The painted walls told the story of the birth, life and death of the Virgin.

Very slowly my eyes began to absorb each individual episode of Her life, a life that unfolded in a landscape where small castles sat on hills, streams ran down to join rivers and trees gave shade for rest. This extraordinary medieval landscape was peopled with richly dressed lords and ladies enjoying courtly pleasures whilst ordinary men and women toiled in the fields. So real was their presence that as I swept my eyes along the great panorama I felt myself being drawn into their world, my eyes going from the marriage of the Virgin's parents to the joy of Her birth, from Her presentation at the temple to the celebration of Her own marriage to Joseph. I drank in every scene like a thirsty man at an oasis, touched by the moving simplicity of the Annunciation, the urgency of the journey to Bethlehem and the glorious birth of the Christ Child in a roofless stable under the stars of a sky filled with rejoicing angels. With the intensity of someone watching a miracle unfold I saw how the angels gazed down on the Virgin as She knelt in awed devotion before Her Child, unaware that, behind Her, and bowed in reverence, were the Three Wise Kings, the shepherds and all the lords, ladies and common people. It was here that the artist began incorporating the Virgin's life into that of Her Son's—initially showing Her as an attentive mother and later as a hovering shadow. Not until the Crucifixion was She once more depicted as the central figure, first as a grief-stricken mother suffering the agony of seeing Her Son die and then, in a powerful Pieta, as a tragic, ethereal woman becoming visibly transformed as She cradles Her Son's bloodied body in Her arms and begins to comprehend the mystery and promise of His Resurrection. The power of this transformation was followed by the mortality of Her last human manifestation: the simple scene of Her own death, surrounded by sorrowing women, a scene that preceded the final, and triumphant, masterpiece of Her enthronement as Queen of the World.

I stood very still, conscious of being surrounded by a work of extraordinary power and instinctively aware that the artist had been inspired not only by faith but by the concept of a young and innocent girl gravitating towards her position at the very centre of Christianity. This Mary was both ordinary *and* divine. Her hesitation, Her humbleness, Her youth, Her devotion, Her grief and Her ultimate majesty were all represented. She almost moved and breathed; Her aura so strong that it seemed to vibrate off the still walls. She was real and I knew, without any doubt at all, that She had been drawn from life, that the artist had used someone he knew, a young girl who was probably no more than twelve or thirteen years old, to pose as the Virgin. And then it dawned on me: *all* the other figures had also been drawn from life and the fresco was not only a remarkable artistic achievement and statement of faith but a record of the people who had lived and died some four hundred years ago. Here, in the Alentejo.

For a moment I was content to let the power of the frescoes radiate out and enclose me in their enchantment. Only when I eventually recognized my need to see each part of the story in greater detail did I walk over to the dark corner beside the sacristy door, the point where the Virgin's story began. And there, as I bent to look closer, something, a small sound or a faint movement, caught my attention and made me, without any undue thought, look round and into the deeper shadows—and so see that a man was standing there, watching me.

Blood rushed to my cheeks, staining them with guilt and embarrassment. I had been caught red-handed.

'I…I'm sorry…I just pushed the…'

'I know. I saw you enter.'

Though my tension still bound me to my predicament I heard the Indian accent.

'I only wanted to look, to see what was here…'

Why was I sounding like a child? I fell silent.

'Of course. Who wouldn't want to see these…?' The man extended an arm and swept it gracefully around him. 'They show a beautiful and remarkable world.'

My body began to relax. I might well be in the wrong but at least I had been caught out by someone sympathetic to my curiosity.

'It is for this reason that I did not disturb you. That you should feel their first impact alone. I'm sorry if I surprised you.'

'I…well…yes…' It was impossible. I was at too much of a disadvantage. Who was this man? And what was an Indian doing here?

As if on cue he stepped forward, out of the shadows of the doorway. He was tall, perhaps in his late thirties, perhaps older.

'Allow me to introduce myself. My name is Satishan. Satishan Nambiar.'

'Oh. I…I am Sophie…Well Sophia actually, Sophia Neville.'

'The ancient goddess of wisdom.'

'What?'

'Sophia. The goddess of wisdom. Like our Saraswati.'

I was beginning to feel completely at a disadvantage.

'Perhaps I should explain. I am here to work on an Indo-Portuguese project. I've been meaning to come here for weeks but only today did I make the time. Even then there was a problem because at first the key could not be found. But in the end I was lucky.' He held up a large iron key, apparently as old as the church itself. 'And it seems that you were too—to have been so blessed.'

Blessed? I noticed the odd choice of word but let it pass.

'Are you interested in frescoes, in murals, in church art?'

'Yes. No. I mean *yes!*' I laughed. 'I *like* frescoes, I *like* church art but I haven't studied it.' I felt suddenly at ease. 'Is this your subject?'

'No, not as such. History is my subject.' He paused as if this was not quite the explanation he wanted to give. 'Yes. But you see my project is the story of Portugal and my part of India. I am from Kerala.' He looked at me to see if the word meant anything. I nodded.

'Portugal believes they discovered us.' We both smiled. 'Now I am here to see *what*—and *who*—they were when they did so—and what can be learnt from that event, what it might tell us about ourselves and how it might remind us that nothing is ever quite what it seems.

'You see,' he continued, looking at me and pointing towards the walls, 'even here there is something to be found. Let me show you.'

He walked towards the scene of the Nativity then stopped and pointed: 'Look!'

I followed the direction of his finger to where it almost touched the Three Wise Men as they came over a small painted hill. There was no need to ask why they might be of interest to an Indian historian. Though two of them rode camels, the third king, the dark Balthazar, walked beside an elephant.

'Of course, of course this is the Bible story,' He looked up to see if I was following, 'but just look at the hills—are they not Alentejo hills? And the castles? And the people. Do you not feel they are from here, that they were *known* people?'

I nodded but kept my eyes fixed on the painted elephant.

'You see elephants were sent from Malabar to the Portuguese king. The most famous of them was later gifted to the Pope and sent off to Rome. But there were others and…' he flicked a finger towards the wall, 'this must be one of them. And perhaps the Wise King is actually a portrait of the pappan who came with him…'

'Pappan?' I interrupted.

'Hah? Oh yes, the mahout,' he paused and then with an extraordinary intensity turned and looked at me. 'You see I feel I know this man.'

I took a step closer to the wall to examine the face of the man on the elephant. Like almost all the faces the detailing was fine and there was a very real sense of the artist having painted someone who had really existed. But he was lost to me. The passing of the centuries had muted his voice and made him a stranger, a man I would never know.

I hesitated before asking my next question, wanting to precisely pinpoint what Satishan Nambiar had meant. 'Do...do you believe that you know his actual identity?'

There was a slight pause and during it I saw, or perhaps just felt, a veil being lowered.

'No. Not exactly.'

I wasn't quite sure what more to say. It seemed that the painted figure suggested something to Satishan Nambiar that he himself was uncertain about. There was a long beat before he continued.

'I suppose it is to do with finding someone like him here—someone who has been on a painted Portuguese wall for more than four hundred years—that makes me wonder who he *really* is—or was. He must—like me—have come from Malabar.'

I looked closer at the painted figure and then up at the man before me, almost as if I was expecting to see a facial resemblance.

'Well it's too late, no doubt. He is gone and were it not for this portrait we would not have known even this much.' He glanced briefly at me and then back to the wall. 'Perhaps it's just that I feel...well how often can I expect to see someone from Malabar in a sixteenth century Portuguese mural?' He gave a slight shrug and once again I got the feeling that a thought was either being suppressed or concealed and that something more than shared origins linked the two men.

♓

Over the next few days I continued my exploration of the surrounding countryside, drawn by its apparently conflicting appearance of being both vast and intimate, a land that, however much it dipped and rolled and stretched away, somehow gave the impression of being small and contained. As a result I found that as I walked—always accompanied by the black dog—I looked out not only over the land towards the far hills but often stopped to examine details, the colour of wild flowers, the texture of a cork oak's bark, a rock, a small pond. I would try to walk in a different direction every day but, like the pull of a magnet, more often than not I found myself turning towards the Cromeleque, sensitive, consciously or not, of the hold its atmosphere had over me. Although I had confirmed that the stony path leading up to the ancient stones did indeed originate just outside the hotel's arched entrance, I never once took this direct, and shorter, route. Instead I took the more random, less frequented path that curved across the land and that, halfway there, brought me to a place marked by an old stone cross standing just outside the shade of a solitary cork oak's gnarled and twisted branches. Since this place was no more than fifteen minutes walk from the Cromeleque I often stopped for a moment, to seek the tree's shade, drawn by the understanding that, for centuries, it had stood as the protective sentinel of this small and lonely hill.

As I usually set out early I would inevitably be the only walker and easily fell into the habit of believing that the Cromeleque was, in some indefinable way, mine. On one occasion, just as I passed the cork oak I heard laughter and the slamming of car doors coming from the Cromeleque's direction. I turned away at once, knowing I could not see the place treated as a tourist attraction, accepting that I went to absorb its atmosphere and benevolence. And, I had to admit, to see if I could find anything that might confirm my initial sense of a personal connection.

On one of these days, when I was walking back towards the hotel, taking a barely used track, I saw a man bicycling towards me, approaching at a steady pace, his face shaded by a dark hat.

When he drew level he looked at me and, without in any way changing his speed or rhythm, said: 'Bom dia.' While it surprised me that he was black I was more aware that he passed me by like a ghost.

♓

On the Tuesday of my second week I decided that it was time to visit Évora. The walks and discoveries of the hotel's surroundings had restored me to the point where my curiosity about the old city at the centre of the surrounding region had been aroused. I drove in early, left the car outside the city walls and walked up a cobbled street, following the small map provided by the hotel. For the first time since I'd arrived in Portugal I felt like a tourist and it was strange to be back in an urban environment after the peace and quiet of the countryside. I'm really not at ease in towns I thought, even though Évora hardly qualified as a bustling metropolis.

My initial intention was to follow the road up to the main square, the Praça do Giraldo where the tourist office was situated. It was only as I passed a small café that I changed my mind and decided that culture and history would have to wait until I'd had a coffee.

Moments later I was seated at a tiny table, a large glass of milky coffee and a Portuguese pastry before me. I drank slowly, watching the locals standing up at the counter and ordering tiny cups of black coffee. The place was new and modern, obviously recently opened, its walls gleaming with mirrors and glossy images of breads and cakes and juices. It bustled with activity, serving people who all knew each other. Gossip and greetings were exchanged with almost everyone. The pretty girl behind the counter blushed once or twice, the butt of a remark about her sweetheart no doubt, the older woman beside her smiling and reprimanding the speaker in such a way that the girl blushed again. I felt a smile cross my face, suddenly aware that despite these people being strangers there was something oddly reassuring about their presence and timeless banter.

I looked around, taking in the people sitting at the other small tables, seeing women with their daughters, older husbands and wives, young married couples, some with small, perfectly behaved children who would solemnly get up and go to the counter when called to collect an order. All's well with the world I thought as my eyes fell on two old men.

They were formally dressed but, though they both wore flat caps and were sitting bolt upright side by side it was hard to tell if they were together or not. The older man had real country eyes, narrowed and used to seeing and understanding what most of us would miss: the hovering hawk, the hidden nest, the gathering clouds. A man who could find the lost lamb, sense the whims of the wind and smell the coming of rain. Yet behind his eyes lurked an innate sadness as if in the shiny newness of the café he sensed himself surrounded by the death throes of all that was familiar to him, aware that his world was vanishing and becoming a universe beyond his comprehension.

The other, slightly younger man sat more stiffly, one hand clutching the side of the table, his legs crossed at his ankles. Though he held his head at a defiant angle and kept his lips tightly closed, his expression was a careful blank. I realized I would like to talk to them. I am, I thought, much closer to them than they would ever realize. Yet it was a wish that could never be fulfilled; we were separated by much more than language. They would have taken months to feel comfortable with expressing themselves—if they ever could—and in any case I instinctively knew they were unlikely to allow themselves too much introspection. As I got up to leave I suddenly remembered Satishan's words, that nothing is ever quite what it seems.

Outside in the warmth and brightness of the sun I shivered slightly before walking almost immediately into the Praça do Giraldo to begin a long morning exploring Évora. From a cursory check of my map it seemed practical to take one of the roads leading off the square that would bring me to the ruins of a Roman temple, the museum and Évora's cathedral. Probably enough for a morning's sightseeing I thought as I walked up a narrow pedestrians-only street lined with shops selling souvenirs, most of which spilled out onto the pavements. The Roman temple took no more than a few minutes to absorb, its remaining columns standing in defiance of time and the indignity of having once been used as a slaughter-house. The museum, on the other hand, took me closer to Évora's slightly more recent past and for an hour or so I peered at objects and paintings, conscious that I was trying to see behind at least one of the many veils distancing me from a true understanding of what life had been like four hundred years ago. Yet all I saw was superficial, simply the façade of what things had *looked* like. I saw the clothes, the houses, the furniture—but never felt the textures or smells of the world they clothed, housed and furnished. I carefully scrutinized paintings that showed faith and miracles, I gazed up at saints who blessed their kneeling patrons and looked carefully at the objects and symbols of the church—but failed to catch the rhythms and sounds that had accompanied them in their daily reality. And even when I came across a series of paintings depicting the life of the Virgin none of them came close to the sense of almost being there as those in the Convento's church. When I finally left and walked out into the bright sunlight I knew that all I had done was look at another world without ever entering or knowing its embrace.

It was in this mood that I went round the corner and into the vastness of Évora's cathedral, the Sé. What is happening to me, I thought? Am I just going through the motions of looking at things simply because they are here to be seen? I shrugged but no answer was forthcoming, despite knowing that what I really wanted was to feel the pulse of the people who had built and occupied this world. And so it was that, with these thoughts in mind, I sat down in a pew about half way along the cathedral's central nave. Is it possible, can I somehow conjure up Évora's seemingly elusive past, can I take my mind back to an age when kings and queens, courtiers and nobles assembled here to watch religious processions and listen to solemn masses? I tried but it was beyond me; the constant droves of tourists infested the vast interior with a kind of virus that eroded all evidence of sacredness. Perhaps it would be different without the people, their flashing cameras and videos. What would it be like if the Sé's later additions, its Baroque features and modern, electrically powered chandeliers were removed? What would happen if they were replaced with pools of candlelight, the wafting smoke of incense, a darker light and, above all, an innate respect for the sacred? Would other footsteps then echo on the paved flagstones? Would the high arches then lift the mind heavenwards and the building start to vibrate, to live? I wondered what happened to the old ghosts; did they hide during the day, seeking some secluded corner, emerging only at night? How effectively we destroy, moving like clumsy bulls in china shops, unaware—and unconcerned—about atmosphere and sanctity, failing to see what *really* occupies a place, the shades that have prior rights to it.

Then something changed and I sensed rather than saw the woman coming slowly up the nave, a woman who was different. At first I thought it was her unnatural slowness that had caught my attention but as I looked closer I saw that she was very obviously, very pregnant. She stopped just after she had passed me, turning her body awkwardly to face a shrine on the other side of the aisle, a shrine enveloped in cloth and behind which scaffolding could just be seen. I watched as the woman went closer, catching her voice as she called to someone behind the cloth screen, sensing the fractional pause before a man's hand took hold of the cloth and lifted it up. The woman leaned closer, an attitude of supplication filling her as she raised her hands in prayer, her lips moving silently. Without thought I angled myself to take advantage of the lifted cloth, to see in towards the centre of a golden, gilded shrine and catch a momentary glimpse of a small sculptured and painted Virgin. Immediately the lifted cloth was dropped—as if I had no right to see what had been wordlessly offered to the pregnant woman. But it was too late, I had seen the Virgin's richly painted robes, I had seen how She clasped them around Her belly. And I had seen that She too was pregnant. I gasped, my emotions suddenly in inexplicable chaos as the woman crossed herself and began to walk away.

♓

By the time I left the Sé I was starting to feel hungry and as I retraced my steps back to the Praça do Giraldo I kept peering into small restaurants to see if there was one that wasn't already full. Only when I came out into the square and saw its parasol-shaded tables did I realize that a snack was all I needed and that in any case I would prefer to sit outside and watch life go by. Seconds later a table became free and, before I knew it a waiter was handing me a menu.

After I had ordered an omelette and a salad I sat back to study my guidebook and check its information against the reality of my surroundings. Apparently the great church behind the marble fountain was dedicated to Santo Antào, the streets off the southern side had once been the Jewish quarter whilst the fountain marked the site of an old Roman arch. Layers upon layers of history I thought, at the same time noticing, just as my meal came, that most of the activity in the square was created by old men constantly forming and reforming themselves into different groups. All of them were dressed like the two men I'd seen in the café, wearing flat caps and very obviously countrymen. What brought them here I wondered?

'May I join you?'

The slight accent not only told me who it was before I even saw his face but saved me from the panic of wondering how to deal with an unwelcome stranger.

I smiled and waved Satishan into an empty chair, seeing out of the corner of my eye that the waiter was already scurrying over to take his order.

'What will you have?' I asked.

'A coffee, just a coffee. I've already taken my food.'

The waiter obviously heard him, making ordering redundant, leaving before anything further was said.

I smiled again, conscious of how relaxed I felt. Was it just because of the sun and my surroundings, of having just eaten?

'Where have you been?' I asked.

'In the library, working my way through the sixteenth century, looking at old manuscripts. In another world.' This time it was Satishan who smiled. 'And you?'

'Well, nothing as erudite I fear. Just wandering around, behaving like a tourist, looking at the landmarks, ticking them off the list, buying the postcards. All the rituals of being away from home.'

The waiter came back and placed a coffee on the table, creating a slight vacuum that made me feel vaguely self-conscious. I stayed silent, waiting for Satishan to speak.

'Tuesday is my favourite day in Évora.'

My expression asked the question.

'These old men,' he nodded towards a nearby group, 'has anyone told you about them?'

I shook my head.

'Today—like all Tuesdays—is São Porco day. It's when the farmers come to Évora to buy and sell domestic animals…pigs, sheep, cows…'

I felt a slight frown knit my brows together.

'It's remarkable,' he paused, 'and all because they know each other.'

My frown deepened.

Satishan looked for a moment at the men, watching as two of them shook hands, one of them slapping the other on the back as he turned to go.

'It's like the Emperor's new clothes. There are never any animals. But, because of trust, they can buy and sell without ever bringing their livestock to Évora. Their word is always honoured and the deal agreed with just a handshake.'

He looked at me, checking to see if I'd understood before continuing, 'In how many places would such a thing be possible?'

I shrugged, thinking *nowhere I know.*

'And here of all places.'

I looked up. 'What do you mean?'

'What do you *see* here?' Satishan asked.

It obviously wasn't a factual question but I hesitated, unsure of how to answer.

There was an unnaturally long pause, as if Satishan himself seemed to consider the answer he might give. I looked around, wondering what clues I could find. I saw the old men, I saw people, locals and tourists, moving across the Praça, I felt the sun slanting itself under the parasol to warm my back. I heard a child's laughter and saw the fountain's spray sparkle in the light as a small dog jumped up onto its rim and began lapping up mouthfuls of water.

'It all looks so normal doesn't it?'

I waited.

'Here we are sitting comfortably in the shade, watching life, chatting in this unconcerned way.' For just a beat he paused, as if aware that he could still change his mind and pull back. And then continuing, 'Oblivious of what happened here on September the twenty-third 1543.'

His next pause was different. He knew he had committed himself and was now merely gathering his facts.

'September the twenty-third, the day of Évora's first auto-da-fe, the day four men and one woman—and even one exhumed corpse—were brought into this peaceful square and publicly burnt. All were so-called New Christians, accused of being Jews, found guilty and condemned to death by the Offices of the Inquisition...'

As his voice trailed off a shadow seemed to move like a speeding cloud across the square and out over the whole universe. Even as the fountain played, children giggled, lovers kissed, tourists took pictures and invisible animals were bought and sold. Even as my mind shivered through the horror conjured up by Satishan's words and caught something he had left unvoiced: *that there was a reason he was so affected by the auto-da-fé.*

Which, I suppose, is why I heard his almost inaudible whisper: 'Sometimes it feels as if I was there.'

♓

Two days later I finally paid attention to the small inner voice that had been pestering me for days: going to the information desk and asking if I could see inside the convent's adjoining church. Minutes later I was slipping the key into the great padlock, ruefully aware of how unnecessarily timid I had originally been, conscious that if it hadn't been for Satishan I might never have seen the frescoes.

This time there was a subtle difference for though they retained their impact, their images still breathed and the processions and colours still lived, I was able to slowly examine each section. And even notice a small unfinished patch in the last panel of the dying Virgin. This time however the main difference was that because they no longer took me by surprise, and Satishan was no longer there to distract me from the aura they created, I could take my time to examine the building that enclosed them.

There was no doubt about the church's atmosphere: it emitted a sense of sacredness, giving space for the divine to be honoured, the murals so obviously a work of faith that they not only enhanced this impression but made it a certainty.

So what, I wondered as I sat down, made me sense the presence of some other element? What else was it that drifted through the dark interior? I looked round. Along the walls. At each panel and its enchanted world. But no, for all their magic, they concealed nothing. The altar. The enthroned Virgin. The altar plain. The Virgin magnificent; golden. Everything seemed to be no more than what it was. The problem was that by then I knew I was right. It was just a question of finding it.

Ironically it was what *wasn't* there. The revelation coming when I stood up and walked round, looking into the body of the church rather than along its walls. I found it almost at once: an empty niche, just above eye-level, on one of the stone pillars. It stopped me in my tracks—its message too clear for me to misunderstand or feel the need to look anywhere else.

The central part of the niche's lip was worn, touching evidence of the countless numbers who had once reached up to the figure it originally contained. I stood back a fraction, almost as if I hoped that I might find a clue as to which saint or—. Or? How was it that I knew the *or* was redundant? That as soon as I half thought I *knew?* It had to have been the Virgin.

I stepped back further, seeing the faint touch of paint within the niche and conscious, quite suddenly, of an indefinable aura of pain. What had happened? Had the statue been stolen? Destroyed? I shook my head, telling myself my overactive imagination had gone too far. But at the same time I remembered the small figure in Évora cathedral. And the pregnant woman I had seen praying to the Virgin. A pregnant Virgin.

♓

That evening I felt at a loss. I had been in Portugal for just two brief weeks. I hadn't actively chosen to come here and yet now that I was about to leave I admitted feeling an inexplicable affinity with this small part of the Alentejo. Something about this land had inched its way beneath my skin and managed to suggest that an ancient and long forgotten connection was being reaffirmed. Perhaps this was why I felt the need to find some way of marking my last evening. To begin with I was unsure of quite what to do and just drifted round the hotel-convent's cloister, believing that its peace and solitude would inspire me. I walked slowly, conscious of the quietness, looking out at the central courtyard's formal garden and seeing how the day's dying light shimmered through the fountain's spray. I breathed deeply to inhale the pungent aromas of heavily scented flowers but, separated from them by the glassed-in arches of the cloisters I smelt nothing. An awareness that made me feel trapped, changing my mood and making me suddenly wonder what it had really been like for the nuns who had lived here. Had they felt a nearness to God within these walls? Did they sense that He also existed outside, beyond them, where perhaps they were not allowed to venture? Were all their mental and spiritual needs satisfied in the convent or did they yearn for more? Did they perhaps long for the rise and fall of the land and its place under the sky, for the joy of running free? Slowly my perspectives changed. I saw how strictly the cloisters could bind, how restrictive their serenity might appear. Nothing was ever quite what it seemed and I knew I had to get out of the convent and walk across the plain, to the old tree and, perhaps even further afield, to whisper my farewells to the Cromeleque's ancient mysteries.

In no time at all I was away from the convent, out on the open heath and walking, almost striding, across the undulating plain. I walked fast until I was completely enclosed by the land, only then slowing down to a more leisurely pace. The late summer air was full of the smells and perfumes of grasses and flowers, of the earth. A gentle breeze barely stirred the leaves in the few trees I passed and, as I walked, I felt uplifted by a sense of the land's proximity. Somewhere unseen birds sang of their summer joys. A few silent breaths of air shivered through the grasses. An occasional scuttling revealed the presence of an unseen animal fleeing to safety. For a brief moment I caught the faraway lowing of a stabled ox. The moon, though not yet high in the sky, was already swollen in fullness, palely waiting for darkness to fall and shine its light on the world below. Everything around me suddenly seemed timeless, peaceful and deeply certain. An awareness that remained even when I heard the heavy, panting breaths and turned round to see the black dog bounding towards me.

As I watched him approach I saw how his glossy black sleekness shimmered in the late summer light and that his pink tongue was his only touch of colour. A colour suddenly startlingly visible when he stopped, his body alert as he looked up at me, his tail wagging and head held to one side. Just for a moment I wondered how—and why—he always kept just out of my reach. What would happen if I managed to place my hand on his lean body? And why did I think that, somehow, he would always evade me? And why didn't this thought disturb me? What instinct assured me that he posed no threat? How did I somehow know he had always been there to protect me when I ventured beyond the convent's walls?

I shrugged, knowing these were unanswerable questions. It is enough that he is with me, I thought, as I walked on more briskly, idly wondering whether I really should consider going as far as the Cromeleque. And then smiling, aware that I was admitting how I felt about the dog, accepting that his presence gave me a sense of security, of being watched over. Yet even so I hesitated. It was going to be a long walk just to reach the Cromeleque. And I had to return, have my dinner and finish packing before I slept. Well, perhaps just a little further I thought, at least just up to the old cork tree.

And so I walked on, feeling at ease and at one with my surroundings until, just before I reached the tree, something strange happened. It was not so unexpected or out of the ordinary that I was uneasy; it was just different. The dog ran ahead of me, bounding up and down in the grass, his blackness rising and falling, a small whisper of sound moving with him. Until he reached the tree. Then, though for only the briefest moment, he seemed to vanish. It is impossible to say that he absolutely wasn't there but the sensation that he had evaporated into thin air was not entirely removed by his reappearance a beat later. The grass was no higher there than anywhere else, the ground did not dip, no rock lay to conceal, no shadow crossed the setting sun. I felt no fear and yet I shivered, suddenly feeling as if I had come up to the edge of another world.

I walked right up to the tree, watching as the dog cocked his head and looked up at me, seeming to gaze right into my eyes. Whose dog was he? Did he have a name, an owner? Where did he come from I wondered, watching him watch me as I leant my body back against the trunk of the gnarled cork oak. Then I looked out towards the old cross, idly wondering why it was there as I sought the tree's support and inhaled the heady odours of the approaching night. Relaxing for just a beat. Until I realized that although I felt no fear I was not alone.

I turned round slowly, knowing without recourse to reason, who would be standing there.

Satishan.

I felt no sense of shock as my eyes settled on him, standing quietly, his darkness blending into the deepening shadows of the evening. Somehow it was as if I expected to see him. As if he belonged here. The only thought that did momentarily occupy me was so strange that I simply let it come and go, a thought that made me wonder if the dog and Satishan were one and the same and that the dog had merely vanished in order for Satishan to appear. But the dog was still there; its eyes still fixed on me. Again I sensed, but let pass, the idea that this dog was more than just a dog and that such thoughts would not surprise Satishan.

He spoke first, but as if in answer to a question: 'You are wondering about this cross?'

How, I asked myself, did he know?

'And,' he continued, 'You are right to wonder for there is, of course, a story about it, telling us that many years ago a very strong man used to regularly walk from Guadalupe to Boa Fé, passing this spot as he did so—and perhaps, like us, pausing here. In those days wolves roamed all over this region and because he knew the dangers it is said that he devised a simple method of protecting himself. He would carry a good stick in one hand and a long length of rope in the other. Whenever the wolves appeared he would simply uncoil the rope and keep walking, letting it trail behind him. This made the wolves curious and they would follow, sniffing inquisitively until he reached the outskirts of the village where, of course, they would stop and disappear. He would then hide the stick and rope in a tree, picking them up when he next left the village. One day the wolves must have appeared sooner than usual, before he had reached the place where he had kept the rope. Nowadays—and constant re-tellings have, no doubt, embroidered the details—it is said that all that was found of him were his boots, well-chewed. The belief is that this cross was erected in his memory.

'We know nothing more, except that it is known as Cruz do Preto, the black man's cross. The strangest irony of all is that this must mean he was an African slave, one of many once found in Portugal. And, though almost certainly a Muslim by birth, presumably converted to Christianity.'

There was a long pause before he continued.

'In Malabar this is the most dangerous time of the day. Sandhya. Dusk. When men hurry home to safety. When uneasy spirits claim the night. You are brave to come out alone at this time.'

We looked at each other, my mind a blank.

'You see even here, in the Alentejo, there are dangers. Tonight is a full moon night, the time when the *lobisomem* are found.'

Even though I stayed silent Satishan saw the question *what is a lobisomem* on my face.

'The Alentejo has many very old beliefs,' he said, watching me as he spoke. 'One of them concerns the curse that affects all seventh sons, the belief being that whenever there is a full moon they are compelled to leave their homes and seek a hidden, isolated place. It is then, almost in a frenzy, that they discard their human form and assume that of a wolf.' He paused to see my reactions but I very carefully kept my face still and empty, allowing only my mind to race. He continued: 'Once the transformation is complete they start running since the curse is such that they must visit seven different crossroads before dawn. Only then, only after this has been done can they make their way back to where they have hidden their clothes and return to their human shape.'

I looked towards the dog, now seated on his haunches, his bright eyes catching the last light of day.

'The dog came with me.'

He smiled. 'So it seems you are not alone.'

I said nothing. It was not so much that I was uncomfortable with all that he had just told me but that I was unsure about quite how to continue. I therefore waited for Satishan to speak again.

'I came here,' he said after a long pause, 'to see the Cromeleque one last time. And to say my farewells to you. For now.'

'To me?' I asked, surprised but choosing not to comment on the fact that he had expected to find me here.

'I leave tomorrow, early. A day or two in Coimbra for some work and then to Lisbon, to India. To Malabar.'

Somehow, though I myself was due to leave I felt caught out, betrayed.

'But I didn't know…so soon?'

He smiled again and, as always, it changed his face dramatically, altering his naturally stern, somewhat aloof features.

'But, for now we are here. The Cromeleque is over there. You have your guardian spirit. Shall we all go together?'

♓

To begin with we walked in silence, keeping a slight distance apart, content and seemingly at ease as we made our way across the land. The dog ran before us and as we walked the moon climbed slowly into the darkening sky and lit our way. All that could be heard was the padding of our footsteps and the panting breaths of the dog and eventually it was this near silence that changed things, breeding strange thoughts. At first I allowed the idea that the dog possessed some strange quality to crawl back into my mind, going over the idea that he was indeed a spirit or some benevolent guardian. I kept my eyes fixed on the bounding figure, watching, almost straining my eyes to follow him as he moved through the dark shadows of the land. Yet though my eyes were fixed on him I could not detach my mind from the growing persistence of other thoughts. Though initially circumspect their innocent tenor changed once they had started inching their way into my mind. At first, thinking that they just wanted to test my reactions—and unaware of their true nature—I let them be. Until it was too late. Until, finding themselves unchallenged, they became bold and rushed in, scudding, slipping, sliding, pushing their way around my subconscious, demanding to be heard—whilst never allowing themselves to be caught, never quite letting me catch their drift, never quite letting me see what conclusion, if any, they might yield. It was only very gradually that one particular thought rose out of the drifting morass and made me recognize, even as I kept my eyes fixed on the darkness of the dog, that Satishan had, however lightly, read and echoed my thoughts. It was a thought that edged me into a discomfort with the silence between us and made me want to say something. For a moment I tried to suppress this unease—even as I tried to isolate exactly what was nagging away at me. Words, ideas, questions began to gather at the tip of my tongue, readying themselves to be voiced until, at the last minute, something made me suppress them and stop their utterance. Every thought that came to mind seemed too trite, too unformed. A word, a phrase would spring up and then, just as I was ready to voice it, I would force it away, aware only of how pointless it was. Nothing seemed worthy of speech and this awareness began to make me even more self-conscious and uncomfortable—and more aware of Satishan's proximity and silence. Eventually I pulled further away from him as if by increasing the physical space between us I could prevent him from sensing my silent turmoil.

It was only when our footsteps crunched on the last stretch of the walk, the dirt track leading up to the Cromeleque, that the silence between us was finally broken. It was then, reassured by the ordinariness of the sound that I began to breathe more freely and allow my mind to start wondering what the ancient stones were going to look like in the moonlight. Perhaps this was what made me unconsciously quicken my pace and scurry forward, hurrying as if someone was suddenly urging me through the dark shadows of the encircling trees. Perhaps I moved too fast. Perhaps if I hadn't been in such a hurry I would have recalled the power of the stones in the daytime and known how much the moonlight would affect them. But, because I did none of this I was caught by surprise when they loomed up before me without warning, the impact of their extraordinary presence stopping me in my tracks. I felt I had stumbled into a pagan realm, that the whole universe had tilted and sent me hurtling into a great primal vastness filled with the whispers of invisible forces. And I saw how the moon heightened everything, how it shone its shimmering light down on the open ground and bathed the stones in a luminous whiteness. For a moment I staggered, stumbling as if I was going to faint or be seized and taken before a high priest and ritually sacrificed. And yet even as these thoughts swirled into and around my mind I sensed enough of a benevolence to know that I was safe. My body relaxed and, though my eyes remained fixed on the stones, I was aware that Satishan, like me, had instinctively stopped outside the enclosing circle, awed by the stillness of the ancient stones and oblivious to the distant twinkle of Évora's lights.

And it was Satishan who eventually broke the spell that bound me to silence.

'Coming here is like coming home. Something here speaks to me. I can almost say that this place is mine.'

As usual I said nothing, just letting formless thoughts drift through my mind as the dog settled onto his haunches and the moonlight glimmered on the stones.

'I wonder if you know what the local people believe about this place?' He looked over at me. I shook my head.

'You know of course that the Moors once ruled this land?' I nodded. 'It's strange but though they were conquerors and people of another faith they appear to have lingered in people's consciousness, and especially in their myths, as benevolent. In all the stories the Christians still tell about the Moors, they are always described as honourable men. Unlike their conquerors. Just look at Évora's coat-of-arms.'

As he paused I remembered the hotel guide's description of the moonless night when a twelfth century knight called Giraldo Sem Pavor ended centuries of Moorish occupation by scaling Évora's walls and opening the city's gates to admit his waiting soldiers. And that Évora's grateful Christians later commemorated Giraldo's courage by putting him on their city's coat-of-arms, showing him boldly galloping his horse over two severed heads.

Satishan waited a moment and then continued.

'Do you know what actually happened?'

Again I shook my head.

'Well Évora's so-called "gallant knight" actually gained admittance by courting a Moorish woman—telling her that if she left a small gate open he would visit her once darkness had fallen. Of course it was his soldiers who entered, who freed the city—none of which is heard in the tales now told. Tales that never mention him killing not only the woman he said he loved and her father but compounding his betrayal by putting their heads on two shields and sending them to the king in order to prove his loyalty. Admittedly this was something the king had good reason to doubt.'

Satishan paused.

'Nothing is ever quite what it seems.'

'For instance,' he continued, sweeping a hand before him, 'people say that these stones are the petrified figures of enchanted Moorish princesses. Perhaps it was a way of them staying here—an admission of how much the Moors loved this land and how sad they were to leave it. Perhaps, well perhaps, it also shows how much the people of the Alentejo themselves respected the Moors and that in some way they too wanted them to remain, to stay...Who knows?' he shrugged.

Once again I knew that though Satishan was speaking to me he was at some other level merely thinking out loud. I wondered what he really saw and felt about this place.

I shivered and, as a small gust of wind sighed across the ground, I saw the black dog get up and walk into the circle. What happened next was like that moment in a film when music slowly creeps in, a tune that is soft and haunting, expressing a mood and creating an atmosphere. In reality of course it was a silent and unheralded moment that began when a small cloud started to creep across the moon and the dog's body suddenly tensed. Then there was another gust of wind and for the briefest flicker I thought I saw a young girl slip behind one of the great stones. She came and went like a wisp of smoke, moving so fast that I immediately questioned having seen her and, even now, I'm sure that if nothing else had happened I would have put her presence down to a strange trick of the clouded moon. I would simply have denied everything. But when I looked again, to see if I'd really seen someone, something distracted me and I glanced at the dog and then up at Satishan. And knew they had seen her too. And more than that. That there had been a connection between them, that something powerful within the stones had vibrated between the girl, Satishan and the dog. Or so it seemed for as soon as the moment passed my certainty went with it, disappearing as the cloud cleared the moon and I could easily see that we were alone, that the place was empty. No one was there. I had imagined it all. The only being within the confines of the great standing stones was the black dog. And he just stood there, looking back at us, as if waiting for us to join him.

'It's all right, it's all right to go there.'

Somehow Satishan seemed closer than he really was and his voice made me jump. Though whether he broke the strange spell or enhanced it is impossible to say.

For a moment, as I stepped into the area enclosed by the stones, I thought I could feel something totally ephemeral brushing across my face. It was like breaking through a thin membrane or pushing aside the thinnest of veils and though there was nothing threatening about these feelings as soon as I entered the Cromeleque's enclosure I sensed something closing behind me. It was as if everything that was about to happen was to be governed by a different sense of time and space, that we were no longer part of the outside world.

As always I was drawn to the slightly sloping stone. It seemed to have some special quality about it, an air of offering protection. The others, especially the large one in the centre, were bigger and more imposing and I noticed that Satishan went and stood beside the largest of them, watching me as I began walking slowly around the circle. Though I kept moving without any apparent sense of purpose somewhere subconsciously I knew I was searching for something. I kept moving, though whether for a minute, for five minutes or even ten or more I have no idea. Nor do I know how many times I went round, whether it was once or twice or if I simply went randomly from one stone to another. All I am really sure of is that in the end I went up to the sloping stone and, very suddenly, sat down and tucked my body into the base of its slope.

It was amazing how safe I felt.

I sank back, putting my hands out as I did so, slowly sweeping them backwards and forwards across the ground, feeling the bumps and sharpness of tiny stones as I looked up at the moon. How eternal it is I thought. For hundreds and hundreds and thousands of centuries, from even before these ancient stones were installed, the moon has gazed down on this land and been a silent witness to all that has happened here. The moon knows every secret of this place, indeed of the whole universe. It knows what is here. And it was as this thought passed through my mind, and as I watched the gauze-like veils of small clouds breathe their way across the sky that I felt my hand touch something smoother than the sharp pebbles. I looked down and saw what looked like a small lump of bone.

Did a shaft of the moon's silvery light actually catch on its surface and cause it to shimmer? Or was it only later that I invested this moment with these qualities? All I am really certain of is that as I slowly lifted the small object up, holding it in the palm of my hand, I saw that it was no more than a few inches high and less than half its height across. And that it had rough incisions cut into it. And that when I looked closer I could see that beneath its ingrained, earthy grime was a carved human figure.

I stared at the small figure, feeling it almost burn into my hand. Then jumped to my feet, barely aware that the dog had been lying close beside me.

'Satishan!'

There was no sign of him.

'Satishan!'

He was standing on the shaded side of the large central stone. Had he been there all the time? I held out my hand. 'Look, look what I've found!'

He walked over and wordlessly took the figure from me, holding it between his thumb and forefinger as he lifted it up to the moonlight. I watched his face, instinctively sensing that his reactions were the only real answers I would get. Which meant that I saw him slip his face behind an invisible mask and become part of something I knew nothing about.

'How strange, 'he said, 'do you know what this is?' He looked at me and there was a slight pause. 'It is ivory.'

He glanced briefly down at the dog and then back at the small figure, a slight frown gathering on his face. Then I saw that, like a blind man reading Braille, he was rubbing his thumb over it, as if trying to extract its secrets. What surprised me was that when he looked at me an expression I am inclined to describe as awe was slowly creeping across his face.

'It is—well you look,' he said, handing the figure back to me, dropping it into my outstretched hand rather than giving it to me.

I brought the heavily stained ivory up close to my face,

holding and turning it in the moonlight as I peered at its carved features. It was a female figure, more precisely that of a young girl. Yet though the barest of lines clearly suggested an enigmatic smile it was impossible to decide exactly what she was wearing or how her hair was arranged or if she wore a crown or a headdress. Had the carver done this deliberately? Or had time simply eroded the details?

Then I re-examined Satishan's words, understanding that he'd begun to tell me about the carving—which meant he knew something—but had stopped himself and handed it back to me so that I could see—or perhaps decide—for myself.

Again I held the figure up, one thumb feeling the still smooth surface of the ivory. What had escaped me? What had Satishan seen that I had not?

It was the hinted presence of the figure's hands that suddenly made it obvious. One was raised, the other pointed downwards in a gesture of benediction. It was an Indian gesture, the gesture I supposed of a Hindu goddess.

I looked at Satishan.

'It is a…' Suddenly I hesitated, doubt shivering through me. An *Indian* goddess here, in the Alentejo, in Portugal? It made no sense.

'Exactly. You know but you don't know.' Satishan smiled. 'Like me you thought one thing and then the other. Like me you thought she is the Madonna.' I looked at him in astonishment. 'And then you saw something Indian about her.'

I stared hard at the figure and immediately saw how right he was. It *was* the Madonna. How had I thought the figure was Indian? It was nonsense. This was a small ivory, a roughly carved image of the Virgin and there was absolutely nothing Indian about it. Except the hands. Except that the Virgin also blesses and offers benedictions. Except that the Virgin *belongs* in Portugal and an Indian goddess does not.

And then the next thought: how, whether Virgin or goddess, did this figure get here?

'You were meant to find it. It is yours.'

Maybe if I'd been outside the Cromeleque's aura I would have found Satishan's answer to my silent question strange, maybe uncomfortable. Inside it felt perfectly normal. Or at least not something I felt worth examining.

'Yes, but where does it come from? Is it old? How can it just have lain here undiscovered?'

Satishan shrugged as though wanting to suggest that his guess was as good as mine. I felt that, once again, something was being withheld from me.

I decided to break the question down.

'Do you think it is old?'

'I am very certain of it.' He never even glanced at the figure.

'Then?'

'Then?'

'How can you say it is mine?' I decided not to enter into the discussion of being *meant* to find it. 'How can it be mine to take? Shouldn't I hand it over to some, well I don't know, some museum or archaeological society?'

'No,' he was emphatic. 'I told you. You were meant to find it. It is yours.'

I looked down at the figure. Mine? Meant to find it? Why?

'Don't think about it. It is a gift.'

I knew I was hesitating, conscious that his certainty was making me begin to believe it *was* mine. Except that now I had another silent question: *If it is a gift who is it from?*

'Take it Sophie, not every question can be answered.'

I closed my palm over the small ivory and turned away from Satishan, struggling to hide my emotions. Up to that moment I hadn't even been aware of wanting it, let alone wondering if I could keep it and yet now that Satishan had so confidently assured me it was mine I was almost overwhelmed with relief.

Then I glanced down and saw that the black dog was looking up at me, the light just catching his eyes.

What on earth made me think the dog was also telling me the ivory was mine?

'Now perhaps we should remember why we came here.'

I turned back, yet another unvoiced question forming in my mind.

'We came to say our farewells, remember?' Satishan asked, a smile forming at the corners of his mouth.

'Of course,' I smiled back.

Since I had no idea what I meant by this beyond wanting to acknowledge the power of the Cromeleque I just stood with my head lowered. It was only when I raised it again and saw Satishan bringing his folded hands up to his chest and opening them palm upwards that I saw how precisely his gestures displayed the respect I had failed to express.

Then we both stepped outside the Cromeleque's aura and, followed by the dog, started walking back to the convent.

It was just after we'd turned to catch our last glimpse of the great standing stones that Satishan asked me if I would have dinner with him.

♓

When I came out of the shower I knew I was breathing too quickly. The formality of having dinner with someone for the first time is like performing in an under-rehearsed play without ever understanding the motives of the other character. I knew I wanted to be entirely myself but was in danger of losing sight of exactly who that self might be. And I knew that though I didn't want to appear unattractive I couldn't be sure that I specifically wanted to appear attractive. Or if I wanted, or expected to be wanted? Or if I was ready to examine the possibility of attraction, of sexuality? And if so what then?

I dressed quickly, fluttering from the cupboard to the mirror, slipping into a longish black dress, aware of its flattering lines and wondering what had made me pack it. Then standing in front of the full-length mirror and knowing my perception of myself was like that of an anorexic's, totally divorced from reality. I studied my face in the bathroom mirror, searching only for imperfections, missing my clear skin, clean hair and wide eyes, seeing only a stranger. Should I use makeup? I would look better without it I thought even as I rimmed my eyes, coloured my lips and asked myself how long it had been since I'd last felt like this.

I was almost proud of myself when I finally walked into the lobby, certain that I appeared calm and collected. But it was a paper-thin facade and it immediately began to collapse when I failed to see Satishan.

'Sophie?'

How had I missed him I asked myself as yet again I was faintly conscious of how often he seemed to appear and disappear even when he was perfectly visible. He was standing exactly where we had arranged to meet, beneath the lobby's large wooden cross. I watched him approach, wishing my hands weren't quite so clammy but gradually relaxing as a slow smile began to cross his face.

'This would never happen in Malabar. I would see you surrounded by relatives. Yours. Mine. They would arrange everything. You look beautiful, Sophie.'

My heart was beating louder than the sound of his voice.

I decided to focus on the ritual of being shown to the table, of seating myself on the pulled out chair, of arranging the napkin flicked open by the waiter and then burying my head in the menu. I'm buying time I thought, wondering when I would have to raise my head and act like an adult. As always Satishan spoke first, asking me if I had any preferences, whether I wanted meat or fish, and then making it easy by saying the fish soup was really a meal in itself.

'That's fine by me,' I said, 'I don't really eat much meat.'

'And what wine would you like, red or white?'

'Red, although I suppose that if I'm having fish it should be white.'

He smiled and said he saw no reason why I shouldn't have whatever I wanted and that if I'd like red then that's what he would order. I smiled back and, as he beckoned to the waiter, I felt the ice had been broken. I watched him order, holding the large menu in his long fingers as he looked up at the waiter and spoke, to my surprise, in Portuguese. Only when the waiter had finished taking the order and was gathering up the two menus did Satishan turn to face me.

'I never knew you spoke Portuguese.'

'Well, I have to; I need it for my research—all those archives I have to go through.'

'But it's an impossible language.'

'It's not easy I agree but just wait until you hear Malayalam.'

'What does Mal—what does it sound like?'

For a beat he looked at me. Then he smiled and spoke two or three sentences, using sounds that were almost liquid, that seemed as if they were bubbling over stones in a shallow stream, so run together that there was no way of telling where individual words began and ended.

'What does it mean? What have you said?'

Again he smiled.

At that moment the wine waiter appeared with the wine, showing it to Satishan and entering into some discussion about it. I watched them talk, almost believing that they were two conspirators, both in league against me, using one foreign language to prevent me from learning what had been said in another. Instinctively I knew that Satishan had never seriously meant to translate what he'd said to me and decided, as the waiter opened the bottle and poured a little into Satishan's glass that I wouldn't bring the matter up again. I wouldn't appear *that* anxious to know. Despite the little voice in my head telling me otherwise.

Satishan indicated to the waiter that the wine was fine and we both watched in silence as he moved round the table to fill my glass. I fixed my gaze on the bottle, seeing how the waiter tipped it and how the wine started flowing, leaving the lip of the bottle and falling in a red stream into my glass. And then I saw how the wine went on being poured even when the glass was full, flowing over its rim, spilling down onto the table, staining the pristine white linen blood red and spreading across the table and down onto the floor, flowing and gushing until the whole room seemed in danger of being flooded.

'Sophie?'

I looked up. My wineglass was three-quarters full. The tablecloth was white. The room was dry. The waiter was putting the bottle aside and Satishan was looking at me, one hand raised with his wineglass.

I shook off the image and raised my glass.

'It's hard to believe that nuns once lived and died here.'

It surprised me that for once I was the one who had spoken first and I was vaguely relieved when Satishan responded without appearing to notice.

'It's strange,' he said, 'sometimes the past truly disappears and is gone. In other places it hangs in the air like the scent of flowers, as if it is waiting.'

Waiting for what—or who—was a question I chose to leave unasked, even though I was the one who then asked a direct question.

'Do you feel it about this place; that the past is still here?'

'Oh yes. Although in some areas more than others. Perhaps not so much in here. I think the spirits have left the dining room don't you?'

I grinned at the idea of ghostly nuns flitting through their old refectory.

'The church for instance.'

My grin faded. It was as if Satishan had suddenly lifted a veil and presented me with something I had resisted seeing. Without ever discussing it I knew we had both accepted the presence of the past at the Cromeleque. The church however was something else, something that edged too close to something I was trying to ignore, or at the very least was uncertain about.

'There is a lot of power in the church,' he continued. 'It has presence—and it speaks both of people's faith and of the sacred. And yet it is full of pain.'

I wished I hadn't started this conversation.

'Pain?' I asked.

'You don't feel it?'

I hesitated, wondering whether to take the lure. And then nodded.

'Did you know,' Satishan asked, 'that in the Counter-Reformation certain images of the Virgin, that most beloved and divine of mothers, were taken from their altars? That the church authorities had Her removed simply because they believed it was unseemly to show Her pregnant?'

The empty niche in the chapel loomed in my mind's eye. Yet I wondered where Satishan's questions were taking me.

'She was called the Virgin of Ó and was a Virgin of the people, a Virgin who knew the pangs of childbirth, who had suffered as they did. A Virgin women could pray to and who would intercede with God on their behalf and grant miracles.'

I listened, interested but still uncertain about what was actually being said—once again feeling that Satishan was somehow speaking on two levels—even though, as he continued, he already appeared to be taking a different tack: 'Portugal has always had an extraordinary relationship with the Virgin. In 1646 a gathering of the Lords Spiritual, the Lords Temporal and the Commons declared Nossa Senhora da Conceição to be not only Portugal's patron saint but the kingdom's true sovereign. Thereafter no Portuguese king was ever physically crowned, All of them ruled in Her name, the royal crown being kept beside them, on a silken cushion, at the time of their coronation. And even now, despite having been a republic for more than a century She has never been deposed; She is still Portugal's queen—no doubt the only monarch ever to rule a republic!' Satishan paused and the shadow of a smile crossed his face before he continued. 'Captains of fleets prayed to Her before setting out on their voyages to India. We were even discovered by men who sailed in ships bearing Her image and in one of our churches there is a Virgin popularly known as Kappalkayariyamma—the Mother who came by ship. When Vasco da Gama landed on the Malabar coast he was taken to a temple dedicated to the Bhagavathi, *our* Goddess, and thought Her shrine was a church honouring the Virgin. And there is another deeper connection: when we address the Bhagavathi we usually call Her 'amma' meaning mother while when the Portuguese refer to the Virgin in the context of the Crucifixion and the Pieta they call Her 'mãe', again meaning mother.'

Suddenly the temptation was to believe he was talking about the small ivory figure.

'The Virgin has so many names, so many manifestations. Some are merely the same as the church honouring Her or of the local village whilst others, like Our Lady of Grace speak of Her position in Catholicism. The official Virgins as it were, the Virgins of the Annunciation, of the Immaculate Conception, of Compassion and Mercy.'

If Satishan had not talked of the Bhagavathi as *our* Goddess I might have begun to think he was Catholic.

'I have made a list of them. There is a Virgin—or Nossa Senhora as they call Her in Portugal—of Joy and another of Consolation. There are Virgins of Sorrow and of Lamentation. In times of trouble there is Nossa Senhora da Ajuda, of Help, and another, Nossa Senhora do Amparo, of Support, Protection, Refuge and Shelter. There are Virgins of Pleasure and Happiness. And there is the beautifully named Nossa Senhora da Luz, the Virgin of Light, as well as the Virgins of Hope, of Succour and Mercy. There is Nossa Senhora da Guia, who will guide travellers and Nossa Senhora da Boa Viagem whose blessings ensure safe journeys.'

Satishan paused again, almost as if he had said too much, hesitating for a moment that would have been charged with silence if the waiter hadn't arrived with the first course. Only when the plates had been placed very precisely in front of us did Satishan continue.

'So many Virgins. It is as if there is one for every eventuality, that every devotee can find the Virgin he or she *needs*—whatever that might be. So while there is a Nossa Senhora da Tosse, the Virgin of Coughing, there is also Our Lady of the Green Lizard, honouring not only Our Lady but a little reptile which used to protect the inhabitants of Bragança from the Moors.'

We looked at each other, and smiled.

'Some of them though are different. Nossa Senhora dos Anjos, the Virgin of the Angels is one. But there are also the terrestrial Virgins, the ones who belong to the land, who are closer to the lives of ordinary people—the Virgins of Fields, of Valleys, of Snows—and even Nossa Senhora da Silva, the Virgin of the Blackberry Bush, of Brambles. And then there are the Virgins whose intercession is sought in times of personal need like Nossa Senhora do Livramento, the Virgin who can assure a woman of an easy delivery.'

Satishan stopped, apparently studying his now empty plate as the wine waiter reappeared and topped up our glasses whilst another waiter came and removed the plates. I noticed that Satishan had a frown between his brows. It seemed as if, once again, he was voicing internal thoughts rather than talking directly to me.

'But in many ways the Virgin of Ó is different, beloved in Portugal even though Her popularity was first recognized in Spain, in the seventh century, in Toledo, when a feast day was introduced in Her honour. Nossa Senhora do Ó. A name that comes, like a sigh, with the start of the chanting that begins Vespers during Advent, just before Christmas, just before She bears Her Holy Child.'

Again Satishan paused, perhaps to allow the main course to be served, perhaps to assemble his facts before continuing. By this stage I had accepted that though I could detect no direct purpose or sense about where this one-sided conversation was leading, my curiosity was aroused.

'For over nine centuries this goddess was at the centre of an intense cult,' he continued, the use of the word *goddess* still unconscious, 'but then came a reforming zeal and with it the idea that showing the Virgin pregnant was unacceptable. Her images were removed and, gradually, or so it was believed, people's devotion to Her dwindled.'

He looked up at me, his expression unfathomable.

'But no one forgets. Not really. Not those who need miracles or who seek succour and protection. It is true that almost all images of Nossa Senhora do Ó were removed, but not all of them were destroyed, some even remained. Even now you can see one in Évora's great cathedral. But Her presence there is one of those exceptions that prove the rule. Mostly Her images were buried, often in the cemeteries of the churches dedicated to Her—or even hidden behind bricked up walls or taken to a safe place, to where a devotee could continue to honour Her and where the prayers of pregnant women could reach Her.'

He looked up at me.

'Perhaps She *is* still here.'

I suddenly had a terrible image of the Convent's Virgin walled up, surrounded by bricks and darkness, sealed off from Her devotees.

Then, once again and as if he had read my thoughts, Satishan spoke.

'But our thoughts can bring Her out—or at least surround Her with light.'

His face widened in a smile and, as I smiled back he raised his glass.

'Let us drink to Her, to Nossa Senhora do Ó.'

The tension that had been tightening my shoulders released its grip and as we lowered our glasses I spoke.

'How do you know all this?'

'Interest.' He shrugged, 'And the people I work with. Most of them are from the Alentejo, from Évora even. I meet people. I ask and they tell me.'

He made it sound so easy but I knew it wasn't. Historical facts were one thing but little anecdotal details about Virgins, myths about Moorish princesses and ancient beliefs about wolf-men were another. He hadn't *read* about them. He'd been told, which meant he knew how to put people at ease and listen once the conversation had been directed towards such fragile and insubstantial matters. And that took skill. I thought back to the two men in the café and how I'd known that to enter the world of someone's deeply held beliefs there has to be mutual trust. And perhaps something else, something less defined. Something I couldn't articulate but felt on the edge of knowing and which, for now, I had to let pass me by.

'What brought you to Portugal?' I looked up, slightly startled by Satishan's sudden change of tack.

I thought for just a moment and then told him about my mother being sick and dying, and how a friend had arranged my ticket and the hotel accommodation.

And how I'd thought it would be a good idea to get away, to take a breather.

'And was it, has it been?' Satishan asked.

'Oh yes, much more than I ever expected. It's been...' I almost let the sentence fade away before continuing. 'Well, it's hard to explain. I knew nothing about Portugal. I'd never heard of Évora. But now it's almost as if something of me belongs here.'

Satishan smiled. 'Sometimes when these things happen we overlook the possibility that perhaps a part of us *does* belong elsewhere.'

Although by now I had accepted the idea of there so often being an undercurrent to Satishan's words I once again let his observation go without comment.

'So, what other family do you have?'

I think I was about to answer when Satishan burst out laughing.

'Forgive me! I'm behaving like a typical Indian, only wanting to know about your family, where you come from and what you do. But now, having asked this much I might as well ask you the most typical Indian question: "Are you married"?'

He caught me completely by surprise and it took a moment to get my mind focused on answering him.

'No, no I'm not,' I said, wondering if this wasn't one of those answers which despite being true don't quite tell the truth. 'And you,' I added, both to cover up my unease and to find out, 'what about you?'

'I was. My wife died in an accident eight years ago.' His face revealed nothing of his inner emotions. I hoped mine was as blank and that my failure to find a response didn't show.

'So you are alone?' he continued.

If you forget about The Bastard, I thought, as I said: 'Yes.'

At that moment the waiter reappeared, saving us from any further unease by removing our plates and asking if we wanted dessert or fruit and cheese, and then coffee. I was about to opt for just coffee when Satishan raised a hand and said: 'No, here I'm afraid there is no choice. It is simply not correct to have anything except a sweet—in fact,' and as he said this he turned to the hovering waiter, 'you will find I have already ordered them!'

The waiter smiled an apology and was gone, once again heightening the impression that the two of them were linked in some unfathomable conspiracy. When he returned, almost immediately, he held two gleaming white plates, both containing what looked like several slightly messy small rectangular shapes, all glistening and deep golden—and not at all what I was expecting.

'I know,' said Satishan smiled, 'this sweet looks, well, how can I put it, unsophisticated? It is called *trouxa de ovos*—and though *ovos* of course are eggs, and *trouxa* is often translated as "bundle", it can also mean something badly arranged. However five centuries ago it was not only a very costly confection—as much as a kilo of sugar being mixed in with eighteen egg yolks—but brought great wealth and power to the nuns of this convent.'

I looked up, amused by the name and aware that disbelief was clearly visible on my face. Satishan smiled.

'So, once again nothing is quite what it seems. Should I explain?'

'Well, I admit I'm intrigued.'

'Then let me try,' he said before, after a light pause, continuing, 'People have certain set opinions about convents. Mostly they appear to believe that nuns were deeply devout and prayed all day or, on the contrary, were forced by their families into convents, condemned as innocent prisoners, repressed and enclosed for the rest of their life. Like all stereo-types there are enough examples to sustain—and feed—both these ideas. But in general the truth was vastly differently.'

He paused. 'You should try the sweet—and taste something of the world it comes from.'

I took a small forkful, aware again of the deep golden colour and the glistening glaze as I slipped it between my lips. And then, as I paused for my tongue to savour and identify the flavours, I realized Satishan was watching me.

'How is it?'

'There is no way I can describe it,' I began and then hesitated, uncertain, 'or rather there are so many different levels of taste that if I try I'll just gush out a rash of clichés: sugar and eggs, sweetness, richness, lightness, all blended together like a whisper. I don't know...'

I looked down at the sweet and then up again at Satishan.

'It's well—different. And not, somehow, as it appears—although I'm not quite sure what I was expecting. It is delicious anyway—and I do admit that I'm now curious to know how something that looks as insignificant as this could possibly make a convent rich.'

'And powerful; most of all powerful,' he said, and then laughed. 'You must feel you are attending a series of lectures but if you can bear one more I'll tell you about this and other such sweets.'

'Please...'

'So let me begin with two facts: one, in the fifteenth and

sixteenth centuries few women entered convents because of religious vocation or any kind of desire to be a nun, and two, they were seldom entirely cut off from the outside world since, in essence, it made its way into *their* world. Women—and they were always from high-born, land-owning families—generally entered convents due to secular constraints, mostly because their families were unable, or even unwilling, to give dowries for their younger daughters, preferring instead to arrange one grand and prestigious marriage for the eldest. Of course the convents expected dowries for these brides of Christ but the amount was, on the whole, reasonable.

'As a result when these young women entered the convents to become nuns it was subtly understood that they were not going to lower their standard of living, they were not going to forgo the food they were used to and they were not going to do without servants. Therefore since vocation didn't necessarily enter the picture they saw to it that their life was a comfortable one. They were used to, and therefore sought to retain, a level of abundance, of plenty.'

He stopped for a beat.

'We are now in a building that was originally a convent and many people might imagine the conversion has been extensive but, in truth, if you allow for modernization, little has really changed. Almost every convent was able to cater for visitors. There was a concept of an open house, and while the professed nuns, and of course novices, lived an enclosed life, adjoining buildings sheltered paying guests: widows, single women who maybe had no close family or children, and orphans of some standing. None of them were nuns, but all desired to live a safe and protected life surrounded by familiar comforts.

'Of course all this cost money and the convents had to find ways to finance themselves.' Suddenly he smiled. 'Perhaps I should add that this situation is not unheard of elsewhere. In all our temples devotees make offerings to seek a deity's blessings. In return they receive prasadam—literally meaning divine grace, a gift from the deity, and usually in the form of sandal-paste, flowers—and sweets. While the devotee is happy he probably is unaware that he has helped finance the temple. The same process for the same end.'

For a moment Satishan hesitated. 'Am I boring you? It is going to take a little longer.'

I shook my head.

'Good! Well, a quick sidetrack then. In Portugal high-born women, even in the grandest houses, did the cooking. Of course servants prepared everything under instruction, but the woman of the house did the actual cooking, and many of them were remarkably skilled. Cooking was an important part of the education of all women—even those from the royal family—and, naturally, they taught their daughters, passing on their skills—and secrets. This meant that a daughter destined to be a nun took her family's recipes to the convent—particularly those for sweets—sweets whose recipes demanded an excessive amount of what was then an expensive commodity: sugar.

'But fate—and a certain buccaneering spirit no doubt—played a major role in all this for by the mid-fifteenth century Portugal was growing sugar on the island of Madeira and thereby becoming not only immensely wealthy but, uniquely in Europe, able to use sugar generously, almost I can say to excess. This in turn meant that sugar began to play an important role in the development and creation of a whole, well, is cuisine the right word? As a result the women, primarily nuns, who had the time—an important factor—to produce these rich and expensive confections came into the limelight. Convents became famous for their sweets—and zealous about guarding their recipes. Rivalries became so intense between convents that though the recipes were written down in a book, only the Abadessa had access to it—and she kept it under lock and key in the Treasury. When a new novice brought her family recipes she was required to sign and swear an oath that should she be transferred to another convent, even of the same order, she would never reveal her secrets elsewhere.

'Now, back to the combination of wealth and power—and the role of the church and the king, and how the convents trod the tightrope between them. Their problem, as with all who seek the patronage of the powerful, was to be certain the power bases never shifted—and that often meant dealing with more than one source of patronage. So convents used the sumptuousness of a banquet to attract the king, the court, the powerful archbishops, the great princes of the church and the surrounding nobility. But, as I said, their ultimate purpose was to support and endorse *their* power and fill *their* coffers. And this meant that though it was the nuns who cooked the magnificent banquets, who produced feasts of extraordinary grandness, and laid out lavish spreads of the sweets for which they were famous, everything was paid for with gold sent by the king and the queen.

'Of course this was only possible once a convent was known for its sweets, since it could then seek the protection of the king by, as it were, permitting him to strengthen and consolidate *his* power with the giving of these magnificent banquets, an act which, in turn, enabled him to win the approval and blessings of the powerful, and dominating Church, without whose support *he* was powerless.

'I realize all this sounds cynical and self-seeking but running alongside all this was a very real fear of divine retribution. People knew that the fires of Purgatory awaited them, and possibly even the eternal ones of Hell. But they counted on the fact that if the sins of this life could be burnt off in Purgatory they might still have the chance of entering heaven. So, though surrounding themselves with the pleasures of the flesh, they sought to mitigate the inevitable retribution that death would otherwise bring. Generally speaking this was achieved through indulgences, a practice that allowed them to buy off the horrors of eternal damnation—although actual salvation was only possible when sins were absolved by confession. It's a complicated process so I'll just stick to our sweet-making convents and see if I can't get to the point!'

We both smiled.

'This practice helped the convents, and indeed all monastic houses, to make money. The belief was that a man's—or indeed a woman's—time in Purgatory could be lessened by acts of charity, good works and the offering of masses for departed souls, the building of chapels, and even grand tombs, and, inevitably, donations. The soul's salvation was ensured through recurring payments which, needless to say, meant that the competition to attract generous legacies from rich and powerful donors was fierce. And, now coming, I promise you, even closer to the point—this is where our *trouxa de ovos* and other sweets like it played their role. Convents sought girls from the most powerful families, conscious of their contact with power, their social standing, particularly with the royal family—and one queen who sent a convent 1,500 litres of olive oil, 300,000 measures of rice and money, termed her gift a "little offering."

'But a high position in society, an old and respected name was not enough: what the convents also sought were girls whose mothers had trained them in the skills and intricacies of producing these little masterpieces of temptation, sinful bites of pleasure that would lure the king and his court, the church dignitaries, the rich and the powerful to patronize and support all those who produced them.'

I looked at Satishan and then, unexpectedly laughed. 'I thought I was to have dinner with you but instead—no that's not fair—in addition, you have taken me into another world. It is wonderful. Really...,' my voice faded away as I ran out of steam.

He smiled but said nothing, giving a barely perceptible shrug.

♓

The rest of the evening passed uneventfully. Conversation was easy, much of what I'd been told meant I had questions to ask and facts to clarify. Satishan answered my queries, filling in, adding and explaining before, somehow without any conscious effort, our talk gradually drifted into the gentle probing of two people getting to know each other. Finally, after coffee had been served and drunk, and the bill presented and paid, we were once again standing in the vastness of the lobby.

'Sophie?'

I looked up at Satishan, aware suddenly of the awkwardness of the moment.

He handed me a card.

'This is my address...' he paused, 'You should come to Malabar.'

I took the card and though I studied it as if expecting to find the secret of some hitherto unbreakable code all I really noticed was that the word *Malabar* wasn't even there. I looked up again.

For just a moment there was an immeasurable beat, a strange pause before Satishan reached out his hand and gently straightened my earring.

Then he was gone.

It began sometime before dawn, somewhere in that limbo of time that separates the darkness from a new day, the time when dreams and reality are one. Somehow I was dancing and instinctively aware of participating in an ancient, pagan ritual, of drifting without thought or reason, of moving in a mysterious darkness and facing someone whose identity was unclear, dancing slowly backwards and forwards as if we were umbilically linked, always keeping the same distance apart. And it was as we danced that I became increasingly aware that this unknown and shadowy figure possessed enormous power. I knew too, that, within this power was energy, and that it was streaming towards me, enveloping, protecting and enfolding, making me conscious both of the overwhelming inevitability of our dance and that the Universe was merely the knowledge of our ritual space, the sacredness of our gestures and of the benevolence they bestowed upon us.

I got up early, packed and finished my breakfast before going to pay the daily incidentals not included in my stay. Everything was ready but just as the cashier was about to hand me the bill he frowned and said: 'Excuse me, Madame—they've made a mistake. I just have to check something. I won't be a moment.' He then disappeared into a side room leaving me standing alone by the counter. In front of me was the large, almost ecclesiastical register. Idly, and for want of anything better to do—and no doubt out of some curiosity—I turned it round and started looking back through its pages.

I only had to turn back two pages. To see the name: Francis Neville.

Francis Neville. The Bastard. My father.

I didn't faint. I didn't do anything. I didn't even absorb what I'd read. I just stood there with both hands on the counter, feeling as if a huge fog had rushed into my head.

And then the cashier came back, smiling. 'I'm sorry, they'd made a mistake but it's all sorted out now.' He handed me the bill, his professional eyes meeting mine. And immediately changing their expression.

'Madame, are you all right?'

'Yes, yes I'm fine.' I wasn't of course; I was struggling with how to ask my question. And finally did so without preamble.

'Who's this?' I demanded, stabbing at the page.

I presume that in an ordinary situation I would have been diplomatically sidetracked and given to understand that in order to preserve the privacy of the hotel's guests they did not divulge personal details. But the abruptness of my question caught him out.

'Why...he, he was an English gentleman. He left before you arrived,' he looked up at me, perhaps hoping to see that this information had satisfied me before continuing. 'Actually he was working, or so I believe, with the Indian gentleman. They were colleagues. They were often together anyway.'

A sickening lurch shuddered through me.

'His address. Do you have his address?'

At that moment he recovered himself and there was a frosty

edge to his voice when he spoke again. 'I'm sorry, Madame, we're not at liberty to give out such information.'

Satishan, I thought. I can ask Satishan.

'Of course, I'm sorry. You see, he's, he's someone I know…I've lost touch with him and…' My voice petered out and I took the bill, glancing at the figures without seeing them before offering up my credit card.

Five minutes later I was outside, watching as the bellboy put my bags into the car. My mind was whirling. How *could* The Bastard have been here, almost under my nose?

'Is that all?' The bellboy was looking at me strangely.

'No, is it possible for the church to be opened? I'd really like to go there, to see it again before I leave.'

'Of course, please wait.'

I got the distinct impression that he bolted back into the hotel with relief. I wondered what he saw in my face. Shock perhaps.

He was back immediately, almost shoving the great key into my hand, saying I could leave it in the door when I'd finished. Not wanting to have anything further to do with me, I supposed.

Despite the fact that by now I knew what to expect the effect of being drawn into another world was still the same. I felt the same sense of awe as my eyes followed the great procession around the walls, drinking in the scenes of faith and humanity until, at last, they settled on the majesty of the crowned Virgin. Nothing had changed, the richness of Her robes still contrasted with the delicacy of Her expression. She still gazed down at me and Her hand was still raised in a gesture of benediction. But it was the other Virgins I wanted to see, the ones who figured in the individual episodes of Her life, the ones that showed Her progress from a shy child to the Nativity and the birth that changed the world. And this time, thanks to Satishan I found Her, the one I was really looking for, the pregnant Virgin, Her swelling belly clearly outlined as She rode on the donkey to Bethlehem. Someone, the priests, the church authorities or perhaps even the local people themselves had taken Her from Her niche but no one had thought—or dared—to erase Her painted image. I breathed more easily.

And yet I felt the pain. What had happened here? Or was it me, was it what had happened to *me*? Was this a place that emitted pain or fed on it? Was it to do with the removal of the Virgin or was it something else? And why, despite this wafting plume of pain, did I still feel a kind of empathy, even a kind of peace here?

I looked round again and as I did so a collage of undefined images began drifting in and out of my mind's eye. The light seemed to intensify, to stream into the space that surrounded me. The frescoes gleamed. The painted figures almost moved. I caught the smell of paint. I sensed the presence of the painter. And wondered how long he had worked. And who he had been. I looked again at the elephant and almost heard Satishan's voice. I looked up and saw the gilded figure in the niche. Where none existed. I inhaled the scent of burning candles. Where none were lit. I saw the wafting smoke of incense. Where nothing burned. And heard gentle voices begin to sing. Where all was silent. And saw the young girl standing before me, one hand stretched out, holding something. In an empty church.

I jerked myself back into the reality of my surroundings, or reality as I supposed it to be. Sweat was pouring down me. I wiped a hand across my brow. I looked up, my eyes wide open. I was alone. But I could not deny. The girl may have gone—she *was* gone—but there was no denying her presence. Because I had seen her before. I could still see her. She was all around me. The girl who had stood before me had the features of the painted Virgins, the same delicacy, even the same darkness. But that wasn't all. That I could have explained, perhaps even tolerated. But what I could neither deny nor explain was that she was the same girl I had so briefly seen the night before at the Cromeleque. And that in her hands lay the small ivory figurine. The figure I had so carefully packed just a few hours earlier.

I stood very still, trying to blank out my mind. And failing. And replacing the images with words, with questions. Was I frightened? No. Had I really seen what I thought I had seen? Yes. Could I explain what had happened? No, well yes, perhaps. Perhaps everything had begun when my mother died. Perhaps the shock of seeing The Bastard's name just a few minutes ago. Perhaps battening down the hatches of my mind hadn't worked. I looked around the church. And saw it's stillness, it's calm. I looked up at the empty niche. And imagined Her. Imagined Her hand clasping the folds of Her gown, imagined the swelling belly, imagined the raised hand and the gentleness of Her smile.

'Holy Mother of God, save me,' I whispered. I, who never prayed.

I turned and left the church, pulling the door shut behind me, relieved that I didn't have to hand in the key or talk to anyone.

I saw him as I walked over to the car, just as I went to open the door. The black dog. Uncurling himself from his place near the church door. Walking towards me, his tail wagging. I watched him, my emotions uncertain. How had I failed to see him when I entered the church? Was he too going to evaporate?

As he came closer I knew I was holding my breath. He was looking up at me. His tail moving as he put his head against my leg. As he touched me. As I felt his body push against my legs. The way dogs do. As I remembered Satishan calling him my guardian spirit. As I bent down, my arms going around his neck. As I choked back the tears. And looked up and into his eyes. And saw the yellow flecks in them. And their expression of extreme and ancient wisdom. And knew as I cupped my hands around his head, scratched behind his ears and stroked my hands along his body that he knew what had happened in the church. And felt my racing heart calm.

It was as if he had come to bless me.

♓

As soon as I walked into my London flat a wave of loneliness swept over me. It had been all very well going to Portugal but now I was back I was going to have to deal with the everyday reality of life. The period set aside to get over my mother's illness and death was behind me. Life had to go on. Except that there were still things to deal with. I sat down, still in my coat and dialled Arthur Boggis, huddling over as I waited for the phone to be picked up, rocking backwards and forwards.

'Arthur, it's me, Sophie. I'm back.'

'Good ter hear yer, gal. We got yer postcard.'

After the usual pleasantries I asked him if everything was all right, if Bertie was being any kind of bother—and how was Mrs Boggis. As always he told me not to worry, that there weren't any problems.

'Arthur, I have to come down and sort out the cottage…it'll take me maybe a week or so to go through all the letters that have piled up here. When it's done I'll call you again and let you know when I'm coming down.'

♓

That night, before I went to bed I took the small ivory out of my luggage and put it on my bedside table. And closed down my mind, shutting out the voices that hissed and whispered and tried to make me listen.

♓

The rain began soon after I left London. At first it wasn't much more than a drizzle, a misting spray that blurred the windscreen and was easily cleared by switching the wipers on and off. It was only when I reached the East End's anonymous sprawl that the grey clouds ominously darkened. My spirits soared, lifting me from the dreary urban stress I was driving through, and making me perversely hope for the drama of a proper downpour. Driving alone through heavy rain has always made me feel secure, as if enclosed in a womb-like warmth, unaware and safely cocooned from all the dangers of faulty brakes, restricted vision or slippery roads.

Yet though I'd seen it coming the impact of the cloudburst still took me by surprise. Within seconds visibility was reduced, the roads awash and glazed with water. I altered the speed of the windscreen wipers to replace their desultory efforts with a frenzy of frantic sweeps but the glass never completely cleared and I drove carefully, feeling the car being buffeted by the storm's sudden fury. And yet my heart was singing. This, I thought, this is more like it. Now I'm on a real journey. I have purpose. I have miles to go, distances to cover, elements to overcome. I have something more substantial than the small is-it-really-worth-taking-the-car trips I usually made in and around London.

Up ahead a traffic light turned to red. I braked slowly, bringing the car to a careful stop on the wet road. The rain was still pouring down. The windscreen wipers still kerthwunked busily backwards and forwards. A slushing of cars swept round and past me. A pedestrian scuttled, head down, across the road. *Thank God,* I thought, *thank God I don't live here. I'd go mad.* The uniformity. The greyness. The scalloped prissiness of net curtains. Then the lights changed to green, freeing me to continue my journey and drive on towards my distant destination.

Two hours later I was off the motorway and driving down a familiar network of side roads. The rain had stopped, allowing a faint sun to emerge, lift my spirits and bathe the wide expanses of the Suffolk countryside in a clear, almost luminous light. The sun had lost its summer brilliance but still lit the landscape up with a rich glow. There was a sense of the seasons changing, as if before we knew it the early, dark days of winter would be upon us. The late afternoon shadows were already long and carrying a whisper of mystery in them, suggesting that the bright clarity of summer was now being subdued by darker forces. And summer *was* over. Stretches of harvested fields were themselves evidence of change, their surfaces a bare stubble, the corn gone and the plough awaited. I wondered, as I always had as a child, how the birds, the small rodents and even the farmer's unloved rabbits managed when their worlds were destroyed by the sudden violence of combine harvesters. What can it be like to have everything you have ever known brutally vanish, without warning or reason?

The nearer I got to Blythburgh the more I knew that I was playing games with myself. I kept telling myself that in another thirty minutes, another twenty, another fifteen I would be able to see the church tower and that another ten minutes after *that* I would be drawing up outside Phoeby Cottage. It won't be long I thought before, whether I like it or not, I'm brought face to face with the new reality of my life. I knew that up to then I'd managed to push everything away, to keep everything at a distance, often muttering 'later, later' as I did so. But I now realized that as soon as I opened Phoeby Cottage's front door I would finally feel the full impact of my mother's death.

For a moment I almost reached down and switched the radio on to distract myself from these awkward thoughts. But it was an unfulfilled moment and I withdrew my hand even before it was fully extended. I was too aware that in a minute, in just a minute I was going to catch my first glimpse of Blythburgh's Holy Trinity church. I wanted nothing, no extraneous sounds or images or thoughts to diminish its impact. I wanted to feel that euphoric exhilaration. I wanted to be ready. And yet, though I was already slowing down as the church tower came at last into view I was, as always, unprepared, braking too sharply as I completed my halt with a final, tightening jerk on the handbrake.

I rested my arms on the steering wheel, hearing the last few mechanical clickings of the engine as it settled into silence, waiting until the only sound was the thump-thump of my heart. Only then did I lift up my eyes and see how completely I was surrounded by the natural and untamed roughness of a flat land tumbled across by coarse grasses and thorny gorse bushes. There was more sky than land and its wide vastness stretched endlessly away, covering the tangled danger of the marshes, the lonely estuary and the distant sea. Slowly, as I gazed out over the heath's wildness and its almost mournful desolation, I marvelled at the distant church, absorbing the tenderness of its steadfast promise. For how many centuries had the sight of this tower signalled journey's end? How many pilgrims, travellers and lost souls had stopped here? How many had paused, as I was now doing, to inhale fresh air and draw sustenance from this sight? How many had felt suddenly comforted, aware that safety, warmth and even sanctuary were finally close at hand? By building Blythburgh's church in harmony with the land's wild and mysterious beauty its builders had not only enhanced its glory but acknowledged that the presence of God existed *outside* as well as inside their magnificent building.

I sighed, sensing a unity with all those who had come before me as, very slowly, I released the handbrake, switched the ignition back on and moved forward. Within minutes the rough, open ground of the heath changed its character as the road narrowed and hedges reared up to block the view. The openness of the heath suddenly vanished, pushed aside by neat and huddled clusters of houses and small cottages. Though aware of my proximity to the church tower I resisted the urge to stop and take a closer look, already too conscious of the curious eyes I knew would be watching from behind lace curtains. I wanted, if possible, to get inside my mother's cottage without being waylaid, before anyone could distract or question me. I needed to get the first few moments over by myself, alone and as quickly as possible.

♓

Though my hand shook slightly as I inserted the key into the cottage door it slid in easily and turned without protest. The latch responded to the lightest touch and, in an instant, I was surrounded by a shadowy interior, the darkening light of early autumn failing to penetrate the cottage's small windows. I switched the light on and watched as pools of light sprang up and brought warmth into the sudden quietness. Then I drew the curtains as quickly as possible, both to avoid the prying eyes I knew were trained on the cottage and to enclose myself in the darkened womb of the cottage, to be in an enclosed and separate space, cut off from the outside world. Then I leant back against the door, seeking its support as I began to look around the home of my dead mother.

Phoeby Cottage was small. My mother had bought it a year or so after The Bastard had vanished. I had grown up in it. I knew every inch of it and yet suddenly it felt as if I was seeing it for the first time. In many ways it was everyone's idea of a small country cottage: cosy, intimate, crammed with objects. My mother had modernized it over the years but her finances—and taste—had not permitted her to make many alterations. She had done what was necessary for comfort and convenience as and when she could afford to do so; a task that had taken her eight or nine years. After which she had left well enough alone. As a result the cottage had a comfortable, lived in and slightly used look about it. At the same time everything was neat and tidy, books I knew my mother would have left strewn across the round table in the centre of the room were stacked in neat piles. Newspapers had been folded and put in the old brass cauldron. Everything that I could see from the front door was sparkling, dusted and clean and I knew I would find the rest of the cottage in the same condition. Thanks to the redoubtable Mrs Boggis, a stickler for tidiness who had often complained about my mother's lack of concern for order. Yet in a way I was sorry Mrs Boggis had seen fit to restore everything to her liking for in doing so she had erased all signs of what my mother might have been reading or doing before she came to live with me in London. By presenting me with a room cleaned up 'for company' she had inadvertently forced my mother to retreat just that little bit sooner, and further, into the eternity of her shadows.

Mrs Boggis had even left a fire made up and ready to light in the fireplace with the huge Mexican mirror above its mantelpiece;

a mirror whose central roundness was rimmed with glass slivers pointing outwards like the rays of the sun. I could still hear my mother's voice on the phone. 'Sophie darling, I've got the most *marvellous* mirror. It's just right, what I've wanted for ages. Jane found it.' Jane was her antique dealer friend. 'No, no it's certainly not an antique—or at least she's not palming it off as such with *me.* Actually it's quite new I suppose. But exactly what Phoeby Cottage has always needed: its very own sun. It's Mexican and all very dramatic. Mrs. B doesn't hold with it of course but I love it and I'm *sure* Montezuma used it for shaving.'

I smiled, remembering how I'd laughed.

But she had been right. The mirror suited the cottage and I felt strangely happy to see my broken image reflected in all its rays. It made me feel secure enough to look round the rest of the room. It was like ticking off a list, checking the familiar and reassuring myself that everything was in order. I looked again at the old round table covered, as always, with a beautiful but worn shawl. Placed very precisely in its centre was a large jug of my favourite Michaelmas daisies, doubtless courtesy of Mrs Boggis. The two long walls were lined with bookshelves, crammed to overflowing with well-thumbed volumes. Piles of books, mostly to do with art, were stacked on a nearby stool. Pictures covered almost all the remaining wall space, hung in an apparently haphazard fashion, more or less as they had been acquired, their subjects reflecting my mother's eclectic tastes. There were Victorian watercolours, mostly of landscapes and rural scenes, there were engravings of Suffolk churches, some fine pencil studies of European monuments in my mother's precise hand and an unexpectedly dramatic picture of a wild-looking Cossack galloping his glassy-eyed horse across the steppes. Half a dozen old photographs had been framed and hung near the door into the kitchen, all of my mother's great-grandparents, wary men and women who, with self-conscious stiffness, squinted eternally into the sun and out at a world that now gazed back at them without recognition. Little knick-knacks, testaments to my mother's magpie sense of acquisition ('I just couldn't resist it, darling') were everywhere. Small boxes—china, wooden, lacquer—were dotted about on shelves, window sills, the mantlepiece, sprinkled haphazardly in amongst figures of animals, pine cones, shells and stones from beaches, souvenirs and memories, the bits and pieces of a life spent 'picking things up'. Postcards, most of which I had sent, were propped up all along the bookshelves.

As I looked around the room I gradually admitted to myself that I was censoring both my mind and my eyes. I was blocking out certain thoughts and trying to avoid the final sweep of my eyes. I knew exactly what was placed where, Mrs Boggis was adamant that 'everything has its place even if Mrs N don't know it'. So it was easy enough to prepare myself and not to get caught out or surprised. So I knew, perfectly well, what I would find on the small table in the corner between the window and the fireplace. I knew this was where my mother kept the three photographs, all of them in silver frames. It shouldn't have been difficult to keep my eyes away from them.

It shouldn't have been. But it was. Because in the end I had no control over myself. My head simply swivelled round, my body turning to follow it, placing me, facing me before the table, my eyes narrowed and focused. Focused down onto the three photographs. It was only at the last moment that I exercised some self-control by deciding in what order I should look at them. The first one was of my mother, smiling, young-old as people were then and holding me, aged about three. Behind her was the sea and somehow it seemed that I'd just run from the water's edge and jumped into the safety of her arms. I looked closer, wondering at the connection between the toddler forever clutching my mother's arms and my present self. A slight sigh escaped my lips. It was safe to go onto the next picture. This was of an older teenage me, scowling self-consciously at the irksome irritation of being photographed. It was a photograph only a mother would keep, let alone frame, for only a mother would know that my stiff and rebellious formality was deliberate, a ploy to mask adolescent insecurities. Now even I could smile when I looked at it. And so I betrayed myself and allowed my eyes to slide down to the third photograph. Of course it was what *wasn't* there, what was missing, that disturbed me. The picture had been taken ten years ago and, once again I was the subject. I was younger, fresher and full of hope. All the things you're supposed to be at that age. All the things you are completely unaware of being if you're lucky. Taking everything for granted. Like I'd done with Richard. Until the day after the photograph was taken. The day he was killed. The day life was crushed out of him in a motorway pile-up.

I walked over and picked up the frame, remembering how, months later, my mother had taken the roll out of my camera and had it developed. And then kept the photographs, worried about upsetting me before—so like her—changing her mind and having this one framed. Well more than this for she'd had *all* of it framed. Both of us. Richard and I, standing with that inane look of people waiting for a self-timer to go off. Holding our breath and waiting. Forever.

It had been too much for me. I had given the picture back to my mother. It wasn't that I wanted to forget Richard. It was just that he was still too real, too near. I could still hear him, feel him, remember his touch. I didn't want to see him frozen forever by my side. Then later on, as grief and confusion withdrew inside me, forming themselves into small, hard knobs of pain, a personal and guarded ache, I found that whenever I saw this picture everything came back. The shock of the oncoming sports car veering towards us, the slow motion crashing, the driver and his girlfriend already terrified, the grinding, jarring howl of metal and then the darkness of oblivion rushing in and, as cruelly, retreating. The terrible precision of details. The fireman's 'Hang on love, we've got you' endlessly replaying in my head. The slow, slow awareness as I regained consciousness that something awful had happened. The glimpse, as they lifted me out, of Richard's feet, just his feet, sticking out from under a blanket. It was to avoid this reminding that I'd eventually opened the frame, taken the photograph out and torn it in half. Then, after a slight moment of hesitation I'd put the half with me in it back in the frame and, without thought, quickly and randomly, shoved the other half into a nearby book without ever noting its title.

Though my mother must eventually have noticed what I'd done she never said anything. Nor did she ever remove what remained. Instead the torn picture stayed, just slightly behind the other two, always disturbing me. As it did now.

It was at that moment, as I stood remembering too much, that the doorbell rang. 'Who the...?' I wondered. I wasn't expecting anyone and I didn't want to see anyone. For a brief moment I considered not answering the door but then, realizing that my parked car was evidence of my arrival, I changed my mind and opened the door.

It was Arthur Boggis. Large, comfortable Arthur Boggis. I smiled, ready to welcome him. Until I saw the drawn paleness of his face and that cradled in his arms was Bertie, my mother's dog.

'Edna musta left the gate open. He ran out, proper quick he wuz, reckon he were coming here...' He looked down at the still body lying in his arms. 'He wuz a gonna. Buggering lorries. They shouldn't have built the motorway so close...The driver never even stopped...'

Somehow I was backing into the cottage, letting Arthur follow me in. He didn't hesitate until he was inside and I'd shut the door, sharply as if in some vain attempt to keep any further horrors at bay. It took me a moment to see that Arthur was in some kind of shock, that he was just standing, waiting and wondering what to do next. Finally I reacted and found my voice.

'Put him, put him here,' I said as I dashed forward, whipping my bag off the armchair and plumping up the cushion.

He lowered him down slowly. Arthur Boggis was no sentimentalist I knew but his distress showed in the lingering way he withdrew his hand from Bertie's head.

'I'm sorry, I'm so sorry Arthur.' I felt my throat constricting and, not knowing what to say stopped, looking down at the pathetic body through glazed eyes.'

'He can't a-known a thing. But he wuz with *us*. Oi shoulda bin sure he were safely inside. He's been a-waiting for months, for weeks, whining at the door, as if he knew. He just waited his chance ter come back to her—and ter you. He just waited.'

I looked at Arthur, at his plain, good face and then down at Bertie. Despite his stillness I expected him to look up, cock his head, jump off the chair and bound towards me. But he never moved. I held my breath to see if my stillness could somehow catch him out and force him to move, to breathe. But the only movements were Arthur's as he shifted uncomfortably from one leg to another.

'Arthur, please, please don't blame yourself. Or Mrs Boggis…it's nobody's fault. Poor Bertie…my mother adored him.' I didn't know what more to say. 'Arthur would you like some tea? Or…?'

'No, don't you fuss yerself. I reckon you've got enough to be doing. Jes you call me if you need me—or Edna.'

He turned, opened the door and went out, closing it sharply behind him. In an instant he was gone and everything was suddenly unnaturally quiet, so quiet that I easily heard the sound of a distant clock striking. I looked at my watch. Seven o'clock. For a moment I hesitated and then, out of habit and not quite knowing what else to do, I went into the kitchen, thinking that perhaps I should eat.

The wonderful Edna, Mrs Boggis to me, had thought of everything. There was fresh bread in the bin. Eggs in a basket. Fruit in a bowl. I opened the fridge: butter, cheese, milk, a homemade pie all ready to heat. A baked apple, a pot of cream. But I knew I wouldn't eat anything. I wasn't hungry and felt I never would be. Instead I filled the kettle, switched it on and then let it boil and switch itself off. Suddenly I was tired and knew I wanted to rest. I gulped down a glass of water, went out into the big room, crossed it and climbed up the narrow staircase.

There were only two rooms upstairs—and a bathroom. The larger one was, had been, my mother's. The other had originally been mine but had later doubled as a spare room when my mother's friends came to stay. Out of habit I walked into the smaller room and was instantly aware of old memories flooding back as I looked around, seeing and remembering. I sat down on the bed, my body sagging as I fought to focus my energy on even the simplest thought, wishing someone would come and tell me what to do. But the cottage was silent; there was no one there but me.

And Bertie.

I jumped up with a twinge of guilt and rushed downstairs to fetch him, finding, almost to my surprise, that he was still lying in the armchair. I picked him up, discovering with something of a shock, that his body was still very slightly warm. I carried him carefully back upstairs and into my mother's room. The door was ajar and I had to push it open with my foot. Of course it was as neat and tidy as the rest of the cottage. The bed was made, the bedspread crisp and smooth, without a wrinkle. A jar filled with what my mother always called 'real' roses stood on the chest of drawers, their rich, heavy pungency filling the room. Then, for a brief moment, as I waited for the door to stop swinging, I saw myself reflected in the large mirror my mother used for seeing what she called 'the full horror of it all'. I was clutching Bertie as if, dead and inert though he was, he could somehow support me. But it was my face I really noticed. It was streaked with tears, tears I didn't know had been rolling down my cheeks.

I turned away quickly, to look for Bertie's basket. It was in the corner, at the foot of the bed, just near the bedside chest of drawers. I placed Bertie down gently. 'Just for tonight,' I told him, almost accepting that I'd really brought him upstairs for my own benefit. Then I sat down on the bed, looking at him, knowing that now he at least looked peaceful. Surely, I thought, the worst must now be over?

But it wasn't. It hadn't even begun.

For a beat or two I sat looking at Bertie, my mind a blank. Then as the moment passed I began looking around my mother's bedroom. Only then, when it was too late, did it dawn on me that there must have been times when my mother felt as alone and as scared as I did, times when she too had no one to turn to. The Bastard had seen to that.

The room was in sharp contrast to the abundance of the 'things' downstairs. It was almost empty. Just the bed, a large table, Bertie's basket, a large armchair and, beside the bed, a small chest with three drawers. On the far wall she had hung one of my photographs, a misty view of Delphi in the snow, reminding me of the only time she was ever able to come on one of my assignments and how much she enjoyed it and how much I had wished I could get sent to Mexico and take her with me. Somehow, though the room downstairs had been totally created by my mother's personality, by her scavenging and acquisitive love of 'things', of objects that spoke to her and delighted her, this starkness was more evocative of her. Generally no one except Mrs Boggis and myself ever came up here and I now suddenly understood that this was where my mother came to lick her wounds. Here she was utterly herself and needed nothing to feed on, to look at, to remember, to touch, to feel or to delight in. Here she was in and of herself sufficient.

I lay back on her bed and stared up at the ceiling, smiling as I saw that the golden stars were still there. I'd stuck them up there when I was twelve, as a birthday surprise, after she'd said that she *had* to see the stars before she slept but was sometimes too lazy to get up and look out of the window. I stretched my arms out, luxuriating in the bed's comfort, feeling the tiredness in my body. Then I let my arms flop down, ouching in surprise as my left hand hit the bedside chest.

I sat up, gently rubbing my hand as I leant over and, without thought or purpose, intention or design, opened the top drawer. It was empty. I bent over further to open the middle drawer. It was also empty. It was the bottom, the third one, which brought me off the bed and onto the floor in order to pull it open. By comparison it was full, containing the large book I'd bought her in Athens, a book on ancient Greece that I'd seen her resolutely put to one side as too expensive. I lifted it out and began slowly flipping through its pages, so slowly that I didn't notice anything. It was only when I increased my speed, flicking through the book like a card dealer that the envelope slipped out.

It had my name written on it. The handwriting was my mother's. Though I immediately questioned its presence in the drawer, in the book, I assumed that Mrs Boggis's tidying up mania was responsible, that her blessed rage for order had made her put the envelope in the book and the book in the drawer. There was nothing sinister in that, I felt sure. And yet I hesitated. How do you deal with a letter from a dead mother? And why hadn't it either been sent to my London address or given to me?

Slowly I opened the envelope and, as slowly, extracted its contents. It contained two pieces of paper, one that was old and faded, yellowed at the edges, plain on the outside. I opened it up and saw the preciseness of the fountain pen ink and how it flowed from the end of the printed words to exactly fill a space that had originally been left blank. It was not a large piece of paper and it didn't contain that many words. But what words it had were enough. Too many even. Enough, as I read them, for the cold sweat of comprehension to begin a feverish ascent up my spine and initiate the clamping down of denial as I desperately tried to close the floodgates of what came pouring towards me. The message, the paper's basic information was simple.

I was adopted.

I sat very still. Cold and sweating. Accepting as I denied. Knowing that there are things in life, dreadful things, things you know cannot be but which are. This was one of them. I did not even question. I just knew.

And then I looked at the other piece of paper. Its words were even fewer. All eight of them, written in my mother's curiously precise scrawl. Only eight: one, two, three, four, five, six, seven, eight words: '*I suppose you'll wonder why I've done this.*'

I looked up and out of the window. It was dark now. I could just see the yew tree black against the sky. I shivered. It was cold. *I* was cold. I looked at Bertie and then got up, pulled the blanket out from under him and wrapped it around him, to keep him warm. He was stiff, all body warmth had gone. Then I sat down again, on the floor, by the bed, leaning against it.

'I suppose you'll wonder why I've done this.'

She had been wrong for somehow I *did* know. Somehow I knew she was letting me know that she'd never been able to tell me I was adopted—that this was therefore some kind of curious admission. Yet even as I began asking myself questions I knew I was wasting my time. I would never get inside my mother's head. Not now. It was too late. The questions would keep coming and, for the moment all I could do was turn back to the other piece of paper and try to focus on what being adopted really meant.

Who, suddenly, was I? Who was I *now?* Was my mother no longer my mother? And had there ever been a time when I had felt that she wasn't my mother? How was I to think of her now that she seemed to be some kind of impostor? And don't, just don't let even one thought of The Bastard into your mind I told myself as I got up from the floor and went to stand by the window. Outside it was so dark that the yew tree's black mass had blended into the night. But I knew it was there. I could sense its wavy, ancient fronds fluttering in the night. I opened the window and lent out, inhaling the slight, sharp catch in the air, the advancing grip of autumn. I listened to see, to sense, what was out there, what moved in the night. But I heard nothing. I lent further out, holding my breath until I was finally just able to hear a distant television. Did it reassure me? Did it tell me or let me feel that I was not completely alone? For a brief moment I stood very still and then, almost in a frenzy, I slammed the window shut and jerked the curtains together in an effort to push away my uneasy thoughts as I retreated back into the room.

But I was not successful. My thoughts continued their nasty little dance just outside my reach and finally I gave up and staggered from my mother's bedroom, crossing the small landing and almost falling into my room. I was asleep, fully clothed, before my body even touched the bed.

But I didn't sleep through the night. Instead I woke quite suddenly in the early hours of the morning, disturbed both by the lightening that flashed outside in the still dark sky and the thunder growling around the cottage. I sat up and looked out to see if it was raining, wondering if I should get up and close the window. But everything was dry. And so, wide awake but loathe to move, I lay back and watched the sky gradually lighten as unseen birds began their joyful singing. I heard how their voices soared above a chorus of cooing pigeons, blending harmoniously together and drowning out the distant thunder. Until, without warning, a blackbird shrieked a strident, panic-stricken cry that silenced the other birds, warning them of some hidden danger. For a strange, unmeasured moment it seemed that the ensuing silence would engulf us all and that the whole universe was holding its breath to see if good would triumph over evil. The wait was almost unbearable and only broken when a single bird began to sing with the purity only the innocent possess. Each note was like a rounded jewel of sound, high and sweet, piercing the thunder's last grumble and rising to the heavens, borne upwards with the certainty of unblemished goodness. Until, as suddenly as it had begun, the singing stopped and it was as if, once again, the fate of the whole world hung in the balance. I tensed, straining myself to hear whatever would emerge from the charged silence. Even so I only just caught the slight sound of something panting for breath and the soft padding of footsteps as it ran beneath my window. Sounds that made me shiver and seek, desperately, to deny.

Somehow I eventually fell asleep, waking again soon after six as my room began to fill with the misty light of an early autumn morning. By then all signs of the night's thunderstorm had vanished, the dawn was pushing away the darkness, replacing it with a fragile promise of fresh hope.

It was a short-lived hope, immediately dashed when I turned over and saw the adoption paper beside the bed. And felt the sudden lurching within my guts and knew that the smallness of my room, even of the whole cottage was too confining, too enclosing and that I had to get out, to get air into my lungs and, if only by physically exhausting myself, walk off some of the tension and confusion. Especially before visitors came knocking at my door with their awkward condolences.

Twenty minutes later I was carefully unlocking the front door and slipping quietly out into the road. I rejected the idea of driving somewhere in the car and then walking, not out of consideration for my neighbours but because I wanted my presence to remain undetected. I feared a well-intentioned early riser offering to come with me. Instead I hugged my light jacket close to my body and hurried down towards the estuary, drawn by a need to place myself within the church's protective aura, wishing that, like some thief of old, I could enter the church and seek sanctuary. But the modern world now values a church's material wealth more than the refuge it once offered and I knew all doors would be securely locked.

I scurried down to the river, following the path beside the church, grateful for the comforting proximity of its solid structure and the whispered promise of its assurance. The river behind the church flowed sluggishly, giving the impression that it wished to conceal its proximity to the open wildness of the sea, a deception belied by the mournful shrieks of the seabirds circling above me.

For a moment I stood looking out across the river and the

marshes beyond. Then, having quickly turned to confirm the church's existence—and protection—I sat down, suddenly feeling as remote and isolated as the river pretended to be. A few gulls, the carriers of dead sailors' souls, called out as they soared above me but otherwise there were few sounds. At the same time the silence was filled with the *feeling* of sound, the sense of life along the river's banks, the idea of scuttling insects, the knowledge of fish beneath the water. Everything seemed to be linked, part of a single, united whole that inhaled and exhaled in tandem with the whole universe. A universe to which I felt even my breathing was joined.

I fixed my eyes on the river, watching its effortless movement, seeing how particular drops of water drifted gently past me as they flowed away to join the waiting vastness of the sea. I saw a stately swan move towards the opposite bank, its regal power unchallenged. I heard a fish signal its presence with a sudden splash and, somewhere, the agitated cheep of moorhens. And a lorry's faraway drone as it thundered along the road, a sound that brought me back to my present reality, reminding me of the lorry that had killed Bertie. Bertie who still lay, alone and dead, in his basket in my mother's room.

'I suppose you'll wonder why I've done this.'

I now saw the complexity of my mother's question. And of her statement. She had said so much—and left as much unsaid. Unsaid forever. Yet it was suddenly so obvious that too many interpretations could be found in the eight words of her apparently simple but enigmatic line. But what were they? And why, why, why? And why did I even ask? I knew no answers awaited me. I was never going to know what had driven my mother to this, what had made her, through her mind's fractured prism, give me the facts that she had previously hidden so assiduously. And then said so little. In the end it was as if she merely sought to absolve herself, to opt out of details yet draw me into her confidence, to admit that she was confused and unbalanced. Allowing me to gain information but withdrawing my right to understand the reasons behind it. I also saw, despite the vastness of the chasm now opening before me, that she *had* sought to reach me, that even in the depths of her despair she had not abandoned me. All I now needed to find was forgiveness, unconditional forgiveness. And I knew it would take time for this to become a spontaneous act. Whatever I had understood of my mother's actions gave, as yet, no comfort. I did not have even the residual thought that most mothers, even dead ones, can bequeath their children: that, after all, she *was* my mother. And then again the circle formed and, once more, I recognized that I would *always* think of her as my mother. And yet even as I acknowledged her permanence in my life I admitted to a growing confusion about my real identity.

And what role, I now wondered, had The Bastard played in all this. He must have known I was adopted. Was that why he'd felt no guilt about simply vanishing? That because I wasn't really his child he'd felt no sense of responsibility towards me? Had he been angry with my mother for adopting me? Then I admitted another strange little thought into my mind: was I perhaps *his* child, adopted because my real mother had died? Or run away? Or been unable to keep me? Married to someone else—perhaps my real mother was the dreadful Mrs Baines? But no, all this was too unlikely. None of it was even possible and I knew I was just trying to provide myself with plausible origins. But then again and again however much I gave my mind a free rein to run down all these pointless avenues I was always pulled back to a basic and more sombre set of facts. One: *I was adopted* and two: *I had never been told.* Until now and in a brutal fashion. When I was trying to come to terms with the death of my mother. Who was not my mother.

I felt a feathery tickling on my leg and glanced down to see an ant scuttling around my ankle. Without thinking I smashed my hand down onto it. And then wondered why I had been so violent. Couldn't I just have flicked it off? Was I looking or subconsciously seeking some way of hitting out at something, anything, on which to vent my feelings of helplessness? I shrugged and looked up, distracted by the swan beating his wings as he rose and began to propel himself along the surface of the river before, with an effortless surge of energy, he was airborne. Slowly he climbed higher, soaring upwards, as graceful in the air as he had been on water, my eyes fixed on him until he disappeared from sight, flying out towards the coast.

It was time I too moved on.

Even though I could hear a distant rumble of thunder I decided to turn inland and walk up to the wood. As yet there was no sign of rain though the smell of it was in the air and I knew I should turn back. I knew I was being warned but I chose to ignore the look of the sky, the signs that were clear, that were there, perhaps, to protect me. But my mind twisted everything round and I choose to believe that the unseen forces were just being fair and alerting me, despite knowing I would keep walking.

I loved this part of the land and as I turned away from the river and the church I felt in tune with all that surrounded me. It was centuries old and ancient, formed by the whims of the elements. Man's hand had touched it lightly and with such respect that it had remained wild, the haunt of strange and unspecified powers. I kept going until I reached the slightly higher ground, the beginning of the slope up to the wood. Only then did I look back, drawn as always by the security of the church. It was still early enough to feel the day's freshness and sense that it was even enhanced by the lurking threat of the faraway thunder's rumble. The presence of other forces was less hidden; their boldness assured by their knowledge that no one would leave their homes once the rain started. Soon they would be free to disport themselves in a world that was theirs by right. Already the sky was growing darker, its blackness suddenly heightened by a streak of lightening shivering down from the clouds to earth itself behind the church. Soon, very soon, Nature would demonstrate her power.

Though I knew I would be soaked I continued walking in the

direction of the wood, already thinking of the mournful journey that had been made so many centuries ago. I wondered if there had been just such a charged atmosphere when a group of men emerged from their night's sanctuary in the wood I was now heading towards. Perhaps they too had sensed the protective security of Nature's fury as they marched forward, staggering under the weight of their dead king's bloodied body. They were tired and weary, some of them were wounded and all of them frightened, hungry and cautious. Above all they knew that the army of the new king, the army which had scattered their forces and put their land to the torch and sword was even now hunting them down. Yet despite these dangers their loyalty drove them to risk their lives and carry the mortal remains of their lord and king to his eternal rest in Blythburgh's church. The pain, sorrow and intensity of that journey, the heartache of the sad cortege was ground into the land; the clandestine carrying of a king who should have been carried before his people, draped in glorious robes could still be sensed. Stories of solitary early morning walkers catching sight of this procession were once commonplace. When I was a child Arthur Boggis told me of the crisp winter morning when he had heard the faint rattle of metal and seen an unknown group of men emerging from the woods and making their way furtively down towards the church.

The first splatter of rain hit my face with stinging intensity as I rushed into the wood, almost deafened by the great crack of thunder sounding directly overhead. I quickly huddled under a sheltering tree, all too conscious that this was not *my* domain. And that I was not alone, knowing as I stood in the shadows that something was watching me, waiting to see how I would react, to see if I would honour its presence. But the ancient, unseen forces, the elemental shadows finally let me be, sensing perhaps my need to draw something from them, to harness their strength without stealing it, knowing that I respected and deferred to their prior rights of occupation. And so the dark trees remained no more than dark trees, their appearance softened by the mosses and lichens covering their gnarled surfaces.

Yet though conscious of being benevolently protected I continued to sense the fury of the battle raging around me. Streaks of lightening forced their way down through the trees and terrifying claps of thunder followed every jagged flash. The rain's buffeting rage whipped through the trees. I could almost feel the palpable anger around me as unseen and powerful presences danced in the branches of the whiplashed trees, waiting to reveal which wild gods would demand to be propitiated. But in the end I was protected. I was welcome. I had not misjudged the nature of the powers around me.

Gradually the storm abated, the lightening stopped, the thunder began a slow retreat and the rain dried to a gentle drizzle. I went to the edge of the wood and looked down to the church, almost seeing the king's cortege nearing its final sanctuary. In a few more minutes the rain would stop completely and allow me to retrace my steps, to make my way back down the ancient burial route.

What is it that tells us we are not alone? What animal instinct do we still cling to so tenaciously, even after aeons of evolution? What is it that still makes us capable of sensing these things? One moment I felt safe, alone and unthreatened. The next I was almost deafened by the thumping of my heart. Even though no sudden sound, no shrieking bird, no sinister cracking of a twig, no sensation of movement through the trees, nothing tangible or audible had alerted me. But it was there. Nearby. Close and waiting. Knowing and watching me.

I turned round, looking back into the heart of the wood unable to make rational queries, conscious only of the sensations shivering through me, my whole being alert to whatever I now knew was about to emerge from within the trees. At first there was no sound, no disturbance, not even a faint padding of feet until, and without warning, a huge dog suddenly rushed past me with the force of a deadly arrow, passing so close that I could feel its breath and catch the great panting gulps of air being pumped through its heaving chest. It was huge, heavy and black, moving so fast that there should have been a desperately fleeing prey running before it. But the terrible dog was alone, bounding in great leaps down the dead king's burial path, heading towards the church. My transfixed eyes followed its course and so saw how it suddenly veered away, swinging out towards the bleaker land of the heath. And disappeared. But not because it had raced into some fold of the land or behind some hedge or into some tree cover. Instead, and I knew this with utter certainty, the great dog had vanished, quite literally, into thin air.

It was not cold but I shivered and then scuttled, as fast as I could, down towards the church. I kept my eyes fixed on its tower and did all I could to keep my mind a total blank, praying that no one would see me and know that the expression on my face was naked terror.

I was lucky. Though people were already emerging from their houses I reached the church without being stopped. Even so when I came into the shade of the porch I was still holding my breath and muttering *Please, please, please let it be open* as I pushed my hand against the great door. Again my wishes were granted and, with a slight creak, the door of the church known as the Cathedral of the Marshes swung open to offer me sanctuary.

Lightness. Space. Peace and tranquillity. The church's interior swept my whole being heavenwards with the sheer impact of its soaring sense of the sacred. It was as if its stark lightness had the capacity to soothe every lost soul, as if some magic within the church could not only nurture all those who sought refuge but confirm them as an integral part of the universe. Like every weary pilgrim before me I felt I was slipping into the arms of an enclosing intimacy and that though, as with all those who had come before me, I entered in awe and as a supplicant, I now found myself recognized and accepted as an equal. Conscious of the benevolence surrounding me I paused, aware of being in the presence of something I could only call divine.

Light was streaming in through the East window, pouring down towards me like a river from heaven and falling on the polished gleam of the flagstones. I raised my eyes to the great arch-braced, tie-beam roof that I used to think supported the heavens. And saw the angels Arthur Boggis once told me looked down from heaven to protect me. I knew each one of them individually, their all-seeing eyes, their long gilded wings stretched out in hovering flight, wings so real I used to imagine I could hear their faintly beating flutter. Only when I began growing up did I very gradually understand that these angels were carved and inanimate, that they merely adorned the roof of the church, that heaven was somewhere else and that students of church architecture regarded them as nothing more than fine examples of medieval art. But I used to wonder. I still do. I accept the reality of their stillness and their painted, wooden features. But I remain certain of their grace and the benevolence of their protective blessings for I believe that the master-craftsman who carved them was God-inspired. My only difficulty had been accepting that the angels would never fly down to gather me up to heaven.

I walked slowly up the nave, wishing I could take off my shoes and feel the coolness of the flagstones, smiling to myself as I remembered a long ago Harvest Festival when I sat beside my mother and her friends as they decorated the church. And how, bored by their chatter, I had eventually wandered off, disinterested in the plenty, the burnished colours of the fruits, vegetables and flowers whose abundance promised survival through the grimness of winter. And how, when I reached the font I had sat down and, after removing my shoes and socks, had twiddled my toes with delight before getting up to walk around, carefully putting one foot in front of the other as I made my way up the nave, savouring the texture of the ancient and uneven floor. Until I stopped and gazed up at the angels, holding out my arms, moving them slowly up and down, imitating their suspended flight. And how, without thought I lay down directly beneath them, feeling not only that we were close to each other but that I was flying up to them and they down to me.

Until my mother suddenly shouted: 'Sophie! What are you *doing?* Get up at *once*! And put your shoes on! *Now*!'

I can still hear the voice of Arthur Boggis. 'Mrs Neville,' he had said, 'let her be. She's bin feeling where the good Lord walked and flyin' about up there with His angels.'

Arthur was like that. He could say such unexpected things but always in a way that left no room for discussion. My mother looked at him and shrugged her shoulders, knowing there was no argument she could use and so left me to wander about, happily barefooted until it was time to go home.

I looked around the church, trying to imagine what it had been like on that fateful early morning when the grieving followers of Anna, King of East Anglia, had entered with his broken and bleeding body. Though the church was then no more than a small wooden building neither the brutality of his death nor the secrecy of his burial in an unmarked grave—or the building of a new church—has erased his memory. The king who defeated him is forgotten. It is King Anna who lives on, carved alongside his four canonized daughters on the present church's choir-stalls, his spirit at peace, his earthly remains long indistinguishable from the earth around him.

I gazed up at the light entering through the high windows, now bright and clear, retaining no evidence of the storm that had driven me here. Yet in my uneasy mind I could still hear the faint echoes of lashing rain, of the wind whipping through the treetops as howling whispers sped over the earth. A storm that, even in this place of peace and sanctuary, would not allow me to forget the great black dog I had seen earlier. And with good reason. I couldn't pretend I didn't know who and what he was. His was a familiar presence. Even in this church. Especially in *this* church. I turned to look at the North door, my eyes unable to deny the long, dark, scorched scratches that this dog, this *same* dog, had made more than four centuries ago. Black Shuck we call him here. Black Shuck the great, dark harbinger of death. The Devil himself some say.

Though he has haunted this land for centuries and lonely travellers have left countless stories of being terrified by his sudden appearances, these seemingly innocuous scratches are the only clear evidence of his power and presence. They were put there one terrible Sunday in August 1577, a day that started with people hurrying into the church for the morning service as a great storm began gathering. Once inside the congregation prayed and listened to the preacher, aware of the growing intensity of a great keening wind. Maybe as the singing began they hoped their voices would drown out the cracking rolls of thunder. But to no avail. The rain began hitting against the stained glass with fury, even as the churchyard trees started beating their branches onto the windows in a rage of desperation. Terrible thunder roared and growled and angry, jagged shrieks of lightning seared across the darkened sky. Outside the church a great crashing and breaking could be heard as if unseen giants were uprooting trees while, from inside the belfry came the wild and frightful clanging of the great bells breaking loose from their restraining ropes. No doubt the congregation believed that inside the church they were safe, directly under God's closest and most immediate protection. A certainty that must have crumbled when they saw the stained glass saints beginning to crack and shatter onto the floor below while the wings of the wooden angels remained in frozen flight. And then, as despair clawed at every heart a great bolt of white lightning struck at the bell tower, heightening the discordant madness of its bells.

It was then, as the South door cracked open with a great bang that the true terror began. First came a streaming streak of fire, rushing into the church and snaking its way down towards the high altar, followed by the awful shape of Black Shuck. The monstrous dog bounded up the aisle with dreadful ease, moving in powerful leaps, killing a man and his son simply by brushing past them as he pursued the hissing flames, rushing towards the altar and his confrontation with the Almighty. And here, at last, the challenge was met. The fire suddenly died to a smoking wisp and the dog ceased his headlong rush. For a charged moment he had stood with one huge paw raised before, with a terrible howl he turned and rushed towards the North door. And here, as he threw his weight against it, a strange and unnatural silence fell. For a moment the door appeared to hold until, with a great roaring howl, Black Shuck hurled himself at it once more, raking his claws down its surface with such force that fire seared into the wood with a great scorching hiss. This time the door yielded and in an instant the dog was gone, out into the remnants of the storm.

Though Black Shuck had vanished the terrified congregation remained transfixed and unable to move. Only very gradually did their fear subside enough for them to begin examining the surrounding devastation. At first they knelt by the dead father and his son, gazing in horror at the terror frozen onto their faces as the wind still toyed with their fears, hissing and whining around the church, blowing in through the broken windows and sending shards of broken glass scudding along the floor. Many of them shivered and began to cry, terrified by the sound of the doors banging open and shut as rain continued to pour down, splashing onto a floor covered with broken masonry.

But in the end their attention was drawn and held by the small fluttering flames still burning on the North door, flames ignited by Black Shuck. And even now, in this age of reason when both God and the Devil are denied, the charred marks of his dreadful touch remain, scorched deep into the wood.

'Thought I'd find yer here, gal.'

I jumped, but only slightly, already smiling as I turned round.

'Arthur Boggis, you know too much.'

'Yer reckon so?'

It wasn't really a question. I liked his sense of being solid, of being certain and unflappable.

'Tell me why, why did I come here?'

'Well, I don't reckon yer'd had a decent night's sleep. And I were up afore you and saw you come out. I knew near enough where you'd go…'

'And why? Why I'd go there?'

'I reckon so.'

I looked at him, seeing his weather-beaten face, his high red cheeks, the broken veins all clustered together, his eternal smile and, most of all, his deep, kind eyes. Sometimes I wondered at his knack of appearing when most needed and suddenly realized how glad I was to see him. And then wondered how long he'd been in the church, watching me.

'He's bin about a mite too often recently,' he said pointing at the door.

'Arthur,' I hesitated, just for a moment, 'Arthur, I heard him, very early, before it got light, going past the cottage. And then...then I saw him, up near the wood.'

'I know. I saw him too, gal.'

There was a long pause. A stranger entering the church would have wondered what we had in common. The old countryman and the city woman. But these were only externals. I'd spent too much of my childhood trailing along behind Arthur Boggis not to be able to dovetail into his mood and as many of his thoughts as he cared to share with me. He didn't have children of his own and when I was growing up I occasionally wondered if he hadn't chosen more or less to adopt me because of my own fatherless state. And now, a huge voice shouted inside my head, my motherless, parentless state. Did he know I was adopted? Was this secret going to be like the one where everyone but me had known about The Bastard and Mrs Baines?

'What does it mean, Arthur? Why is he about? Is it, is it anything to do with my mother?'

'Maybe. Meself I reckon its more that in these godless times we have to be reminded. If we see Old Shuck and see his marks upon us, well, it stands to reason we'll think of the Almighty and our eyes get opened and we'll see what He's given us, what's really here. And when yer see Black Shuck you's afeared and yer look at the land, yer look at the rivers and yer remember the creatures we're supposed to share it with and see what greedy buggers we are. I ain't so sure we shouldn't be seein' a lot more of Black Shuck than we bin doing.'

I looked at Arthur in awe. He was a man of very few words and in all the years I'd known him he'd hardly ever said as much as he'd just done. Yet nothing came as a surprise. He'd lived his whole life by the tennets of what he'd just said.

'Well, gal, why don't yer come back and have breakfast with us? The missus is fretting about you. Then, after that we can go and give old Bertie a proper send off.'

♓

It had been years since I'd been in Arthur's cottage. There had hardly ever been a reason for me to go there, even as a child. It wasn't anything to do with him not wanting to ask me in or me not wanting to go but more that whenever I went to see him he was always outside in his garden. His wife, who I never called anything but Mrs Boggis was often out 'doing' for my mother. As a result going inside the small and spotlessly neat cottage was always something of a special occasion.

Mrs Boggis was waiting for us, beaming in the doorway and wiping her hands on her apron as we approached. She stood back to welcome me, gesturing towards the one large, downstairs room where it was immediately obvious she did not believe in restraint. Though there was hardly any furniture it was all far too big for the room and, as in my mother's cottage a large table was set squarely and precisely in its middle. It was groaning with generous abundance, laid out like an advertisement for the English Tourist Board. Breads, buns, toast, butter as well as jams and marmalades—all handmade and in neatly labelled jars—crowded together. The roundness of the Boggis' was hardly surprising.

'Sit down. How about some tea? You look proper dun in…I told Arthur, I sed she'll not be getting a proper night's sleep…Yer go and see if she's wantin' anything. But he sed "Let her be…if she wants anything she'll ask." But cum mornin' I told him, I said yer *haf* ter go and bring her here. No matter what.'

As if suddenly satisfied that she'd exonerated herself from any suspicion of not having had my best interests at heart Mrs Boggis stopped speaking and looked at me with concern as I squeezed round the table and into a chair.

'Mrs Boggis. I...I'm...I was so grateful. Thank you so much for...for all the food in the fridge. And the flowers. The cottage looked...I don't know what my mother and I would do without...I mean what we, I, would do without you.' I paused, uncomfortable that perhaps I was making Mrs Boggis uneasy. I could still hear Arthur outside cleaning his boots. I decided to stick to specifics.

'I'd love some tea.'

Instantly a huge teapot appeared, brown, ancient and comforting. As soon as it was on the table a great knitted tea cosy descended onto its plumpness.

'Jes let it brew a bit,' Mrs Boggis advised, 'And what'll yer be havin' ter eat? I'll be certain that yer didn't eat last night. You young people don't look after yerselves. Well, I'm gonna see to it that you get a proper meal...'

She turned and went off into the kitchen, which almost immediately began reverberating to the sounds of cooking. It appeared that the food already *on* the table was to be discounted for my ears caught the noise of eggs frying, of bacon sizzling, of sausages spitting in fat. I listened to Mrs Boggis cutting, chopping and cooking as Arthur came in and sat down opposite me, at ease but looking faintly out of place. It was obvious that he was an outdoor person and would never quite fit into a house, even his own home.

'Pour for yerself, gal, and give me a cup.' He indicated the covered teapot and I followed his order, standing up to get sufficient weight behind my arm to lift it.

I watched as he spooned sugar into his tea and began stirring. He was marking time, waiting. But any speculation about his motives was swept aside by Mrs Boggis' triumphant glee as she surged out of the kitchen and placed a large plate in front of me. It was filled to overflowing with enough food to feed us all.

For a brief moment I thought of saying that I couldn't, I simply couldn't eat so much but as I inhaled the deliciousness of all she had cooked I remembered that I hadn't eaten since the day before. To my surprise I accepted that I was ravenously hungry.

I finished everything, even reaching out to take some of Mrs Boggis' homemade bread and marmalade and then washing it all down with more tea, understanding the comfort and nourishment of a good, square meal. Yet once I'd finished I looked up, somewhat appalled at what suddenly seemed like greed.

'There Arthur Boggis, didn't I tell yer she needed ter eat?' Mrs Boggis was positively glowing with pleasure.

He smiled and pushed his own empty plate to one side.

'So, where'll it be then?'

'Bertie?'

'He were a gud'un.'

I thought of Bertie. Though I'd always preferred the idea of big dogs I had to admit that Bertie had had a big heart. Perhaps he wasn't quite the dog for a grave out on the heath but equally I wasn't quite sure about my mother's garden. Then I had an idea.

'Arthur, what about under the yew tree?'

His nod settled the matter and as I got up to go he said: 'I'll be right along in about an hour. Don't you worry about a thing.'

I thanked Mrs Boggis profusely, and left.

♓

The shift began two days later. The first evidence of it appearing without warning when I was holding my hand under the kitchen tap, looking out of the window, my mind more or less blank as I waited for the water to heat up. Suddenly I realized that I couldn't see clearly, that my vision was beginning to blur. I blinked—and found that tears were streaming down my cheeks, flowing of their own accord, so separate from the rest of me that though I could hardly see I found myself asking 'What on earth is going on, what is happening to me?'

I went and slumped down in the large armchair, curling my legs up under me, peripherally aware that the crying seemed to have stopped, as it had started, without involving me. I looked vaguely around the room, subconsciously seeking something that could reassure me, could give me some semblance of something, somewhere being normal. It surprised me that, of all things, it turned out to be the mirror, Montezuma's shaving mirror. I heard someone giggle and it took a moment to realize it was me. But by then it seemed as if my body was acting completely independently.

But not my mind.

My mind was full of swirling chaos, filled with so many unclear, half-formed thoughts that they seemed to ebb and flow in a thick mist. It took ages for me to realize that I should make a list to clarify what I *had* and what I *needed* before I could work out what I should *do*.

It was—eventually—a very short list:

My mother was dead.
My mother was not my mother.
My father was not, I supposed, my father.
And if he was he was also 'whereabouts unknown'.

It was not encouraging but I consoled myself with the notion that at least these were all incontestable facts. Until the inner voice asked: *What about the hotel ledger?* What about it I screamed silently to myself. Well, I answered, don't you think it rather suggests that though your father might once have vanished he has now shown signs of re-appearing? That the Bastard therefore lives I giggled inanely to myself. Before the next thought came hurtling back at me: *so what are you going to do about him?*

♓

The morning passed. The clock ticked on, the hours were chimed. A newspaper came through the door. Junk mail arrived. The deep freeze purred on and off. The odd beam creaked.

And all the while I sat in the chair trying to empty my mind so that I could see things clearly. Of course I was deceiving myself because I wasn't being completely honest since, somewhere deep inside me, my decision had already been made. Long before I accepted this fact I knew exactly what I was going to do. But I played a game with myself, dodging what I didn't want to see, pretending to be honest and level-headed. And at the same time seeking within myself to have my decision condoned and accepted.

I would go to Malabar. I would find out about The Bastard. I would find out who and what he was, where he lived—and whether or not he was still with the dreadful Mrs Baines. Then, perhaps, I could get at least one parent back. And then maybe, just maybe, I would find out who the couple were who had once pretended to be my parents. And then perhaps, just perhaps, I would find out who *I* was.

I paused—and in that brief hesitation just caught the thought that whispered: *And what about Satishan?* Did I blush? I don't know—but I did concede that behind all the other thoughts was the one reminding me that by going to Malabar I would be able to see him again. There, I thought, I've said it. Then immediately—as if one side of myself was trying to fool the other side—I rushed in to justify everything by adding that well, after all, Satishan *had* been working with The Bastard. He knew about him and, I supposed, where to find him. And he'd said I should come to Malabar. Beyond that I cheated and played with a loaded deck. I arranged the cards so that they would appear in the order I wished them to. I even asked myself about Mrs Baines and wondered if she'd also been in Portugal. Had this been yet another time when everybody knew about everything except me?

Eventually I got up, fetched my bag, reached into the inner pocket and pulled out Satishan's card. *T. Satishan Nambiar* it said in embossed letters with below, in smaller type, an address, a telephone number—and an email address. As soon as I saw that he had email I felt trapped. Somehow I thought, so far as I thought at all, that I would just arrive on his doorstep with some unlikely excuse about...well I just hadn't thought it through. Now I was forced to. And it unnerved me that if I sent him an email I might have an answer within a few hours. Yet if I was going to go I had no other choice but to email him. And this brought me back to examining my real reason for wanting to go to Malabar.

All that I was very clear about was that I did not want to mention The Bastard. Somehow I had the idea that he might just possibly be with Satishan and that if he knew I was on his trail he might disappear again. Once I'd thought this out I came to accept that my only option was to ask Satishan if he had been serious when he suggested I should come to Malabar.

Dear Satishan,

I hope you have reached home safely.

I'm now sorting out my mother's home and hope to be finished in about a month's time. I feel I'd like to go away for a break once it's done and I wondered if you really meant it when you suggested I should visit Malabar? I thought I might go around South India for a couple of weeks and then, if convenient, I would love to come and spend a day or so with you.

With best wishes,

Sophie

Dear Sophie,

I have been expecting to hear from you for quite some time and of course I was serious. You must come here. And there can be no formality. You will come and stay and there can be no nonsense about a day or two. India is a large country and if you haven't been before then may I suggest you spend all your time here? I think you will need a rest when you have finished in your mother's house. You are welcome to stay as long as you like.

Yours,

Satishan

> *PS the festival of our Goddess will be in two months' time—it would be wonderful if you could be here then.*

It was the postscript that decided me.

For the next few weeks things were easy, or easier. I had plenty to do in the cottage, sorting and shifting through my mother's things and then making separate piles of what to keep or give to people and what to throw away. Though I was always wary that there might still be some surprises waiting for me I did what had to be done as methodically and as unemotionally as possible, moving through the cottage room by room. I went through all of my mother's papers carefully, searching for more signs of what, by then, I thought of as her double life. But she had either buried her tracks remarkably well—or simply never made any for I never found anything that threw any more light on either my adoption or her marriage.

In between I made calls to my travel agent, went briefly to London for my visa, had the necessary jabs and gradually prepared myself for India. Every few days I emailed Satishan with some query or another and gradually felt more at ease about going to Malabar. I kept silent about The Bastard. I thought as little as possible about almost everything I was doing, working until late at night and only going to bed when I felt so tired that sleep was a certainty. Otherwise I went for early morning walks, I saw Arthur and Mrs Boggis almost daily and met my neighbours and found that though their words never diminished the ache that lurked permanently within me, there was a comfort in talking to them about my mother.

Finally one evening just over six weeks later I realized everything had been done. Everything that was obvious was accounted for, bureaucracy was satisfied, everything was in its proper place. All that remained was to go and say goodbye to Arthur and Mrs Boggis and, as usual, leave the spare key with them. Arthur was digging in his garden when I arrived but stopped as soon as he saw me.

'How are yer, gal?' he asked, 'you look all dun in.'

I smiled. Arthur always came straight to the point.

'Yes, I am. I'm exhausted. Why do we all have to deal with so much paper work? Anyway it's all done now. I hope.'

I put out a hand with the spare key and Arthur took it without a word, looking down at it, appearing to consider it before shoving it into his trouser pocket.

'Reckon it'll be a while afore we see yer again.'

It was hard to tell if this was a statement or a question.

'I've decided to keep the cottage,' I said in case it was the latter, 'at least for now. I'll decide about it later, after I get back from India.'

'Its good that yer' going.'

Again I was noncommittal, though rather surprised that Arthur should voice such an opinion. It certainly wasn't shared by most of the other local people.

'Do yer good to get away. Portugal wasn't no holiday. Yer've bin through a lot gal. Now you look atta yerself for a change—and don't worry about a thing here. Me and the Missus'll see to everything.'

When I left him my idea was to go straight home, have a light meal and sleep early. I wanted to make an early start and be back in London in time to pack before another early night and the flight to India. Yet, as I walked slowly back towards the cottage I knew something was drawing me to the church, that perhaps I should go and seek blessings for my journey. *Blessings?* Where had that word come from? Then I remembered Satishan saying how I had been blessed to see the murals in the convent's church. Well, I thought, it's an English word—although as I examined it I saw how rarely anyone used it as he had done.

This time the interior was shadowy. There was not enough light left in the evening sky to penetrate the windows. But there was still that extraordinary sense of stillness and calm. There was no feeling that the encroaching darkness would dispel any of the church's certainty. The shadows and the ghosts, if any existed, were benevolent.

I sat down in a pew, caressing my hand around the well-worn figure carved at its end. Then I slumped back and looked up at the angels. How could they always be so still? Were they not a blessing too? Had they not always protected me? Then I remembered the painted angels on the convent's chapel wall, hovering above the Nativity scene. They hadn't moved either. Portuguese angels, English angels. Did angels give blessings or were they, themselves, the blessing? And would these angels come with me, would they protect me on my journey to India?

I made a mental pause. I had to be careful. I was edging out into dangerous territory. For weeks I had been dodging the real issue of why I was going to Malabar. Only now, seated in this quiet church and absorbing its enfolding calm did I finally begin to skirt close to the subject.

So what am I going there for?

To find The Bastard, I answered, glibly. To find out, if possible, who I am.

Oh yes, and is that all, is that really all you're going for, my other side asked?

Again I looked up at the angels, up at the one hovering directly above me.

'Help me,' I whispered, pretending that it was not a prayer.

♓

It was in the limbo of the plane, as it droned through the long hours of the flight that the last of my ghosts finally appeared. He came back like a sigh, suddenly breathing his way up through my subconscious and then just settling on the edge of my inner vision so that I could feel his presence. *Richard.* I shifted in my seat and turned towards the window, seeking perhaps some blankness. But it was too late. He had caught me, however gently, unawares and I knew there was no escape. The time had come to face him.

Richard. Richard and I. It has been nine years now, nine years since the accident. Isn't it, I thought, about time that you finally examined your thoughts about him and looked at what really happened? Isn't it time you were honest? But have I lied, I asked myself? Oh yes, I answered, you know you have. How, I asked next—and trapped myself. The part of me that was uninvolved smiled at the uneasy crossroads my mind had reached. I knew that if I'd had these thoughts elsewhere I would have gone and distracted myself, found something to do, made a cup of coffee or a shopping list or thought of someone to call. But here I was helpless, and yet, though tied down in my seat and vulnerable I also saw that I was now facing what I'd so often simply side-stepped.

Richard. What had he really been like? You know, you know, I screamed to myself. Good-looking, amusing and, and—yes, what else? I raced to find ways to describe him, ways I could live with. Well he knew so much, he was clever, he—yes, yes we all know that—but what else? I was caught. I had to answer this time.

Richard Shelton was my husband for six years. Until the accident killed him. And saved me. There, it had slipped out. Or begun to. Maybe now it was going to be easier. Yes, it was true, he *was* good-looking, amusing, clever. But he was also unkind, judgemental, critical. *'Do you really think your idea is a good one?' 'Is that the best you can do?' 'How do you ever manage to do anything by yourself?'* No, that's not true—I rushed to defend him. Perhaps, perhaps sometimes, once in a while he would speak like this. So what? It didn't mean anything. But it did, I screamed. And anyway it wasn't just that, was it? I mean what about Catherine? And Julia? And...well did they really matter? Did any of them finally matter? No. They didn't. Here I made the last pause. It was time to say it, to admit it. What mattered, what really mattered were the put downs in public, the sudden bursts of temper, the control. They were what had made life intolerable. That and his final legacy: the guilt he had bequeathed me. Guilt that he had died, guilt that I didn't have to struggle with the decision to leave him and hating myself for these feelings and not setting them aside and being stronger. No wonder I'd locked him away.

No wonder I'd torn that misleading photograph in two and hidden half of it. No wonder I'd denied him for so long.

Now part of me also wondered why he'd chosen to ease back into my life at this precise moment. What had made him do it now, at a time when I'd almost managed to erase him altogether? Was it that everyone else in my life had been revealed as some kind of impostor? Was it that Richard was somehow all that was left? I longed to subscribe to this idea because, somehow, it was a comfortable notion, one I could live with. The trouble was I already knew there was another reason—one whose truth I knew I would be forced to face. The truth was all to do with Satishan.

Satishan. I hesitated. I was now out on very thin ice, slipping and sliding, aware that at any moment a sudden crack could open up and I'd be sucked down into a dark oblivion. I had to do this fast and then get out. Satishan, I whispered silently, almost as if I was testing myself, not quite knowing, even then, if I would admit to anything. I waited, waited to see how far I'd go, knowing that if I opened the door to that inner region where the answer was waiting I'd never be able to close it again. Satishan had brought some part of me back to life, he had shown me something I hardly dared to think about, he had made me aware of myself again. And that frightened me—even as it attracted me. And now because of the emotions he had aroused I was forced to face the unfinished business with Richard.

The irony was that the fear of finding something awful proved to be less terrible than what I discovered. For an hour or so I summoned up memories of my marriage. How it had started and what its attractions had been—and how long it had taken me to realize that I had deceived myself. And how, as part of that deception, I had sidestepped reality, realigned my perceptions, adjusted and adapted them—and then kept silent, unable and, I thought, unworthy to confront an unpalatable truth. When all these thoughts had finished and their slow procession through my mind had been examined in greater or lesser detail, I was left with a kind of peace. I knew their vibrations would continue to affect me, but I also knew that now I'd brought them out into the light I would begin to see them for what they were—obstacles which could be overcome.

♓

Hours later, sometime just after midnight according to Indian time the plane landed at Mumbai and I stepped out into a night of heavy, cloying dampness, the air in the terminal so humid the air conditioners did little more than suggest coolness. At Immigration I stood dutifully in line, hearing the repeated thunk of passports being stamped, knowing the innocent's fear of alien authority as I inched my way towards being officially allowed into India. In the baggage claim area I joined gaggles of people waiting restlessly for their luggage under the gaze of paunchy policemen feigning disinterest. As soon as my suitcase appeared I went effortlessly through Customs to take the shuttle bus to the domestic airport and the four hour wait for my Calicut flight. In the ensuing limbo of time I fought sleep, watching as a portly saffron-robed man sailed by surrounded by men and women clutching garlands and sari clad women tidied up recalcitrant children while businessmen read papers. I began to get a sense of a different world.

♓

When I woke up the next morning it was still dark and for a moment I was confused. *Where was I? What was I doing here? How had I arrived in this room? Who had brought me here?* Then the drowsiness of sleep retreated and though the unsettling emptiness of jet lag remained I knew I was in Satishan's house. Or, as he had called it, his ancestral home.

Malabar. I'm in Malabar. I smiled and let the tiredness settle, knowing that I still had sleep to catch up on. And there's plenty of time for that I thought, letting my mind slip back to yesterday's journey. The arrival at Mumbai, the wait and flight to Calicut where the blast of humid heat hit me like a wet towel. And Satishan.

I had wondered if I'd be able to find him, if he might again deceive me by being invisible. But he was there, standing by the exit, his stillness drawing me like a magnet and pushing everything else into the background, Only in this room, hours later did I remember how unaware I'd been of the jostling crowds, the people meeting other passengers, the people with offers of taxis, of demands to take my luggage, to find me a hotel.

'Welcome to Malabar,' he had said, 'You have been lucky; for once the flight was on time!'

Was it then, just as I was about to say something that I noticed the woman standing next to him in a blue sari? And the young girl holding his hand? A young girl, of perhaps eight or nine who looked just like Satishan. And caught the thought *My wife died in an accident eight years ago* shooting through my mind?

'Sophie, this is my sister, Jaya and this—this,' he said, looking down at the girl,' is her daughter, Ammu.' *In Malabar I would see you surrounded by relatives.*

I turned on the bed, watching the outside sky lighten, feeling the quietness, comfortable with my thoughts as I recalled Jaya's extraordinary eyes and the warmth of her welcome. And how Ammu, torn between intense curiosity and shyness had been gently encouraged to raise her hands in the Indian style of greeting and say: 'Namaskaram, Sophie-aunty.'

And then the drive, seated beside Satishan with the other two in the back and thinking for the first time *I'm in Malabar* and then saying without thinking: 'I don't think I ever thought I'd get here, that I'd really come to Malabar.'

'Why, did you doubt this place existed?' Satishan had asked, 'That Malabar is a figment of some cartographer's imagination?'

I'd shaken my head, smiling. 'No, it's not that—it's more that I'm here so suddenly. I left London less than a day ago.' Then I'd hesitated, not exactly sure what I wanted to say. 'Maybe it's something to do with the fact that when you talked about

Malabar it was as though it was a specific place on a map. And it's not. I don't know why but it took me time to realize it was a region.'

Then there had been a pause and I'd gazed out of the window, sensing the heat and seeing dry patches of red earth and the greenness of vegetation and coconut trees, of people moving, walking, on bicycles, on scooters, in auto-rickshaws, buses, cars. And somehow I'd been aware of just accepting what I saw, not necessarily without curiosity but simply as if it wasn't strange or—*when did I last sleep? Hours ago,* I'd answered, knowing in my heart that this wasn't the reason.

'You know I haven't even looked at a guidebook, I haven't read a thing,' I'd continued, looking sideways at Satishan, wondering what his reaction might be. 'Usually I arm myself with information before going anywhere—about the region, the country, its history, culture, customs, beliefs. And always their myths. I always want to know what their myths are.'

'Malabar is different. I doubt you'd get much from a guidebook—just names of towns, where to shop, beaches, hotels, the usual stuff. None of which you need. And some nonsense about culture, a little history maybe,' he'd looked at me then, a broad grin spreading across his face, 'but then I'm here for that.'

I'd laughed. 'And the culture?'

'That too.'

♓

I sat up in bed, seeing how quickly the room was now filling with light. I wanted to get up and look out but first I needed to finish off my thoughts. Not that too many were left, my recollections of the rest of the drive were a blank, erased by the jet lag sweeping through me and lulling me to sleep. And, although I woke up when the car stopped, I was too tired to absorb anything beyond the fact that we'd arrived at the place where I was going to spend the next three weeks, a huge old wooden house.

Now it seemed as if I was going to make my discoveries from the inside out.

Starting with the room I was in, a room that was almost monastically austere, the walls a dull colour, less painted than coloured by the warm patina of age. The door was wooden and the glassless window had just three wooden slats; the only furniture was a small round table, a chair and the bed I was still sitting on.

Then, remembering how I always needed to check whatever a room looked out on I slipped off the bed and padded over to the window. As I gazed out on tall palm trees and a tangle of undergrowth memories of the view from my room at the convent-hotel came drifting back. *It's the same,* I thought, *it has the same sensation of calm and quiet, of inner peace, the same regard for the landscape.* Even though it was so different. Here there was no sense of the land beyond, only the closeness of trees, of being held, surrounded by them. Then I looked back into the room and saw the goddess on the wall. Not the Virgin this time but a simply framed picture of a Hindu goddess. *Is this is why nothing feels so strange or unexpected,* I wondered? *Is it all somehow familiar, the same? Or is it something else?*

♓

An hour later I was downstairs, drawn by the sound of a house coming to life, wide-awake and ready to explore. In many ways that first day and the ones that followed it echoed those I had spent looking around the convent-hotel. The one major difference was that I had to learn not only about my physical surroundings but also the people they enclosed and to begin with I was uncomfortably aware that, except for Satishan, all of them faced me with a slight air of hesitation. Only when I observed myself doing the same did I relax, accepting that they were displaying nothing more than the hesitation of shyness, of strangers getting to know each other.

♓

They referred to their house as their ancestral home, their tharavad and explained that their system of inheritance was through Satishan and Jaya's mother and that, in time, it would be passed onto Ammu—and that this would have been the case even if she had had a brother. I never met Ammu's father, and wondered about him until it was explained that because he worked for a bank which, every three years, transferred him, he was presently in Trivandrum and seldom able to visit them. It was Jaya who explained that it was easier for them make the journey and that they all hoped his next posting would be to Kannur. I also learnt that though Satishan traditionally had what he called 'rights' in the house he did not live there but on the campus of his university in Calicut. 'I'm here for a year,' he said, 'taking a sabbatical and doing some writing, or trying to since the general perception is that I'm being idle.'

♓

One morning as we were having breakfast Jaya came in to tell Satishan that a group of men had just arrived to see him. He got up at once, giving a resigned smile as he did so. Jaya smiled at me as if I knew what their visit was about, making me angle myself to be able to see what was happening and observe that, though the men waited deferentially for Satishan, one of them, who was holding a small pad, waved it forcefully and appeared to be using a certain degree of persuasion as he talked. After a short time Satishan laughed and came inside.

'Donation time,' he said. 'And of course no escape.' 'Donation for what?' I asked.

'For a festival, at a nearby shrine. They come every year for contributions.'

When he came back from giving them the money he shook the receipt that had obviously been torn out of the pad, saying: 'Safe—until the next lot turn up!'

'Is this for the festival you emailed me about?'

He laughed again. 'No, no—and if it was *we'd* be the ones

going from house to house and doing what they're doing. And then *you* wouldn't escape!'

'When is your festival?'

'Next week—which is why your visit is so perfectly timed.'

'And what does it celebrate—and what happens?' I asked, happy that the topic had presented itself so naturally.

He looked at me for a moment and then waved a hand towards one of the empty chairs.

'*What* I'll tell you about later although of course you'll anyway see that for yourself when the time comes. For now I'll tell you something about *why*,' he said watching me as I sat down.

For a brief moment there was a pause and though at first I thought Satishan was allowing me to settle myself I later realized he was preparing me, alerting me however subtly to the fact that what he was about to tell me was important and demanded my full attention.

'There are so many stories here,' he began.' No one can ever say they aren't true because every single one has its truth—whatever the contradictions might appear to be. Our stories are about what people feel and what we see around us, they are about faith and belief, about what we feel in our hearts regardless of whether or not the plots are logically possible. And what is belief anyway? Every single one of our myths and folktales has emerged out of our land, the land that surrounds us. Their *emotion* is always true.'

There was a slight pause before Satishan spoke again.

'And I must also tell you that there are numerous complex layers in all of this. I can—I will—tell the basic story. But you would have to live here and get to know us before the further depths can be understood. But in the back of your mind keep this thought: our Bhagavathi is the whole universe.

'But let me not get too serious. You want to know about our Bhagavathi not get a long, dry lecture on either the nuances of every aspect or on why we feel the way we do,' he said with a smile. In the slight pause that followed I took the chance to shift my body.

'First all you should understand that Her story is many centuries old and, as sometimes happens with some of our other gods and goddesses, the belief is—or at least it is generally said—that She originally incarnated Herself on earth, specifically in this instance, that She manifested Herself in a Namboodiri family.' Again Satishan paused and looked at me. ' I hope I'm not going to confuse you too much with all our caste complications—all you really need to know for now is that our so-called Malabar Brahmins are more correctly known as Namboodiri Brahmins. Anyway her family's illam—that is their traditional ancestral house—was not so far from here and, like all Namboodiri women until really very recently, she was strictly brought up. There was never any question of her seeing a man from another family or going outside the house, even escorted, except in exceptional circumstances. In many ways it was a cruel existence for these women; many of them were never married because though the eldest son of the family could marry—and sometimes did so more than once—none of the younger sons were ever supposed to do so. This enabled the Namboodiris, who are both patrilineal and patriarchal, to keep their property intact and not have to divide it up amongst younger sons. Needless to say these younger sons—despite being expected to devote themselves to spiritual and scholarly pursuits—almost always took mistresses. These women were *never*—well certainly never openly anyway—Namboodiri women. Instead they were invariably women from my community, the Nambiars—and what is more, being the mistress of a Brahmin was not only socially acceptable but desirable for them. We call it having sambhandam.'

He paused. 'Is this making sense so far?'

I nodded.

'Well as far as this girl was concerned—and she was only very young, about twelve or thirteen—her misfortune was not only to be very beautiful and very devout but very intelligent. And it was this last quality that was her undoing, the fatal flaw that made her elders and teachers jealous of her. Or so the story goes. Of course once they felt like this about her it was only a matter of time before they began looking for ways to destroy her. Or better still to get her to destroy herself. And this they eventually achieved by asking her two questions, knowing that she would not only be able to give correct answers—because of her innate intelligence—but would give them *despite* also knowing that her answers would be deliberately misinterpreted and therefore bring about her undoing.'

'But,' I interrupted, 'I'm sorry—these men, her teachers, were they also Brahmins?'

'Oh, yes, I'm afraid so,' Satishan said with a smile.

'And the questions? What were the questions?'

'The first was: what is the most important rasa—and rasa is a word that we usually more or less translate with the word "emotion", of which in the Indian scheme of things there are said to be nine—anger, fear, love and so on. And the second question was: which is the most dreadful of all of pains?'

He paused as if waiting for me to come up with an answer myself. I shook my head.

'She said—and you must remember her age and upbringing—she said that the most important rasa is sringara which means eroticism. And then went on to declare that the most unbearable of all pains is childbirth.'

I gasped and put my hand over my mouth. It took little imagination to realize the reception such an answer would get in a conservative and traditional environment.

'And then—what happened?'

'Well from their point of view they'd succeeded, no doubt beyond their wildest dreams. They pounced on the fact that she was, or was believed to be, a young virgin and triumphantly declared that she could never have given such answers unless she was sexually experienced—even though they were well aware that she had the power to answer truthfully.

'It is at this point that the story takes different forms. In the most commonly told version people say she was thrown out of her family's illam and made an outcaste, something that virtually condemned a Hindu to a living death since to be without family and caste was terrible. It means you no longer officially existed and had to live outside—and beyond—society. It is said that when this happened the girl wandered until she came to a shrine dedicated to Lord Shiva. And that she took refuge there, praying and meditating until, after forty-one days Shiva appeared before her and pronounced her to be innocent.'

'So did He then make her a goddess?'

'Yes and no. According to this version He told her that being innocent wasn't going to solve her existence on earth and that she should end her life and merge with Him in infinity.'

My eyes widened. 'And so?'

'Well, it is believed that she then built a huge pyre of wood and, after seating herself on top of it, calmly waited for someone to come along and light it for her. Although the first man she asked refused to help, saying he would not be responsible for the death of a Brahmin woman, the next man, who was an oil-presser, at least stopped when she called out to him. Initially he too hesitated, caught between his reluctance to carry out her wishes and the deep conviction that it is wrong to disobey a Brahmin woman's command. In the end however, despite his misgivings, he emptied his pots of oil over the wood. And it was then, before he could do anything else, that the whole pyre spontaneously ignited and, as the man watched in awe, and no doubt horror, the girl soared miraculously heavenwards, completely untouched by the flames.

'Within hours people began gathering, all with reports of auspicious omens and very soon it was recognized that the girl was not only innocent of the charges that had been made against her but, more importantly, had revealed her divinity. And now,' Satishan said with a sweep of his hand,' She is one of Malabar's most sacred deities.'

It was as this story slowly sunk into my mind that I remembered his mention of there being more than one version.

'And what is the other story, what do others say happened?'

'Well as I said—and it is inevitable that when a story is told and retold as it is passed down over many generations numerous little differences begin to appear. Often all that remains is the central theme. In the story of our Bhagavathi everything stays more or less the same up to the point when the girl is questioned. What then occurs—at least in the version told around here—is that after she has answered the questions and been accused of sexual misconduct she *walks* out of the illam of her own free will,' Satishan paused, looking straight at me before continuing.

'You are from England, you move freely, mixing with who you like, going where you like, without any social judgments being made. Yet no more than a mere hundred years ago things were very different even in your country. A woman who fell from grace had few options open to her and independence was rarely one of them. That this girl did such a thing here, in Malabar *and* so many long centuries ago, is extraordinary. Even the *idea* of a young Brahmin virgin walking out, leaving of her own free will is virtually inconceivable. All I can say is that so much of this story is probably just that, a story, so who can say what the truth may actually have been? We will never know what really happened. Any explanation we give now, any story we tell is just conjecture, we have no way of knowing, one way or the other.'

'But even if she really *did* walk out as you say she does in your version, what happened next?'

Satishan gave a twisted smile. 'The ending, the going to the shrine and so on is more or less the same except of course that everything has become her *choice* rather than something she is *forced* to do. Yet one never knows. Despite the girl being elevated to the divine—which naturally makes her different to all other women—the fact is that she dies. It could be that the ending is a warning, designed to ensure that any woman who might consider questioning the status quo thinks twice. Who knows?'

I sat back to let the power of the story sink in, trying to reach into myself and imagine what it could have been like to make such a choice, to wilfully give answers knowing what the repercussions would be, to imagine being a young girl with such power and conviction. What was the real truth?

And then I suddenly recalled Satishan telling me there was a connection with his family and that this was why they worshipped Her.

'And then there is our family,' he said as if my thoughts had been read. 'And that story is not so easy to tell.'

Somewhere far away I seemed to hear a strange sound, nothing I could recognize but which I can now think of as having been a small warning whisper.

'I've given you the basic outline of the story though I could easily spend hours listing all the numerous embellishments attached to each and every aspect of it. For instance I could tell you how this Goddess connects with so many other deities and the meaning and symbolism, the layers and levels and complexities behind everything concerned with Her, and even *who* She really is. Once you start these things there really is no end to them. They're all part of a vast ocean.

'However. The belief here is that our Namboodiri girl was in some way betrayed and lured into a situation where, as in the other versions, she was asked the same questions. Although how that happened isn't known or at least isn't mentioned, what *is* still believed is that the person responsible for this was a young Nambiar girl, a servant in the illam. And more to the point local tradition says this girl came from my family. And for all I know it may be true. There are no details. Other, strangely, than the fact—which once again may be nothing more than some fanciful later embellishment—that the girl was called Nanikutty. Of course that's a somewhat old-fashioned name nowadays but, whatever actually happened you may be very sure of one thing: since then no girl in our family has ever been given this name. And further more—or so it is said—the family ceased to directly worship this Goddess, the association of guilt being, perhaps, too much for them.'

'Then why? I don't understand. I thought…'

'I know you thought that my family now very much worships Her. And you are right,' Satishan paused again. 'But that is *now.* Our worship recommenced much later and is said to have begun when the Bhagavathi brought a long lost relative back to the family. Only then did we seek Her forgiveness, understand Her benevolence and truly honour Her, even taking Her as our bhara devata, our family's protective deity.'

'Do you know who this was, this relative—or when exactly it happened?'

'That is the mystery. It was certainly a very long time ago but who she was has long been forgotten. If indeed it was ever true in the first place—although I am inclined to believe it. Perhaps,' he laughed, 'more as a devotee than a historian.'

♓

A few days later, as we were having breakfast, Satishan said he had to go into Kannur and would I like to go too. 'You've had some culture,' he said, 'now how about some history?'

'Where are you taking me?' I asked as we drove off, breaking the silence as Satishan turned the car out into the road.

There was a slight pause. As always I thought, it's as if he has two parallel conversations going, one for me and one for some listener within himself.

'To Fort St Angelo.'

We were behind a bus and another one was speeding towards us.

'It's a fort built in 1505 by Francisco de Almeida, Portugal's first viceroy to India,' he continued when the road was clear again. 'What you'll see now is not much more than a shell, mostly just the ramparts and the walls. Once Portugal's power declined the hungry sharks of various nations moved in. First were the Dutch who captured it in 1663, holding it for just over a hundred years before selling it off to Malabar's only Muslim royalty, the Arakkal Rajas. Twenty years later the British took the fort and largely rebuilt it in order to use it as a military base. Of course the tourism people would love you to believe it's untouched, that the Portuguese have just departed but the truth is that little of their original construction remains. What you will see—and what the place will give you—is an idea of *where* they settled and *what* they looked out over. In that respect almost nothing has changed.'

He glanced quickly at me. 'And it'll give you a link, show you how Portugal and the Alentejo connect to Malabar.'

It crossed my mind, as it so often did with Satishan, to wonder what else he was telling me. As usual I let it pass, feeling the notion was anyway too insubstantial to be voiced.

When I did speak, just a moment later I took myself by surprise.

'Do you know someone called Francis Neville?'

Satishan kept driving, carefully overtaking a car as I looked ahead, hardly noticing the elephant lumbering along on the other side of the road, my mind as near to a complete blank as I could get it.

'Yes I do. Why do you suddenly ask?'

Because he may be my father, I screamed to myself.

'I saw his name in the convent-hotel's register. They said he worked with you.' Was that true enough I wondered?

'Well, we *know* each other. But we don't work together.'

It suddenly seemed hard to continue. And anyway I still couldn't quite believe I'd brought up the subject without even thinking about it.

'What is he like?'

'He's a friend of mine. He lives in Lisbon and is interested in history, particularly the Discoveries,' he paused and I felt him look across at me. 'He's about my age.'

'What! How can he be?' I was stunned.

'What do you mean, Sophie? What is this about?'

'I, well, I thought, I mean I think…' I hesitated, aware of being about to put my thought into words for the first time, 'I think he may be my father.'

Only later did I realize that Satishan had immediately slipped the car onto the side of the road and come to halt. All I see, even now, is him looking at me.

'That's impossible, Sophie.' Somehow I noticed that he spoke very gently. 'He's in his thirties and has lived in Portugal all his life. He was born there. He grew up there. He belongs to one of those English families connected to port. English in name only, Portuguese in most other respects.'

I wished I couldn't feel the frustration well up. *The Bastard had eluded me again.*

'My mother always referred to him as The Bastard, ' I said with a strange half laugh, the words suddenly tumbling out. 'She said, I mean she always *used* to say that he just pissed off after I was born. Of course what she *never* told me was that she wasn't even my mother. Only when she died, when I went back to Suffolk, after Portugal, did I discover this. I have absolutely no idea who I am.'

There it was, in a nutshell. I'd finally voiced it.

Satishan's expression was unreadable. No emotion seemed to register, nothing that I could even guess at anyway. Until, to my surprise, I saw the faintest suggestion of a smile creep across his face.

'You are Sophie. Remember? Like our Saraswati? The Goddess?'

Somewhere far away I heard myself giggle. Like a monkey laughs when it's in pain.

'A Goddess? I don't think so.'

'Did you know that in many of our small shrines it is not uncommon for the Goddess to be swayambhoo? That means the image isn't manmade but believed to have been divinely manifested. You are who you are. In that way it is not necessary to know who you are in the way that you mean.'

He paused.

'But I can feel for you. It is not that I can't understand how painful it must be.'

I just nodded. *He is right,* I thought.

'I don't think—well I *know*—that anyone else in the world would ever see this situation like this. Not knowing who I am and then well…' For a moment my voice petered out. 'What you say makes sense and eventually I'll probably believe you. I just never dreamt of there being another Francis Neville out there. I thought when I came here that I might, well, find out from you where he was—that I might find the man who was, or was said to be, my father. And from *him* I hoped to find out about my mother and why she never told me I was adopted but just left me to find out. It's odd, it's been like having a welling dam inside me, everything just waiting to burst. I've wanted to ask you about him ever since I saw his name in the register. The morning I left Portugal. But I suppose I was afraid to. And then when I found out about my mother it was as if I didn't know where to start. It's strange, I never knew him. I don't know if I ever saw him. Now I suppose I never will. He's just out there. Maybe. Or maybe not.' I waved a hand. 'And anyway I have no idea if he even is, or was, my father.'

I wasn't so foolish as to believe that I'd got the lid back on the Pandora's Box of finding out who *this* Francis Neville was but Satishan's words had somehow given me some kind of an identity. A starting point from which I could look forward rather than going back through the invisible past of my two non-parents, one dead and not my parent, the other vanished and almost certainly not my parent either.

♓

Throughout the rest of the drive I felt calmer. I knew I would eventually start picking away at the bones of my identity again but I also accepted that *not* finding The Bastard had been a discovery of sorts. And talking about it had changed something between Satishan and myself. My initial reluctance to speak, to almost never be the one to ask a question or ever tell him about myself had evaporated and we talked easily. I finally told him about Richard and what our marriage had been like. I even, after a strange moment of hesitation told him the one truth I had always kept so tightly locked inside myself that I usually denied its existence: that I'd been three months pregnant when Richard and I had been in the car crash that killed him. And that I'd lost the baby two days later.

I was looking straight ahead as I finished talking, wondering how long it had been since I'd even admitted to this pain. And realizing that, having mentioned it I was able to let it float gently back into the inner recesses of my mind, that the pain was fading and that when I looked down I saw Satishan's hand on mine.

'It's been strange how we've told each other about ourselves. We've both told the truth.' He looked at me. 'But it's been a selective truth, not so much to withhold information but to protect ourselves.' I felt his hand tighten around mine. 'I told you my wife was killed in an accident. But I never told you what she was like or anything else. I never told you about the accident.'

I waited.

'Vasanthi was very beautiful,' he paused and I could sense how carefully he was proceeding. 'Our marriage was arranged—my parents knew her parents and it was something that seemed to have been fixed so early on in our lives that there was never any thought of anyone else. And, as we say here, we pulled on well enough. She had no interest in history but...' he shrugged, a shrug that probably encompassed his whole marriage. 'We'd been married about five years when we had to go to Calicut for a cousin's marriage and after it was all over we were crossing the road, to go and buy her a sari. It all happened so suddenly. A bus came too fast round a corner and seemed to swerve to avoid something, someone, I don't know...One moment she was beside me, the next she was...gone, knocked over, dead, killed instantly.'

I shivered and pulled my hands out from under Satishan's and placed them around his, linking his fingers with mine.

'And we'd just heard that she was expecting.'

The silence that united us was filled with ghosts.

♓

Satishan had already told me enough about Fort St Angelo for me to have some idea of what to expect and once inside the enclosure of its high and imposing ramparts it was obvious he had been right; little remained beyond that uneasy emptiness often left by long demolished buildings. Only the dark laterite stones of the ramparts were untouched, the passing of time having done little more than cover them with small lichens and green mosses. What made the fort remarkable was its position as the sentinel surveying both the wide curve of the bay and the open sea. As we stood gazing down on the bay, seeing the beached fishing boats and just catching the fishermen's laughing chatter it was easy to imagine the power the fort had once evoked. But it was a desolate place.

'There are ghosts here,' I told Satishan, 'did any tragedy take place?'

'Well, no famous ones at least.'

What happens in such places, I wondered, do we catch some whisper and conjure up forgotten ghosts, giving them spectral flesh as it were? And was it then, as I looked out towards the furthest tip of the land, the little finger that took the fort out to sea, that I saw the woman standing under the casuarina trees? And was it then that all sounds dulled until I could hear no more than the sea's pounding roar? And was it then that I sensed the woman's terrible sadness? And turned and looked at Satishan? And saw that he was looking at me, knowing I had seen the woman?

I looked briefly away to pinpoint the woman before turning back to Satishan, suddenly conscious that the expression on his face was one of confusion. That he knew the woman or at least had seen her before was somehow obvious but beyond that I knew they were strangers. I turned and looked back at her, wishing I was close enough to see her features whilst guessing at her beauty, seeing she wore the traditional mundu and that her clothes were fine. Otherwise all I knew for certain was that she radiated loneliness and an intense unhappiness.

And then I saw that she was no longer alone. That running towards her was a young girl. And that I had seen her before. I had seen her at the Cromeleque, and in the portraits of the Virgin, and in the church the day I left Portugal. I closed my eyes, swaying slightly, almost unable to breathe. Before looking up to find them both gone and knowing with utter certainty that Satishan had brought me here to see if I would—or could—see them.

The moment that passed was immeasurable but eventually I was the one who spoke.

'Who are they?' I asked.

'I had hoped you might tell me.'

♓

In the end we walked up to the place under the casuarina trees, not so much to be where the woman and the girl had been but to be as far away from everyone else. Even in the warming heat of the sun it was a bleak spot. The breeze from the sea hissed mournfully through the trees and the air of desolation was marked. We sat down on a low part of the wall, far enough apart not to be touching but close enough to be able do so. For a moment I looked out to the sea, wondering how many others had been in this place and felt the same vibrations. Or was it only us?

'Why,' I said, returning to the question again, 'why do you feel I know?'

I felt rather than saw the muscles tighten in Satishan's face and wondered why I'd so often felt his expressions to be inscrutable.

'I've seen this woman whenever I've come here,' he said, opening his hands in a gesture of acceptance, 'not of course that my visits are frequent. The girl only came later. After I returned from my first visit to Évora, to the Alentejo. At some level I accepted—I still do—that this is how things are. I live in Malabar, such things are not so strange.' Our eyes met as he said this. 'Yet I knew there was—is—something about her—and the girl—that connects to me, that their presence is to do with who I am, or was. Again I can accept this for who are we to know everything anyway?'

I looked down and then up and out at the sea.

'What changed everything was when I met you. Even when I first saw you, in the church when you came in to see the frescoes I sensed something. And that night at the Cromeleque when we both saw the girl and I knew she was giving you the little Madonna-Goddess I was certain. And now here…,' his voice tailed off.

I shook my head.

'Did you know,' I asked, 'that I saw the girl again? It happened the day I left. I went into the church and she was there. Or,' I shrugged,' maybe not there. I can't tell.'

'There is something here and something in Portugal and something between us that forms a circle. And it's an ancient circle. Maybe that's enough. Maybe we're looking for explanations when that *is* the explanation.'

Finally I looked at Satishan. Properly, meeting his eyes, knowing his hands were on mine and feeling myself begin an inner fall, remaining still and upright even as my whole mind tumbled and turned, plunging me deep into a realm where the circle closed and where we found our spirits and souls and joined with the universe. And, as I did so I saw that light surrounded us both. And that within that light was power and energy, streaming towards us, enveloping and enfolding us, showing us the overwhelming inevitability of our dance, telling us our place in the universe was merely the knowledge of our ritual space, the sacredness of our gestures and the benevolence they bestowed upon us.

Later, when the sound of the sea came back into our ears we looked around and wondered where the desolation had gone. We were in a changed world, held in an invisible enchantment, secure in a crucible of peace and calm. *And of knowing,* I thought, when I looked down at Satishan's hand and saw how his long fingers were woven in with mine.

♓

What I hadn't understood until Satishan told me more about the festival was that it would last for five days, and that not only was their Bhagavathi to be honoured but so too were other gods and goddesses. Another discovery was that each deity, each Theyyam, came in two forms: one a preliminary manifestation who would sing the thottams, the songs of the deity's life and presence in the shrine and that later, and in different costumes and with intricate make-up, the actual Theyyam would appear in what Satishan referred to as 'the full form'.

So it was that three mornings after our visit to Fort St Angelo I was woken up early by Ammu bursting into my room, bubbling with delight and saying that *at last* the day had come and insisting that I *had* to come *right now.* 'Don't worry,' said Jaya who'd come in behind her. 'She's over-excited I'm afraid and ran up here before I could stop her. I think she sees you as a willing victim, someone she can drag off to the festival hours before there's any need to go.'

I placed my arms around Ammu, feeling the trusting way in which she sagged back against my body. 'Well, she's right—and I think I'm the lucky one to have someone who will drag me off.'

Jaya smiled, 'Well, don't say you haven't been warned. And there really is no hurry. We don't have to be there until the late afternoon.'

I was taken aback, feeling a little shiver of disappointment.

'So take your time and come down when you're ready,' she said, pausing briefly before handing me a piece of folded paper and saying: 'Satish asked me to give you this.'

I waited until she was out of the room.

Sophie,
Despite all the things I've told you
I never mentioned that our family has
certain traditional duties to perform
at the festival. I have to go to the shrine.
Jaya will bring you along later,
Satishan

At one point I thought *later* would never come. Finally, about an hour before lunch I asked Jaya if she would allow Ammu to take me to the shrine.

'I just don't think I can wait another minute,' I said.

'Well you don't have to ask twice. Have lunch and then take her, she's just longing to go. And enjoy everything. I'll wait and come later,' she smiled at me before speaking again.

'Sophie?'

I turned and looked at her just as she picked up a flat packet. 'This is for you,' she said handing it to me, 'for the festival.'

I took it wordlessly, not knowing what to say, opening it at once. It was a setu-mundu, the white two-piece version of the sari that Jaya wore to go to the temple in the evening.

'I got one with a red border and just a little zari,' she said pointing to the thin gold stripe on either side of the red line, 'you said you liked the colour of mine—and it means you can borrow one of my blouses. I'm sure it'll fit you.'

I just stood looking at her before stammering, 'I don't know how to thank you...'

'No mention. Come, I'll help you put it on.'

♓

Half an hour later I walked out of the tharavad feeling like someone transformed, amazed that though I felt different I also felt comfortable and at ease. It was as if my whole body had automatically adjusted itself to the mundu's restrictions, as if it was familiar to me.

I was glad to have Ammu with me, her hand in mine as we walked along the dirt lane leading out from the tharavad.

'Oh, Sophie-auntie,' she squealed, half turning to look at me as we walked, 'You are looking *sooo* pretty. Uncle will like it *verrry* much!'

I am sure I blushed.

It took us about twenty minutes to reach the shrine and the nearer we got the more people we met, all going in the same direction and all dressed in their best clothes. Although I soon became overly conscious of being openly stared at Ammu was in her element, constantly answering questions about me. At first I found this disconcerting but gradually, because the questions were in Malayalam, I ceased to be concerned. Only occasionally was a direct address made to me, usually from a child calling out 'What is your country?' or 'What is your name?' Ammu appeared to revel in all this, answering as if she had proprietary rights over me, treating even these questions with a laugh and a smile, making me aware not only of the wideness of people's smiles but of their welcoming gentleness.

The shrine, when we eventually reached it, was set in a clearing, the surrounding trees so thick and dense that they appeared to offer it both seclusion and protection. A low wall defined the edge of a large, open compound that was bare except for two small central shrines, a couple of altar-like pedestals and, in one corner a low, hutch-like shrine. On one side, just outside the far wall reared the thick trunk of a huge tree while on the other side I noticed a somewhat temporary looking shelter made of what appeared to be dried coconut leaves.

Though people were streaming towards and into the shrine I suddenly felt diffidence and hesitation. Perhaps I *should* have waited for Jaya and come later. Now, because I was alone I was forced to consider whether or not I was allowed inside the shrine's precincts. I tightened my grip on Ammu's hand and stopped, making her turn and look up at me.

'Ammu,' I said, 'are you sure I can go in? Should we perhaps find Satishan and ask him?'

'No, no aunty, why are you worried? Come! There's no problem.'

But I held back, asking myself if I was wise to accept a young girl's word as sufficient authority.

'So, you couldn't wait!'

Satishan. I sighed with relief as I turned and saw him, noticing at once that he was traditionally dressed.

'No, I couldn't—and Ammu was dying to come and...,' I said, smiling at the amusement in his eyes. 'It's just that once we got here I wondered, well, am I allowed to enter the shrine—Ammu said yes but...'

'I told her not to worry, Satish-mama,' Ammu piped up.

'And you told her very correctly,' Satishan replied, bending down to her. 'So, shall we now take her inside?

'All you will have to do is remove your chappals,' he said, glancing at my feet. 'Come, I'll show you where you can leave them.'

Without a backward glance he set off, heading round the wall towards the coconut leaf shelter. As we approached it the handful of men standing outside raised their hands to greet Satishan and, as he returned their greeting, I saw that despite the men's ready smiles they held themselves with a certain wary aloofness.

While they talked I stood clutching Ammu's hand, aware that she too was listening as Satishan spoke to the men. I knew I was under surveillance since they made no effort to conceal their curiosity about me. Yet what really disconcerted me was the sensation that they could somehow see right through me, that there was no way I could hide myself from them.

Then as Satishan finished talking and the men nodded and smiled I heard my breath sigh out, knowing, that whatever he had asked them for had been easily agreed to.

'Sophie, take off your chappals and put them just outside. They'll be perfectly safe there,' Satishan pointed down at my feet.

I picked up my shoes and did as he said, putting them near the open doorway of the shelter, following the pointed hand of one of the younger men. Out of the corner of my eye I could see that inside there were small cloth bags and what I assumed were pieces of elaborate costumes hanging all around the interior walls. I also saw that a man was lying on a mat and having his face painted. Intrigued but too nervous to openly stare I hurriedly backed out, only to be brought up short by the unexpected closeness of the man who had shown me where to leave my shoes.

He was young, maybe twenty-five, maybe a little older yet his features were in many ways ageless. He wasn't particularly tall or fine-bodied and, like everyone else, including Satishan, he was bare-chested. What set him apart were his eyes. They were restful and though their gaze was open there was a curiously enigmatic quality about their expression. For a brief moment it occurred to me that they resembled the eyes of the goddess in the picture hanging in my room.

Somehow I waited until we were out of earshot before, almost hissing with intensity, I whispered my question to Satishan: 'Who, who is he?'

'He is to be the koladhari of the Bhagavathi.'

The blankness of my expression made Satishan smile and, for a moment, I tightened my grip on Ammu's hand. Then, as suddenly, I let go of her and stepped away, to hear whatever Satishan was about to explain in isolation.

'His name,' Satishan continued, 'is Kunhiraman Peruvannan. In English there is really no alternative but to describe him as a *performer* since your language simply doesn't cover the concept of what he is or who he becomes.'

Satishan paused and looked at me as if to check my responses. 'I cannot even translate the word.' The second pause was almost imperceptible. 'To put it more plainly: he is the man who has taken adayalam, who has accepted the contract to—as you might say—*perform* the Goddess but'—and here, he paused again, '—what we actually say is that he will *carry* Her and it is at that time that he becomes Her. I fear none of this sounds right in English since we don't really use words like "trance" or "possession" although the belief is that the human element has been replaced by the deity.' I now know that this was the moment when being able to *choose*, to *decide*, ceased to exist. There were no alternatives; I had to trust. Trust without reservation; perhaps without even understanding, certainly without questions. Of course I knew that doing so wouldn't be enough to let me simply subside comfortably into the universe whose abyss now loomed before me. Things might remain as they were, or become even more complex but, somehow, instinct, that gut and primal knowing we occasionally still have enough sense to heed, told me I would at least be taken forward. One small step.

♓

During the days that followed a whole world passed before me in a blur of fire and light, of heat-soaked days and dark nights. The normal markers of everyday time and space were replaced by the pounding beat of drums, the hissing flames of fire-torches, the reds and golds of fantastic costumes and the intricately painted faces of other-worldly beings. And somewhere, somehow, all this was interspersed with alternating bouts of sleep and tiredness, of walks to and from the house, quick baths and grabbed meals and of such total assaults on the senses that I could not even begin to process all that I saw and heard.

The Theyyams, the gods, were the embodiment of splendour and power whose appearance—their elaborate costumes and masking make-up—effectively distanced them from their devotees—even as they moved amongst them. Almost all evidence of an individual's human features were erased, no part of their bodies seemingly unadorned while headdresses crowned their painted faces. One powerful goddess even had burning tapers rimming her headdress and great fire-torches blazing around her waist. Another goddess—who Satishan first said was a tiger goddess but then confused me by saying she was really Shiva's consort, Parvathy—whirled and leapt around the shrine, sometimes struggling against the restraining arms of her attendants to run in great athletic leaps, apparently disdainful of the costume's restrictive weight and bulk. An incarnation of Vishnu roared into the night, a warrior god moved in a fiercely crouched walk, his eyes raking across the shrine, seeing all, piercing every heart. And all the while, a strange thread ran through these primal manifestations of powerful and divine beings, a steel cord which whispered of the splendour and vastness of of an unfathomable and deeper realm.

I initially caught—but did not immediately identify—these whispers on the first evening when the preliminary 'form'—explained by Satishan as being the Bhagavathi's thottam—entered the shrine. She advanced slowly, swaying very slightly, precisely placing first one foot and then the other. Although Kunhiraman's face was clearly visible I never doubted the true identity of the red-robed figure: *he* held part of the red cloth over *his* head but *She* moved in a state of liquid grace, in what I later thought of as a kind of silence, a stillness. The face was closed off, shielding, concealing—the word *protecting* slid across my mind—something that, despite its external power, appeared to be of inherent fragility.

These processions took place in the evenings and mornings and always ended before the sanctum where a small crown-like headdress was tied around Kunhiraman's head. After streaking his body with turmeric paste he began a series of low-key rituals placing what I assumed were offerings on a large and heavy stool. After this he began to sing whilst slowly beating the chenda, the drum that had been placed horizontally across the stool, accompanied by the handful of men who stood behind him.

These were the bare facts. They cannot hope to give even the faintest impression of the intensity and sombre atmosphere that this small group created. The low and serious singing was more of a chant and though all I knew—of course from Satishan—was that the Bhagavathi's long and complex story was being told—I felt myself drawn into its plangent aura. It was a song of aching sadness and purity which, though it appeared to draw from an enormous well of emotion, never once displayed any overt feelings. The almost fitful drum beats, the harsh voices of Kunhiraman, and of those accompanying him, made no concessions to the uninitiated but what I felt, along with an overwhelming sadness, was that I should be still and listen. It was as if by so doing I hoped to absorb the meaning, the real meaning of this extraordinary chant.

What followed it was no less extraordinary. To say that it was a procession is to mislead for though it correctly conjures up an image of formal splendour and pageantry it gives no hint of the other element that was present: a deeply solemn sense of the sacred, a sacredness so eternally intact and undiluted that it drew everyone into its ancient world. The participants moved in unison, the drummers, lamp-bearers and attendants all linked by invisible threads to the small figure of Kunhiraman. He was, to my eyes at least, the main and central figure even though walking backwards before him were four remarkable men. Each one appeared to have incarnated himself from a world few of us can even imagine; their costumes, their expressions and the great curved swords they carried echoed the dictates and compulsions of another world and time. Although, like Kunhiraman they too wore red, they had golden ornaments hung over their chests, gold bands across their foreheads and heavy, and harshly jangling, belts of bells around their waists. Somewhere Satishan's words came back to me—that they were the komarams, the representatives of goddesses, men who moved between the worlds of gods and men, able to commune with and interpret the divine. One of them was 'attached' to the Bhagavathi, the others to the three goddesses whose mythical lives intersected with Hers and were also being honoured as Theyyams.

Once again I have given facts, not emotions. I cannot for, despite being aware of all those who accompanied the procession, I barely registered either their solemn expressions or whether Satishan was among them: my attention was too fiercely gripped by the player at the centre of the universe they surrounded.

By this stage Kunhiraman was being more supported than held by his attendants, moving under a long awning, making the first of three rounds of the shrine. Though with each round these steps changed in style—and became progressively faster—the spatial relationship between Kunhiraman and the komarams was rigidly maintained, remaining as constant as if they had been physically linked to each other. Kunhiraman held his head slightly back and to one side, a stance that, with the stillness of his expression and the swaying pattern of the dance, created an effect of an almost surreal beauty. Even the increased speed of the last round, when the need for Kunhiraman's attendants to support him became more obvious, had no effect on the flowing sensation of their movements. My one barely conscious thought was that the line between man and god had blurred and that to even think of denying the existence of the divine within the small red-robed dancer would be a sacrilege. And yet when it was over, and the small headdress had been removed, and I watched him being led away, still visibly supported, I felt that he was being held like a small lost child.

♓

The last day began early, the heightened tension within the shrine's precincts underlined by the knowledge that Kunhiraman had spent the night in seclusion, preparing himself for the line he would soon cross, the transformation that awaited. Devotees poured into the shrine to pray, receive blessings and make offerings while in the vast covered space outside the shrine the great fires began cooking the food that would be given to everyone as evidence of the Bhagavathi's protective benevolence. Meanwhile, at the temporary shelter where I had first left, and continued to leave, my chappals, there was an atmosphere of anticipation and calm. It was obvious that everyone there was an expert; that centuries of interacting with their gods had ensured that everything needed for the Bhagavathi had, long before dawn, been taken to the smaller shelter where Kunhiraman had passed the night and where his physical transformation was already in progress.

It was now that Satishan came more directly back to my orbit. Up until then he had generally kept his distance, occasionally coming to wherever I was standing and then either explaining something or moving me, along with Ammu, to another, and better, position. *In Malabar I would see you surrounded by relatives.* By this time I had realized that though Ammu was undoubtedly a self-assured child we rarely moved of our own volition. Instead, whenever she knew we should change our position, and Satishan did not immediately appear, she would run to find him. On this last day however I could see that she was reluctant to make her way through the crowd already gathering in one corner of the shrine's compound and kept asking me if I could see Satishan. Inevitably, since there was no sign of him, her tension transmitted itself to me and though, equally inevitably, he finally appeared without me ever seeing him visibly walk across the shrine's compound, the only word he uttered before turning back into the thick of the crowd was 'come.' As we drew closer people parted, smiling as we passed through to the circle that had been formed around a small, low pedestal. Even then Satishan kept going, edging his way around it until we were close to where several of the Theyyam people were standing, the slight movement of their heads imperceptibly acknowledging our presence.

No sooner had we taken up our positions than a man appeared beside us, carrying a long woven basket containing costume accessories, garlands, bangles and a small hand mirror. And then, once again the crowd parted, many of them respectfully folding their hands together as a group of men approached, holding up a white cloth that carefully shielded Kunhiraman from curious eyes. Only when they reached the small pedestal and Kunhiraman stepped onto it did I realize that only his legs were visible, red-painted and with small silver bells tied below his knees.

The white cloth stayed firmly in position with just enough light shining through it to give a shadowy impression of the activity it attempted to conceal, making it obvious that everyone was huddled around Kunhiraman.

And it was then, as the sun beat down and surrounded me in a cocoon of sweat and discomfort that the singing began. It came from behind the shielding cloth; the voices were low and while there was no attempt to make them audible to anyone except Kunhiraman, I recognized the aching song. I leaned forward and, in the strain of trying to hear, separated myself from my surroundings, allowing the singing to enfold me and run down veins and touch nerve ends until it felt as if the chanting contained words I was *meant* to hear, that something was forcing me to listen. Only when someone's hand pulled at my arm was the spell broken, making me turn in time to see the fierce tiger goddess approaching, slicing her way through the crowd, ignoring its proximity and forcing everyone to peel back from the dangers of her sweeping headdress. She came, as Satishan had said she would, to bless the Bhagavathi and bestow the strength of Her divine powers on Her.

But I had no chance to examine my thoughts. I could see that the Bhagavathi's great headdress was being raised and knew that, as the singing began to swell and the drums to pound that the moment had come, that the Bhagavathi's seclusion was almost over.

And then, gently and without fanfare, the cloth was lowered.

I gasped. Just in front of me, and bent forward, was a transformed being. The Bhagavathi, a divinity from another universe. Here on earth. Her huge red and gold headdress almost touching the ground, streams of tiny red flowers dripping from it like rain. Nothing remained of Kunhiraman. His—no *Her*—red-painted hands held two blazing fire-torches, exquisitely intricate makeup covered Her face, small silver eye-masks concealed Her eyes, silver canine teeth glinted at the edge of Her mouth and a magnificent costume encased Her body.

And then, as if emerging from the depths of the earth, She began to rise, slowly, with everyone round me crying, showering Her with rice as She drew Herself erect and drums pounded to underline unfathomable emotions. And with Her rose the sense of a sacred mystery, of a distant world, of an enveloping power, of something ethereal and delicate, something that, deep within its core, was cast of iron, solid, real, powerful, ancient and forever.

♓

Throughout the long hours that followed I moved and stood and watched with the detached consciousness of a sleepwalker, perfectly able to see and hear but apart from everything, entrapped in another world. A world that spun itself around the extraordinary figure of the Bhagavathi. She moved slowly, protectively surrounded by Her attendants, led by one drummer and a man carrying an oil lamp to honour Her presence. And all the while, despite the heat and the pressing crowds, with sweat and tiredness seeping into me, my eyes followed Her.

She circled the shrine nine times, each round with a different step, placing Her feet precisely, carrying Herself with regal solemnity, supported by Her attendants—perhaps because of restricted vision—and with Her hands holding the fire-torches. At first I could just catch the sound of Her anklets, a disquietingly gentle sound that was soon lost as Her speed and the number of drummers increased. Only after the last round did She move to stand alone, before Her shrine, free from Her attendants, raising and crossing Her fire-torches in a gesture of blessing.

The spell was finally broken when Ammu began shaking my

arm and I caught the urgency in Satishan's words: 'Come! Follow me!' He never waited for a response but surged through the vast crowd, firmly holding Ammu, who in turn clutched at me. As he did so the Bhagavathi, once more under the care of attendants, made Her way in the same direction and it was only when She stopped that I found that we were facing each other. Satishan had brought us to the far side of the shrine's well, opposite Her and close enough to see how the silver eye-masks, by hiding Her eyes, gave Her an unreadable and enigmatic expression.

For a moment She was still and silent, holding Her head up high, perhaps waiting for the two men either side of Her to reach up and support Her headdress before She bent forward, over the protective wall, to look down into the well.

'She is quenching Her thirst,' I heard Satishan say. 'At this point She goes down into the water.' And such was the power of the illusion that when, once again, She leaned over the wall I felt She was already moving down into its depths, into its darkness. Even as I saw, quite clearly, that She stood straight and that the older of the two attendants was reaching up to the silver eye-masks. What followed was a moment of such intimacy that I felt I was prying, intruding on Her privacy. Yet, unable to look away, I watched and saw how, with great respect, the eye-masks were removed and a damp, cooling cloth placed tenderly, one by one, on each eye. And that, for the first time, I could see that the eyes of the Bhagavathi, encircled by black, were now gazing out into an eternity, suggesting a vastness of untold depths as a small still voice whispered to me of love and compassion, of an extraordinary promise.

The hours that followed were again filled with ritual and movement, dance and re-creations of important episodes in the Bhagavathi's life. They were hours full of sombre joy and splendour, a time where I watched in awe as She progressed around the shrine, interacting with the komarans and bestowing blessings on Her devotees.

Yet, as I watched and absorbed, unbidden thoughts floated in and out of my consciousness and I felt a small nub of stillness growing within me, an ache, a pain, a certainty that sustained me even as my defences began falling. It was like being on a high and distant plateau where I could see, far below, a path that would eventually lead me to an extraordinary and sustaining energy. Except that to find it I had to jump into the limitless void. And trust, knowing that concealed within these thoughts was the growing certainty that something else would, finally, be revealed.

♓

At last all the rituals were complete and it was time for the Bhagavathi to receive offerings and give Her blessings. She did this before the small shrine, seated on the special wooden stool, flanked by Her attendants. By this time there were, according to Satishan, at least twenty thousand devotees waiting to approach Her. Yet, within a short time, the apparent milling chaos was reduced to two long lines; one—into which Ammu and I were hustled—for women and children, the other for men.

It took over an hour to reach Her, an hour in which the sun beat relentlessly down, dust eddied constantly and the stickiness of sweat clung to bodies and drenched clothes. Ammu stood quietly beside me, one hand placed on me as if to support herself. The women around me were as silent, perhaps to conserve energy, perhaps in order to focus on the Bhagavathi, to be in communion with Her as we gradually edged closer to Her presence. Of Satishan there was no sign. I tried to detach myself from the cloying discomfort for I knew better than to retreat into the thoughts already seeking to attract my attention. Initially I tried to replay all I had seen, to conjure up details, sounds and reactions. But this proved to be an uneasy occupation and in the end I just allowed my mind to empty.

And so, finally, just as I thought we would never reach the Bhagavathi, I found myself almost in front of Her. Somehow I pushed Ammu before me, so that I could see what to do. It was simple enough: Ammu bowed and respectfully gave money into the Bhagavathi's red-painted hand—which was instantly handed to an attendant who, as quickly, held a container before the Bhagavathi. As soon as She had taken a pinch of pale yellow turmeric and given it to Ammu, the Bhagavathi raised Her hand in a gesture of blessing and intoned a few words.

And then She turned to me.

Time stopped. What happened next cannot be said to have taken me by surprise because by then I had no thoughts, preconceptions or opinions. I just saw the Bhagavathi raise one reddened hand, take one of my hands in Hers and begin pulling me towards Her, drawing me down onto Her large and ornate chest covering. For a timeless moment my head was kept there as She rocked me, like a small child, from side to side. A multitude of ungraspable emotions arose. And subsided into distant oblivion as I felt myself released. But still kept close, able to see the red-smudged silver canines, the slightly uneven teeth behind the moving lips. And into the great depths of the black-rimmed eyes. At the same time, as if from a vast distance, I saw that one of my hands was still being held, that the Bhagavathi's other hand was being raised and that something was being rubbed into my head. Then my mouth was opened and—again like a child—gritty turmeric was placed on my tongue as the Bhagavathi began speaking in a ritualistic high-pitched cadence. The intensity was extraordinary, compelling me to listen, to catch and absorb every syllable of a language I could not understand.

Then the bubble burst and the world began to turn again. I held out my offering and within seconds I was spun away from the limitless space I had entered and was no longer even within the Bhagavathi's immediate terrestrial orbit.

'Sophie?' The voice was quiet.

I looked down at my clasped hand, slowly opening it to see the pale turmeric. Then I looked up, smiling.

'You were blessed,' he said.

'I know.'

♓

That night it began again, sometime before dawn, somewhere in those uncharted hours before darkness begins yielding to a new day, the time when dreams and reality are one. Once again I was dancing, a participant in some ancient, pagan ritual, moving in a mysterious darkness, facing someone whose identity was now clear, dancing slowly backwards and forwards, umbilically linked, always keeping the same distance apart. And it was as we danced that I became more and more aware that this figure possessed enormous power. I knew too, that within this power was energy and that it was streaming towards me, enveloping, protecting and enfolding, making me conscious both of the overwhelming inevitability of our dance and that the universe was merely the knowledge of our ritual space, the sacredness of our gestures and the benevolence they bestowed upon us.

I woke to a feeling of enormous peace. It was time to accept myself as I was, to ignore the doubts and pains, to acknowledge the connections and know I was protected.

♓

The day after the festival was strangely quiet. People moved slowly and spoke less, as if taking their time to return to the normal, busier rhythms of everyday life. I felt grateful for the silence and the chance it gave me to let my feelings about the Bhagavathi still and settle within me. In ways I did not even bother to examine, I recognized the need to let the last wisps of my thoughts about Her find a place where they could rest, even store themselves.

Just before nightfall when Jaya brought out the evening lamp I was already seated in the spot I had come to think of as mine. As usual I leant against the same smooth wooden pillar and gazed out at the compound, listening to the day's sounds growing gradually quieter as the sky darkened and other sounds emerged. I felt the coolness of the slight breeze shivering through the trees and caught the faint rattling of palm leaves and, at one point, the sudden crash of a coconut leaf falling to the ground. It was then, as the full moon began to rise, lifting itself into a clear and star-sprinkled sky that a thought came to me: that though I could easily imagine the same moon and stars shining over Suffolk and the Alentejo it was impossible to think of them above any city, anywhere.

Suddenly, at eight-thirty sharp, the whole world changed its rhythm. Somewhere far away in a distant town an unknown technician pulled the lever or pressed the switch that cut off all power. In an instant nothing mechanical could be heard, nothing hummed or hissed, nothing extraneous remained, no light could be seen. It was like being alone in the silence of snow. Every nerve end vibrated as, without fear, I sensed the presence of something very old moving stealthily closer. The breeze whispered to me, telling me that out in the darkness I was being watched, that there were forces and energies all around me. I could almost feel them sighing through the night, their echoing voices blending into the earth's pulse, rising and falling with every breath I took. It was a time that spoke of an ancient world, of things so old that they were intertwined with the earth, of powers and spirits that could not be denied. And it was then that I heard the sound of distant drums, pounding to a beat I now knew, speaking of powers I now sensed.

And then the thought came to me, dropping into my mind like a stone falling into the depths of a pond. I was happy. I was content. I was at peace. *Now.* At this precise moment. This was not a time I would only later think back to and say *I was happy then*; it was *now.* The thought surrounded me and took me into a world where I floated weightlessly, where time and space were measured with meaningless calculations and the world was without borders.

I looked up at the moon, now settled in the night sky. I

looked at the billions of stars. I saw how they spread themselves across the vast expanse of sky like a silken net. And then I saw the Cromeleque. And the moonlight on the roughness of its standing stones. And the angels in Blythburgh church. And then, at last, my inner eyes opened and I saw the black dog. And the young girl. And the Virgin in the empty niche. And the Bhagavathi.

And knew what I must do.

I now believe that I went into the tharavad like someone in a trance. I have no memory of going up to my room, of what I did there, or of leaving it. I remember nothing until I stepped outside and saw Satishan standing there, waiting for me, just as I expected him to be.

I never hesitated.

'I have something for you,' I said.

He smiled and said, 'I know.'

And held out his hand.

I placed the figurine of the small ivory goddess on his palm. Very carefully.

'She was given to me in Portugal. But this is where She belongs, where She was always meant to be. I was merely the one to bring Her home.'

And felt the thought flutter through my mind: *As She has brought me home.*

Book Two

INÊS

I still see Her. Immaculate and serene, the stars arched above Her head, the moon beneath Her holy feet. I still see the sky-coloured cloak gathered around Her swollen belly, one hand stretched out towards me. I still long to reach up and feel Her arms enfold me. And I still call out to Her. Mãe. Mother.

Mãe. Even now I call Her Mother. What indeed has changed? The sky still arches over the universe. The stars still glitter in the night. The moon still shines. My prayers still reach Her.

How else would I be here now if it were not for Her blessings?

♓

Many long years ago when I was still a child, I was forced to watch a man die a brutal death. Against my will I saw his face contort into a dreadful mask of pain. Against my will I saw him writhe and strain against the ropes that sawed at his arms. And against my will I endured the most unbearable of all these enforcements: watching the flames as they enclosed his broken body, terrified of showing emotion, soaked by rivulets of sweat and, above all, wracked by the sensation that it was my body the flames were consuming. And finally, though time has dimmed some details, one memory has never faded: his last, long agonized scream. Even now that awful reverberating howl will sometimes, and without warning, echo its way through my mind. Child though I was, I knew it signified a last gathering of strength, a final declaration that his spirit was about to soar free, that they had not won. It was also the moment when all innocence was irrevocably lost and the pain of knowing, of knowledge truly began.

Like all of us who live in troubled times, Death has been my constant companion. He has walked beside me like a shadow, always present, always waiting to reach out and pull someone I love into his terrible darkness. Because of Death I have raged in sorrow. I have known pain and grief. I have mourned and sobbed and queried the wayward carelessness of his casual choices and lost count of the days and nights I have lain alone as my furiously churning thoughts formed that eternally unanswered question: *Why?*

And yet now, in the last few hours of my own life, I feel no fear, no sadness, no regret, no inner pain. My time has come. It is that simple. All I need do is sit quietly and wait for Death to fold me into the mystery of his final embrace. Until then I close my eyes and look inward. I mark time and harbour my thoughts, conscious that I have no desire to speak, that I am content to sit within the shadows of this house and listen to its familiar rhythms. Occasionally I sense the concern around me and know they are wondering if I still remember everything or if I have forgotten all that happened so long ago. Sometimes a hand will rest on my arm or I will catch a sudden shiver of whispers and know that I am watched. At other times they talk more carelessly, more certain that I do not even listen as they wonder out loud if I can still hear, if I can still see, if I can still remember, if I ever think back to before, to then.

And they are right to wonder; my mind does wander and the old memories do come back. Crystal clear, untarnished. Even though my eyes are dim, my body frail and my ears barely able to hear my mind roams freely. I remember the journeys I have taken, the distances I have travelled, the changes I have undergone. I remember everything—indeed it sometimes seems that I am separate from my body, existing in another time and place. Especially now, as the old memories become clearer. I see colours. I hear sounds. I smell the air. In a few hours I will go to Death as eagerly as a maiden runs to her lover and I will gladly allow him to gather me up like a wild flower—even as I am slipping back into my past, to a time that is filling my mind's eye. As it does right now. Right here, right in front of me, where I can almost touch them, are the wild irises, the flowers I have not seen for many decades. And they are not a memory. I have not dreamt about them or conjured them up. They are real and, despite the cloudy dimness of my eyes, I see their abundance. I see every detail of every tender petal, the depth of their colour and how it echoes the blue and velvet richness of Our Lady's robes. And I catch the earthy scent of the marsh they grow in and feel the warmth of that sun shining over the overwhelming vastness of the land that once more surrounds me.

And so it is that even as I feel Death's breath upon me I am alive and conscious. My memories are asserting themselves; at first in a disjointed way, without beginnings or endings, lasting for no more than a few moments, rushing towards me like a river in full spate, so fast that they are without sense or sequence. Only gradually do I feel that an order is forming and that after so many, many years my life is being lived again, the door to my past unbolting, swinging open to release everything I once kept isolated and unvisited. Finally I am going back to where it all began, to make a last pilgrimage through my life, a pilgrimage that will end sometime before tomorrow's dawn.

Already the changes are happening; already my legs are young and strong again. I am running free, the wind catching my hair, my arms outstretched as I seek freedom and inhale the fresh air far from the convent's restrictions. Then the moment vanishes and, once again, I feel the aches in my tired body. But only briefly, for, almost seamlessly, I am slipping back to another day, the day when I first ran over the rolling hills, over the grass and the flowers, seeing but hardly caring for their tender blooms, not even looking to see how they turned themselves up to the sky, the clear blue sky that stretched to forever, spreading over the whole universe. It is a blue my inner eye has never forgotten, a blue that even in the darkest shadows of this house still surrounds me—even as I still hear the nearby burble of idle chatter, the rise and fall of laughter, the giggling of the children and—sometimes—the sudden sharpness of a correcting voice.

Occasionally one of the children will take my hand or crawl into my lap and demand a story, pestering me with small kisses until I yield. I belong here. I know that and am thankful for the life this place has given me, the peace it has offered me when none was ever expected; the love and affection that surrounds me, that encloses me. I have been more blessed here than I ever dreamt could be possible. I have no regrets. And yet I look back and remember.

My memories are now finding an order. I catch glimpses of that day when I lay on the summer grass, watching as the great vultures lumbered and lurched until their ungainly bodies were finally airborne. I see how one particular bird soars, gliding on the warm thermals, circling in a sky full of birds, all darkly ominous, the moving markers of Death's presence, informing all who see them that somewhere on the plain below is a gutted carcass. And I see how this one vulture turns in the vastness of the sky and veers off towards the distant Sierra, to a high place where digestive juices will break down the torn flesh already moving through its long gullet, giving it strength for its next scavenging foray.

How many times did I watch these vultures circling? And how many times did I imagine myself to be one of them, soaring high above the land to gaze down on the world below? A world I used to think stretched—such was my ignorance—to no further than the distant horizon, east towards Extremadura, west to Lisbon. Places I never expected to see or travel beyond. Yet though my imagination lifted me up to soar with the great scavengers, I identified myself more closely with the earth below.

And it is my memories of this earth that make me hesitate. Even now. Even after all these years I am too aware of the dangers. I know what pain awaits me but am powerless to hold it back. My mind has already raced ahead and is searching, desperate to see, to find, to know.

I have never forgotten. It is part of the pain that will be with me to the end—and perhaps beyond. Though I know how pointless my search will be I am forced to make it one more time. In this matter I am helpless. Despite everything, despite all that has happened, this is the moment when, quite suddenly and without warning, the pain comes swooping towards me, claiming my attention and forcing me back to the old unanswered questions. First: *Who was my mother?* And then: *How was it possible that no one ever knew who she was, that no one ever saw her?* But why do I ask these questions when I have always known the absolute futility of doing so? The truth is now—as it was then—that no one even looked for her. How could they when no one knew where to look or who to ask for? There was never any way of finding out who she was or where she had come from. There was nothing for anyone to find or remember, no description, no clue, no shadow to substantiate her existence. It is not so much that my mother vanished but that she never so much as ever appeared. After all she never held me in her arms, never suckled me—perhaps she never even saw me—and if she gave me a name it was never known.

All that confirms her existence is that I was born. Over the years and out of this single fact, the one simple truth that is known about her, I have drawn on a whole series of imagined images to describe both my mother and the events leading up to my birth. By doing so, and by endlessly layering and embroidering this one known certainty, I have almost made my mother real and so pulled her back from anonymity. From that precise moment when she was torn away from me, the very moment of her death, the moment when I was quite literally separated from her, I have given her not only life but shape and substance. I have so filled out the stark facts of my birth that I believe I can see how that fateful day began. A day on which, as I near the end of my own life, I now relive, turning my almost sightless eyes up to the heavens and seeing the pale moon's crescent lingering in the dawn of that particular morning. I feel the last frost of winter quickly melting away as the sun rises. I see the grasses waving, the trees beginning to blossom. I hear the birds singing, a shepherd calling to his flock and the jingling of their bells. And, once again, I see the vultures circling in the sky, drifting weightlessly. And I sense their dark shadows skimming across my inner vision as their outstretched wings cloud over the sky and obscure the sun's light. And, perhaps for the last time, I shudder as I am forced to acknowledge why the great carrion eaters float across the sky, why they endlessly drift, why they hover and why and for what they wait. And then, though I know what will happen, I withdraw my mind's eye from the great circling birds.

It is at this point that I bring on my mother, that I yet again catch my first glimpse of her. As always she is walking very slowly towards me, holding a protective hand over her swollen belly. Soon she is so close that I can hear both her gasping breath and the faint rustle of her clothes. And, though I often hope otherwise, I see that she still keeps one hand before her face, perhaps to stifle her pain and keep from crying out. Other details are, as always, forever indistinct; perhaps her hair is gathered into a tangled mass at the nape of her neck, perhaps it hangs loose. I know neither the shape nor colour of her clothes or if there are shoes on her feet. These are vague and unimportant details, unconsciously overlooked as I surreptitiously shift my attention to her face, hoping to catch her unawares. But in vain. All my life I have tried to imagine her eyes, the tilt of her nose, the shape of her mouth, the sheen of her skin. Yet never once has she raised her face or lowered her hand. I have never managed—however hard I have tried—to see what my mother looked like. She has always eluded me and remained in the shadows—even though I am sure, absolutely sure, that she possessed an unusual beauty.

It begins when she is almost within touching distance. Everything goes quiet, a strange and unnatural stillness. The birds cease to sing, the insects to chirp, the distant sheep to bleat, their bells to ring. A tenseness slithers through the air like a strange smell. Even the vultures have vanished from the darkening sky and for a moment I am deceived, distracted by my mother suddenly clutching her distended belly and staggering forward, falling to the ground with a single cry of pain. My invisible, watching self edges closer, seeing how she begins to writhe and twist, gasping for breath, one hand held over her face as she leans back against the wall of a tall building.

And it is now, as my mother's labour pains begin to overwhelm her, that I hear the sound of the earth growling and groaning beneath her. Sometimes I think this is my only real memory, that deep within her womb I really did hear those sounds and so actually remember the terror of the shuddering tremors, the grinding and grating, the great howling. That I really felt the whole world shift and lurch before, and without warning, the earth heaved open, yawning wide in cruel imitation of my mother as she strained to give me life. It is now that I feel myself hurtling down a dark tunnel, racing against time, tossed and thrown about as my mother heaves and strains, falling and tumbling, slipping and sliding as, in spite of everything, her body fights to give me life. And then, with one last heave I am free, thrown out into the light, into the world. A world as mysterious as the inner darkness that has so suddenly rejected me, a world enveloped in dust, filled with the sounds of falling rubble, of cracking beams, of shattering walls and the yelling, howling, groaning cries of the injured and dying. And then a merciful silence. As my mind and memory shut down, leaving me to remember only what I have been told: that my mother was an unknown woman crushed to death by falling masonry, that she was buried by the earthquake, killed as I was born. And that somehow, in all the death and mayhem, I was found in the rubble, screaming and covered in blood—though whether from my mother's womb or her crushed and broken body no one ever knew.

♓

Throughout my early childhood, no one ever allowed me to forget how the land had broken open on that cold January morning in the year of our Lord fifteen hundred and thirty-one.

And how, almost before the earthquake had ceased its after-shocks, and even as the dead were still being counted and the injured attended to, certain priests began declaiming from their pulpits. These men of God declared the disaster to be God's punishment for people's ungodly ways. They shouted that hellfire would soon consume the land's surviving sinners. No one, they thundered, would be spared the torture of eternal damnation. At once all those who heard these awful threats fell to their knees and began praying to the Virgin, beseeching Her to intercede with our Lord, to ask Him to at least grant them the hope of divine forgiveness. And so it was that as they were praying a man came running, shouting that an innocent newborn baby had been found in the rubble. It was a cry that brought everyone rushing to see me, all of them sobbing like drowning men grasping at straws, seeing my survival as the miracle they needed, the sign that God had heard their prayers. Redemption, they believed was possible, forgiveness was at hand.

Yet what do I really know of this? Only that while still covered in blood and dust—and no doubt still bawling—I was brought to the local priest, a kindly man known for his compassion. 'Tell us father,' everyone must have begged him, 'tell us who should care for her?' It is not hard to imagine the weariness of the bedraggled group that gathered around this priest, each one of them jostling to catch his reply. Some had just lost their loved ones, others were still searching and all of them were terrified, in shock, unable to comprehend the violence that had torn their lives apart. The sight of my tiny body must have made their tears flow anew, blurring their vision as they grasped at the one, fragile ray of hope I appeared to represent.

Is this where my memories really begin? Is it here, in the arms of the priest? Do I actually remember how, in the first few hours of my life this priest spoke to the weeping crowd, telling them: 'I will take her to Joaquina. Her husband died two months back and just four days ago she gave birth to a stillborn child. Though she is now wet nurse to Dona Briolanga's newborn baby she will welcome a child of her own and this babe will ease her pain.'

Is this a real memory, or something still lingering in that strange, uncharted realm between memory and the constant retelling of old tales? Is it a true whisper or a deception of time? Is it not possible that the memories of my early years are simply the dreams of a long ago past, conjured up, like the images of my birth into a confection of imagined thoughts?

Was Joaquina ever real? Should I perhaps now question even her existence? Decades later what remains to substantiate her presence? Who still lives to sit and talk about her? Who can tell me of her laugh, who can help me pull her out of the shadows? And yet it seems that the very act of thinking about her brings her back and helps me catch the faint echo of her voice and the softness of its particular lilt. And it is as this happens that I feel my body soften and know once more the peace of lying in her arms, of being held close to her body.

But Joaquina's features still escape me, her face is indistinct, a blur that remains as no more than a presence. Only her voice still lingers, faintly reminding me of how she laughed when she picked me up, tickling me and calling me her solemn child as she settled me into her lap and began to tell a story. In the early days she would tell me how I had come into her life, how I had been found and brought to her at a time when she was consumed with the grief of losing first her husband and then her child. 'You were my blessing,' she would say,' Without you how would I have survived? And how would you, a little motherless soul have survived if our Lady hadn't watched over you and brought you to me?' Then she would bring me close to her face and whisper that even as she, Joaquina, cared for me here on earth my mother, her husband and child were all seated up in heaven, gazing down on us from beneath the protective cloak of our Lady.

Those first few months of my life were lived in the small, enchanted circle of Joaquina's arms. It was only very gradually that my world spread outwards and my boundaries widened like slow ripples moving across a pond. And only as these ripples grew did I begin to sense, to feel and finally to understand that I was different. It is hard to pinpoint the moment when I sensed that first tremor of uncertainty in my life. Did someone else pick me up one day and whisper the implications of my birth? Did someone else tell me that as soon as I was found I was given the good Christian name of Inês to protect me from eternal damnation? And when did I learn that no one had expected me to live, that naming me was a kindness designed to give my tiny soul the chance of entering heaven? And when did I grasp that since my mother was unknown the stain of illegitimacy was assumed? Perhaps if someone had come forward with my mother's name I might, like some foundlings, have been renamed. But this never happened. Or at least not until many, many years later when all those who knew of my orphaned status were gone, did my earth mother finally reclaim me.

♓

It is now that I pause, aware of the worn and fragile rope time has thrown across the vast chasm between the year of my birth and my impending death. I am waiting, waiting to see what memory will now come back to me, allowing my mind to drift quite effortlessly until I feel myself once again being rocked in Joaquina's arms, listening to the sound of her voice.

'I am going to tell you,' she is saying, using the words with which she always began, a story already beginning to tumble out. In the summer she would tell me about a bold young prince who rode a white horse and braved dragons and sorcerers to win the most beautiful princess in the land for his bride and how they married and lived happily. She would describe their castle and their kingdom, a land of plenty, with flowing rivers and great forests full of gentle beasts, of distant mountains and cool water—everything that we longed for when the burning sun scorched our land and forced us to seek the darkness of shaded interiors. She would tell me of the beautiful storks who flew vast distances, following their ancient instincts to journey from faraway

Africa to spend their summers with us. Even as a tiny child I knew how anxiously people looked forward to their return and the re-building of their tangled and untidy nests and how, once their young were hatched, their parents brought small creatures to feed them, all the while uttering an endless clicking of reassurance. Joaquina's tales stressed the benevolence of these birds and how, soon after people married, they would be brought a baby by a stork—and that a very special stork had carried a baby girl to the prince and his bride. And it was here that Joaquina confused me for she never stopped to explain how the babies brought by the storks were always white-skinned and pale while the slave Balthazar, who Joaquina said had also come from Africa, was so dark and different. And now I wonder whether this was when I first noticed him. Had it happened on a rare summer day when he came into the *quinta* and so a marker of when my boundaries began moving further back and I began to grasp that a great house enveloped us, that there were retinues of servants and that though Balthazar's duties were outside, looking after the horses, he also belonged here?

♓

But the weeks passed and the sun began setting earlier and, as the days darkened sooner, a slight tension started to enclose us. In the evening Joaquina would seat herself by the warmth and security of the fire and tell me frightening tales about our land, a land that had so suddenly become cold and inhospitable. This was the season when dustings of powdered snow sometimes fell and covered our world, and Joaquina would describe how the great soaring vultures sought sustenance, and how packs of hungry wolves hunted across the High Sierra, their keening howls echoing across the land. But, though I was small, and my world still tiny and enclosed, I remember that on full moon nights, Joaquina would draw me closer to her body. Her voice would be hushed and she would keep looking up and away, towards the outer doors. But I was only a child and the demands of tiredness were soon met despite the little unexplained tremors of fear I instinctively felt. Soon enough I slept and when, hours later, I awoke it was to a crisp morning with all tiredness gone. Yet Joaquina's moods sometimes remained dark, a mood often reflected in her stories of strange monsters and fierce beasts. On one cold and bitter day, she whispered to me that faraway, beyond distant Lisbon, there was—or so she had heard—a vast, heaving stretch of water, a great ocean that roared and surged and was filled with terrible sea-creatures which would rise up from the depths to devour even the greatest ships, that whole fleets were lost. Here she crossed herself and, in a barely audible voice, said that sometimes men *were* fortunate and their voyages did end safely. Such men were the lucky captains and sailors whose devotion and prayers brought them the protection and blessings of Mãe, our Mother, whose image sailed with them, keeping them safe not only from the terrors of the deep but from the frightening dangers that awaited should they set foot in Africa.

Africa. Africa was somewhere far away, wrapped in darkness and mystery, a land that, according to Joaquina, was made up of jungles and ravines and mountains, of great rivers and barren, burning deserts, a land filled with mysterious and bloodthirsty beasts, peopled by fearsome and sometimes even monstrous men and women. These horrors transfixed me, filling me with fear until, one evening I looked up and caught sight of Balthazar standing in the shadows, listening to her words. For the briefest moment his eyes met mine and he smiled a sad and secret smile, imperceptibly shaking his head.

♓

Although Joaquina's supply of stories was seemingly endless the demands of her work meant that she would often be busy elsewhere and it was then that Balthazar would sometimes come and pick me up. On one such occasion, an evening just after a summer storm, he gathered me into his arms and took me outside. There he pointed at the large numbers of storks standing a short distance away, all holding their black-bordered wings away from their bodies, as if waiting to begin a mysterious dance. Balthazar looked at me and smiled before telling me that because of the rain the birds were earthbound and merely hanging their wings down to let them dry.

We had watched in silence until, after a very long pause, he looked at me and said 'We have storks in my land' before again falling silent. I feel now that he was deciding how far he could allow himself to talk, and therefore think, about his homeland. Only when a large stork suddenly flapped its wings did he speak again. 'We respect them for we believe their presence augers well for the future, that they are auspicious and herald the coming of rain.'

As time went by Balthazar, when not busy taking care of the *quinta*'s horses, would tell me other stories about his land, stories that spoke of a world far beyond anywhere imagined or described by Joaquina. And here, with utter clarity, I see again the morning when he sat me down beside him and began describing a long and powerful ceremony, one attended by not only nobles and princes and kings, all wearing their most costly and magnificent robes, but by the *jalis* who, he said, were the court praise-singers, men whose songs and music brought them great respect. Once every seven years these men would gather together so that the history of the entire world could be recited and everyone was reminded of how the earth had been created. It was at this point that Balthazar looked down at me and cupped his two hands together as he told me how a divine egg was formed, of the seeds it held—along with two pairs of beings—and how the male being of the first pair was called Pemba and had wanted to take over the work of creation. And that Pemba ripped himself away from the egg-womb and came down to earth, keeping with him all that surrounded his umbilical cord. And that from this he created the earth, but that it was barren, and though he planted the seeds the earth was contaminated by them since they drew on the cord's blood for sustenance. And how, in order to purify the earth, the male of the other paired being was offered as a sacrifice and came to earth as water, which cleanses everything. And that this spirit of the waters is called Faro and is symbolized by two catfish, the fish that move with the waters when they surge out from the rivers and flood across the land after the rainy season. And that this spirit came to earth in a great ark which settled on the mountains of Kri, and that with him were animals and plants and flowers and four pairs of humans, and that where this ark rested is now a sacred shrine. And that from this ark came three other beings, Surakata, the heroic ancestor of Balthazar's people, the first blacksmith and, lastly, the first of the praise-singers. And from their prayers and drumming and singing, and the blacksmith's beating on a rock, came the great gift of life-giving rain. And it was at this moment that Pemba's female twin, who had remained in the egg, came down to earth and, though no one knew why, immediately fled away to the east.

Although, after many years had passed, one of the four men from the ark became the first being on earth to die, one of his companions made a musical instrument and restored him to life. Yet though he returned it was as a great serpent, which, wordlessly, and quietly, slithered away to a cave in a distant mountain. Finally, the last of the ancestors from the ark went east and met up with the female who had been paired with Pemba and how because she tricked him into killing one of the sacred catfish, he died. Faro then sent an antelope to restore the land's fertility, and wherever it roamed the land blossomed and bloomed, becoming lush and green. But Pemba, the first unruly spirit, and the continuing cause of the world's pollution, was always haunting them, leaving a trail that Faro followed as he hunted him down the great river, tracking him from the mountains to the delta where he finally fought and overcame him.

♓

When Balthazar finished this story he sat without moving, almost like a statue, as if the slightest movement, even breathing, would destroy something he was trying to hang onto. Then something passed through him and he turned and looked down at me, his face so close I saw the full effect of the question I then asked.

'How,' I said, 'did you hear this story? Who told you?'

His stillness almost frightened me for though I saw how my words had affected him the actual truth is that, for the briefest moment, he closed himself down so completely that there was nothing to see. It was instinct that told me he was protecting himself. Then the moment passed and he smiled.

'It has,' he said, 'been a very long time since I have spoken of him. And you are a child. And yet...perhaps you will understand. Perhaps his name should be spoken again, perhaps our terrible story should be told.'

I sat quietly, wanting so much to hear more but knowing things hung on a knife-edge—even as I wondered how terrible the story would be.

♓

It took another long pause before Balthazar, very slowly, began to speak, telling me of the royal family he belonged to and mentioning once again that all noble families had, as part of their entourage, a family of *jalis*, bards who sang praises of the royal family's founders, of their great ancestors and history, and of their exploits and bravery, always singing to the accompaniment of a many-stringed kora. These men, he said, were poets and storytellers and it was usual for the young sons of the kings and nobles to grow up alongside the young sons of the *jalis*, and for their lives to be interwoven from birth to death. Such men were held in high esteem, as much for their singing and music as for their spirituality and knowledge and, because they were so respected, they would sometimes be sent as emissaries to a neighbouring kingdom, to bring peace and reduce the threat of war.

Then he stopped, as if trying to find a way forward, knowing that he had to finally decide whether to continue or stay silent. When, at last, he continued, his voice almost chanted the words that followed.

'His name,' he said, 'was Souleymane. We were born in the same month, just two days apart. Almost twins. We grew up together. Inseparable. Although I had to learn my royal duties and he had to study and become proficient in his calling, we were never far apart. And as we were boys together so too we became men together, both marrying, having children—each of us content that our sons would also grow together and continue the tradition, and that the same story I told you, that Souleymane's father and grandfather told my father and grandfather, would be passed on for all time by his son and grandsons to my son and grandsons.

'But it was not to be. My son will never hear Souleymane's son sing or play or tell stories. And neither of them will ever know their fathers or grandfathers.'

I sat quietly, aware that my hand was almost touching his.

'It happened, after a decade of peace, first with the rumblings of war and the decision that a dialogue between ourselves and the ruler eyeing our wealth and fertile lands could halt his advance. And so Souleymane was sent to his court, of course with our blessings and an escort. There was no danger in this; we knew his return was inevitable since even harming a *jali* is a repugnant, unthinkable act. Yet time passed and as we watched the moon move through its phases, waxing and waning, our concern slowly mounted, eventually growing deeper when, for the second time, the moon began growing to fullness. And then, just as once again it began waning there came that dreadful dawn when, with the moon still in the sky and the first clouds of the coming rains swelling closer, a single camel came staggering into the palace compound and, as it collapsed, its rider tumbled off and we saw he was Souleymane's young cousin. Had he been less weak, less bloody and wounded he could have given us his terrible message in the blink of an eye. But thirst had made him speechless and his blistered lips were barely able to part. Yet, all too soon we knew that Souleymane had been murdered, that the terrible and unthinkable had been done: a king had disregarded tradition, had ignored the belief that the most abhorrent, the most obscene of all crimes is to kill a *jali.*

'For the rest of that day, and until well past nightfall all we could hear was the sound of weeping in Souleymane's house, the keening howl of the women. I could barely stand the pain. Yet I was present at all the discussions, listening to my father and uncles, to the wise men of our court, aware all the while that a river was sweeping towards me, its waters roaring, its sounds beating into my head, telling me what I must do. In a moment of silence I stood up, bowed before my elders, and sought permission to speak. Perhaps it was grief and exhaustion that made my father finally nod his agreement for what I then asked: permission to go and avenge Souleymane; something they were initially against. Yet I persisted until, at last, they granted my wishes.

'And so it was that, even before the dawn, before a whole day had passed, I was readying myself to leave. Taking my farewells of my wife, my mother, my children, of Souleymane's wife, of his family, and, had I but known it, of my land and people.

'I cannot speak of the journey or even of my feelings when I saw my father's warriors were following me, or of the fury with which we all rode, our camels racing as if to outrun a sandstorm.

'But it was all for nothing. They were waiting for us. And knew we were exhausted.'

Again Balthazar fell silent. This time, some instinct told me what was coming, that, in fact, it was obvious. I edged my hand even closer, slowly inching my fingers over his.

'Of course we fought, slashing in every direction, striking each blow to avenge Souleymane. But we were outnumbered and it was soon over, all but three of us were either dead or with lives ebbing away, their blood staining the earth. I was put in chains, kept imprisoned and barely fed for six months. Until the morning when a caravan appeared, a caravan which, once its business was over, and its camels were rested, set out again, taking me—and many others—with them. While still half-bound I was forced to walk the long miles to the coast where, along with all the other unfortunates, we began the terrible voyage which brought us to Portugal, to the Lagos slave market.'

♓

Many of Balthazar's stories were of his distant home. He had a low, deep voice and he would sometimes talk as if in a trance. Often he would fall silent and it was in between these pauses and the habit he had of waving one arm that I unconsciously picked up a whole, hidden range of emotions. Years later I realized that they spoke of his pain and the walled up ache that forever reminded him of his own people, his family and of Souleymane, his music and his songs. Balthazar's Africa was different to the one Joaquina whispered about for in his own land he had been a man of substance—a fact that had caused his captors to mock him, taunting him for the haughty reserve that suggested he was more familiar with the giving of orders than following them. It was for this reason that, by the time he reached Dona Briolanga's house—and he never, ever spoke of the great humiliation of the slave market, of being bought—he had been renamed Balthazar in memory of the darkest of the Three Kings who had journeyed, following a star, to bring their precious gifts to the newborn Christ Child.

Balthazar was always slightly apart from us, secluded in the darkness of a shadow we could barely see, inhabiting a place where we could never find him, where part of him could be kept closed and hidden. When I think of him now I see him sitting alone, silent and very still, his head turned away. At one time I thought that perhaps he was waiting for someone—or something—but now I believe he was simply protecting himself, preventing us from discerning the terrible depths of his loss and pain. Although I never really saw the full extent of all that he kept locked away I believe he allowed me closer to him than anyone else—once he even told me that his real name was Abd-al-Rahman and whispered that it was one of the ninety-nine names of God and meant the servant of the merciful. Though at the time I knew too little to understand all that the name implied I grasped that it was further evidence of him having had another life and existence. Perhaps he told me because he knew I was too young to understand the emotions he hid from everyone else and would therefore accept him and innocently see his truth. But what was it, I now ask myself, that made me aware that this truth was Balthazar's most secret side, that whatever external mask he wore, and regardless of which face he showed the world, I instinctively knew what I did not then understand: that what he was deemed to have been forced to repudiate, still lived within him?

♓

It is now many decades since I last saw Balthazar but his face, unlike Joaquina's, has remained clear to me. His voice still whispers close to my ear and if I reach out a hand I can feel the springiness of his tightly curled hair. And I still smile when I remember how safe I felt when he took me in his large hands and held me up high and told me to look 'far, far into the distance.' He made me feel I could *almost* see Africa, the stories he told bringing to life somewhere I instinctively knew was real. Sometimes Balthazar would stop and ask me if I had understood everything, encouraging me to ask questions, answering and explaining and telling me how things were and had been, repeating favourite stories, painting a world I was never likely to see and he would never know again. Only much later did I understand that the stories he told me were the stories that, in another life, he would have told his own children. And, as it eventually dawned on me, that Souleymane would have told *his* children.

But then, when spring finally came and the wild flowers began to bloom, Balthazar was busier and Joaquina would always be the one telling tales. They were often about the surrounding land and the mysterious men who had once lived here. 'They were Moors,' she would say—before adding that long, long ago they had come from a distant land as conquerors, that they had ruled Portugal and were infidels. 'Until,' she explained, 'our brave Christian knights drove them away.' Yet though she said this with assurance, even a touch of pride, I can still catch the faint query of doubt in her voice as she continued. 'Or so the priests and knights would have us believe. For where could our Moors go? Was this not also their land?' She looked at me quizzically, pinched my cheek and pulled me closer to her. 'Anyway they stayed here, almost disappearing from our sight, living beneath the ground in great houses made of gold that are filled with precious things.' Sometimes when she told me about them she would suddenly pause and declare: 'They are honest men—but it is unwise to cross them.' This was always the signal that she was about to describe the hot summer afternoon when she had gone to fetch water and had met one of them, a small dark man.

'He just appeared,' she said, 'right before me on the path.'

For a moment she paused, looking down into my eyes, to see if she had my attention. I shivered and snuggled closer in case the story might be too frightening.

'He was just *there*. It was a shock but he was polite. "Please, you must come with me," he said, "I have a child and it needs to be bathed". Well, what could I do? I was frightened of course but knew I had to follow him. So I agreed and off we went. For a little man he moved fast and I had to run to keep up with him. Eventually we came to the ancient stone, the great dolmen the Old People built long, long ago, even before the Moors came. There he stopped and looked up at me, telling me to walk carefully. Then, for just a moment I thought he had vanished until—can you believe it—I saw he was walking down under the dolmen. I hurried after him, my heart beating as I scurried along, moving down a long, long corridor until—well, what do you think I saw?' she asked.

I drew even closer to Joaquina's body but said nothing.

'It happened so suddenly, he just stopped and there right in front of me was a huge and beautiful house, built entirely of gold—the doors, the windows, everything; all was gold. Then, as if by magic—for I saw no one—the great golden doors swung open without a sound and there inside I could see so many costly things, all richer than anything I'd ever seen before—or since. But I had no time to look around. "Wait here," the little man said, going out through a door for just a moment. How he came back so fast I'll never know. He'd hardly left me before there he was again, with a small baby in his arms, a tiny little girl. 'Come', the man said, walking towards a great door off the hallway. Once again though there was no sign of anyone, the door just opened and he took me into a room in the middle of which was a large golden basin filled with fragrant water. Then, after handing me the baby, he stood watching me as I washed the little mite and dressed her in the beautiful, silken robes that suddenly seemed to appear in his arms.

'After I'd finished he took the baby gently back from me, and told me to wait again. Why he bothered I can't say because he was back no sooner than he'd gone, holding two bricks in his hands. "These are for you," he said, "for the trouble you've taken." I took them because, well, though he'd been so courteous, I didn't know what might happen if he was offended. It's not wise to offend them. Then he took me back down the corridor and up to the dolmen. And there, without warning, he suddenly vanished and when I looked round there was no sign of where he'd gone to or come from, nothing at all.'

'So what did you do with the bricks,' I asked, finding my voice at last.

'I was a foolish woman,' she said, 'I threw one away as I was walking home. 'What do I want with a brick?' I thought. The other I decided to keep, to fill up a hole in the lane outside the house.' She sighed. 'And when I'd done this and gone into the house what do you think I saw the next time I came out? Well, I'll tell you: there where I'd put the brick was a great bar of gold! Of course I ran off to look for the one I'd thrown away. But I never found it.'

Years later I wondered what benefits she'd got from even her one brick of gold but at the time all I wanted was another story.

Because of Joaquina's stories, the Moors became a familiar—but mysterious—part of my world. She even told me of the great Cromeleque, a great gathering of huge stones that stood within walking distance of the *quinta*, and that her family had lived near it for generations. Yet she also added that it was a dark place, that no one who went there would ever return—despite the probably untested belief that if the forces it contained were truly respected, they might permit entry to their realm.

All this I accepted—for what child can discriminate or really question? Then came that particular spring morning when she told me something about the Moors that changed everything—and opened up a wound which, until then, I never knew existed but which has since—and despite everything—never completely healed. The day began earlier than usual, just as the first rays of light started pushing away the night's darkness. Now, when I look back, I can see that there had been signs that it was not to be an ordinary day. My sleep had been restless and throughout the night I had tossed and turned with fever. In the circumstances I should not have been surprised when I opened my eyes and saw Joaquina looking down at me. But when I did so I shrank back, immediately seeing—and am still seeing—the expression on her face. She was looking at me, gazing at my face without really seeing me. Sensing a tension I couldn't understand I pulled my blanket closer to my body. I could see her concern. But I could also see that there was something behind her scrutiny. It was as if she was looking at me for the first time and I almost flinched when she reached out a hand to draw back the cover and stroke my face.

'You poor little mite,' I heard her whisper under her breath, 'Where do you really come from? *Who* are you?' I held myself still, conscious that she was talking to herself, understanding that, despite her closeness, she was not really aware of my thoughts and mounting confusion.

'You just appeared,' she muttered to herself. 'Out of the earth. Had you been living there? Are you a child of enchantment?'

I sat up, wide awake, my fever forgotten as I scrabbled towards Joaquina, my words tumbling out, begging her to explain.

And, in a way, after giving me a long look and reaching out to gather me into her arms, she did.

'There are people here,' she began,' people we don't always see. I've told you about the little Moor whose baby I bathed and how he apparently appeared from nowhere and how he later disappeared. But there are others, other Moors.' She paused for a moment. 'They are people who have a curse upon them; a curse that some say can only be broken if a good Christian kisses them. They are—or so it is said—Moorish maidens, some even say that they are princesses! But how can one know? All I can tell you for certain is that they are young and very beautiful and have long black hair which they comb with a golden comb.' There was another pause. 'They are rarely seen for they only appear to be in a human form. Their real shape is different.' At this point there was a long beat, a moment when Joaquina hesitated and it was obvious that she was struggling to put what she had to tell me into words. 'You see,' she eventually whispered, her voice so low I had to strain to hear her. 'The curse that binds them is a terrible one.' Here she stumbled, stammering as she continued. 'You...you see they are held—enchanted—trapped and enclosed for all eternity in the old standing stones of the Cromeleque. They are petrified. They are stone.' Her voice was practically inaudible by then and her final words were almost lost in the swallow she gave before she finished. 'And that is not all. It is said that if we dare seek them out they can be found but, as soon as they realize we have seen them, they quickly vanish, slithering suddenly down into the earth, transformed into serpents.'

Her words drifted away, moving from faintness to silence but even before they were gone I knew the damage they had done, that they had already wormed into my mind. It was then, and for the first time, that I consciously asked myself who I was, a question that as it insinuated its way into my mind was made more terrible by Joaquina's own question about my origins.

♓

Yet despite the heavy weight that had descended upon me I was still a child. And Joaquina, for all the unease she had created, was someone whose company—and stories—I sought. She continued to tell them and it would often happen that by the time she had finished a story the light of day would have vanished from the sky and a shiver of wind would be eddying through the house to hunt out and slam shut any carelessly unclosed door. Their distant banging would make Joaquina tremble and doubtless remind her of the precariousness of our existence and the tragedies of her own life. Yet whether it was summertime when the sun set late or springtime when the night was filled with the songs of unseen birds or winter when the dark mysteries of the world moved closer it was inevitable that as day ended Joaquina spoke about Our Lady, Mãe, mother as she called Her. Joaquina loved Her with passion and it could easily be imagined that every step she took and every breath she drew was with the word Mãe on her lips, every word tinged with awe, every phrase halfway towards being a prayer.

So absolute was Joaquina's faith that though I knew Mãe lived up in heaven I also knew She was down here on earth, caring for us. Because of Joaquina I knew the joys and tragedies of Mãe, and of the Son She bore, and the cruel death that led to His Resurrection. I knew too of the time Alvaro, Dona Briolanga's oldest son, had fallen out of a tree and lain unconscious until She appeared and blessed him and how he had then risen up and run off, unaffected by his fall. I knew too that She had brought home a nearby landowner's lost oxen and how he had fallen to his knees when he saw Her herding them towards him. And I knew how Maria, the childless wife of Joaquina's brother had prayed to Her and been given the blessing of a daughter. And, above all, I can never forget that night at the end of a long, cruel rainless summer when, holding Joaquina's hand, I had gone with her to the church. I can still see myself watching in awe as the priests took down the statue of Mãe, our Lady, and how, along with so many others, we set out in a long procession, our Mãe held high, carried and surrounded by men bearing great fire-torches. Slowly, accompanied by musicians, and with all of us singing and praying, we made our way to the dried-up river bed for Her to be shown the ravages of the drought. I see the statue being carefully lowered and how we then murmured our heart-felt prayers, beseeching Her to send us rain.

My inner eye still shows me how, three days later, we gathered in the church's incense-filled darkness, our eyes gazing up at the light filtering in through the windows to fall on Mãe's *resplendor*, her halo, highlighting the slight trembling of Her hands. Even now I can hear the straining groan of the wooden doors being swung open and the singing and rejoicing, the music and banging of drums. I look closer as the villagers burst into the church, all of them soaked through to the skin as they rush towards to our Mãe, our Mother, hands raised as they cry out their gratitude. And then my eyes follow Her outstretched arm, moving past Her pointing finger and on, out through the open doors to the sheets of drenching rain, rain brought to our parched land by the love our Lady.

It is as I think of Her that I feel an expression of joy spreading across my face for it was our Lady, our Mãe, that Joaquina loved. Our Lady, *my* Lady. The Lady who had watched over me at my birth and has been with me all my life, who will soon guide me back to Her and who is, even now, waiting to greet me.

Nossa Senhora do Ó.

I feel I have given a somewhat unbalanced impression of my childhood, suggesting that the only people around me were Joaquina and Balthazar who did nothing but tell me stories. This is not so, the house seethed with constant activity, servants and slaves working ceaselessly to follow Dona Briolanga's orders. I lived, discreetly and generally unnoticed in the large and bustling household where Joaquina's duty was to provide the milk needed for Leonor, the child born to Dona Briolanga just a few days before my birth. The house was large and sprawling, a place where numerous people came and went at all hours of the day and night. It was only as I became older and more curious that I understood that Dom Martim, the rarely seen husband of Dona Briolanga, was a close advisor to the King and therefore often away in distant Lisbon. Indeed it was only when the court moved to Évora that he was ever much more than an occasional visitor.

Leonor grew up alongside me, sharing Joaquina's love and often sitting beside me when stories were told. She was always brought to Joaquina's breast before me since she was the child Joaquina was employed to suckle. But there was no jealousy between us; Leonor was a gentle, quiet child and though well aware of the void that separated us she never asserted herself or demanded more than she was given. Of her own mother she saw little and it is now tempting to believe that she looked upon Joaquina as more of a mother than Dona Briolanga. It was Joaquina who cared for her, soothed away her childhood hurts and pains and banished the terrors of the dark.

Although Leonor was only two years younger than Catarina, her only sister, the birth of several stillborn babies had placed a gap of almost eight years between Catarina and her brother Pedro, the youngest of Dona Briolanga's seven sons. It is hard to say how I always instinctively knew there was something different about Pedro. I barely ever saw him—neither he nor any of his brothers had much to do with the more domestic side of life within the great *quinta.* And yet from my earliest days I somehow sensed that there were times when he was watched as if it was feared that some dreadful accident might befall him.

It was only very gradually, probably sometime after the beginning of my third year that I started to understand the meaning of the whispers that wafted around Pedro and grasped that he lived at the centre of some kind of recurring terror. A child is like an animal, using senses that will later be discarded once words are understood and questions can be asked. Devoid of the necessary vocabulary—and aware that since I could never ask questions I could not expect answers—I began to watch both Pedro and those around him, Joaquina and the other servants, especially Balthazar.

And so it was that, one morning I was able to creep close enough to hear what Joaquina was whispering to Balthazar.

'She has ordered us all to stay with him,' were the first words I caught. 'She says that this time the curse must be broken—though I fear he will once again be too cunning for us.'

'We all fear that,' Balthazar agreed, raising one arm in a gesture of inevitability.

'But tonight you must try. May our Blessed Virgin have mercy on him.'

Bit by bit the pieces began falling into place and yet, though every move Pedro made was dogged, soon after the full moon had risen it seemed that Dona Briolanga's wishes remained unfulfilled. People ran out of the house, the hounds barked, there were shouts and cries and the banging of doors before, quite suddenly a strange silence fell. It was a silence that very slowly turned into a shivering whisper that ran through the *quinta* telling us that, once again, Pedro had eluded his watchers—though why this should be necessary was left unexplained.

All I knew was that by the next morning Pedro was not only back in his room—but stayed there for most of the day. When, towards evening he finally emerged he looked pale and exhausted, drained. During the day Dona Briolanga, a woman we all believed to be above displaying emotion, was seen weeping. Balthazar kept his distance, as if fearing Dona Briolanga would suddenly turn and vent her disappointment—or anger—on him. Yet, by the following day everything seemed to be forgotten. Once more everything appeared to be normal.

Until the next full moon. And then the next and the next.

The truth eventually came, slowly leaking out like oil from a cracked jar. I would catch the word *cursed* from time to time. Then *seventh.* And *moon.* And *man.* Words I could not link but which I soon realized hovered around Pedro every month. Then I noticed that the approach of a full moon night was not only accompanied by a sense of tangible fear but when Pedro was both closely watched and his face marked with an expression of haunted terror. Now, all these years later it feels as if I am somehow suggesting that at the tender age of three I cleverly assembled facts and reached my conclusions. This was not so. How could it be? Nothing was ever spelt out. Nothing was ever voiced or made clear. All that surrounded me—and indeed the entire household—was an atmosphere of recurring tension.

In this way more time passed and by the time I had entered my fifth year more words had been dropped into my ill-assorted collection: *son* was added to seventh, *full* to moon and *wolf* to man. Finally, as I toddled, often unseen, around the kitchen, half hidden in the folds of Joaquina's skirts and listening to the servants' chatter I assembled the last of the pieces I needed to make a terrible whole.

Pedro was a seventh son. And therefore a *lobisomem,* a man cursed to suffer every full moon night. A curse that made him seek some concealed place to disrobe, that made him nestle into the earth and transform himself into a wolf. A curse that made him run to seven different crossroads before returning to regain his human shape. And, last of all, I discovered there was one more horror: that though Pedro was aware of this curse, and though he longed to break it, and even knew how to do so, the moment the moon took possession of his soul he was driven to hide his clothes from all those who might save him. Only if a *lobisomem*'s clothes can be found and burnt whilst he is in his wolf-form can the curse be lifted. And yet, though he knows this and longs for it to happen it is the one thing his wolf cunning always guards against.

♓

Eventually a time came when Leonor began spending time with her mother in the *quinta*'s vast kitchen, learning the required skills of cooking and, most especially, those of sweet making. Joaquina would often help in the kitchen, usually working alongside Catarina, Leonor's self-assured sister, who was already nearly as capable as her mother, often preparing simple dishes by herself. As part of the household, and now learning to be a servant, I was expected to help: cleaning, chopping and peeling vegetables, fetching ingredients, removing empty bowls and bringing dishes, sometimes even stirring pots or pouring water. Initially I was wary of Dona Briolanga, well aware of how vigilantly she ordered and controlled every aspect of life in and around the *quinta*. Yet I soon discovered that in the kitchen she revealed a softer side of her character, suggesting that she found pleasure in cooking, perhaps because it took her away from constantly supervising the work created by Dom Martim's long absences. Her moods were lighter and, very occasionally, she would hand me an apple or a perhaps a pear. One morning, when she seemed particularly happy she suddenly bent down and, with a laugh, gave me one of her sweets, a confection of sugar and eggs, and therefore costly.

I soon began to realize that not only was sweet-making Dona Briolanga's greatest pleasure but that it was Leonor, even more than Catarina, to whom she was teaching the elaborate and complex art of making them. On the days when they were being prepared there was a special atmosphere in the kitchen. At first I believed this was because the required delicacy of touch, the correct beating of eggs and especially the careful measuring of sugar was dictated by the expense and rarity of these and other ingredients. Later I understood that though these factors certainly played their part, Dona Briolanga's attention to the smallest detail was deliberate. Many of the recipes had been part of her inheritance, their preparation and ingredients not only unique to her family but preserved as a closely guarded secret. I soon observed that with one or two particular—and rarely prepared—sweets no one except Leonor ever really knew quite how much sugar was used—or how many eggs, or precisely which spices or even how they were combined and in what order. When these recipes were prepared Dona Briolanga would make Leonor stand close beside her, often turning to whisper instructions to her.

Yet regardless of whether or not sweets were being made, the cooking of everyday meals continued as usual, ensuring that the kitchen was always heavy with the smell of either fish or meat, of garlic and herbs, of oil and cheese and the rich warmth of freshly baked bread. These were familiar, comforting smells and though they remained when sweets were prepared they were then joined by other richer and deeper scents. While I soon learnt their names, their intangible qualities remained undefined: the pungency of cinnamon, the bitterness of cloves, the succulence of ginger, the richness of saffron and the sharpness of pepper, aromatic and black, all gave not only their distinct flavours to Dona Briolanga's different sweets but filled the kitchen with the mystery of unknown and distant lands.

♓

Time slipped slowly by, the years passing until that fateful morning when I woke to find Joaquina weeping and, instinctively, knew my world was threatened. My fears were justified for as soon as I sat up and began rubbing sleep from my eyes she swept me into her arms. 'Well,' she eventually said, 'I knew it would happen. How could it not?'

It took a while but she eventually explained everything.

Leonor was a second daughter and while Catarina would marry, she, as was customary, would enter a convent. Once I had absorbed Joaquina's words there was a short pause as I began to comprehend that Leonor would soon leave us. Slowly I began to rise in denial but, as I did so Joaquina bent forward and cupped her hands around my face.

'And you, you are to go with her.'

♓

At first I failed understand the full import of her words: that Leonor was to stay, as a Bride of Christ, in the Convento da Nossa Senhora da Boa Fé for the rest of her life and that I—though never as a nun—would stay there with her, as her servant. Forever. Perhaps if I had not felt a quiver of apprehension—and seen the unhappiness etched deep onto Joaquina's face—I might even have looked forward to going since I imagined that she would be coming with us.

A few days later Dona Briolanga assembled the servants and ordered them to begin packing up a mattress and sheets, candles, and even dresses and ornaments, and spices. As they did so she ticked them off a list that carefully detailed everything Leonor's family had contracted to send to the convent as her dowry. The recipes of all the sweets she had been so diligently taught to prepare would be taken with her, a valuable part of her dowry and the reason, I now realized, why she, rather than Catarina, had been taught to prepare them. At the same time I suddenly understood the real reason for Joaquina's tears: she was not coming with us. My first reaction was that this was a mistake and that, somehow, she would be able to keep me with her, at the *quinta.* In despair I ran to Balthazar, hoping he could help, that he would understand my distress. And change things.

Did his words comfort me? I hesitate. Even as I remember how he picked me up and took me outside and that, for a moment, he just stood there. And how he then turned his face to me and told me to look out, to really look—even as he asked if I could see his faraway house. I stayed silent, confused—though I turned my face and gazed towards the far horizon. But everything was as it had always been, no strange house had appeared. And then, even as I felt my confusion growing Balthazar placed his mouth close against my ear and whispered: 'Look again.'

I raised my eyes, listening to the softness of Balthazar's voice as he continued whispering, telling me of the desert whose sand rolled endlessly for untold days, stretching away from us like a frozen sea, and that if we travelled across this vast expanse we would eventually see an oasis around an ancient well and that, a day or so later, the walls of a city would appear, high walls of dried mud through whose arched gateways people came and went, their billowing indigo robes eddying around them as warriors on caparisoned horses galloped past them and into the great square. And that once in the square—a place I suddenly saw was full of activity and noise, of buying and selling, of colours and music, of scents and life—we took a turn and made our way down an alley of cool and shaded houses until we came upon another set of walls. And it was here, at the entrance of a great house that I saw two tall imposing guards, both holding spears, alert and ready to defend those who lived within. Men who, as we approached, smiled and drew back, lowering their spears and bowing with respect even as the carved doors of the house suddenly swung open and a beautiful woman came running out. Running and almost falling, her robes floating like liquid around her, running towards us, her arms outstretched, laughing and weeping, followed by her children.

'Can you see her?' Balthazar whispered.

I buried my head in his shoulder, nodding as I did so. Understanding.

♓

But, of course, since I was still little more than a child, the remaining days were filled with tears and sadness. I stayed close to Joaquina, watching and following every move she made, somehow believing that something would happen and she would come with us to the convent. Yet, even as I repeatedly sought to bury myself in her love I also began to sense her distress and to notice how often she tightened her arms around me to stifle her crying or turned away to hide her tear-streaked face. And it was then, even as she continued to comfort me, that I finally understood the extent of *her* loss: that she was once again losing those she held most dear. Only Leonor's expression was unreadable for though her face was pale and drawn I felt she was hiding something, somehow deliberately concealing an emotion behind an unexpectedly impenetrable veil.

Time edged forward at a cruel speed and, all too soon, the morning of our departure was upon us, dawning with the sounds of activity, of men shouting and horses milling outside the *quinta*, champing at their bits. Somewhere in the midst of everything was Dom Alvaro, Leonor's eldest brother who was to come with us, standing in for his father who, as usual, had been forced to bow to the king's dictates and remain in faraway Lisbon. Used, as perhaps she was, to an almost permanently absent father, Leonor seemed to unemotionally accept reality until a horseman galloped into the *quinta*'s courtyard and handed her a small missal, sent by her father. For a moment her face blushed and tears sprang. I turned away and saw that just outside the house, and close by, attending to the horses and checking their harness, was Balthazar who was to be our coachman. Although, by then, almost everything that constituted Leonor's dowry had been sent to the convent, Dona Briolanga's servants ran in and out and backwards and forwards, scurrying to obey her orders. She was not coming with us; her farewell to Leonor had already taken place and her expression was so carefully composed that not one of us could read her mind. Not for a moment was anyone able to guess how she felt, knowing that once Leonor entered the convent, she would never again see her for more than a few fleeting moments.

At last, when there were no more delays or excuses for prolonging our departure, Dom Alvaro led his sister out of the house and helped her into the waiting coach. Strangely, he was the one who hesitated, taking a last look round—as if he too was leaving forever—before getting in and sitting opposite his sister. It was while all eyes were on Leonor, and with everyone perhaps wondering at her thoughts, that Balthazar, having lifted me up onto the coach, climbed up beside me and gathered the reins into his hands. It was then that I turned back and looked towards the *quinta*'s great doors, just in time to see Catarina backing away into the house, her face ashen. For a terrible moment I thought Joaquina was also inside, that I had missed her, but then my eyes settled and I saw her tear-streaked face and felt her sadness and knew the bravery of her smile as our eyes met.

Then, at last and without any discernible sign of lives being forever changed, the two heavy horses surged forward and we set out. As we passed under the gateway's arch, and took the well-worn and dusty road towards the convent, Balthazar reached out a hand and briefly placed it on mine. Nothing was said—indeed what could be said—but just that light pressure gave me the peace to sit quietly and keep my mind a merciful blank during the immeasurable half-hour our cavalcade took to reach our destination; a journey that transported us to another world.

The worst moment came as Balthazar handed me down and, as my feet touched the ground, my hand slipped out of his and I knew I was losing him forever.

♓

We had halted before a church set into high walls that so obviously enclosed the convent within. Beside the church was an arched and imposing entrance whose great doors were open, revealing three wide marble steps leading down to a recessed entrance that contained another large and imposing door with, to one side, a much smaller door. Nobody appeared to greet us and no-one spoke. The only sound was of a horse distractedly shaking its head up and down, jangling its harness as Dom Alvaro helped his sister out of the coach. In an effort to stop myself from turning round, I fixed my eyes on Leonor, and saw, with some surprise, that there was no sign of her normal timidity, indeed that she was walking forward with a calm formality I had never seen before. As she approached the door she appeared almost to float, one hand resting on Dom Alvaro's wrist, moving as if in a formal dance. I struggled to imitate her poise, attempting to still my apprehensions while all too aware that I could not only hear the clattering of hooves behind me but the groan of the coach being readied to leave, alerting me that Balthazar would soon be gone. The urge to swing round and run into his arms, to be lifted up and held was overwhelming and, for a moment, I faltered, uncertain. Then I heard Leonor gasp, a sound that was little more than a caught breath as she tripped on the uneven ground. But it was as she gripped her brother's arm to maintain her balance that my eyes caught the small indent of a tooth etched into her lower lip, an indent that unmasked the thinness of the veneer behind which she sought to hide her emotions.

Time was again immeasurable, making it impossible to know how long Dom Alvaro and Leonor took to step down into the great hallway and reach the grille I now noticed beside the smaller, and still firmly closed, door. Although for a fleeting moment nothing really registered there was, quite suddenly, the faintest suggestion of a presence behind the grille. Immediately Dom Alvaro withdrew his hand from Leonor's and walked forward, leaving his sister standing, as if only his support had enabled her to move. I saw him bring his face close to the grille and heard a low murmur of voices, first his and then, from within, the sensation of a barely audible whisper. Seconds later an unseen hand opened the door, revealing nothing but an empty darkness. For a charged moment everyone was quiet and still, almost frozen. The only movement, the only sound was from Leonor who, without even glancing at her brother, or turning round for a last look at the outside world, simply walked forward, seemingly drawn in by an invisible—and irresistible—power. Then, without warning, she was gone and the door was closing, almost silently, behind her.

I felt the breath sighing out of me. Leonor was gone but I was still outside the convent's walls. Perhaps it had all been a mistake; perhaps I would now return with Balthazar and be with Joaquina. It was a cruel moment of hope, soon broken by the door reopening and two young women emerging. There was a moment of hesitation, when, though they started coming towards me, they almost immediately stopped and looked round. It was then that Dom Alvaro, so clearly in charge, stepped forward and spoke to them, pointing to me before handing one of them a small packet. It was as it was being taken that I quickly glanced round, finally unable to prevent myself from wanting to see Balthazar, knowing I would run to him if our eyes met. But he was standing close to the horses, calming them and carefully preventing himself from looking in my direction. I turned back towards the two women, just as they again approached me, gesturing for me to follow them.

The door opened again and, within seconds, the darkness within had swallowed me up, the only sound being a faint click of the latch catching. Behind me.

♓

It is hard to describe the emotions of that day; indeed to do so I must now stop and deliberately summon up my memories of the convent. It has been many years since I so resolutely obliterated everything, even the tiniest of details. Everything has been locked away, not just the incidents and experiences that eventually brought such pain but the smaller memories that might otherwise bring back an individual voice or the turn of a particular body, the grace of a hand, the glance of an eye, the details that might remind me of the sound of a door, the heaviness of incense, of candles, of flowers and even of torrential rain. They have all been sealed and bolted down, buried deep in the darkest regions of my mind. The miracle is that to some extent I always believed I had been successful. I did forget. But here I pause, suddenly aware of my self-deception as the word *almost* surfaces and I see how fast it is all now flooding back, erupting. Without warning I know again the body that turned, the hand that moved, the eye that glanced. I know which door groaned, where the incense burnt, the candles flickered, the flowers bloomed and the rain fell. I admit what I would most hope to deny: I have remembered everything. All I can now hope to do is recall that time without dwelling on the pain it brought me.

♓

It all began, invisibly, when I truly entered the convent's world, when I followed the two women, hurrying after them, barely able see, moving by instinct and the rustling sound of their skirts. Then, as suddenly as I had been plunged into darkness, another door opened and I was blinded by light. We had emerged into a large open space and, as my vision returned, I was surprised to find myself in a garden, in a kind of paradise.

At first I thought I was in a vast orchard of various fruit trees, many of them heavy with fruit—apples, pears and quinces—but, as I walked I saw that there were also shaded arbours and trellises of climbing plants, roses and vines. Instinctively I inhaled the denseness of heady scents and saw the delicate play of light and shade and the sun shimmering through leaves, heard the singing of birds and felt an unexpected sense of peace and quiet tranquillity. Yet though this abundance assaulted my senses there was no time to look around. The determination of the two women forced me to hurry after them, down a well-tended path which seemed to take us away from the convent standing close beside the church. My uncertain reactions were still unformed when, without warning, we veered off down a less tended, but well-worn path, and headed towards a single-storey building which we had no sooner reached than we were inside it. Here I found myself in a long room, almost bare except for two rows of simple beds, a fact I blankly absorbed as both women swivelled round to face me, their unconscious precision so marked that it was immediately obvious that they were twins. Equally obvious was the fact that though neither of them spoke this was where I was to stay. Which confused me since there was no sign of Leonor—and surely I had come to the convent to be with her? I waited, uncomfortable and unsure, but still expecting one of them to explain everything. But all that happened was that, without a word, they turned to leave and as they did so I realized one of them was holding the packet containing the most precious part of Leonor's dowry: the recipes of Dona Briolanga's sweets.

♓

Now, all these years later, I once again hesitate, wondering if I can go further for though—as yet—there is nothing to fear I still sense the need for caution. But then, foolishly, and for the briefest moment, I relax and wait to see which thought, which memory will surface. And it is, of course, of the church and the sound of singing and, before I can stop it, the smell of paint. And with it the old searing pain, still as fresh now as it was then. Should I perhaps avoid all this? Yet why do I even ask the question? I find no answer and so whisper a prayer, accepting that if I am to find peace I must complete my journey. Then the thought occurs that perhaps I should once again gently acquaint myself with the world of the Convento Nossa Senhora da Boa Fé: the world of enclosed nuns belonging to the Cistercian order, a community of highborn women living lives dedicated to worship.

In many ways it was like being in a small walled city whose only inhabitants were women with, as it were, the Abadessa as their leader. The eighty-four professed nuns, all uniformly dressed in white habits, their short hair concealed by black veils, were the most important citizens—and the ones who guided and instructed the younger generation, the novices who dressed in all-white habits and whose numbers, with Leonor's arrival, became twenty-seven. In addition there were the *aias*, the servants, like myself, who attended to the nuns—and there must easily have been about two hundred and fifty of us. Finally there were at least as many *escravos,* lowly slaves—a handful of whom were black—and who, as with the *aias*, attended to the needs of the nun or novice with whom, like me, they had entered the convent, bringing the grand total to somewhere in the region of just under six hundred. And yet there were others: the young girls who stayed within the convent to be educated and might, depending on what they or their family decided, either leave to be married or stay and take their vows. And last of all there were the women, either unmarried or widowed, or even some whose husbands were away and who, for assured security and protection, paid to stay as guests. While some of these women were rich enough to live in some considerable style, others lived a more frugal existence, staying within the convent's precints rather than cause their families inconvenience.

♓

Like all those within the enclosing walls—whether nun or novice, servant or slave—I looked up to the Abadessa, Dona Imaculada de Almeida, an aristocratic and haughty woman who never appeared to forget the nobility of her ancestry. She was set apart from the other nuns as much by her demeanour as by the elaborate embroidery on her black veil and the crozier she carried in all processions. Eventually I discovered that she had been elected from within the ranks of the perpetually professed nuns, chosen and appointed for life because of her religious and spiritual qualities. As an Abadessa she was uncompromising, her duty being both to ensure that the order's rules were scrupulously followed and to administer the convent. However, though her powers were far-reaching she could not always act alone. In most matters she was assisted by a handful of the older professed nuns, wise and experienced women who assembled every day in the Chapter House and whose collective support enabled the Abadessa to maintain the smooth and harmonious functioning of life within the convent.

Of course, a servant was certainly not expected to think about such matters—or in any way be party to them—but it eventually seemed obvious that, though the opinions, complaints and suggestions of the nuns who sat with the Abadessa were taken seriously, she probably always had the upper hand since she had appointed each one of them to their particular post: the Prioress, the Mistress of the Novices, the Storekeeper, and, of course, Dona Benedita, the venerable and vigilant nun who guarded the entrance to the convent. However the Abadessa was not necessarily all-powerful since while all Cistercians, both men and women, were bound by the same rules, the strictness of enclosure enforced on women was such that it was necessary to have a bridge between the interior of the convent and the outside world—where the nuns were neither allowed to venture nor wished to do so. As a result, the Abade of Sta Maria in Alcobaça, the nearest Cistercian monastery, was not only responsible for the material and moral well-being of the nuns and novices but acted as their spiritual guide. In this capacity the Abade appointed three monks with special duties in our convent: a Confessor, a Chaplain who conducted all religious services and an Overseer, who dealt with all financial matters. Although I learnt all this gradually it took me many years to grasp that without these arrangements enclosure would have been impossible: the order's rules did not admit to the principle of the nuns being independent, since, as the scriptures tell us, St Paul 'would suffer not a woman…to usurp authority over the man, but to be in silence.'

Since the Alcobaça monastery was some five days' ride away these monks who, had the monastery been closer, would have come once a week, stayed nearby, in a house just outside the walls. They were the only men who regularly entered the enclosed areas. From time to time there were others, but they were all ecclesiastics. Otherwise no man, except in very extreme cases, a doctor was ever permitted to come further than the small door beside the grille. On designated days and times close relatives of the professed nuns could stand in the special parlour set aside for them to meet their relatives, separated by a great iron grille—through which no hand could pass and which was covered by a large black, semi-transparent veil. It was in these surroundings that the nuns could talk to their family, exchange news and learn who was to be married, who had given birth and who had died, while a listener nun stood close by, ensuring that no talk was unseemly or any physical contact made. For the novices not even this was possible.

All these decades later it is possible for me to acknowledge and understand the complexity of what enclosure represents. As such I can allow myself to recall those early days and *why* I eventually so feared and fought its restraints. The difference is that I can now understand how the walls of a convent's outer limits can also protect and nurture what lies within them, can indeed even bring the calmness of order to a separate world where the spirit and the sacred can find the time, the peace and concentration to unite. The breath sighs out of me. I have found my way forward. I can now take my thoughts back to my early days in the convent, to a time when it was impossible for me to comprehend any of this.

A week after entering the convent I was both wiser and calmer. The twins—who I soon realized to be both deaf and dumb—were, like me, servants in the convent. But with one important difference: I had come into the convent as part of Leonor's dowry contract, 'attached' to a novice who would eventually take her vows and remain enclosed within the convent for the rest of her life. This made me of a higher status than the twins, and others like them—including the two girls from Leonor's home who had also been sent by Dona Briolanga to perform the most menial of tasks: mostly cleaning and washing. A marker of this was that though they were also bound to stay within the walls—and, like me, for life—they were housed in a separate building; nearby but apart from my dormitory which was reserved for servants, *aias* whose duty, like mine, was to serve our individual mistresses. As such every nun and novice had at least one *aia*—and while some nuns had two or even three or four, our Abadessa was served by seven.

Meanwhile I also discovered that on entering the convent Leonor had been met and escorted by special servants to the dormitory whose space she was to share with twenty-six other novices. When I innocently asked Úrsula, the oldest servant in the convent—and one of those who served the Abadessa—why Leonor could not have a room of her own she contemptuously replied: 'Is she the Queen or an Infanta of the royal family then? She had better be if she is even to dream of such luxury!' Yet, within all my initial confusion one fear was banished: the fear of being totally separated from Leonor. It was true that though we were now more apart than we had ever been, it soon transpired that she had insisted that I should be her *only* servant, despite Donna Briolanga wanting, because of my extreme youth, to appoint at least another two. In this way it gradually began to dawn on me that the gentle Leonor was both asserting herself and adjusting to the prospect of becoming a nun.

♓

Gradually, day by day, I became more familiar with both the layout of the convent and the rhythm of life within its confines. Every moment, regardless of what was actually happening, was directed towards Our Lady and, through Her, to Her blessed Son. These emotions both comforted and distressed me, the comfort reminding me of My Lady's love even as distress brought back memories of Joaquina's devotion and stirred the ache of my longing for her. Often, as I walked through the convent I would hear, coming from the cloister, music and singing, hymns and songs of praise. Occasionally a song would come to a sudden end, stilled no doubt by a reprimanding hand, but though I never considered the mistake to have been Leonor's, I was content to be aware of the proximity of her presence.

The church was the centre of our world and, as such, generally reserved for all those living within the enclosing walls. Only on Sundays, and special feasts and saints' days, and those celebrating Our Lady, was it open to those living beyond the walls. On these days the nuns, to avoid the inconceivable possibility of being seen by outsiders, especially men, entered from within the convent, moving almost directly from the cloister to the choir stalls, their presence shielded from all eyes by a great grille. It was from behind this veiled area that the choir's singing billowed out to fill the entire church, wafting into the hearts of all those who heard it soaring, like a rising dove, up to heaven itself. Those of the grand nobility, and important church dignitaries, made their way into the church from the large recessed entrance, taking the three steps down and then entering through the large door to the side of the grille behind which Dona Benedita kept guard. Once inside they turned away from the concealed choir to seat themselves near the high altar. The local people used the less imposing doorway to reach an area where they had to stand throughout the service.

♓

As time passed I realized that, more than anything else, I was becoming conscious of an unending sense of continuous prayer. Sometimes it seemed as if no one ever really slept. The office of Lauds, though celebrated as the night's last ritual, came just before dawn, signifying that the first thoughts of the new day would be of God and the desire to praise Him and that as dawn lifted into the full light of day we would again be reminded that Our Lord's radiance will always banish the forces of darkness—even as we remember that glorious dawn when He rose from the tomb, from death to Resurrection.

The office of Prime, the first true prayer of the morning was for the consecration of the day's work and began early, as the sun slowly rose, gradually moving high enough to light our world and guide us all to worship—for, unless detained by pressing and urgent work the *aias* were, like the nuns and novices, expected to attend all services. Prime was also when excerpts from the rules written by St Benedict—and followed by all Cistercians—were first read and then commented on by our Abadessa. It was also when any nun who had violated the spirit of these rules could either confess her shortcomings or be denounced. The Abadessa would listen and consider before pronouncing the penance deemed appropriate to any nun found guilty. Needless to say no servant was ever present at this time—something I accepted with relief, all too aware that if lowly *aias* were made to declare their faults I would always have been found wanting.

After Holy Mass had been celebrated between Prime and Terce—the third hour after dawn and the hour when our Lord was condemned to death—the Abadessa, accompanied by her senior nuns, retired to the Chapter House to make administrative decisions and assign duties to particular nuns; a gathering that concluded with the singing of the prayer De Profundis. Meanwhile all other nuns attended to their daily tasks until Sext, the hour seen as the most conducive for prayer and contemplation. It was at this time that Adam and Eve ate the forbidden apple of knowledge and so lost their innocence, an hour of Grace when the high sun blazes most strongly, its blinding light reminding us of divine power and splendour, while haunting us with the memory that this was also the hour when Our Lord was nailed to the Cross.

Gradually I grew to understand something of the rest and contemplation Sext both inspires and offers, and why it is followed by the nurturing of our physical bodies. Later still I began, hesitantly and imperfectly, to realize—for who teaches a servant?—that all these liturgical hours contain mysteries and symbols which though I would never fathom or comprehend them, somehow gave me the feeling that within them lay a whole universe of understanding and benevolence. I did, imperfectly and slowly it is true, become aware that though the next office, of None, was sanctified by great mysteries and was, like Terce and Sext, consecrated to prayer, it is also the hour that commemorates the death of Our Lord. Yet almost as mystical to me—perhaps because I could somewhat more easily grasp its inner meaning—was the belief that as the sun begins setting the spirit sinks and is less resistent to temptation, making it both the hour when demons appear to lure us from the path of grace and when Adam and Eve were driven from Paradise. And it is at None that fasts are broken and there is Mass and Communion and the closing down of the day commences.

Vespers was in many ways my favourite time, the evening office that truly ends the day, for it is then, as the sun sets, that the oil lamps and candles were lit, and the darkness repelled. Ancient hymns would be sung, each one devoted, according to the day of the week, to praising the days of Creation: Sunday honouring the creation of light, Monday marking earth's parting from the waters while Tuesday reminded us of the creation of plants and Wednesday of the sun and moon, leaving Thursday for the creation of fish and Friday for all the beasts of the earth. The one exception, Saturday, was kept to honour the Blessed Trinity with a special hymn.

Compline was the time of introspection when we made peace with God, sought His forgiveness for our sins and, as the darkness surrounded us, envisaged Christ as the divine Sun and ourselves as the children of that Sun. These images occur in all the offices but at this time, with the night beginning to enfold us, they are realized as the reverse of light, forming a cloak under which Satan can hide his evil power. Only prayer and faith can aid us by helping us to understand that we are like tiny fledglings nestling safely beneath their mother's sheltering wings. And as we recognize the source of our protection we face our knowledge of the evil that haunts the night, the spirits that lurk in its blackness, and so pray not only for our own salvation but that of all mankind. And finally we are aware that sleep reminds us of death and therefore pray that Our Lord will grant us a quiet night and a happy end, safely sheltered by His love.

Eventually the last night prayer would fade away, the final verses seeking the blessings of Our Heavenly Father as we offered our farewells to Our Lady. Each antiphon was sung as a beautiful and moving farewell, the last note leaving like a sigh as the choir stilled into a soundless calm and the Triple Prayer took our cloistered world into the great silence.

♓

Now I pause. Was it really like this? Was it all prayer and worship? How hard it is to pull all the memories together, to gather a balanced picture. What do I see if I let my mind go, if I do not, as I have been doing, keep it tightly under control? I wait. And then, to my surprise it is not something that I see that comes to me—or even what I hear. Instead it is the welling of silence, an empty hush that comes like an enveloping cloud, caught most beautifully as the day ends and sighs away—and which so often, and like an invisible cloak, surrounded us. I recall that though sound often filled the stillness—be it of music and singing, of voices, a bell or even birdsong—we were always bound by silence. It was with silence that the convent maintained an atmosphere conducive to prayer, ensuring that we were kept constantly aware of Our Lord and His Holy Mother by subduing all idle and distracting chatter. Though the ideal of silence existing throughout the convent was seldom attained it was generally enforced in the cloister, an area invested with sanctity by virtue of the nuns using it to meditate and read sacred texts. While there were times set apart for silent and individual prayer, it was also maintained by the nuns when they ate, barring the voice of the nun chosen to read from the scriptures. And, importantly, silence fell like a blanket after Compline.

Inevitably when sounds were heard they often appeared to contain a freshness they would otherwise have lacked. A solo voice would pierce us with its beauty, soaring with the delicacy of a fragile bird. The bell that summoned us to eat, to pray, to announce would catch our ears uncluttered by other sounds while, in the late spring, the same was true when the storks, who nested on the church roof, endlessly clicked to their young. These were the balances and counter balances within the convent and it was in the same way that my emotions shifted from what drew me to what caused unease. While I knew I belonged in the convent I had to accept that, like all servants, I was unable to truly participate in the life of prayer enjoyed by the nuns.

♓

The Abadessa was a distant figure, someone who would never normally have shown the least sign of interest in a servant belonging to a girl who, however wealthy and highborn, was still only a novice. Yet, one day, as she passed me by someone must have whispered in her ear that I was the child found in the earthquake. She stopped and for a moment her disdainful features softened as she lowered her face close to mine. 'Never forget child', she whispered, 'that you were only saved by Our Lady's compassionate mercy. Be worthy of Her grace.' Although the initial effect of her words was to remind me of the earthquake's devastation and the miracle of my survival they also made me feel the loss of my unknown mother and that in some curious way I had been as much birthed by the earthquake as by her, that I had somehow come *from* it.

Meanwhile, even as I learnt the order of the services, the holy days of Our Lady and those of the saints and the days of their feasts and the fasts, I became more familiar with my duties, my assigned tasks and what I was expected to do. Although very occasionally there was work outside—though within the walls—I was mostly in the convent's great kitchen. And it was here that I found my time with Dona Briolanga had served me well, instilling in me an alertness that enabled me to anticipate what would be needed. Despite being the youngest servant, I was capable—not only here but elsewhere—and often useful to the nuns, since Leonor seldom needed me to help her—either because she was still only a novice or, as I began to suspect, had begun to reveal that behind her undemanding exterior lay an innate austerity. As a result some of the nuns would sometimes send me on an errand or give me a small task, to fetch and carry.

Very gradually I realized I was at peace, and that—though I still missed Balthazar and Joaquina—I had settled into life within the Convento Nossa Senhora da Boa Fé. It is true that I never became close to any of the other servants—and no one made any effort to befriend me. Perhaps this was because of my own nature or maybe because, in the same way that Leonor was the youngest and most recent novice, I was much the youngest servant and so seen as only a child. The truth was that I did not seek to make friends due as much to my growing awareness that life within the enclosure suited me, and that I was in tune with its rhythms, that it was from them that I drew intangible sustenance, not other people.

♓

Then, one morning, without any sign of what lay ahead, the sun eventually rose on the day destined by fate for turning my increasingly well-ordered life turned upside down.

Ironically it was a day already ordained as being special, one the convent had spent weeks planning and preparing for, the day when the King, Dom João, and his Queen, Dona Catarina, would enter our enclosed world. The royal couple would come not only with members of their family but with courtiers, noblemen and an accompanying retinue of ecclesiastical dignitaries: archbishops, bishops and priests—and a host of servants carrying thrones for the King and Queen and great chairs for those whose status demanded them. After attending High Mass in the church the King, because of his unique position and symbolic association with the Church, would enter the convent's otherwise fiercely restricted interior. There he would be able to see, and be seen by, the nuns. Once he had been received by the Abadessa and demonstrated his piety by paying his respects to her he would, along with his immediate family, partake of a sumptuous banquet.

This banquet was a meal full of delicacies and specialties and fine wines never tasted by the order's austere founder but which were now considered the very least that could be put before the highborn. Ironically although it was the King who came to the convent he also bore the costs of his visit, gold having been given in advance. It was only many years later that I grasped that these royal visits, and the great feasts that were laid out, were all part of a delicate power game in which the King, powerless without the approval and blessings of the Church, sought to strengthen and consolidate his power with the giving of banquets in famous convents. A further outcome of this subtle half-hidden manoeuvring was that the convents, by permitting him to do so, and by providing food of the highest quality, ensured that they were protected, and that their own power was endorsed by royal favour.

♓

On that morning work started early in the kitchens and soon after dawn its vast space was a hive of activity, an orchestrated frenzy of cutting, chopping, peeling, kneading, grinding and mixing. Fires were stoked and spits were turned as pots bubbled and boiled and sweat poured—for it was mid-August and the sun which scorched the land around us forced its heat into the deepest recesses of the convent. As a result tempers were short and those in charge spoke with sharp tongues. I, in common with the other servants, kept a wary eye on the senior nuns, knowing that just the suggestion of a shortcoming would bring instant punishment. But, despite my vigilance, I earned the displeasure of Dona Maria de Jesus who was in charge of the kitchen, simply by failing to bring the eggs she needed quickly enough. She shouted at me and, hurrying to obey, I tripped and fell. Though in an instant I had pulled myself back onto my feet it was too late. I was surrounded by a sea of broken eggshells, the mess of their yokes already oozing across the floor. I stared at them in horror, freezing in terror—and so took the full brunt of the vicious hand that flew savagely across my cheek. Yet it was neither the hurt nor the terror that registered. All that penetrated my consciousness were the words that came spitting at me.

'You clumsy little bastard, what kind of man ever fathered *you?*'

Was this really the first time I became aware of being not only without a mother but also a *father*? Was this the first time that I really wondered who he might have been? Were these the words that opened my mind to the existence of the man who had fathered me? It seems unlikely—though I have no recollection of an earlier time when I had given the matter any thought.

♓

Somehow the rest of the day went by in a strange mixture of heart-stopping confusion churned and beaten in with the excitement of seeing such splendour and pageantry in our midst. One moment I would almost sweat with the possibility of having had a father and the next I would be straining to see the uneasy bustle that endlessly eddied around the royal party, watching as servants with wary eyes were ordered about by overseers before a sickening lurch took me back to the frozen moment of Dona Maria de Jesus' words—even as I registered the King's unfathomable expression and the Queen's fixed smile and saw how her pale hand was forever touching the jewelled pendant around her neck. How strange, I thought, all these people know exactly who their parents are.

That night, when all the tensions created by the royal guests had subsided, and when everyone within the convent was asleep, I finally allowed my mind to consider the implications of a second parent. So much had been made of the circumstances of my birth and the simultaneous death of my mother that it was strange to now consider my father and his identity. I tossed and turned, my mind racing backwards and forwards. Of course in the end I was unable to do much more than accept the basic fact that no more was known about my father than about my mother. Yet though my mother was shadowy I had at least some sense of her having been real, of her having nurtured me in her womb for nine months. I had been able to conjure up images of her and make her, however intangibly, real. Now to do the same with my father was impossible. There was no way I could pull him out of the thin air he had vanished into. And yet, in all this hopelessness, one small fact presented itself. At first it was only a small seed I hardly dared to nurse—something I was almost too scared to admit to—a thought that was both dangerous and bold in its simplicity. It took time but when I finally lost my instinctive fear of the implications behind this thought I was left acknowledging an extraordinary possibility:

Perhaps my father was still alive.

It was a thought that changed everything. At first I avoided it, not certain of quite how it could be pursued. But it was like a blind worm who, though it has no hope of sight still crawls up to the light. A thought that inched its way into my mind and then lay at the base of all other thoughts, slowly and gradually consuming me until I became certain that my father must exist and that all I had to do was look until I found him.

From that moment whenever I heard that a stranger, a man, had come to the convent, I would imagine myself examining his face, searching for any common features that might suggest he was my father. Of course though I accepted the pointless futility of what I was doing, the intensity of my longing meant I sometimes dreamt up the shared similarity of a nose or a mouth or the arch of an eyebrow. Then, as my heart began beating faster my inner eye would stare at the man, trying to match his features to mine. Occasionally I would shrink back against a wall, wondering what I would say or do if I felt I had found a match. But the cruel bitterness of reality was too strong and either my imagined shadow would move or the light would shift and force my foolish dream of a fleeting resemblance to evaporate.

After a month or two I understood and accepted both the futility of my delusion and the hopelessness of my search. Or so I thought. The truth was that my hopes were only suppressed and, somewhere in my subconscious, I retained the conviction that I would one day find my father—even though this was as unlikely as discovering my mother's identity.

And yet the question about my father changed me. It made me understand one certainty: neither my father nor my mother would ever be found inside the convent. Neither would any nun—or even the occasional visiting priest—ever help me discover their identities or confirm their existence. As a result I became more conscious of the world outside the convent's enclosing walls. This in turn caused something to slither out from behind the thoughtlessness of the question put to me in the convent's kitchen, something that presented me with another and darker question: *Who was I?* For the first time I really began to ask myself who *I* thought I was. Perhaps I was a Moor—and a bastard too. I had come from the earth, I had not been birthed in a Christian world, and neither of my parents was known. Questions tormented me, circling endlessly around my mind, leading nowhere. Exhausting me.

Until the day I instinctively sensed that I must go outside and look at the land from which I had emerged.

♓

Now, though a lifetime has passed my memories of the day when I first stepped outside the convent are still clear. Everything is fresh in my mind, everything is still *now* and of *this* moment and it is once again *that* early morning. Dona Benedita, the gatekeeper, is, as always vigilant but when I haltingly tell her I have been sent on an errand the door she guards opens and I am already slipping out. It is early summer but the air is cool and the dew still carpets the grass. Light is just beginning to appear in the sky—though the full moon still lingers as if reluctant to leave for her dark quarters. For the briefest moment I hesitate, wondering whether to continue into the unknown or return to the safety of the convent's enclosing walls. But it is already too late. I draw a deep breath and walk forward.

It is then that I see the black dog for the first time. Small, wiry and undistinguished he is curled up near the door that has just closed behind me. Apparently disturbed by the sound he lifts his head and looks towards me, his eyes clear and bright. For a fleeting moment I feel I am being judged, that he is considering whether or not I am worth following. Then he gets to his feet and slowly yawns and stretches before trotting towards me, gently wagging his tail. Only then do I find that my unconsciously held breath is sighing away. And only then do I start walking away from the convent, relieved and aware of the new thought now shivering through my mind, telling me that the dog's accompanying presence is some kind of honour or even, a blessing. Even as I realize how very black he is.

That morning it was as if the whole world rested in the palm of a great magician, a sorcerer who had cast a spell upon the light and tinged it with a delicate shimmer that made the early sunlight find ways of catching on small stones, shining on the last of the dewdrops clinging to the grasses and on the wing of a bird startled by my presence. A magician who played with sounds, drawing far off noises close to my ear and making them clear and sharp. A magician who puts enchantment into the sweetness of birdsong, the breeze and even the small sounds of my own breath, making each small blade of grass and every leaf seem distinct and individual, a special part of paradise. I drank it all in and, as I did so, found that my feet were suddenly moving faster and faster and that I was breaking into a run, that I had spread my arms wide and flung my head back, letting my hair flow free as the magician's power carried me effortlessly across the land.

The black dog bounded ahead of me, part of the magic

perhaps, soaring over the grasses and small boulders. Only much later did I understand that I had followed the dog, that I had gone where he led me, without any concern of where that might be. Until, quite suddenly and without warning, he stopped. Caught unprepared I almost stumbled. My exhilaration vanished and I found I was out of breath, unable to run another step. I sank down to the ground, gasping as I wiped a hand across my sweating forehead, feeling the dank mass of my hair tangling down my back. Something had happened. What madness had brought me this far? And where was I? Was I lost? Where was the convent?

I got back to my feet and, for just a moment, it seemed as if there was nothing to be seen but the eternity of the rolling, grassy plain and, far, far away, the distant mountains. But when I looked again I saw that in front of me there was a low dip leading down to a small pond surrounded by a marsh. A small stretch of water that, even in the dryness of summer, lay like a giant mirror, its surface reflecting nothing but the brightness of the sun as a small ripple crept across it, made by the dog slaking his thirst.

I walked down to the pond, wondering how it could exist in the heat, wondering if it was not perhaps an illusion created by another sorcerer, someone who had emerged to contest the power of the magician. Everything was suddenly too still, the air too quiet. Nothing moved but the gentle ripple and the dog's lapping tongue. I shivered. Though the sun was now hot a cold clamminess swept over me. Too far from the familiarity of my normal everyday world I was suddenly thankful for the dog's presence—and the way he quietly paused in his drinking to look up at me. As if to remind me that I need not be frightened.

Reassured, I moved closer to the edge of the pond and looked at its marshy surrounds. I saw how water had oozed in between the clumps of the plants and then, as I peered closer, I saw the irises. Their blue petals were of an extraordinary delicacy, first reaching up to the sun before, as suddenly, curling backwards to reveal their luminous colour. The sunlight shone through them, showing every vein. I edged closer and was just reaching out to touch one when, in a sudden frenzy, the dog began barking. Instinctively I jumped back, my heart jumping into my mouth, my eyes widening in terror as I saw the snake slipping out from between my feet and slithering down into the lake.

My heartbeats were like the pounding of a drum. My skin was clammy and cold and yet the water was now still, without the slightest ripple. I turned away, first towards the iris I had almost touched and then to the dog. He was sitting on his haunches, quiet and contained. My whole being calmed. Suddenly I knew that I was safe if the dog was with me. And so turned my attention back to the irises. And saw how their colour echoed that of My Lady's cloak, and thought how beautiful She would look clothed in iris flowers, wrapped in the pureness of the colour that reflected the beauty of Her gentle gaze and the eternity and infinity of the universe She protected.

♓

From then on the convent's walls ceased to hold me. Instead they became mere markers of the space I lived in. I followed the daily rituals of worship; I honoured My Lady; I did my work. Occasionally I glimpsed Leonor—and noticed how contented she seemed, and finally understood that the life of a nun would suit her gentle ways. But, for myself, there was one great difference: I now knew I was free. It was not that I often ventured out—instinctively I knew I had to be cautious—but that I knew I *could* go outside and roam across the land and find a refuge beyond the constraints of life within the walls.

The next time I set out I simply left the convent and, without having any sense of choosing a particular direction or that I was to find somewhere which would eventually give me a feeling of security, of being *my* place. How can I explain the instinct, the urge that made me, on that particular day, go in that direction, made me go just that little bit further than I might have otherwise gone? Perhaps it was the familiar presence of the black dog and the sense that I was in safe hands.

I had left the convent late, sent on an errand justified by the approaching preparations for the festival of St John, that day in high summer when the earth bakes, panting like a thirsty dog to find water and when the sun punishes the earth by drawing out every drop of moisture, leaving the land gasping, turning it into an exhausted wasteland. The grass had already withered into straw-like tangles, the wildflowers had died and their dry petals had faded. There was little shade. Few birds sang. No animals were seen. Only the vultures endlessly hovered in the sky, knowing the terrible generosity they would reap in the summer's heat. Yet I ran with such joy, knowing I would not be missed, delighting in the air around me, stopping just once under a lone tree to stand in the shade and get my breath back. Then, when I saw the black dog was looking at me, alert and waiting, I moved, going after him as he trotted determinedly forward, uncaring about where we might be going, idly noticing that the landscape was becoming wilder, filling with small trees and bushes all clustered together, that our way had narrowed to a small path.

What was it that made me suddenly stop? Was there a small warning voice? An instant of knowing? Yet it was too late. Quite suddenly I saw that looming up before me was a vast circle of towering, and ancient, stones, as near it seemed to the convent as Joaquina had said they were to the *quinta.*

And then I remembered, indeed could almost hear Joaquina whispering in my ears, telling me who and what they were and warning me that no one who ventured near them ever returned but that there was a belief that if one waited with respect permission might be given to enter their realm.

I stood and waited. There was no warning, no vibration but, somehow, I knew I was safe and walked slowly forward, cautiously—in case they changed their minds. The sun beat down with a fierce intensity. Sweat trickled down my neck, soaking my hair against my skin and making my clothes cling to my body. The sun's glare bleached out the sky and forced me to screw my eyes up. I shifted uncomfortably, my dusty feet feeling the dry, brown grass crumpled against the earth. Nothing stirred, nothing could be seen or heard. The silence was unnatural. It was as if the whole world had ceased either to move or care for any living creature. I put my hand against one of the large standing stones, both for support and to ease myself into the shade of its leaning tilt, wondering what had happened as I rubbed my hand against the ancient, rasped surface. Then, very slowly I sank down to the ground and lent back against the stone's roughness. I felt strangely safe, almost protected. Or so I thought until I looked at each one of the great, standing stones and realized how motionless they were, how eternally still. I found I was holding my breath, as if trying to catch them out, as if, by keeping absolutely still I could deceive them and so lull them into forgetting my presence. For a moment I was confused. Should I not expect them to be still? Why did I hold my breath and wait for them to move? Why did I feel that once my presence was ignored or overlooked they would release themselves from their imprisoned stillness? But my questions, half-formed and vague went unanswered. The stones were too cunning, too knowing and, of course, too ancient to be so deceived. They stayed motionless and kept their secrets, silently watching me with their unseen eyes as the sun burned into my flesh and sweat trickled down the side of my face, under my chin and around my neck. My thoughts shifted and made me feel uneasy. I began to sense that I was in alien territory where different ways, different rules held sway. I closed my eyes both to deny these thoughts and to shield my eyes from the glare.

I was not successful. My uneasy thoughts lingered and I could still see the sky through the thin membrane of my eyelids. Then, quite suddenly, things were imperceptibly different and I knew I was no longer alone. Like a hunted animal I sensed movement and seemed to hear a sound. Instinctively I sensed that someone—or something—was watching me. I listened but could catch no more than the nothingness of a silent sigh, the echo of an unspoken whisper. My body tensed and, at last, I opened my eyes. I looked around—but saw nothing except the stillness of the stones. Again I held my breath, straining to hear or see some movement that would tell me where the faint sound had come from. But beyond the heavy, sun-soaked stillness there was nothing. I let my breath out slowly. And then quickly sucked it in so fast I heard it hissing through my teeth. A strange shadow had fleetingly crossed the sun. I was right. I was not alone. Something, someone was close by. I swung round but though a shiver of light danced past my eyes there was still nothing. For a moment I hesitated. Was I imagining things? I looked out over the open centre of the circle. Nothing. And then up at the sky to see if a bird, a lone vulture perhaps, had been hovering above me. Of course I knew was deceiving myself. I already knew who I expected to see, though I hardly dared to acknowledge their existence. Yet no one was there. I hesitated. Perhaps I had merely imagined the sensation of movement.

It was then, just as I tried to dismiss my imaginings, that I raised my head and turned it, just slightly, towards the biggest stone. And saw the standing woman. I saw her without any sense of surprise or shock or fear and yet, as I looked at her and saw how she stared, her eyes locking into mine, an icy sweat slithered down over my whole body. How close was she? Perhaps no more than a few feet away, perhaps miles away. Distance, time and space had shifted beyond my reckoning. Beyond her presence, her aura of fragility, almost of intangibility, nothing else registered. She was simply standing there, gazing at me, her eyes large and wide as she drew a great golden comb endlessly through her long, dark hair. Not a leaf stirred, not a blade of grass moved, not a breath of air whispered through the trees. Only her fingers moved and all I was conscious of were the limitless depths in her extraordinary eyes and their expression of almost unbearable pain. And that behind her pain I sensed an understanding so profound that the tenseness eased out of my body. I knew I was safe, unthreatened. I sighed deeply and drew a hand slowly across my eyes. When I lowered it, she was gone.

Or almost gone, because, since I now knew who and what she was, I looked down in time to catch the movement at the base of the stone. And so saw the last flicker of a scaled tail disappearing beneath its shadows, the final uncoiling before she slipped away and vanished into the earth's darkest regions, to the realm that held her trapped in the awful enchantment of an ancient curse.

The silence was terrible and so intense that I felt I could hear her slithering descent as she moved further and further into the earth. Then, somewhere far away, a bird called and the spell that bound me was broken. Slowly I got to my feet and walked over to the stone. I look down at the small hole, knowing I would never have noticed it had I not seen the woman transform herself back into her serpent shape and withdraw into her world, the world of the *mouras encantadas.*

Then a shiver of sunlight suddenly glinted nearby and I saw that her golden comb was lying almost hidden at the base of the stone. Without thought I stretched out a hand to touch it—and quickly jerked it back. There were too many tales about the dangers of the *coisas dos mouros*, the things of the Moors, and the curses they brought upon those who stole them. The comb was not mine to take. For a moment I squatted, looking at its intricate design, seeing how beautiful and well-worn it was. Then I reached out and carefully picked it up, feeling the weighty beauty of the gold—and seeing the one long black hair caught in its teeth. The comb was valuable—but it belonged to the vanished woman and I knew that if I did not return it to her someone might come and steal it away. After a brief moment of hesitation I began scooping out the earth around the hole, widening it until I could squeeze my hand through its opening. Then I quickly pushed the comb down the hole and let it go. In the silence all I heard was the faint nothingness of it falling, hurtling down and down, spiralling into the hidden vastness of another world.

♓

When I came back into the convent I found a weeping Leonor.

Joaquina was dead.

Joaquina who could soothe away every ache and every hurt was dead.

Joaquina who could tell tales and hold me close and cover me with a million *beijinhos* was dead. Dead, a word that had been meaningless suddenly became so terrifyingly real that I began to howl. Even as I shouted at Leonor that it could not be, that she was mistaken. *How could Joaquina be dead?* I yelled at her in defiance of the pain on her tear-streaked face, screaming my denials—even though within me a near silent and tiny voice was already beginning to betray me and I was already accepting, knowing she had not lied or been mistaken. Her grief was too real. And yet and yet, how could Joaquina, *my* Joaquina, be dead?

That night, surrounded by darkness, and as everyone slept, was the first of the many nights that followed, the nights when I gathered Joaquina to me, held her close and smelt her body, drew her face down next to mine, traced a finger around her eyes and mouth and along her nose, trying to keep her. Listening to her voice, hearing her, watching her, trying to keep her. Trying to keep her and make sure she would always be with me while knowing that somehow, and too soon, she would slip away. And something has gone, the shape of her face is now an unfocused blur, the lilt of her voice has almost disappeared into silence. But I have never stopped loving her, or thinking of her as *my* Joaquina.

Joaquina. I smile and think of that night when I finally discovered how to keep her, of how, as I tossed and turned, I suddenly cried out to My Lady, to Mãe. And how I then wept and began telling Her about my Joaquina. And how the miracle happened: that I suddenly knew She was listening, that I could feel Her nearness. Only then did I remember how often Joaquina had told me that Our Lady lived up in heaven, keeping my mother and her stillborn child and her husband under the protective and enveloping vastness of Her cloak. At last my spirit lifted and my tired body softened, finding the comfort it craved, sinking into the overwhelming certainty that Joaquina was now enfolded in Our Lady's cloak, watching over me. And with this thought came another certainty: that Mãe, though as unseen as Joaquina, as unseen as my mother, would always surround me with Her love and Her protection.

♓

One morning, a few months after Joaquina's death, I woke up to find an uneasy sense of suppressed excitement eddying around the convent. The quietness of the nuns, the novices, and even the servants, as they scurried demurely to Prime was deceptive since this excitement, once spotted, was almost palpable. At first the near total darkness almost concealed the sly glances that slid back and forth between the younger women and it was only when I noticed the steely severity of the older nuns and the heightened vigilance with which they watched their charges that I knew this invisible tension was real. However it was not until just before Compline, the last of the day's holy hours, the time when protection from the darkness is sought, that the mystery was solved: an artist, some said from Flanders, others from Florence or perhaps Siena, no one was sure, was coming to paint the walls of the convent's church.

It is now, all these years later, no longer possible to conjure up anything more than frail shadows of the emotions that, over the next few weeks, started fluttering through the cloisters, wafting around the refectory and, most of all, slithering in and out of our sleeping quarters. Yet though nothing was ever said openly what hung in the air, however intangibly, was that a man would soon be almost within our midst. It was a thought that festered and, even though we all knew the Abadessa and the senior nuns would ensure no one would ever have—at best—more than a fleeting glimpse of him, the slender possibility of them doing so gnawed away at the even tenor of our lives.

Slowly, insidiously the whispers and stifled giggles could be sensed if not actually heard. So often a corner would be turned and a young novice would move too fast, seemingly suddenly finding a need to hurry somewhere else; or a young nun would quickly glance up towards the doors, as if hoping to see someone standing there. And so, before he even arrived, before we even knew if he was young or old, handsome or not, the artist began to affect and change our lives.

In all this I was an uninvolved outsider; neither a nun, a novice—or even a servant, merely an onlooker. The reason for this was that though I saw and was aware of what was happening, the death of Joaquina was still far too raw, her loss too recent for me to really be involved or have any deep curiosity of my own. Also, I now believe, I was too young. It is therefore ironic that I eventually became the main player in the drama that very slowly, and tragically, began to unfold. A drama I slipped into unawares, innocent yet guilty.

♓

Lucas van Domburg—for such was his name—arrived in October on the feast day of St Luke, the apostle of our Lord and patron saint of painters—evidence surely of the rightness of appointing him to his work. He came soon after Sext, the midday hour when we remember the agony of our Lady standing beside the cross on which our Lord was nailed, sharing His pain; a time when we surround ourselves with prayer and beseech Her to relieve the world's suffering. On that first visit the Abadessa, along with two senior nuns, received him in the parlour room, half-concealed from him by the veiled grille, and where they no doubt discussed not only the nature and demands of his assignment but the restrictions that governed its execution.

Of course no nun or novice ever admitted, not at this stage anyway, to having seen him but by the mid-afternoon celebration of None, the holy hour when Jesus cried out from the cross to ask why God had forsaken Him, it was known that he would be staying nearby, that his access was only to the church and, most explicitly, that he was never to have contact with anyone except the Abadessa. By the time of Vespers, when the evening star rises to announce the call to prayer and Heaven's fading light proclaims the falling of darkness, it was common knowledge that he was, if not handsome, good-looking and, if not young, at least not yet old.

It finally began the next morning when I was summoned by the Abadessa. As might be expected I was apprehensive and came before her with a racing mind, wondering why I had warranted her attention. Except for the one finger that beat a tap-tap on the carved arm of her chair she sat without moving, looking me over, as if seeing me for the first time. I felt my fists clench and my spine straighten.

Her words, when at last she spoke, were framed as a question and, though they were addressed to me I felt she was really talking to herself.

'Child,' she said, 'Are you honest? Can you be trusted?'

I kept quiet, sensing she would repeat herself.

'Can you be trusted?'

I nodded, certain that no words would come if I tried to speak, noticing that her finger had paused mid-beat.

'Come closer; let me see your face.'

I moved one, two, maybe three steps closer, seeing that her hand was now clenched around the arm-rest of her chair. For a moment the silent scrutiny continued. Then her arm came out, her fingers splaying open to take hold of my face and turn it first one way and then the other.

'You know that an artist has come?'

I nodded, wishing she would release my face.

'And that he is to paint the life of our Blessed Lady on the walls of our church?'

I gave another small nod, exhaling as the Abadessa's hand slipped from my face.

'It seems there is a problem in applying the paint to the walls that requires him to carefully prepare them and then, without pause, immediately and directly to apply the colours...' She paused, as if suddenly aware that an Abadessa is not required to explain anything to anyone, especially not to someone like me.

'He is therefore obliged to remain in the church throughout the day,' she brusquely continued. 'He cannot leave to take his meals...' There was a fractional pause, 'I have therefore decided that as soon as he begins his work you will be the one to take them to him.'

Somehow I swallowed my small involuntary gasp.

♓

From then on I wondered when I would be sent for—even as whispers declared that though the painter had brought his materials to the church and spent time studying the walls and looking at the space, he had then left. A day or so later the rumour that wafted its way into the convent was that he had been seen in several different places, walking here and there, looking at trees, at plants and flowers, at buildings, even talking to peasants and then taking out paper and making sketches of them. Then that though he was again in the church nobody knew exactly what he did there or why he needed to be there the whole day and had even brought his own food. Inevitably, although all kinds of opinions were formed about what he might actually be doing the most common question was: why doesn't he begin painting? Of course when it was known that he had gone to see the Abadessa again there was a surge of conjecture. Was he giving up, leaving?

The truth was nowhere near as interesting as they had hoped. He had simply announced that as the walls were now prepared there was no alternative but for him to wait several days for them to dry. He was therefore going elsewhere to prepare his preliminary sketches, after which he would be back and ready to start.

And so finally, and in so many nets, I was caught.

It began on a beautiful late autumn day. A day when the sun shone down into the cloisters, catching on plants and herbs and the spray of the small fountain where a bird perched to drink. A moment broken by the sudden sound of forbidden laughter. And then, as if startled, the bird flew up, beating its wings frantically as it soared higher and then away, out over the walls. A lump caught in the back of my throat and I knew that I too must somehow slip out.

With a suitable excuse on my lips, I hurried away from the convent, aware of my relief when I caught sight of the black dog bounding after me.

I did not go far, just to the old tree that stands by itself, less than half way to the Cromeleque. Once there I sat down, feeling the gentle sun on my skin, inhaling the scent of grasses, hearing the birdsong and trying not to cry.

And then something, a small sound perhaps, made me look up. To see a man standing there, watching me. Not close, but just close enough to see his features and know that he was, as rumour had declared, if not handsome, good-looking and, if not young, at least not yet old.

It was in that split second before I moved that I understood that though he knew I'd seen him, he never stopped looking at me, never lowered his eyes. And that as I stood up I saw, out of the corner of my eye, that the black dog was just behind me, alert and watchful.

Lucas van Domburg—for so I knew he must be—smiled and then waved a hand towards the dog. 'You must be Nehalaennia, accompanied by your faithful dog and guardian spirit.'

I said nothing, but my expression must have shown my query.

'For centuries she was the goddess who protected my homeland, seated with her faithful dog beside her, worshipped by those who ventured out on angry seas.' Though his accent was obvious his Portuguese was fluent; it was what he was saying that remained unclear. Yet he made no effort to explain and my attention shifted to the piece of folded paper he held.

He saw the angle of my eyes and smiled.

'So,' he said, 'as an all-powerful and, I hope, benevolent goddess you may know who I am?'

I nodded, still uneasy and confused while relieved by the sudden thought that he could have no idea where I had come from.

'Are you also all-knowing, omnipotent?'

Confused by what he meant I made no indication, one way or the other.

'I have been searching for you, looking for your devotees. And I have found them, almost all of them. You are the only one who has really eluded me,' he paused, looking at me intensely and more directly than I liked, although without actually looking at me.

'But now,' he said, with a slight flourish, 'I have found *you!'*

'Me?'

'Yes! But tell me what name you are known by,' he said before adding with another, though lesser, flourish, 'I am Lucas, Lucas van Domburg.'

I hesitated. I did not want to be traced. But I also knew the certainty looming before me: when he began to paint the church he would find out. I reasoned that all I could do now was try and find some way of, if not explaining, at least making sure he never told the Abadessa about meeting me. I would have to give my name.

'Inês.'

'Inês. Meek and chaste. Of course, it had to be,' he smiled, 'Inês, you are my Madonna. It is fated,' again he smiled, his eyes still fixed on me. 'I have come to do a series of frescoes on the walls of the convent church, to show, to tell the story of the Virgin's life. My difficulty has been to find Her. But now,' he said, with an air of discernible triumph.' I have found you! You have to sit for me.'

'*Mestre*,' I gasped,' that I cannot do, it is not possible.' The very suggestion horrified me.

He laughed, almost as if this was now going to be a game.

'You will and must! You cannot say no; I have looked for you for too long. You are my Madonna!'

I felt uneasy and unsure of how to continue; it was obvious he was going insist, that he was never going to take no for an answer.

In the end it was Lucas van Domburg who came up with the answer.

'Where have you come from? Tell me and I will go and speak to your parents and assure them that my intentions are honourable.'

'That cannot be done. I have no family,' I paused, trying to decide whether or not to risk any more unsolicited information. 'I am a servant and they would never give permission. Never.'

'But I cannot lose you. Not now.'

There was a long silence. My mind closed down. I could see no way of convincing this man of the impossibility of his wishes—and by now I was uneasy about the fact that my acquiescence was somehow being assumed.

I could feel him still looking at me, again without seeing me. The difference now was that he seemed to be looking for imperfections, reasons to abandon wanting to paint me. Until he shook his head.

'It is no good. You must agree!' he declared. Then his face brightened. 'But if you are a servant you must work nearby. So it is my guess that you are not supposed to be here. '

My reaction was so small he should have missed it. But he did not.

'Hah! Now we are getting somewhere!'

There was a slight pause.

'Then let me suggest this,' his look was intense, 'I do as many sketches as I can now and then you can come another time and I will do more.' He then added, more to himself than to me, 'I suppose I can find someone else for the poses. It just means I must be very certain to cover all expressions.'

Then he laughed. As far as he was concerned the solution had been found because he was already unfolding the sheet of paper.

I made one last attempt.

'*Mestre*, you are correct, I should not be here. But I do not come often…' I almost bit my tongue. I had, in effect, admitted that this was not my first escape and he would therefore know it was unlikely to be my last. 'I cannot come again,' I added, desperately, with as much force as I could muster.

'Well then we have no time to waste. Sit there,' he indicated a large flat rock nearby.

I had lost the fight. I moved over to the rock, the only relief being that as I did so the black dog came to lie beside me.

♓

It was a strange sensation. To be so absolutely the focus of someone's attention, of their very being, whilst never once being seen for oneself. As it was, having begun to sketch he barely spoke, just occasionally telling me to keep still, to slightly move my head this way or that. Once, apparently dissatisfied with how I was holding myself he came over and, without a word, took my head in his hands to shift it backwards and sideways, tilting it up and down without the slightest awareness of my existence.

At first I believed I could stop my thoughts both because I did not want to consider my situation as well as to prevent my attention from wandering and the pose being lost. But it was hard. It was as if my thoughts were just watching and waiting for an unguarded moment so that they could establish themselves and whisper that I was playing with fire and that at some stage I would be found out. The other thoughts, though less precise, were also more complicated, circling around the fact that Lucas van Domburg was planning to give my features to our Blessed Lady.

Time passed in a strange hourglass in which it could not be truly measured. An hour, maybe more, passed before the dog quite suddenly got to his feet and, after looking up at me, went over to Lucas van Domburg and gave a low growl. Without thinking I stood up and brushed my hands down over my clothes. Lucas put his sketch paper down, looked at the dog and then at me and said:

'Madonna, when do we meet again?'

I struggled to find what answer to give, uncomfortably aware that it was no longer *never.*

'Perhaps, maybe, in a week's time. If it is possible.'

Lucas van Domburg smiled and said: 'In a week, less than a week in fact, I am supposed to start painting, or at least be in the church and making my preparations.'

'I can promise nothing. It depends on…'

'…on you being able to find a way of getting away unseen,' he finished the sentence.

For a moment I kept quiet.

'I will try and come the day after tomorrow. In the morning. But it has to be the last time. If it's not possible I will try again the next day—or until I can.'

♓

I did not sleep well that night. Instead I constantly replayed my meeting with the painter as if, in the darkness, I could freely examine his features and look at him as boldly as he had looked at me. Though it was easy enough to say that he was of average height, that his thick hair was lightly streaked with grey and that his nose had perhaps been broken I accepted these facts as being no more than descriptive externals. It was his eyes I most wanted to see. And there, though it was obvious that they contained laughter there was also an accompanying sense that things were constantly being looked at and examined. It was only many years later that I put all this down to a certain detachment, that he took little at face value. I also saw that his blunt directness was at odds with the delicacy with which he had sketched, contrasts suggesting that, for all his apparent openness, he was withholding and concealing a part of himself, and therefore making it impossible for me to catch who he really was.

♓

Although three days were to pass before I was able to leave the convent, I found Lucas van Domburg waiting for me, seated on the flat stone. He did not get up as I approached, perhaps because he was more absorbed in studying how I moved and walked, rising only when he saw that his examination was making me self-conscious. As a result by the time I reached him I deeply regretted having come.

He smiled: 'So, you are a reliable goddess!'

I waited, realizing I wanted to regain lost ground, to retrieve myself, not be too open with him. I had already given away far too much.

'But, I suspect, a difficult one.'

Immediately I offered an explanation—that I could not get away—and immediately I regretted doing so. I had given back the upper hand.

He smiled.

'So may I now humbly request you to be seated on the stone?' he asked with exaggerated politeness.

I went and sat down, determined so say as little as possible.

This time he laughed.

And this time something was different. He was more relaxed, the drawing seemed less a priority and was, perhaps, why he began speaking.

At first he tried to ask me questions, where did I work, did I like being there, was it a big family? Of course I was evasive and unforthcoming. My answers being, quite nearby, yes I liked it and yes it was a big 'family'.

'But more than that you won't tell me I suppose!'

I shrugged.

'So what *will* you tell me?'

'I will tell you nothing,' I said with such sudden vehemence that I surprised myself, 'I will ask. And about you. Where do you come from?'

Although it was obvious that my words had amused Lucas van Domburg I also knew that using a question to deflect his probing had not gone unnoticed.

'I am,' he finally said, 'from Zeeland and, of course, more precisely, from Domburg.'

As he spoke a shadow seemed to flicker across his face. Or perhaps it was just that though he had planned to make light of something he suddenly changed his mind. Instead, for a moment, he concentrated on his drawing, working a line. Then he raised his head and, for the first time, he looked at *me*.

'How does one speak about the place one comes from to someone who has never been there?' He smiled but there was no lightness in his eyes. 'It is many years since I left. There will have been changes that I may never see…'

He shifted and moved his head from right to left and back again, loosening an apparent tightness in his shoulders.

'What kind of answer do you seek? That Domburg rests on the northern part of a small island that fights to stay above the sea? That, though seemingly isolated, people have lived there since very ancient times, that they were raided by Vikings seeking the wealth that came from trade, that power now rests within the castle of the Abbots of Middelburg, that the monks were involved in reclaiming the land, that the city's charter dates from the thirteenth century, that because the lords of Domburg are the Dukes of Burgundy we are under the Habsburg yoke and Spain and while most people are now God-fearing followers of reformist priests their ancestors worshipped local deities, making offerings to ensure their protection. Is this what you want to know?

'Or do you want to know that Domburg is a place of openness, of the sea and a vast sky and an extraordinary light. That this sea is greedy and changes its mood and must always be watched, always respected and sometimes even fought. And that the light varies from darkly ominous to piercingly intense; from the bright shining of a summer day to the shimmering of the moon on a winter night; that this light is always shifting, reflecting the moods of the sea, changing with the seasons, affected by the sun, the clouds, by storms, by thunder and lightning and, in winter, by the veiling of snow.

'For me that is Domburg. My Domburg. For others it is where they take shelter from all this. In their houses; neat and orderly; everything clean and tidy and in its proper place.'

Only years later, when the pain of what finally happened had almost gone, did I begin to understand something of the depths of Lucas van Domburg's emotions, and how much he suppressed in his outburst. And why he so quickly moved to play down the force of his words. I can now no longer recall if I realized how he had laughed to hide a certain bitterness before he spoke again: 'Well, there you are: a quick sketch of Domburg!' Instead I still see how he appeared to push something away with his hands, and how he looked at me before continuing.

'It is a hard land. Just to keep it from the sea takes an annual toll of lives; yet, in truth, it is a willing sacrifice.' He then stared out at the land around us, perhaps to see if he could find any similarities between the Alentejo and Zeeland. 'But it is now almost twelve years since I left, since I began travelling, working my way here, moving like a leaf blown by the wind.'

Though there were many questions I would have liked to ask, especially *why have you been travelling for twelve years,* I sensed that just the sound of my voice would silence him. Only by being quiet and waiting would I learn more.

His pause was a long one and even when he did begin to talk again, his voice was almost inaudible. 'It is always fine until you disagree, until you question or have a doubt. Mine were, I suppose, doubts I was not supposed—allowed—to have. It was not acceptable—and certainly not advisable—to question their way of seeing God. Even though I have never questioned that God exists...For me the divine, the sacred is all around, and within us...'

At this point he suddenly stopped and stood up.

'But I bore you no doubt. Talking of such serious matters when the sun is shining!'

I shook my head.

There was a very long pause before he spoke again, softly: 'At least I am able to paint. That joy is still mine.'

He looked at me. And smiled: 'And Madonna, I now have you to paint.'

♓

The next few days were outwardly calm but inwardly turbulent. I fluctuated between excitement and fear, wondering how Lucas van Domburg would react when he arrived at the convent and saw me. At times I wished I'd told him about myself, where I'd come from and why I was so apprehensive.

Meanwhile, though I assumed I was safe, I lived in constant terror of catching a whisper, of hearing someone describe how Lucas van Domburg had been heard talking about the girl he was going to use as his model for the Virgin.

♓

A false sense of security came on the day of St Martin. As always it was a special day, one I had happy memories of celebrating with Joaquina, roasting chestnuts while those around us drank the first of the new wine. The magic is that though this day comes in the middle of winter and always dawns with overcast skies they soon disappear leaving everyone to enjoy a beautiful sunny day. Joaquina used to say that it was an ancient day, linked to Roman times, when St Martin gave half his cloak to warm a cold and shivering beggar and that in the same way this cold winter day is always transformed into a warm one, becoming a day of plenty and celebration, a time when meat is eaten.

Yet, a few days later, in the last week of November, it was particularly cold and bitter when Lucas van Domburg finally arrived to start his work. Who welcomed him, who saw to his immediate needs we never knew. All that filtered through our enclosing walls was that he had come and would remain as a constant but unseen presence for some weeks, perhaps months. Unseen except by me even though a powerful force seemed to direct everyone's attention towards the church, giving us strange thoughts and pulling us away from our duties and daily prayers. Meanwhile the church was made off limits to everyone, our daily devotions, and where our confessions would be heard, being shifted to the Chapter House and outside people kept away.

It may even have been that on that first morning I was the only one who truly prayed. I beseeched our Lady to protect me, to save me from whatever unthinkable punishment might come my way should it be discovered that I had been leaving the convent and meeting Lucas van Domburg. And all the while, as the morning hours ticked slowly by and the sun moved across the sky, I felt that a dark shadow was moving over the earth and would soon surround me and take me to an unspeakable and terrifying hell. When, at last, I was summoned to the kitchen and handed a heaped plate and a jug of wine I knew the time had come to go into the church and face the fate that awaited me. The only consolation was that, despite sweating with fear, I found myself thanking our Lady for the fact that since everyone around me was nervous, no one suspected me of having any uniquely personal fears.

I walked slowly, ostensibly to be certain that nothing was spilt but in reality to delay, impede, perhaps even prevent the inevitable of having to enter the church. In any event the door betrayed me, opening like silk, swinging soundlessly before me, instantly revealing that Lucas van Domburg not only had his back towards me but was obviously intent on what he was doing. For a strange and almost joyous moment I thought he hadn't heard me and that if I was careful I could put the food and wine down and escape before he was aware of me. But then, without turning, he spoke:

'Madonna, put what you've brought on the trestle table.'

I almost dropped everything—even as a jealous sharpness asked *did he call every woman Madonna,* even as he turned and I knew he had known it was me.

I trembled, unable to move, standing and hearing the faint click-click of the jug knocking against the plate, watching as he came towards me and, without a word—but smiling—took them from me.

'You need not be frightened,' he said, 'Your secret is safe. I worked it out when I examined your reluctance to tell me where you came from. And how odd it was that you knew about me, that you expressed no real surprise when I told you what I have come for…And when I asked myself to think what—or more correctly who—might prevent you from going outside it occurred to me that you might work here and then, of course, it was obvious!'

He paused, looking at me with an expression I could not define, before almost whispering: 'Just as it is equally obvious why you might take the risks you do.'

This time I was the one who smiled, even as I knew that somewhere deep inside me the nervousness of an unspecified fear remained.

'But let me be direct. Sooner or later they will understand that you have been my model and will, I do not doubt, demand to know how this could have happened. And you will be the one to suffer…

'I cannot let that happen. I will therefore change your features—the shape of your mouth, the colour of your eyes, your hair. With such adjustments and the addition of imagined dresses and costly ornaments no one will ever be absolutely sure it is you. And, if, just if, some resemblance is spotted, it will be so faint that it will simply be thought I caught something of you when you brought my food.'

For an extraordinary and strange moment I was torn, balancing my thoughts, caught between the idea of being painted as our Lady and the shadow of fear, the threat of an unknown punishment. So total was the division within my mind that even when I started to speak, my voice a soft and stammered whisper, it was as if I was speaking on someone else's behalf.

'No, *Mestre.* You should paint as you wish to paint. The risk—if there is one—will always be there, even if you disguise my features. Besides' and here my voice and involvement began to grow in strength,' who will really identify me if I am shown in costly robes and jewels? You forget, I am no more than an invisible servant in a convent of aristocratic nuns, some even from the royal family. Do such people really see me?'

He looked at me, just looked. Then he leaned forward and took both my hands in his: 'Madonna,' he said,' I will paint you as you really are. Then they will see who and what you are.'

I lowered my eyes, my mind whispering the question that always lurked somewhere deep inside me: *ah, but* who *am I?*

'Madonna?'

I looked up again, into Lucas' eyes, feeling the prick of tears.

'Madonna, let me explain. Over the next few days I will complete my preparations—the sketching out of the whole fresco, drawing it onto this *arriccio,* this under-layer,' he said, pointing at the few drawings he had already done, all in red. 'Although at this stage I can take my time, once I begin the actual fresco the process becomes more complicated. Every day I will prepare the area I can, as I must, complete in a day. The *giornata*—the day's work. This means applying a fine, smooth coating of plaster, the *intonaco* they call it, through which the sketches can still be seen, and then leave it to dry, just enough for me to paint on, but not too much. Generally I can start around an hour after the application and continue painting for, maybe, up to seven hours. If it dries out it is useless since the plaster is then unable to absorb the colours. If this happens—or if I should make any mistake—I must remove the whole *giornata* and reapply the plaster. It is painstaking work—and why most artists have an assistant…'

He paused. 'I fear that once I start we will not be able to talk…but at least we have the days, perhaps a week, maybe longer, whilst I work on the *sinopia*, the sketches…'

♓

By their very nature those days were precious, each one giving us around twenty minutes—once or twice stretched to thirty—before I had to leave and so be sure no questions were ever asked about what was taking me so long.

What I saw during those minutes was a continually extending procession of people being outlined along the walls, flowing from Lucas' hand to occupy their allotted place. Though it was easy enough to see that these men and women were all individuals there was little to define their height or shape or station in life since they were all so lightly sketched, without features or identifying characteristics. Surrounding them were brief hints of trees and hills, faint signs of small streams and churches, just enough to suggest the richness of detail that would eventually fill up the empty space. Yet even at this preliminary stage one figure stood out: the recurring presence our Blessed Lady, already holding a position central to all others—despite Her face being simply a blank oval indicating how She held Herself and in which direction She faced.

This was what I saw. What I heard, in the all too little time available, was very different. Though his words opened my mind to a universe I may never have known existed, he often spoke of matters far beyond my comprehension and many years were to pass before I understood the hidden depths of what he talked about. Lucas van Domburg's words took me into a world that though almost as indistinct and unfinished as his initial sketches, was as rich as the one I knew would eventually replace them. He said little about himself, his childhood or family except that as a young man he had been apprenticed to a painter in Haarlem and that, without saying exactly when, he had eventually made his way to Italy to acquire the techniques of fresco painting. He described the externals of his time there, the Tuscan towns of Florence and Siena, the glories of their palazzos and churches, their love of wine and good living. And when he said he had even travelled to Spain and painted portraits, he mostly commented on their stiff formality and pride, their passion and religious fervour—almost making me see and feel the pomp and emotional power of a High Mass in Toledo's great cathedral. And finally, and with a laugh, he told me that, just over a year ago he had come to Portugal since it was now considered fashionable to employ artists from the Low Countries. Ill winds may blow he said but the breezes are often good. But of himself he said almost nothing.

Almost, but not quite nothing, for slipped, maybe unwittingly, in between these traveller's tales were snippets of opinions, observations, even stories and, very occasionally, judgments about what he'd seen and experienced, small but significant details that offered brief glimpses of Lucas van Domburg's inner world. For instance although he told me of the burning hot August when he had gone from Florence to Siena to see a horse race held in honour of our Lady's Assumption he also, in a few insubstantial phrases described meeting local writers, artists and thinkers. In Toledo he found his way to a church and it was with almost sensuous praise that he described the intricacies of its decorative details, the dazzling woodwork, the windows of exquisite tracery, the glorious arches and alabaster pillars. And then he surprised me. All this beauty, he said, all this devotion and dedication had originally been to house a synagogue built by a wealthy merchant, one of the many Jews who had once flourished in Toledo, but whose generous contributions to the city's greatness ended violently when the Moslem caliphs were driven out by the Christian kings. And more was to come. Somewhere along the way he was introduced to the writings of a long dead Toledo physician, a man who, inspired by both the

Song of Songs and the devotional literature of Arab poets, had written Hebrew love poems on the mystical elements which, he told me, were common to both a true marriage and the love of God.

And then there were other times when somehow, very subtly, he touched on more ephemeral matters, weaving them into whatever subject he appeared to be discussing. He suggested—and it is hard to give form and substance to the opaqueness of what he said since, as I later realized, he must have known the dangers of being explicit. He told me, as a story, of a man, a lover, who knocked at the door of the Beloved. 'Who is there?' asked the Beloved. 'It is I,' the man answered. 'This house will not hold Me and thee,' came the reply. The lover left to weep and pray in solitude. Then, after a long time he returned and knocked again. Again the Voice asked, 'Who is there?' 'It is Thou.' Immediately the door opened and the lover and the Beloved stood face to face.

And it is now that I finally come not to what I saw, not to what I heard but to what I felt. A more dangerous territory. Again I remind myself that much of what Lucas said was beyond me. Even so I often wondered uneasily about so much of what he told me, remembering how he himself had said it was unwise to talk about such matters since the thoughts they contained were considered unacceptable—and, though the word was never mentioned, heretical. But explaining my uncertainties like this is a deceit, suggesting that I was more concerned about how such statements might affect Lucas. Which was not the case. The difficulty was, and still is, to pull together my reactions and clarify the thoughts and emotions that went through me as I listened to Lucas. To see them clearly and then, of course, to face them, to understand what was really meant by the mystical marriages of gods and their devotees, of the saints and the devout of all faiths who entered into these unions. Men, and women, whose truth-seeking souls journeyed along what Lucas said one Spanish Jew had called the 'path of light'. The recurring theme of love and the Beloved, of love and God and the intensity of the physical longing for that god. The suggestion of sensuous passion, of the forbidden. Love. Marriage. Married love.

And so it was that, day by day, as I walked the short distance from the kitchen to the church I, in truth, ventured further and further towards the edge of another world. A world which reached out and into my mind and played havoc with my thoughts. A situation that increased and deepened once Lucas began painting the actual frescoes since, by the time I entered the church, at around midday, the prepared *giornata* was dry enough for him to have started, carefully and intensely, applying a whole palette of colours to a small section of the wall. As a result, though he would look up and smile a welcome, he immediately returned his attention to his work. For the first two days I lingered, expecting and secretly hoping that he would pause and talk to me. But he never did.

Once again my mind was divided, trapping me in a no-man's land somewhere between my fascination with the emerging beauty of the fresco, its detailing, the fine precision of every face and my festering awareness that I was growing increasingly resentful about being ignored. This, in turn, brought me uncomfortably and reluctantly, to a longing—initially devoid of any understanding of the why behind my need—for Lucas van Domburg to acknowledge my presence. One morning I even dropped his empty plate deliberately, just to make him look at me; a ruse that produced no more than a brief, almost unconscious glance before his attention returned to the wall. For the next two days I went in and out as quickly as possible.

The following day I again lingered simply because I could not help myself. I had by then missed three days of Lucas' work and in that time he had almost finished a complete episode of the Virgin's life. Of course I was anxious to see Her face but in this I was disappointed since the panel depicted the marriage of Her parents. Even so, I was torn between wanting to go right up to the fresco and the uneasy awareness that if I did so I would be much closer to Lucas than I wanted to be. Or so I tried to tell myself.

And so more than a week went by, long days of Lucas painting without pausing, short moments of me bringing his meals and always lingering just past the time when I had promised myself I would leave. During these days I barely looked at the frescoes or even, it seemed, at Lucas. And yet my thoughts revolved around them both and the ways they were affecting me. And as always, though the time inside the church dominated my whole being, the hours elsewhere still required me to attend to my usual duties. And, inevitably, I was subjected to answering whispered and furtive questions about Lucas.

Then another panel was completed: the birth of the Virgin. And then still more days passed before, quite unexpectedly one morning I heard Lucas clear his throat just as I was about to leave. I looked back over my shoulder.

'Madonna?'

Was it then that I saw how tired he was, how drawn his face had become?

'Madonna? Somehow make sure you can stay a little tomorrow. I will have something to show you...'

Of course I knew what it would be; what it had to be. Finally I would see the face of the Virgin. And know what She looked like or, more precisely, who She looked like.

♓

In that respect I was destined, once again, to be disappointed for Lucas still did not really reveal Her face. He had painted Her as a slight figure, little more than a child with a face too small to see if we shared any common features. She had been set in isolation, moving confidently away from Her parents, making her way up a steep flight of steps for Her presentation in the Temple, a thanksgiving for the blessing of Her birth. By placing the young Madonna apart from everyone else Lucas had stressed Her importance, while by making Her a tiny figure he had ensured that Her tenderness and youth were heightened. I found myself moved and for a moment it was easy to imagine myself *in* the painting, following Her up the steps.

'So now you begin to see Her? Is She as you expected Her to be? Are you perhaps disappointed that you cannot see anything of yourself in Her?'

He paused and I turned to look at him.

'It is best that it is so. It is a beautiful painting.'

He smiled and slightly inclined his head towards me before saying: 'You will, I fear, have to wait several more days to see what She really looks like.'

The next scene was the Marriage of the Virgin and though the subject meant that She was closely surrounded by other people, Her presence was still central and unmistakable. Yet, somehow, Lucas had managed to suggest that She was, very gently and very subtly different from everyone around Her and, once again, there were too few details that might show how, if at all, we might resemble each other.

Afterwards came the Annunciation; and it was as the rich and glorious colours of the Angel Gabriel began emerging from the *sinopia* that I began wondering how, if the Virgin was given my features, Lucas could camouflage our resemblance. And yet he did so, by the simple device of depicting Her shrinking in withdrawal from the words the angel bore, giving Her an expression of awe and humility and stressing these emotions with the denial of a hand that shielded almost half Her face.

In this way he played with my curiosity.

♓

But the day finally came when Lucas, having completed one length of the church, started working on the single fresco that was to cover the entire wall behind the altar. Even before he began I knew it was to show the Coronation of the Virgin, to place Her in seated majesty and so glorify Her as the Ruler of our hearts. It was painstaking work and as the days stretched into weeks I saw how, small section by small section, Lucas slowly revealed his vision, instinctively sensing that he was pouring himself into the colours, transferring part of himself onto the wall. Perhaps something had shifted within me, changing my mood and finally opening my eyes to just how much this meant to him. I now brought his food quietly, taking care not to disturb him, simply placing the plate and jug on the trestle table and, as often as not, slipping away without a word. Only at the door would I stop and turn back, not to see if I had been observed, not to try and elicit a look or a word, but to see the progress he was making. Common sense as much as instinct told me that with this fresco he could no longer evade showing the face and features of the Virgin. Yet by then I had sensed that something deeper was happening: that the painting would express something whose identity, at that stage, was still a mystery.

♓

How is it possible to describe my reactions, to express my feelings? How, even now, can I detach myself from the finished painting, a painting that drew me so powerfully into its fold? And what words can I find to describe the central and magnificently robed figure? None. It is beyond me. All I can do is ask myself a few questions: Did She resemble me? Yes. Did the painting suggest that Lucas had used me as a model? No. But how can I be so certain that this is a true and correct answer? And if I am certain how can I explain it? I cannot. Yet, even though I question my ability to put what I felt into words, there is something I am very sure about: Lucas van Domburg had merely taken my features and given them to the Virgin and, in the process, he had invested them with an expression, a persona I knew nothing about. He had subtly suggested that Her face was a delicate mask behind which lay the vast depths of an inner life, a quality that took the onlooker beyond externals and into another dimension. Past me, as it were, to reveal a level of understanding, of compassion that, with a shock, I realized came not from me, but from him. It was the painter who was depicted, not the model. It was Lucas who revealed the qualities, the spirituality, the intensity of the Virgin's love; not me. And even though he had, perhaps, painted this way to protect me I do not, in truth, believe he could ever have painted any other way. It was as if he had painted his naked soul and then clothed it with my features.

'Madonna…' his voice was little more than a whisper.

I barely heard him; my whole being was absorbed by the splendour of Our Lady and Her enthronement as Queen of the World. I gazed in awe, knowing that though my eyes acknowledged the gleaming gold and precious stones of Her crown, the opulent magnificence of Her robes and the adoration of the two angels at Her feet, what was really affecting me was something deeper and less tangible. The more I looked the more I felt that my whole being was in the painting, that I too was bowing in humility before the young girl at its centre, seeing Her depths, Her remarkable eyes, Her youth and Her majesty, Her tenderness, compassion and love. What I saw before me was the absolute centre of the universe.

When I turned and looked at Lucas I could not see him for the tears.

'*Mestre…*

♓

I had said nothing more. I could not. Instead I had turned and run, or more correctly, fled, from the church. Even now it is hard for me to say, to admit, what I fled from. Only at night, when the convent was still and quiet and I was surrounded by darkness, did I whisper his name: Lucas.

Lucas. I was in love with Lucas. I almost cried out my awareness of this knowledge—even as I stifled all sounds in case anyone should hear me. And yet though I cried in pain I was filled with joy and though I wept in despair I almost laughed at the great happiness suddenly engulfing me. Throughout that strange night there was no emotion that did not rush from one side of my consciousness to the other; no feeling that did not fill me up and, as suddenly drain itself away. It was like being simultaneously lost and found.

Despite eventually drifting into troubled sleep I knew, even before I opened my eyes that I was shaking with fever, my head was throbbing and every limb ached. I also knew that I had to get up. But I was too weak, my body betrayed me and, even as I tried to stand, I collapsed back onto my bed. For a brief moment I clung to the belief that a few more minutes of rest would restore me. Yet as soon as I tried to stand I fell, and awkwardly, the noise I made bringing one of the servants to investigate. She placed a hand on my forehead and then left to inform the nun in charge of the infirmary, who immediately ordered me to the hospital, to contain my fever she said, in case it was contagious.

For days I tossed and turned as fever raged throughout my body, a fever which, had anyone but known it, was less deadly than the thoughts that scorched their way through my mind.

♓

The final act began a week later when I was declared well again and asked who, in my absence, had been taking Lucas his food. It was Dona Maria de Jesus, the nun in charge of the kitchen. My heart sank. She was, perhaps, a logical choice but not, apparently, one made by the Abadessa. In fact, as I later discovered, the Abadessa was never even informed that I was ill, let alone of the necessity of replacing me. And I knew why. Right from the very beginning when we heard that an artist was coming to paint the frescoes Dona Maria de Jesus had been one of those most affected. Often, when I collected the meals prepared for Lucas, she would ask questions about him, what was he like, what did he talk about, was he married or did he have a mistress. I was in any case wary of her, her viciousness was well known, and if, as I had learnt to my cost, she was not instantly obeyed her spite and venom were quick to strike. Instinctively I knew she had seized on my illness as a chance to see him. And, while still unwell from the fever and confused by my own feelings for Lucas, I felt a strange fear sweep through me. I felt threatened. Dona Maria de Jesus was beautiful.

She was also, I realized as I walked into the kitchen on the day I resumed my duties, jealous. She immediately made a remark about 'the little nobody' having deigned to return. I kept quiet, seeing the looks shimmering between the lay-workers and a couple of nuns. Then I picked up the plate and wine jug and left. As I entered the church I knew I was nervous and unsure of myself; I was about to face uncomfortable truths: that one fever remained uncured and while my feelings for Lucas were clear, his for me would not have changed.

He was, as I had expected, carefully and intensely painting, now working his way down the last side of the church. He made no movement, gave no indication that I had reappeared. I went quietly to the trestle table, only taking my eyes off him as I put everything down.

'Madonna…?'

I looked up, colour flushing across my face, my heart leaping as I saw the welcome shining from his eyes.

'Where have you been?'

I fenced, answering a question with a question.

'How did you know it was me?'

He smiled. And for a moment said nothing before repeating his question.

'Where were you?'

I frowned: 'No one told you?'

He shook his head.

'I was sick; with fever.'

I saw the frown; and the concern.

'Madonna, she never said—and I did not wish to make too much of it in case it caused you trouble…She was, in any case, more intent on making herself noticed…'

'And so is she now to appear on the wall?'

Lucas gave me a strange look and, no doubt, saw that a fresh rush of colour was staining my face. There was an uncomfortable pause before he spoke again.

'Madonna,' he said,' it is true that she is beautiful enough to go on any wall that glorifies beauty but within her there is torment. The anger she feels will one day burn away her looks. She has no vocation—but why should she have? No one can possibly believe that she ever had any choice about becoming a nun. Have some pity for her.'

Although I heard his words clearly and knew the truth of them, I was not willing to listen. Instead I allowed myself to twist them around and into something else. I allowed my own feelings for Lucas to obscure my vision, extracting only that he found her beautiful and felt pity—and perhaps more—for her. I also knew that Dona Maria de Jesus was nearer to Lucas in age, whilst I was little more than a child. Surely it was likely that he would be more attracted to her?

♓

Yet the next day, when I returned to the church, I did so with a sense of repentance. I had acted badly; my question had been a bitter one. I resolved to follow Lucas's advice. He rewarded me by looking up as I entered.

'I have been waiting for you,' he said, 'I need to make sure of your face in repose. Soon I will start on the Dormition of the Virgin, Her earthly falling asleep before Her Assumption.'

The breath sighed out of me as he gestured towards a bench.

'Place your head on that cushion and lean back as far as you can and close your eyes.'

I did as he directed, but apparently not quite as he wanted for, as he had done when he made his first sketches, he came over and shifted my head, moving it to a different angle. But this time, more than the feel of his firm fingers adjusting the position of my head, I felt the faint touch with which he then fleetingly laid one hand on my hair. It was a touch that ran through me like lightning.

Although at night, and in the dark, I made much of that touch, when the light of day dawned I was immediately reminded of reality. It was a reality my brief time in the church did nothing to alter. Lucas greeted me warmly but was obviously driven by his work and the constant race to complete the *giornata.* And yet, and yet, each night I would return to a different world where hidden dreams blossomed, where hopes were realized and I lived in a happiness where Dona Maria de Jesus did not even exist to disturb my dreams.

But as the weeks went by a new and more substantial reality slowly began to establish itself. Day by day the walls of the church were filling up with glorious frescoes and it was with a sense of shock that I suddenly understood that Lucas had almost finished. And that he would soon leave, would go away. At first I tried denying this, refusing to accept or believe it could happen while at other times I had unrealistic dreams of running away from the convent, of going with him. Of course in my heart I knew that could never happen, if only because Lucas himself never showed any sign of suggesting it, of desiring me. And yet the thought of him leaving was unbearable, making me feel as if life itself was ebbing, draining away from me. And worst of all was the knowledge that once he left it would be forever, that I would never see him again.

By the time he began the last panel—of the Dormition of the Virgin—I could barely conceal my unhappiness. I kept praying that something would keep him from going. But the fates laughed at me as time kept draining away, minute by minute, moving towards the inevitable day when the last brushstroke of colour would be applied.

It was just a day or so before this was about to happen that, very early in the morning, I saw Dona Maria de Jesus moving towards the cloister. That in itself was nothing to comment on but what transfixed me was the smile on her face, a smile that though it contained a host of shifting, fast changing emotions was dominated by satisfaction and a sense of having got what she wanted. A cold sweat iced its way down my spine as I instinctively drew back behind a pillar, not wanting her to know I had seen her. Had she, somehow, been in the church? And if so how had it been possible?

In an instant the passing of time did what I had been praying for: to slow down. Instinctively I knew I could not risk going into the church and confronting Lucas—and why, I wondered, was he there so early unless...unless. I couldn't even think about why. I would have to wait until it was time to take him his meal.

During the interminable hours before I went to the kitchen I could barely form a coherent or complete thought. Almost everything I wanted to do I dreaded doing. I wanted to see Lucas. I wanted to ask him about Dona Maria de Jesus. I also wanted to see Dona Maria and ask what was happening. Yet though I knew I would see them both I accepted that I would never ask either of them anything.

I was wrong about expecting to see Dona Maria de Jesus, or at least in the kitchen. Instead she was just outside it, almost as if waiting to catch me by surprise. In this she was successful and, although I tried to suppress my gasp, she must have been aware of it. Her smile was still in place, its presence as troubling as it had been earlier. But there was nothing I could do, no question I could ask. I had to continue on my way—and ignore the laughter that came sniggering after me.

Only when I pushed open the door to the church did I see how violently my hand was shaking.

Lucas was standing there. Waiting for me, his hands held out to take the plate and jug.

I stood, empty-handed, not knowing what to do, unable to move or speak.

'Madonna...'

It was as if I was frozen.

Lucas took my hands and led me to the bench where, just a few days earlier, I had stretched out to pose as the dying Virgin. This time I just sat.

'I don't know what she has done or said—though I can guess.' There was a pause before he continued. 'She is, as I said before, an unhappy and frustrated woman. She is also beautiful and I am not a saint. But I know the dangers that would exist if I responded, She is now, I fear, in a state of delusion, of believing that, somehow, she will come away with me…'

I looked up in disbelief. Was he also aware of my delusion?

Again Lucas reached down and took my hands.

'Listen to me. Listen to me and understand—and most of all remember—not everything is as it seems.'

What was he saying? My head ached; everything was suddenly beyond me and, because I could not help myself, I began to cry.

'Listen to me.'

I looked up, gulping back a sob, wishing I had controlled my tears.

'I am older than you by many years. Your life stretches before you; mine does not. I am…' and here he hesitated. Later I realized he had been about to say something but then changed his mind.

'I am, well, soon to leave; within three days. I will leave Portugal. I have to. And this time I will go back to the Low Countries, to Zeeland. It is better there. I will not insult you and say your life will change, that you will forget me; you are not like that. And I, in truth, will not forget you. Painting you, discovering you has changed my life, has settled me. Through you, and because of you, I have been able to express my feelings about so much. My request then is that you *will* sometimes think of me and know how much I am in your debt.

'Perhaps, who knows, it will be different in another life. But this time…it cannot be…'

What Lucas said was not, of course, what I had dreamt of hearing. But despite the dull and throbbing pain that still surrounded my heart I instinctively knew he had said—and given me—something remarkable, something that, had I known it, would sustain me when the pain became unbearable.

He reached down and pulled me to my feet, smiling as he walked with me to the church door. Here, just as I turned to go, he handed me the empty jug and plate. I looked up at him, surprising myself by smiling, and then was myself surprised as he cupped my face in both hands and, very gently, kissed my forehead.

♓

Would things have been different if I had known I would never see him again?

♓

As it was I took the jug and plate and went back to the kitchen. Where I saw Dona Maria de Jesus. She came over and looked at me.

'Did he tell you he wished he'd seen me before he'd started painting? That I have the perfect face for the Virgin? That I am beautiful?'

I ignored her, while wishing she hadn't mentioned being beautiful, that it was something Lucas *might* have said. And yet I heard his voice: *remember, not everything is always as it seems.*

She followed me out. I walked away hoping she wouldn't follow me. At the end of the passage I turned round. There was no sign of her.

I breathed a sigh of relief and continued walking, to go about my duties, my thoughts already making their way back to Lucas.

♓

The next morning, an hour or so before I was to take Lucas his meal, I saw the Abadessa coming towards me. I drew back against the wall, to let her pass me by. But to my surprise she looked towards me, hesitated and then stopped.

For a moment she frowned, then knew who I was.

'You have come from the kitchen? I am looking for Dona Maria de Jesus. Is she there?' she asked.

I felt deadly calm.

'No, she has just left. I saw her going towards…into the church…'

She paled and was about to say something more. But stopped herself, before hurrying away.

Only then did I see what I had done. In truth I had not seen Dona Maria de Jesus enter or leave the church. I had simply answered spite with spite. I had made a statement based on assumption. Without any thought of the consequences.

♓

It is almost impossible to take myself through everything that followed. I have hesitated, side-stepped and evaded everything for so many years. Days, months, years, decades have passed and yet I still, despite everything, struggle to deny that the small handful of words I uttered had such terrible repercussions, created such turmoil and gave such inconsolable pain.

♓

I never took Lucas his meal. By the time I should have gone to the kitchen it was known he had left. Dona Maria de Jesus had, we believed, been taken away to the infirmary, weeping and screaming. Rumours bred rumours, yet strict and absolute silence was ordered. The tension about what was happening; the lack of information, the growing suspicion about Dona Maria de Jesus having been carnally involved with Lucas fell on us like a dark and terrible blanket. By then I was feeling the full weight of my guilt, of having initiated the situation that was unravelling. Sooner or later I was certain I would be dragged into the limelight to give facts and explain myself.

Meanwhile I was gripped by the question: *where was Lucas?* What did they mean by *he had left?* Why? The frescoes weren't finished. Where had he gone?

After his disappearance—and it was soon established that he had left by himself, and without informing anyone—the convent's enclosing walls finally fulfilled their purpose and prevented all contact with the outside world. Ten days passed before, somehow, a whisper slipped in and breathed its way around the convent and we learnt what had happened: Lucas van Domburg had been arrested and was being held in Évora by the newly established Holy Office of the Inquisition.

After this a total silence descended and for weeks and months no further information ever reached us. The unknowing, the waiting and the fear affected us deeply and was almost as terrible as the physical torture we feared he was being subjected to.

But what only I suffered was the awareness that though my spiteful remark had started everything somehow I had not—so far—been seen as being either responsible or involved in whatever crime Lucas was accused of. During the early weeks I kept expecting to be summoned, if not by the Inquisition itself, at least by the Abadessa. Had it been possible to talk to people about the arrest of Lucas, of Dona Maria de Jesus—who, having lost her mind was being kept apart from us all—and what she had or had not done—things might have been easier. But no one dared since the knowledge that the Holy Office was involved made everyone wonder not only who was listening but why.

The nights were the worst, full of terror and despair. A time when I could barely tell my daytime thoughts and fears from the nightmares that sleep, if it came, brought me. It was also when, so often, Lucas seemed very close, when I could almost hear his voice, almost feel his hand rest lightly on my hair and his kiss on my forehead. At times he was so real I would sit up and look around, only to lie down again when I saw the cruel reality of empty space. It was too terrible to think of him confined, perhaps in chains, in darkness, tortured. Almost all that was known about the Inquisition was that their powers were far-ranging and absolute, that trials were secret, that the accused was never informed of his supposed crime and that there was no appeal. Once I even found myself wondering if Dona Maria de Jesus was not better off than me, at least she was lost in delusion, rather than surrounded by the agony of silence and the unknown.

When the news finally came it was told to us, formally, by the Abadessa. Somehow she kept all emotion from her drawn and haggard face, speaking to us in an almost lifeless voice, uttering words so terrible that when she finished no one moved: Évora was to have its first auto-da-fé and, though his crime was still undeclared, Lucas van Domburg was amongst those who had been condemned to be burnt at the stake.

After the initial stillness it was as if a small dam had broken. Quiet gasps. A few faint sobs. Suppressed cries. The sound of a novice sliding to the floor, fainting. The clicking of a rosary. Whispered prayers. A sense of loss. Of bewilderment. And most of all the sudden awareness of a fear too terrible to be voiced, a fear that pushed each one of us into ourselves and where all that united us was the darkness.

♓

And so it was that, a few days later, and though cloistered within the convent, I saw Lucas die his brutal death. Against my will my mind's eye showed me, all too clearly, how his face contorted into a dreadful mask of pain. Against my will I saw how he writhed and strained against the ropes that sawed at his arms. Against my will, and soaked by rivulets of sweat, I endured the most unbearable of all these enforcements: watching the flames as they enclosed his broken body, wracked by the sensation that it was *my* body the flames were consuming. So many years have passed but I can still hear the sound of his voice, his last, long agonized scream. Even now that awful howl will sometimes echo through my mind for, child though I was, I knew it was a last gathering of strength, a final declaration that his spirit was about to soar free, that they had not won.

♓

But what comfort did I really draw from this knowledge? The pain of despair, of grief was savage. Hope had died. My body ached, my skin felt raw and inflamed, nights were sleepless, days grief-stricken. My tangled thoughts of death, of Lucas were all-enveloping, cascading over each other as they fought to push me into the horrors of a dark and bottomless abyss. A sense of loss swept over me with waves of such height that each one threatened to crush my very soul. I was so tired, so weary that once I even looked down expecting to see blood draining out of me. I barely ate, my hands shook. Yet I could not cry or call out. I was numb and lost, alone and adrift in an empty hollowness, at sea in a vast, uncharted nothingness of grief. And guilt.

♓

Sometimes bad news comes directly, suddenly and when least expected. Occasionally you are prepared, even expecting it. But maybe the most dreadful time is when it creeps towards you so that, for a moment, there is no sign that something awful is about to happen. As it did late one morning, less than two months after Lucas died, that as I was coming out of the kitchens, I saw Leonor. Despite still being almost consumed with overwhelming grief I managed to greet her with a faint smile. A smile that quickly evaporated when I looked again and saw that she was just standing there, and that though her face was pale and drawn—like everyone else's—it was obvious she brought bad news.

'Catarina. It's Catarina...,' her voice was barely audible, her skin seemingly whiter than her habit.

I felt the blood draining away. The moment of innocence was over and, though I really didn't know, I *knew.*

'Balthazar came...early this morning...just now...He came with a message from my father...to be given to the Abadessa and after he left—about an hour ago—she...she sent for me,' there was a pause, enough time for me to think *please don't let it be true.*

'Catarina...Catarina has died,' she stammered, the tears now pouring silently down her face. 'She was hardly ill. Just for a few days. It seems no one was really worried. Now she's dead, gone...my sister.'

A rush of emotions gripped me. The longing to hold Leonor. To comfort her, even though no comfort could be given. The rules about touching were strict—and a small part of my mind had already accepted that the Abadessa must have allowed Leonor to come and tell me. She would never have done so without permission, she followed rules, was obedient and devout. I hardly knew what words to utter.

Then Leonor spoke again. 'My vows, my final vows have not been taken. And now never will be...How could, how could my sweet Lady do this?'

Even as I wondered at her question I knew the answer. Catarina was the eldest daughter and therefore the one destined to marry. Her death meant that, since Leonor was not yet a professed nun, she would now take her sister's place and that a husband would be found for her. Her wishes were of no consequence. She would be expected to do her duty, even though that meant leaving the convent—where she was happy and at peace. Where she wanted to be. A fact that made my guilty mind pause—even as it made a small leap of joy and told me that I would soon be free.

♓

Free was a word I wondered about on the cold morning a few days later when we were finally ready to leave. I saw the misery on Leonor's face, her short hair how concealed by the secular headdress I had helped her arrange and which had been sent, along with a dress, from the *quinta.* I remembered how she had made her entrance into the convent, her apprehension and how she had tripped. And I thought of how she had settled down into the rhythms of worship and prayer and how I had seen her gently grow into a sense of calm assurance. Now all that had been ripped away from her. A time would no doubt come when she would regain her serenity but for now she was too young for it to have settled within her. A suspicion that was underlined as we both heard the door shutting behind us and I saw how she stiffened and bit her lip and how it was that her time within the enclosing walls had come full circle. But then, and to my surprise, I realized that I too felt nervous. What after all was I returning to? Joaquina was gone. I was older. And therefore more alone.

Until I saw Balthazar, standing quietly, holding the coach horses, waiting for me; even as Alvaro, Leonor's brother, waited for his sister.

The ride back echoed the original journey, yet so much had changed. I felt more formal, even slightly shy with Balthazar, conscious, maybe for the first time, of being female, of the strangeness of a man's proximity. I could no longer imagine him holding me in his arms, of running my hands across his hair, of going to him for hurts to be smoothed away. And I knew he felt it too for I sensed a slight hesitation before he lifted me up onto the coach, placing me in a perfunctory way. Nothing was said as he climbed up beside me; he merely shook the reins, setting us on our way. The irony was that as a wave of overwhelming sadness ran through me I instinctively and without thought, placed my hand on his arm and, for the briefest moment, put my head against his shoulder. And felt him relax. Some things, I told myself, are as they should be. At least for now.

♓

I had all too glibly assumed that only after we returned to the *quinta* would a husband be found for Leonor, a suitable man from a good, aristocratic family who lived no more than a few days' ride away. However it transpired that Leonor's family already had someone in mind: the man who had initially been proposed for Catarina. At first all I knew was his name, Dom Duarte da Cunha, and that he was the nephew of the wife of Dom João de Castro, a man known and respected for having distinguished himself in military encounters on both land and sea. At this time it almost appeared that Dom João was of more importance than the prospective bridegroom. Certainly more was known about him, importantly that he had not only already served in India but was likely to be the next Governor of India. While this rumour alone was enough to make the marriage a desirable one there was another, more personal factor in its favour: Leonor had been named after Dom João's wife who, in turn, was closely related to Donna Briolanga. Yet, despite all these connections it transpired that it was only after Catarina's death that her family discovered Dom Duarte was in India. Although they had initially been happy to propose Leonor they appeared to hesitate when his family made it clear that Leonor would be expected to join him there. While it was obvious that both Dona Briolanga and Dom Martim considered the alliance a good match it was not hard to sense the doubts they harboured, that they were struggling to strike a balance between a prestigious marriage and their remaining daughter going to India. Of course, while the ramifications of all this were beyond me, it was soon clear that the idea of a girl like Leonor, whether married or merely betrothed, sailing to India was, though not unheard of, extremely rare.

Dona Briolanga voiced her concerns: it would be impossible for her to accompany her daughter, and how could she send her off on such a long voyage, moreover one with very real dangers? Would it not be possible to delay the wedding until the bridegroom returned to Portugal? Or could there be a proxy marriage? Dom Martim brushed her worries aside by disclosing that Dom João de Castro, had just been confirmed as the new Governor of India and would leave to take up his appointment on the next sailing to India. Leonor could therefore not only travel safely under his personal protection but be assured of residing in his official residence and having her marriage conducted by him.

And so it was agreed that she should go. And that, once again, I would accompany her.

♓

Eventually all pain settles into its personal corner, a place where the ache continues to linger but where, outwardly, life starts to go on as it did before. Time went slowly by as we waited, and prepared, for the next sailing to India and on one of those days, a day not so very different from those that had preceded it, I woke and though thoughts of Lucas and the acid grief of loss began sweeping through me as usual, I sensed a change: it had found its place. Yet with this understanding came the realization that I had to find some semblance of daily peace and this, I somehow knew, meant going outside the house and seeking the Cromeleque's protective enclosure, aware that though my only visit had been from the convent, Joaquina had explained its nearness to the *quinta.*

I left early, noticing the troubled sky as I slipped away but accepting that while it signalled the brewing of a summer storm it merely heightened my need for the sense of a separate world. As I ran I kept one eye on the gathering clouds, aware that the nearer I came to the Cromeleque the more the skies were darkening. The first drops were already splattering onto the earth as I approached the great standing giants, sending me hurrying towards the protection of the leaning stone, to huddle beneath it and take what little shelter it could offer me.

It was a futile attempt. Without warning there was a loud crack of thunder and the heavens opened. Great bolts of lightning hurled themselves down from the sky even as sheets of heavy rain hit the parched land and, as if dancing, bounced back up again. I shivered, pressing myself into the stone, watching the pouring rivulets of water. I was soon soaked through, my hair plastered against my face and the thin cotton of my clothes almost transparent. I crossed my arms, held myself tight, and waited.

I knew the rain had to stop, that such a heavy downpour could not last forever. But it just kept coming in tumultuous sheets, falling with such fury that it seemed be taking revenge for the long months of drought.

And then I sensed a change, that a faint whispering was coming through the rain and slowly turning to a strange rumbling. A sound that made me strain my eyes to peer through the downpour and out over the plain.

I saw it at once, a huge dark shape, so far away that it was no more than an indeterminate bulk, a vastness that moved slowly, lumbering in my direction. I stood up, placing my hands back against the wet stone as if to hold onto its solid presence. What could this shape be? And how was it making such a deep noise? Fear iced through me, transfixing me as this terrible beast—for so it obviously was—came relentlessly closer, moving like an incoming tide, slowly and inevitably. I strained to see through the rain—mercifully now easing—my whole being focused on the monster. By then it was close enough for me to see that on either side of its great head were constantly moving flaps and that in its mouth were two large white scimitars and that as the rain splashed onto its back steam rose into the air while the grumblings, hissings and strange rumblings that had first alerted me to its presence gave evidence that fires burned deep within its bulk. I wanted to run, but to where? I wanted to look away but my eyes were held by the need to watch the monster's every move, to check each step of its relentless advance. And by then it was close enough for me to see that the two huge swords were in fact round and thick, more for impaling than cutting, and that between them swayed a huge thick rope. Tears of pure terror began to well up in my eyes. It seemed inevitable that this awful monster would soon reach out and snatch me away as its prey. I would be punished for my sins and savagely devoured. My last moments had come. I started crying, beseeching my Lady to save me.

But then, just beside this awful beast, I noticed a strange, dark-skinned man, a man who, without fear or apprehension, was casually resting a hand on one of the great impaling stakes. And that he was smiling at me. And that the beast had stopping moving.

'Do not be afraid,' he said in heavily accented Portuguese. 'There is no danger. We too seek shelter.'

Then, quite suddenly, the rain finally stopped and I knew I was safe: I had seen this man before, dressed in rich clothes, adorned with gold and precious stones, standing before the Christ Child, offering Him costly frankincense. I had seen Lucas van Domburg paint him onto the wall of the convent's church.

♓

A long trickle of rain ran down my neck. I shivered, perhaps from the cold dampness, perhaps because of my lingering apprehension. I was safe but my tongue was locked and, in spite of myself, I was still wary of the beast. Then the man spoke again, one hand on his chest.

'My name,' he said, 'is Thayathu Chandu…My ana'—and here he indicated the beast, 'is named as Kesavan. I am his pappan.'

Somehow, though fearing no sound would come, I answered, managing to splutter out that my name was Inês.

'So now we are introduced.'

But my concern was that I did not know how to address him, Thayathu Chandu was going to be difficult to pronounce. I asked him to repeat it, slowly, so that I could hear exactly how to say it.

'But mollay, there is no problem; you should simply call me as ammavan,' he said with a smile.

For a moment it seemed that though both words were easier to say they bore no resemblance to our names. Yet even as I wondered how to ask, he was providing the answer.

'In my country I would call you as mollay, daughter, and, in the same way, you would call me Chandu-ammavan, uncle. But ammavan will suffice.'

I kept silent as a rush of unsteady emotions rushed through me. I was unsure of how to continue, already calmer and beginning to wonder from where the elephant and this man had come. My curiosity must have been transparent for Thayathu Chandu, ammavan, smiled and, as Kesavan stood quietly, the rumbling by then less obvious, the inner fires quelled, he began to tell me how they had come to Portugal. It was a story that brought back memories of Joaquina and her tales and, even more so, of Balthazar and his.

♓

It seemed that far away, across many seas and lands there was a country called Malabar. It was hot and humid but cooled by gentle breezes and watered by seasons of intense rain. It was not like Portugal and yet many years back great ships had arrived from there seeking spices, gold and ivory—and as he said this he rubbed his hand along one of the great impaling stakes, the ana-kombhu he called it. Some of these men were great sea-captains, men whose dealings with the Thampurans and Rajas were quarrelsome and often devious. A fort was built so that soldiers could be garrisoned and where the wealth, the goods demanded by the Portuguese king could be collected and stored whilst awaiting shipment. Yet, as far as Thayathu Chandu's family was concerned, these facts were really little more than insubstantial rumours, fragments of news, snippets of gossip that eventually, by word of mouth, made their slow way to his home, a day's journey from the fort. His family were landowners, feudal lords of some repute and power who owned, he said, three elephants, all tuskers. One of them was an ana-kutty, not yet quite full-grown but already a beautiful animal and, more importantly, his particular favourite.

It was as Thayathu Chandu began to speak of his home that he became more expressive, stumbling to find the right Portuguese word even as he appeared to erase all emotion from his face, something that might have escaped me had I not seen Balthazar use an identical tactic to conceal pain.

For a moment he stopped talking, still moving his hand gently up and down the tusk before raising his head and looking directly at me. There was a pause in which I felt myself studied, feature by feature, as if he was looking for something.

'Then, one morning, a man, an agent of the Portuguese, came to see my family,' he continued. Again, though he struggled with words and grammar his story was clear and simply told. There had been little preamble: the man had come about the youngest of the three elephants. He simply announced himself as having been sent by the Governor—a title quite meaningless to them—and that he had been ordered to acquire the elephant, adding that though some financial consideration would, of course, be entertained they must understand that there was otherwise no choice in the matter. His uncles had shouted, declaring that they were not at the beck and call of foreign pirates and freebooters and that their elephant was theirs to keep. What finally happened, how the matter went against them, was unclear. What however was indisputable was that the Governor was going to send the elephant to Portugal, as a gift to His Majesty, King João. It was this last fact that was most clearly understood. That and the fact that a pappan would be required to go too for what, the visitor had said, do such people know about elephants?

There was then another pause which seemed, by its very silence, to provide clues to the anguish behind the words that followed. 'And so,' he said, 'I begged my family to let me go too. How could I allow my Kesavan, *my* elephant to go across the black sea to a foreign land where he would be alone, where he would understand nothing of those people?'

Then again silence, before he whispered: 'And so—eventually—we came to Portugal.'

Just one short sentence to describe the massive upheaval that had changed his entire life.

I let a moment pass before asking my first question:

'How long have you been here?'

'Nineteen years…or thereabouts…'

Longer by a handful of years than my own life, I thought, as I watched how he turned to the elephant, fearlessly walking round to its other side, with one hand caressing the trunk as he did so. How had I been so frightened I wondered, looking up at the small, soft eye that, to my surprise, was gazing down at me.

'But, ammavan,' I asked, 'Why are you *here*, now?'

He answered, after a quick look up at the elephant: 'Mollay, it was like this: when we arrived we were taken in a grand procession with musicians beating great kettledrums and sounding golden trumpets—music perhaps but of course nothing like our melams. Accompanying us were richly dressed men on prancing and caparisoned horses, standard bearers with fluttering banners and lance-bearing soldiers marching before and behind us. Cheering crowds lined the streets, all the way from where we disembarked to the King's Palace. On arrival we were grandly and ceremoniously received by high officials. The Governor's letter was read out and I was given a gold coin by the King. Everyone was in awe of my Kesavan—although when some courtiers came too close I had to gesture for them to stand back. When they made no sign of moving, I made him raise his trunk and trumpet to impress his might upon them. The crowd shouted and cheered, amused by the fear shown by the highborn.

'For some months, just over a year perhaps, we were a great novelty. The King would often come to see us, sometimes accompanied by his Queen and their children, always surrounded by attendants and courtiers as well as noblemen and their ladies. Whenever there was a royal procession through the city we too would parade, surrounded by great pomp. But life was not easy for us. I could not follow Portuguese and Kesavan took time adjusting to new ways. I missed my own food too. But, in their way, and despite their ignorance, we were well-treated. It was when the plague came to Lisbon that life began to be very different.

'Everything, absolutely everything in the palace was packed and loaded onto mules or into carts and the whole court, the King, his Queen, her ladies-in-waiting, the entire extended royal family, their father-confessor, other priests, officials, servants, cooks, grooms, musicians, everyone, set out for Évora. We went in one long procession, a cavalcade that soon left Lisbon behind, moving as quickly as possible to flee the plague.

'Two or three days later, when we entered the walls of Évora, our problems began immediately. The whole court was distracted, everyone hurrying to get everything in order, unloading the mules, checking provisions, preparing meals and, in all this, neither I nor my ana were of any consequence. The truth was that by then the royal family and the court were no longer so fascinated by us; our novelty had worn off. No one had the time to attend to us and so finally I simply took my Kesavan and we left the city to find him fodder and, indeed, something to eat for myself. When we came back four or five days later I expected things to be different, in order, that arrangements would have been made. But nothing had changed; nobody was concerned with our needs…

'And so,' Chandu-ammavan said with a wry and twisted smile, 'A new life began for us. Since then we have gone here and there, moving across the Alentejo plains, fending for ourselves. And I have understood the blessing of being with my ana. What, I often wonder, would have happened to him if I had not been here? Who would have cared for him? We grew up together; we know each other; we speak the same language and so are not, in that way, alone. Everything is in God's hands.'

He stopped talking quite suddenly. It was if the telling of his story—probably for the first time—had not only drained him but opened the inner doors he had, until then, kept tightly locked. Again I thought of Balthazar and his ache for his home and family, watching as Chandu-ammavan turned to his elephant, placing an arm on one foreleg, speaking to him softly in the language only they could understand. I saw his leanness and how he moved and the grace with which he carried himself and felt that the deep lines on his face made him look older than he probably was. Had Chandu-ammavan regretted his youthful decision? Balthazar's exile had been forced on him; this man had chosen his.

My reverie was broken by Kesavan stretching out his trunk—and how had I ever mistaken it for a rope? For a second, though I instinctively stiffened when it touched my face, I quickly sensed both the elephant's gentleness and ammavan's lack of concern even as, and with a kind of awe, I felt a soft dampness begin to lightly feel its way around my features, accompanied by an almost tender blowing.

♓

The advantage of being back at the *quinta* was that, unlike the convent, getting in and out was relatively easy, and I usually managed to slip away every other week or so and make my way to the Cromeleque. In this way I was able to meet Chandu-ammavan and learn more about his life and the ways of elephants. I, in turn, would tell him about Joaquina and Balthazar and how I had gone to the convent with Leonor. One morning I even mentioned the frescoes and 'a painter' who had come from the Low Countries to paint the walls of the church, deliberately sidestepping any mention of Lucas' name or the role I had played, fearing that doing so would betray my emotions. Ammavan then told me—as I had hoped—how he had met this painter, and that he had made several sketches of both him and Kesavan, a moment that brought me up short, reminding me of how little I had actually known about Lucas, of what he did and who he met outside the convent's church. Too late, and with regret, I wished I had paid much closer attention to the figures with whom had Lucas had peopled his frescoes. I had, it was true, recognized ammavan but how much real attention had I given to his place on the walls? Ammavan meanwhile was already describing how he had told Lucas about the temples and shrines of Malabar being richly decorated with the lives and exploits of gods and goddesses, and of the interest Lucas had shown, demanding to know about techniques and colours .'He wanted to know everything, even the smallest detail,' ammavan told me, adding with a laugh, that he soon realized how little he himself knew. 'I was,' he said,' better suited to telling him about elephants. Until, that is, he showed interest in our beliefs. At least those questions I could answer.' Here he again smiled and, quite suddenly, I felt I could easily imagine them sitting together, Lucas, seeking knowledge of how people worshipped and the deities they honoured and ammavan, perhaps after decades of silence, being able to voice his feelings for the gods of his homeland.

♓

Most of my time of course was spent at the *quinta.* Though I had come to the house as a foundling to be nursed by Joaquina and, as such, had no official position in the family it had been casually assumed that my place was with them; an assumption heightened by my closeness in age to Leonor and the time we had spent in the convent. In the same way that she was now of an age to marry I was considered old enough to be her maid. As a result as her mother began assembling her dowry, the fine embroidered linen, the robes and jewels, I was the one who first laid them out and then, as carefully, folded them away in camphor chests brought specially from India. One morning I saw Dona Briolanga gently smoothing a hand across a piece of embroidery originally done for Catarina. In the way of these things I also saw Leonor glance up at her mother and catch the brief flicker of sadness that shivered between them as they read each other's thoughts.

♓

Gradually the preparations required for the long sea voyage to India were completed, edging us closer to the day of departure and the need for Leonor and I to make our farewells. For the first and only time I was glad Joaquina was not alive, that I did not have to, once more, see her grief-stricken face. For the moment I pushed Balthazar to the back of my mind since he would be coming with us to Lisbon. Which left just ammavan.

I set out to see him early on a cold afternoon in the middle of February, the week before we were to leave for Lisbon. Although, as usual, I found him at the Cromeleque, I knew at once that something was very wrong. Kesavan was lying near the centre of the stone circle, his great bulk a still and sunken mass. Ammavan squatted before his head, close to a burning oil lamp, one hand resting lightly on a tusk, his face ashen and tear-streaked. 'He is no more,' he said, 'he left his body early this morning. And I cannot properly honour his passing.'

I let a long pause go by before venturing a question, as gently as I could: 'What would happen in Malabar?' For a moment ammavan appeared to ignore me, his face an unhappy blank. Then, with a twisted smile, he turned to me and said: 'There would be pujas and we would cremate him.'

'Then can we not do this too? Do you know what has to be done, the pujas you call them? And can't we gather enough wood?'

This time the pause was much longer but I saw that within him a light had been lit, that he was considering what might, perhaps, be possible.

In the end it took us just over three hours to assemble what we hoped would be enough wood and place it over and around Kesavan's body. Leaves were gathered and a tangled apology for a garland was woven and laid on Kesavan's head. And then, when we were as ready as could be, ammavan stood bare-bodied in the cold winter afternoon and intoned the prayers to release his ana's soul. Finally we lit the pyre, grateful that the air's dry crispness helped the wood ignite even as I was secretly grateful that people's fear of the powers believed to occupy this place would prevent anyone coming to investigate. Almost at once the flames took hold of the wood, and began hungrily consuming the blurred shape that lay within them, the acrid smoke justifying the stinging of our eyes as we watched silently, lost in our own thoughts. Though, soon enough, we were surrounded by night's darkness the leaping flames continued to roar and blaze.

I stayed with ammavan until early morning when a wintry sun rose on the dying embers and showed us that, miraculously, all but Kesavan's tusks and his largest bones had been consumed. No more would be expected in Malabar he told me, adding that when the ashes cooled he would gather them up and take them to a river to be immersed.

By then I realized I would have to leave and attempt to slip back into the *quinta* without causing undue curiosity. But first I asked the question that had crept into my mind during the night.

'Why,' I asked, 'why don't you now come back to Malabar, sail with us?'

He shook his head, almost fiercely. 'No, mollay, it is too late. I myself will soon be gone. My duty is done, Kesavan has not been left to die alone.'

I didn't even try to dissuade him. Yet as I hesitated, wondering how I could leave, ammavan spoke.

'Mollay', he said, 'I have prepared a letter for my family. From what you have told me it appears that your destination is Goa but perhaps you may meet someone there who is trustworthy, someone hailing from Malabar to whom you can hand it over, someone who will ensure it is delivered. We are known people.'

I left with a heavy heart, clutching the cloth-wrapped bundle to me as if trying to prevent it escaping, hurrying towards the *quinta* with tears blurring my vision.

♓

I could not sleep the night before our departure. I was about to leave everything I knew and enter a world where nothing would be familiar—even Lisbon would be alien. And yet it was not that I truly feared the unknown but more that I was apprehensive about possibly never seeing Portugal again. Not knowing if, as had happened with ammavan and Balthazar, I was, in fact, leaving forever. A possibility too vast to contemplate and therefore something I had tried to avoid by looking closely at everyday objects and seeing how they then changed and became invested with qualities previously unnoticed. I examined without discretion or choice: a door, a tree, candlesticks, light on a window, darkness in a corner, a crucifix, a jug in the kitchen, anything and everything, even sounds: a fire cracking, distant bird calls, a scraping chair—and smells: wax candles, burning wood, a rose in bloom—and textures: a clay bowl, fine linen, polished wood. I saw and heard and smelt and touched and stored it all furiously away—knowing all the while just how futile it was.

♓

The first stage of our journey would take us to Lisbon, three days ride away for, although the fleet would not sail until the end of March Leonor's family had matters to attend to and needed time to oversee the final arrangements for both the voyage and her future marriage. In many ways our departure was to be an echo of the time we had gone to the convent—though on a far grander scale. Many more people would come with us, not only a whole host of servants and retainers, horsemen and grooms but Dona Briolanga, Leonor's mother, and even her father, Dom Martim, who had meanwhile ridden out from Lisbon in order to return with almost the whole family and oversee his daughter's departure. Five of Leonor's seven brothers were also to travel with us—the eldest, Alvaro, remaining to look after the estate, along with Pedro, her still troubled youngest brother.

♓

We finally left on a bitterly cold Monday morning, rising early, well before dawn, driven by the storming and shouting of Dom Martim as he urged everyone to hurry, anxious to be on his way to Lisbon. Although his practiced retinue eddied around him, their movements choreographed to perfection, the household servants, less familiar with such apparent urgency, ran backwards and forwards, ordered into action by Dona Briolanga. After helping Leonor dress I waited inside, standing near her, seeing how pale, tense—and silent—she was until, at last, her mother came and hurried her out, instructing her to hold up her skirts as she climbed into the lumbering coach that would carry them both to Lisbon. I kept myself still and quiet, not daring to think or consider the journey stretching before me.

♓

And in all this the only other person who stood as still and quiet was Balthazar, holding the horses.

I did not dare think beyond the immediate: that I would not only be riding with Balthazar but escaping the dust and discomfort of the open wagon carrying the other servants and Leonor's baggage.

When the time came I walked towards him, trying to make my mind as empty as possible, but knowing, absolutely knowing that this, now, was where it really all began, that this time something irreversible was happening. I saw, almost as individual acts, how Balthazar turned and saw me, how he gestured to another groom to hold the horses, and how he then watched as I approached. And how it was that when I stood before him he wordlessly lifted me up onto the coach and then climbed up beside me. It was an unreal moment, suspended in a time of its own making—a moment then instantly broken by the already mounted Dom Martim swinging his horse round and riding out of the great open courtyard. At once grooms shouted, whips cracked and men leapt onto horses that reared and foamed at the bit, their hooves clattering and sparking on the cobblestones as they slipped in panic, reined in tightly until the moment when they were spurred into their place in our cavalcade.

♓

It was a strange journey, reminding me, to begin with, of Chandu-ammavan's description of the King and his court moving to

Évora. Yet, once the horses and their riders had settled, our cavalcade made steady progress with even Dom Martim—who rode beside the coach—allowing his air of unremitting vigilance to lessen and his body's ramrod stiffness to relax. Riding beside him was Diogo, Leonor's sixth brother, who, at Dona Briolanga's insistence, was to accompany us to India. I briefly wondered about Leonor and what thoughts were in her mind and whether anxiety and unspecified apprehension kept her body as rigid as mine. I was also over-conscious of Balthazar beside me. I had too much to say to him—but could find no words and it took the sudden lurch of a wheel falling into a pothole, and Balthazar's reaching out of a restraining hand, to release my tension. For a moment nothing was said, though his hand remained on my arm. Then with a slight smile he said: 'We have over a month and you must never forget that we also have forever.' The ache within did not lessen but his very closeness and understanding gave me the comfort I needed. For a while the silence remained and we stayed lost in our own thoughts, wrapped around us as tightly as our bodies were clothed against the cold. Strangely when the words finally came they were mine and inconsequential. I simply turned to Balthazar and said how wonderful it would have been if we could have ridden to Lisbon. He laughed and within moments we were talking as we always had and there was an ease between us.

It took three days and two overnight halts for us to reach Lisbon. The evening of our first day's journey bringing us to Montemor-o-Novo where, as was customary for many wealthy men, Dom Martim owned a house. Only after Balthazar told me our second night would be spent in another of his houses, did he also explain that this enabled Dom Martim to shadow the King whenever he shifted between Évora and Lisbon. Our arrival had been well planned; servants rushed to greet us, meals were waiting and beds were prepared—even though none of us had a peaceful night's sleep.

The next morning, and again just as dawn was breaking, the

previous day's bustle and activity was repeated. But with one difference: by then our journey seemed settled, possessing its own life, purpose and rhythm, thereby making it possible, once we were on our way, for me to calmly take note of the land we were passing through; even to feel sorry for Leonor enclosed in the stuffiness of the coach. Not that it was comfortable next to Balthazar, the condition of the road brought constant shaking and lurching, the wheels either slipping in and out of potholes or up and over large stones, actions which in turn distressed the horses who had to bear the brunt of the coach's weight. This in turn, along with a lengthy halt for lunch, slowed down our progress, bringing us to Setúbal just before the sky began darkening into night.

As soon as Leonor got down from the coach I could see she was unwell; her face was too pale and covered with a fine dusting of perspiration. Dona Briolanga gestured for me to come as she hustled her daughter into the house, pushing her way through waiting servants, only slowing down when Leonor stumbled and would have fallen had I not been close enough to hold her. Her body was hot, evidence of a fever racing through her.

We sat on either side of the bed we laid her on, watching as her slight body moved restlessly from side to side, shaken by the fever. From time to time a worried Dom Martim would appear, stand wordlessly at the door and then leave. The house meanwhile acquired a strange tension, an unnatural silence that almost cried out to be broken as everyone held their breath and waited. All sense of time was lost and I cannot say if it was after one hour or several that something made me look towards the door and see Balthazar standing there. He did not even beckon or make the slightest gesture. It was Dona Briolanga who looked at me and nodded as I got up to go to him.

He stepped back as I reached the door, drawing me with him as I finally voiced the words that had been racing through my mind all night: 'If only Joaquina was here.' He barely moved his head in agreement; instead he lifted his hands to show me the glass they held, a glass half-filled with a dark liquid. 'She would,' he said, 'have given her this. Take it to her now and make sure she drinks it all. She will sleep but stay with her. It is possible she will sweat even more before she calms.'

He paused and then, as I took the glass from him, he spoke again. 'I will be here, outside. Come at once if you need me. At once.'

Dona Briolanga asked no questions when I showed her the glass; she simply turned towards Leonor and said: 'We must lift her head.' Though Leonor briefly struggled, showing her distaste for the medicine's contents, she was too weak to refuse and within a few moments we were settling her back onto the bed. She seemed to sleep at once, perhaps exhausted by her slight efforts at resistance.

It was a strange night. Dona Briolanga on one side of the bed, holding one of her daughter's hands and me on the far side, clasping the other. Neither of us spoke, both of us no doubt all too conscious of the frailty of human existence, aware that Leonor could as easily die as live, that her fate would be decided by factors beyond our control. Yet as the new day dawned, and after, as Balthazar had warned, a sudden sweating had shivered through Leonor, she opened her eyes and we saw that danger had passed, that our prayers, and the medicine, had restored her.

To give Leonor a chance to rest and have nourishing food, the last stretch of the journey began late. As a result, though we made good time to Alcochete, the point fixed for us to cross the Tejo, we arrived there well after nightfall. However Dom Martim's frequent journeys to and from Évora, and no doubt his court connections, meant not only that his retinue but all those engaged to take us across the river, were well-versed with making such manoeuvres. The entire area was lit with huge flaming fire-torches, investing everything within their orbit with a sense of drama and urgency, despite it being obvious that most people would have a long wait to board their assigned boat.

We watched nervously as loading began, it being no easy matter to handle the horses, some of whom reared and plunged in fear, an emotion echoed by us all. Because of Leonor's condition I was inside the coach with her and Dona Briolanga, the three of us to be kept there until the time came to heave it onto the boat. Whilst this was being done, and until it was safely secured on board, we huddled on the quay, anxiously waiting for Diogo, Leonor's brother, to escort us over the wide gangway and back into the coach. Soon enough we slipping away from Alcochete, accompanied by men shouting and calling to each other, many holding fire-torches, their light dancing on the water as, like moths to the flame, we made our way across the great river, drawn by the pools of flicking light waiting for us on the opposite side of the river, the Lisbon side.

♓

One month later, when dawn broke on the morning of Saturday, the twenty-eighth of March in the year of our Lord fifteen hundred and forty-five, I knew we were finally within hours of beginning our journey to the other side of the world. Somewhere nearby a fleet of six *naus* lay at anchor, their crews no doubt already fretting and anxious to begin the annual *carreira da India*, the India run. Today we would leave Portugal, leave all that was known and familiar and journey for months across unknown seas, sailing past dark and dangerous lands, occasionally calling at mysterious ports, journeying until we landed in Goa and began a new life. Yet as I looked around the still dark room I sensed that the familiar had already begun to recede. This house and the room I stood in were unknown to me; the people who lived and worked here were mostly strangers; the bulk of Leonor's baggage had already been taken and stowed on our ship. All that remained were the last few things we would take when we embarked.

Gradually light filled the room and the day began in earnest. Well-trained servants came and went, efficiently at ease with the heightened activity. Leonor's mother, once more on the brink of perhaps never seeing her daughter again, moved from room to room and up and down the stairs overseeing, instructing and relentlessly issuing orders. Dom Martim, who had left early, was already down at the quayside, with his sons, preparing for our final departure, supervising the arrangements not only for our quarters and well-being during the voyage but having discussions with the captains of the five ships, reminding them that he was placing his only daughter in their care. As one of the fleet's investors he was also no doubt concerned about the cargo their ships would bring back as much as for the daughter they would leave in India.

And all the while, Leonor, the chief focus of this concern and attention, remained still and quiet unless told to go here or there, do this or that—or just sit and wait. Nearly a year had passed since we had left the convent and in that time Leonor had matured. She had recovered much of the serenity lost after her sister's death and learnt to wear the mask behind which a woman of her status is expected to hide her personal feelings. But I knew her too well. I saw the clenched hand disappearing into the folds of her skirts, I recognized the stiffness in the angle of her head and, most of all, I saw the little indent of a tooth on her lower lip.

I also saw the rosary slipping through her fingers, bead by bead. Yet this apparent passiveness was instantly broken when her mother suddenly appeared. She got quickly to her feet, extending a detaining hand as she leaned forward and quietly whispered to her mother. Dona Briolanga's immediate response was a frown of irritation, due no doubt to being preoccupied with all that still had to be done. But by then Leonor was sure of herself and, when she spoke again, her voice was strong and firm.

'Mother, I wish to pray.'

For a small moment her mother's mask slipped, revealing a glimpse of the pain hidden behind it, the pain of her first daughter's death and her second one's imminent departure. Though no one could deny that her diligence in overseeing Leonor's departure was essential it seemed that at least some of her frenzied activity was to protect herself from her own emotions. Her face softened.

'Go, my child. And take Inês with you,' she said, pausing for the briefest moment before adding: 'And pray for us all.'

Minutes later Leonor and I were slipping into her family's private chapel, taking the narrow interconnecting door from the house rather than the imposing entrance facing the street. In doing so we moved almost seamlessly from an atmosphere of tension and stress into the softness of a silence thick with the richness of incense. At first I was taken in by the coolness of the blue and white *azulejos* covering the walls and the apparent aura of calmness. It was a fleeting sensation, a deception instantly confirmed by the huge figure of a crucified Christ looming above the altar, dominating the chapel. I hesitated, caught off guard by the sudden fear that this powerful figure would swoop down like a dark bird of prey and tear at my flesh. The agony of the gaping wounds, the streaming blood, the haggard face and the pain were too real. I shrank back in terror, my mind plunging into disturbed memories of Lucas and the tortures I knew he must have endured. I fought to remember that our Lord had died for our sins, but failed, doubting that mine could ever merit forgiveness.

I stood, uncertain, hesitating as I watched Leonor crossing herself, sinking to her knees and wrapping herself in the familiar and comforting rituals of prayer. I knew she was content, that she had none of my reservations. She was already at peace in the certainty of her faith, her lips moving, silently intoning, seeking blessings, entrusting her body and soul into the divine care of the saints, our Saviour and, of course, our Lady.

And so I finally sank to my knees, bowed my head and folded my hands in prayer, only to find I could not pray. To do so would release a torrent of pain, would admit the need for help, would bring my fears gushing forth, releasing everything I had locked so fiercely away. For now all I dared risk was the whispered shadow of a prayer: 'Bless and protect me, Mãe.'

♓

Eventually word came that everyone in the house was to assemble in the great hallway, that Dom Martim was on his way back and the time had come to leave. Moments later he arrived like a whirlwind, striding in pursued by scurrying retainers, all struggling to run and absorb the reams of instructions he kept issuing. Leonor stood up as he entered, showing respect for a father she barely knew and hardly ever saw. Would she, I wondered, miss him?

'Are you ready? We have to leave.'

'Yes, Father.'

Although without further ado Dom Martim turned on his heels and left the house he did so without the urgency that had been so marked when we left the Alentejo. He simply went outside and waited, surrounded by his retinue until Dona Briolanga emerged with Leonor and he stepped forward to help them into the coach. And this time, though I was to travel with them, Balthazar was assigned to ride beside us, as part of our mounted cavalcade. Even as I sat down the door was closed and, for a strange moment, there was complete silence. No shout, no sound of an order being given or a whip being cracked, just a slight lurch as the coach moved forward. Little could be seen, the streets were narrow and the riders, their faces stern with concentration, blocked our vision as we slowly rattled along, making the occasional unwieldy turn until, just before we stopped, the horses were urged into a sedate trot, taking us briefly across what was obviously a wide open area. Then there was a slight jerk as the coachman reined in the horses; a click as the door was opened and Dom Martim asked us to get down. Beside him was Balthazar.

We were close to the edge of the river, the Tejo, a vast

expanse of dark water, running fast and deep, speckled with ships and boats of every size and description. It was extraordinary, used as I was to the dryness of the Alentejo, to see such an expanse of water. Once we were all gathered together we began walking the short distance to the river's edge, our way cleared by Balthazar, giving us an easy passage through a frenzied bustle of activity, the last-minute loading of cargo, much of it fresh vegetables, fruits and casks of water. All around were crowds, some just watching and some, huddled into small groups, were obviously families whose fathers, sons, brothers or husbands were about embark on a voyage that—should they be lucky enough to survive—would not bring them back for more than a year. Women, young and old, had strained faces, many of them tear-stained, while small children, ignorant of the dangers their elders faced, ran about, playing, until suddenly gathered into the fierceness of a farewell embrace.

By virtue of his closeness to the King, Dom Martim could take us directly to the ship we were to sail in. A boat, its crew in Dom Martim's livery, awaited and, within minutes we had clambered into it and were being rowed across the river as a dull March sun struggled out from behind the clouds. I could see and hear that the river's tidal waters were rapidly rising, rocking the surrounding boats and causing even the six great *naus* ahead of us to ride gently up and down. Leonor grew increasingly tense and was a deathly pale by the time we drew alongside the *nau* we were to sail in. Although we had been told that we would be individually seated in a chair and then winched up, there was no sign of such a device. Instead it was suddenly obvious that we were expected to climb the rope ladder dangling down the side of the *nau.* Leonor froze, too frightened even to reach for the outstretched hands or listen to the voices encouraging her to take the rope ladder. It was, of course, Balthazar who came forward, well aware that her real fear was far greater than the distance between our boat and the deck looming above us as he gathered her into his arms and carried her up the ladder, her face buried in his shoulder.

I stumbled, and had anyone noticed, they would have assumed it was due to the motion of the boat. It was not. It was the sudden ripping off of my mask, the cracking of the veneer, the skinning and peeling back of all my denials. Joaquina, Lucas and now Balthazar; everyone I loved I lost. I could no longer delude myself. Although the fleet was not yet ready to depart each passing moment was already reminding me that once we set sail all hope of ever seeing Balthazar again would be gone. Tears blinded me and for a crazed moment I thought of asking Leonor to insist that he came with us. But I knew I could not, that it wasn't possible. And then I felt the safety and security of arms enclosing me, lifting me, carrying me up to the *nau*, one arm firm against my back. Balthazar.

He set me down, carefully and without a word. There was a pause. Then he took my hand and walked with me to the far side of the deck, facing away from the shore we had left, where the river was at its widest. He spoke, very softly, still holding my hand:

'Remember what can always be found, and how you can see it, how you can travel to reach it. And know that I will always be there with you.'

There was a slight pause before I heard the words he had once taught me in his own language, the words of farewell that actually said 'God be with you.'

As he began to turn I remembered the response: 'And God protect you.'

For how many decades have I gone on seeing that slight hesitation as he walked away? And for how many decades have I resisted running after him?

♓

In normal circumstances the closeness between Dom João de Castro's family and Leonor's—coupled with the fact that she was to marry his wife's nephew—would have meant that she would sail directly under his protection on the *São Thome*, the fleet's flagship. Yet, although two of Dom João's sons were with him there were no women, his wife was remaining in Portugal, pregnant with their seventh child. Leonor's father had therefore made enquiries and while he soon discovered that the wife of Jorge Cabral, captain of the *São Mateus*, was to travel with her husband, the ship we finally boarded was the *Burgaleza*, under Simão Peres De Andrade. And with good reason for, listed amongst the passengers was a married couple, Dom Francisco de Mariz and his wife, travelling not only with their four children but chaperoning a handful of women and girls of varying ages, all destined to marry in India at the King's expense and, as such, referred to as 'orphans of the King'. Dom Francisco's responsibility was to care for them until they were handed over to whoever eventually came forward to marry them in India, a prospect enhanced by dowries in the form of land and a small government post. Dom Martim therefore met Dom Francisco who willingly agreed to take care of Leonor. While this absolved Dona Briolanga from having to re-consider accompanying her daughter to India, it left Diogo as not only the sole relative sailing with us but ill-pleased at missing the glory of accompanying Dom João.

The hours we waited once on board were invested with a terrible and ill-defined restlessness; we were lost in a strange limbo, since neither were we on the dry land of Portugal nor were the ships beginning to sail, starting the voyage that would take us to India. Since Dom Martim's servants had stowed all our baggage in the small cabin we were to occupy next to Dom Francisco, his family and the orphans—and even as Diogo was already establishing his presence with them and our captain—I went to stand on the deck, next to Leonor, close enough for her to barely move when she extended a hand and linked her fingers with mine. It was obvious that though her reserve and timidity made her reluctant to intrude on the arrangements Dom Francisco was making, I sensed she wanted to quietly say her farewells to Portugal. For some time we stood together, silently watching the riverside crowds fading away as the last preparations to leave were made. What, I wondered, were her emotions? Was she, like me, relieved that there was no sign of Balthazar and that the coach had gone? That her father was not to be seen? Suddenly, and for the first time, I was glad I was with her. Yet it surprised me when she turned to face me, the shadow of a smile shifting so briefly across her gentle face that it hardly showed.

'How different all this would be if our Joaquina was with us.'

I could do no more than tighten my hold on her fingers.

♓

Long before we even embarked it was known that the fleet expected to sail with the ebb tide, harnessing the power of its natural force to carry the ships down the river and out towards the open sea. But when the time actually came and the tide started running we barely moved; the wind was too weak. Rowing boats were brought, ropes were attached to each *nau* and, very slowly and under enormous strain, they were pulled down the river. Finally, beneath the dark grimness of a fort standing high on the headland, we anchored and the wait for the wind began in earnest. For the captains, the pilots and seamen this was, however frustrating, something they understood and were familiar with. For us, journeying without any knowledge or understanding of the sea, of its currents and tides, or even from which direction the desired wind should blow, this wait bred an unease that bordered on despair. It was as if everything was suddenly beyond our grasp and we began watching the sailors with a strange suspicion, inwardly beginning to believe they were apprenticed to powerful sorcerers, bent on luring us into a web of deception, keeping us imprisoned until some dark pact had been fulfilled. These feelings gripped us so fiercely that even when the wind rose and finally began to blow—and that too from the northwest—many of us felt it was merely gusting to torment us. A further unease arose as darkness descended: the fear that night would engulf the whole fleet and sea monsters would rise up to devour us. This terror was almost palpable, heightened by the *naus* suddenly beginning to shudder and groan.

It was then that one of the sorcerers took hold of the wind and, just slightly, shifted it, bringing it in from the north—a change that caused orders to be shouted and sent men pounding along the decks to their stations. Activity began again; lanterns were lit, the rolling of the freed ships making their lights dance like fireflies. Then, without warning, a single cannon shot rang out from the *São Thome,* followed by a rising crescendo of shouts, of men calling in jubilation. Immediately, and in quick succession, the other *naus* fired their cannons, releasing waves of cheering and roaring that rose and fell as the sound carried across the water, from ship to ship. It changed everything. Suddenly we felt the swelling of a great primal surge, the urgency of an extraordinary energy being drawn from the elements as the great sails began billowing like ghosts in the darkness, taking us out and over the bar, riding the sea and sailing, at last, for India.

♓

We were up at first light, after a restless and almost sleepless night, to find we had left Portugal behind and were out on the open sea—though with screeching birds following in our wake. Only two of the other *naus* could be seen but Diogo, who shared our cabin, soon explained that while the *Burgaleza* was sailing as part of a fleet it did not mean it would always be possible to stay close to the other ships. While he said this with regret, no doubt still disappointed that we were not on the *São Thome,* he was responsible, and mindful, of his sister's well-being. His youth and enthusiasm had already endeared him to Dom Francisco's plump and worried-looking wife who, I soon realized, was relieved to have a young man more or less at her beck and call. In any case it was Diogo who smoothed the meeting between Leonor and all those occupying the overcrowded cabin next to ours. Dom Francisco was a soft-spoken man, seemingly overwhelmed not only by his wife and four children, but the 'orphans of the King', some of whom his wife was already suggesting to be of questionable character and therefore a threat to the sensibilities of Isabel, her eldest daughter, a plain girl of around fourteen.

Our first full day at sea soon revealed the reality of life on board the *Burgaleza* and by nightfall we were all too well aware of how grim the voyage would be and of the risks and discomforts that would accompany it. Most of all we understood that the shadow of death would haunt every moment. Indeed Diogo, secure in the optimism of his youth and health, seemed to delight in rattling off a whole series of unhappy statistics. While he laughingly assured us that we would survive and that Leonor would marry her beloved, he nevertheless pointed out that 'seamen get washed overboard, they fall sick, get killed in attacks by pirates—and of course ships are often wrecked and all lives lost.' Leonor, though not the only one to pale, was the one who held up a hand. 'Please Diogo, please stop it. If it is the will of God for us to perish then let it be, But, I beg you, do not tell us of what may not happen.'

♓

Even now I can recall the stench that soon permeated the whole ship. Within a few days sea-sickness had claimed many of us, including Dom Francisco's children and two of the orphans. Water was precious and though several wooden barrels of water had been stored for us, we already knew its taste would become more and more unpalatable and that tiny worms and small bugs would soon appear. The crew, who had the raw ingredients for their meals rationed out to them, were expected to do their own cooking. So too were the passengers, except that they had to provide all they wished to eat. Since there were only two stoves there was considerable jostling and confusion to even get near one—and the crew tended to strong-arm their way to the forefront. Since meals had to be prepared for Leonor, Diogo and myself, and as Dona Maria, Dom Francisco's wife, was already coping with sick children and the orphans there was no alternative but for me and the more capable orphans to do our best. Yet it was dangerous work; the crew had no respect for any woman—perhaps why so few of them ever ventured aboard. Had Diogo not taken his duties seriously and come with us the cooking would have been next to impossible. As it was he was constantly struggling to push back lecherous sailors, occasionally even declaring me his sister to ease off the man reaching for me. It was a far cry from the generous kitchens of both the *quinta* and the convent.

♓

Gradually we came to understand the world that by then enclosed us—and something of those we shared it with. Our captain, Simão Peres De Andrade was of noble birth, appointed by the King, the *Burgaleza's* owner, to protect his interests. While, according to Diogo, Dom João de Castro was a great observer who worked in conjunction with his pilots and kept his own precise log books, he was an exception. Simão Peres De Andrade had little nautical knowledge and, as was customary, delegated such matters to the pilot, a master mariner who kept us safely on course, using experience and constant calculations to seek and confirm our position in the heavens and guide us across even the most turbulent seas. An ill-assorted company of around fifty men and as many ship's boys endured unimaginable hardships, doing dangerous work in all weathers and conditions as they laboured to physically sail the *Burgaleza.* Also on board were men without any navigational skills: a clerk to keep various records, a chaplain, even a barber, an apothecary, carpenters and caulkers to carry out repairs on board, two hundred and fifty soldiers bound for India and, much to Diogo's excitement, a constable who had under him thirty or so gunners, mostly Germans.

♓

Most of the time we stayed near our cabin, our minds overwhelmed with boredom listening as the crew shouted to each other from deck to deck, watching in awe as they clambered up to the crows' nests of the two main masts. Sometimes they would stay there, legs dangling over the side, far above us, in another world. At other times, when the great sails, each marked with the Order of Christ's blood-red cross, came billowing out we could see their tiny figures running nonchalantly along the spars, seemingly unaware that one missed footing would throw them down to the deck, or into the hungry sea, a sea which, Diogo assured us, 'ate people.' There was a fascination in watching the vast sails ballooning out as they filled with wind and propelled us forward. The slightest slack and a strange whipping of canvas would be heard. As it was the *Burgaleza* provided us with a constant symphony of sounds: creaks and groans, shouts, often of sailors cursing profanities or someone howling down in the lower decks, the cranking of chains, the ringing of bells and the regular beating of the drums that announced our progress. And, above all, there was the unceasing sound of the sea slapping against the ship, accompanied by the hissing and gusting of the wind and, often enough, the eerie, even mournful crying of seabirds.

♓

And it was as our true journey began that we began to comprehend the role the sea and the winds and the currents would play in our progress, that they were the elements that would most affect the *Burgaleza.* The relative calm of leaving Lisbon and making our way southwards was over. We were about to venture into an area where one set of currents ended and another begun, exposing us to the threat of unexpected and violent storms.

And, finally, this was when the whispers about Africa began, seeping insidiously into our consciousness though never quite emerging from the shadows. Almost nothing was said that had any real form or substance. Or not until Diogo mentioned the sailor who had informed him that, somewhere far away in the interior, there was a kingdom ruled by a gold-bedecked king who dressed in ornate robes and sat on an ivory throne surrounded by magnificent and aristocratic warriors. Yet was this true? He was speaking of a kingdom no white man had ever seen, whose wealth and mysteries—even if they existed—lay far away from a shore that could not even be seen from our ship. But I wondered, conscious of the deep ache spreading its tentacles around my heart. Were we near a land Balthazar had known? Was this why I could almost hear him telling me of the beautiful royal princess who had fled to the sea with her lover and lived with him in a cave? A princess who, though by then pregnant, was finally accepted back to her kingdom after the king agreed that her unborn child would rule. And how, since she gave birth to a daughter, all kings now descend from their mother's family.

♓

Soon enough, as we came to terms with the reality of life on the *Burgaleza*, I became aware of another passenger, a middle-aged and corpulent man whose eye I once accidently met. Yet though I had immediately lowered my gaze, I was always ill at ease whenever he was nearby. What made matters worse was that though he seemed to sense this, he misinterpreted my reactions and increasingly began to smile at me in a suggestive and unpleasant way. He often appeared when I was going to the kitchen area and, though Diogo was always with me, he sometimes tried to start a conversation. As a result I was surprised when, late one morning he came into our cabin unannounced. Yet, as I drew back into the shadows to watch him unobserved I understood that, despite his unprepossessing exterior, he exuded a certain aura of power. After bowing elaborately before Diogo he introduced himself as Henrique de Sousa and announced that he was both the cousin of the present Governor, Dom Martim Afonso de Sousa, and related to Dom Francisco's wife, a de Sousa by birth and the sister of Dom Martim. It was obviously done to impress us.

At this point Dom Francisco joined us and, still in my corner, I could see from his stiffness that, though polite, he was not happy to see Henrique de Sousa. His further efforts to impress soon provided the information that he had been serving in India for more than twenty years and, since his knowledge was therefore extensive he had come to assure us of his help on arrival in Goa. Although the offer was accepted and followed by some formal phrases about how families must help each other no move was made to detain him and he soon left, a strange silence remaining in his wake.

'No doubt we will hear from him again,' Dom Francisco eventually declared, 'though I doubt any help will be forthcoming unless it gives him some advantage. What strange relatives my wife has. One cannot but assume he has benefited by having a cousin as Governor.'

The immediate benefit to me however was welcome: he ceased his attentions and innuendos, no doubt aware that making unwelcome advances to a servant when he had designs on Dom Francisco's family was unwise.

♓

For once Diogo gave us bad news without his usual smile. He had spoken to our captain, Simão Peres De Andrade, and been somewhat cynically told that there would be no stops before Ilha Moçambique—and to get used to the taste of the water. 'Think of it as a soup,' the captain had sneered, 'and perhaps it'll settle your stomachs.' But he had at least explained why they had to keep going. The fleets, it appeared, were always driven by the need to round the Cabo da Boa Esperança by, at the very latest, early July, in order to reach Moçambique and have enough time to make the inevitable repairs before the last stretch, the crossing to India in early August. Any later and though they might leave Moçambique with the southwesterly monsoon winds there was the very real risk of being caught when the winds reversed their direction.

Before any of us could voice the thought that, surely, at the rate we were going, there was ample time, Diogo was already explaining that we were about to cross the equatorial calms where, in stifling heat and without the slightest breeze, ships were often becalmed for weeks, weeks that could too easily throw all other calculations into chaos.

When Diogo finished all that could be heard was a kind of silence, broken only by the usual sounds of the *Burgaleza*, her constant groaning and the slaps of the waves. It was a moment when we knew real fear, the great fear of something unknown and threatening. I turned and looked at Leonor and what I saw on her face was more eloquent than any words. She was unnaturally still, one hand clasped across her mouth as if to stifle a scream, her face deathly pale. It showed me her desolation, the impact not only of this terrible journey but of leaving a world that had given her peace and tranquillity in order to marry a man she had never met.

It was Diogo who went to her. Diogo, the brother who showed no care for danger, who saw everything as an adventure, gathered his sister into his arms, and held her as she released a torrent of tears, as much for what she had lost as the dangers she still faced, the unknown life that awaited her.

♓

Diogo's news at least meant that we knew what to expect. Yet, though there were soon days—and nights—when we barely moved, our pilots used their skills to seek out even the smallest movement of air and current to keep us moving. But no warning or description could prepare us for the heat. It became hard to even breathe or move; every action drained us, and our clothes were perpetually soaked with sweat. We craved water but could barely bring ourselves to drink it while the food we forced into our mouths was as rotten and foul. Almost everyone felt unwell, their vomiting adding to the terrible conditions and heightening the stench that permeated our cabin and indeed the whole ship.

Then tragedy struck, starting with Dom Francisco falling sick. In the circumstances this was hardly surprising but what shook us all was the speed with which his health deteriorated. By the morning of the second day there were such serious doubts about his survival that the chaplain was called. He was dead within minutes of the Last Rites being administered and, within the hour, his body, wrapped in a sheet, was being slipped over the side, his family so stunned they barely reacted, unable to comprehend let alone face, what would now happen to them.

Other than the shock we realized that we were now confronted by a situation of there being, between our two cabins, only one adult male to help and protect nine women, almost all of whom were unwell. Diogo, aware that the task was beyond his capabilities, asked me, with a twisted smile, if he should perhaps find Henrique de Sosa and request his help. I shook my head. 'As I thought,' he said, 'but how will we manage?'

As it happened the matter was soon dealt with. The chaplain had, of course, told Simão Peres De Andrade of Dom Francisco's death and, unknown to us—and because of the orphans—Dom João de Castro had been informed. At this point the fleet was close together, almost huddled on the limpid sea. We therefore noticed when a small boat was lowered from the *São Thome* and began rowing its way towards us.

'It's the Admiral-*mor* himself!' Diogo exclaimed, pointing to the man with a long dark beard.

We watched as Simão Peres De Andrade welcomed him on board and how, in turn, he introduced him to the man accompanying him. Initially we assumed that Dom João had come to offer his condolences to the flustered and sobbing Dona Maria and her children since he went directly to bow before her, speaking so softly that none of us could catch his words. Diogo stood nearby, his eyes fixed on his hero.

It was soon obvious however that he was making more than a

courtesy call on a bereaved widow. The death of Dom Francisco had deprived the 'orphans of the King' both of a protector and someone to look after them once Goa was reached. As the fleet's admiral Dom João sailed as the representative of the King and was ultimately responsible for the well-being of these orphans. He was therefore, he said, appointing Dom Estévao de Leão to take up these responsibilities—and here, and with a gracious gesture, he requested the man beside him to come forward.

I could feel the tension easing out of Diogo. Dom Estévao de Leão was middle-aged, of short stature and a grave and courtly presence. He bowed before Dona Maria and assured her, in a clipped, precise voice, that he was honoured to be able to assist her and that she need not further concern herself with the safety or well-being of the orphans.

At this moment there was a sense of movement nearby, of people being pushed aside for someone to reach the front of the circle around Dom João and Dom Estévao. It was perhaps not unexpected that the man who emerged was a flustered and obsequious Henrique de Sousa who immediately assured Dom João that he, as the cousin of Dona Maria and—as he might perhaps already know—of Dom Martim Afonso de Sousa, would count it his duty to provide all the support and assistance required for Dom Francisco's grieving family and the orphans.

Dom João stood for a moment before, with an enigmatic smile, he offered his profound thanks to Henrique de Sousa but professed himself sadly unable to avail of such generosity since the role of protector had already been accepted by Dom Estévao. The mistake we all made was to believe that Henrique de Sousa's attempts to infiltrate Dona Maria's life had again failed.

Meanwhile Dom João took his leave of Dona Maria, and indeed of Dom Estévao who was to remain on board. It was as he turned to make his way back to the waiting boat that he caught sight of Diogo and came forward to shake his hand. 'I trust all is well with you and your sister?' he enquired. Diogo spluttered and nodded his head, happy to have been so noticed, doubly so when Dom João added that he looked forward to having us as his guests when, God willing, we reached Goa.

♓

It later became obvious that Henrique de Sousa had bided his time, waiting until Diogo and I, and the healthy orphans, had gone to make our daily, and largely futile, attempt at producing a passably edible meal. Leonor was resting and Dom Estévao had gone to see our captain—whose cabin he now shared. How long, we afterwards wondered, had Henrique de Sousa watched and waited to seize his moment?

He did so with deadly effect. When we returned we found him ensconced in Dona Maria's cabin, seated—and making no show of rising—with a visibly proprietary air. We stood confused as the orphans laid out our unappetising meal; it was somehow obvious that something had been agreed between Henrique de Sousa and Dona Maria and it was as we noticed the simpering look on the face of Isabel, her eldest child, that an unthinkable thought began forming. At that moment Dom Estévao entered—and stopped in his tracks at the sight of the man seated before him—a reaction which finally propelled him to his feet.

Henrique de Sousa wasted no time, the urge to display his satisfaction and success, his moment of triumph was too great for any delay.

'I have,' he said, 'wonderful news: my offer of marriage to Isabel de Mariz has been accepted. I am the happiest man alive.'

♓

The wedding took place the following morning. The chaplain, so recently called to bury Isabel's father, now came to unite his daughter in marriage with someone he had actively disliked. Yet, in truth, it was possible to see the advantages of this marriage: Isabel would be safe and provided for, and so would her family; they would not be alone in Goa once Dom Estévao's responsibilities of settling the orphans were over. What was less certain was whether Henrique de Sousa had cast his mind over the benefits to his new wife or, as we all suspected, had merely weighed up those he would receive. Isabel, however, seemed well-pleased with herself, apparently delighted at suddenly becoming the centre of attention and able to flaunt a husband. But her wedding cannot have been anything she had dreamed of: there was no hope of a feast, of wine and merry-making and dancing. Leonor was ready to lend one of the dresses she was bringing for her own wedding but, due to Isabel's plumpness, nothing would fit her. Meanwhile, between bouts of sickness, her mother fluctuated from weeping for her husband and trying to take joy in so seamlessly marrying off her daughter. At one moment she became so distraught that she stumbled, almost fainting even as her older son tried to support her. Yet although Leonor and I instinctively moved to help she managed to seat herself, somewhat clumsily, on a chair. It was then, as she clasped her ample stomach that we gasped in shock realizing the true source of her sickness: Dona Maria was with child.

One immediate benefit to Henrique de Sousa was that he could move into his new wife's cabin which, however overcrowded, was undoubtedly an improvement on his existing arrangements. It was Diogo who made it clear, by standing in our doorway, that he did not, as he initially appeared to assume, have free access to our cabin. As a result we saw little of Dom Estévao de Leão beyond the few daily pleasantries we exchanged whenever he came and went—and we soon observed that his visits were increasingly only made in accordance with his sense of fulfilling his duty.

♓

Throughout our long voyage a day seldom dawned without a reminder of the thin line between life and death. The possibility of disaster—and death—was a constant we had to live with and accept, knowing that the seas we sailed on were peopled with the ghosts of drowned men and scattered with the wrecks of lost ships. But the place most feared by all seamen, and a fear we were soon party to, was the Cabo da Boa Esperança. Rough seas, high waves, strong adverse winds, a rocky coast and violent thunder storms had made rounding the Cape a dangerous and fearful business. As a result everyone, especially our small group of passengers, became punctilious in their devotions, praying not only to our Saviour and our Lady for protection but to St Elmo, regarded by all seamen as their patron saint. The closer we came to the Cape the more frequently this saint appeared in everyone's prayers whilst many seamen could be seen fingering an amulet bearing his image, or recalling the numerous occasions he had appeared to save drowning men, even in the most violent of storms.

We were right to pray and be frightened for, as June slipped into July, the sea began swelling up, its waves growing in size and making our ship, so familiar to us all by then, suddenly seem as insubstantial as a toy boat. It became dangerous to go on deck but, at times, we could look out and see how hard the seamen were straining to keep us on course. But worse was to come. Soon enough we felt the full brunt of the wind howling down at us, refusing us entry to the seas that lay ahead. And all the while the intensity of the wind kept growing, roaring up into a violent rage, keeping us inside our cramped quarters, throwing us from side to side. No one spoke, and had they done so, their voices would not have been heard. Worse still were the sounds around us, those of the wind's howling fury and the continuous cacophony, the great shuddering, creaking groans that came from deep within the *Burgaleza* as she bravely fought the elements, struggling to keep afloat, to make her way through waves that reared up in huge walls of water, only to smash down again to pitch and toss and roll. Every moment felt like our last, that we had no hope of survival. But Nature's fury had not even begun, and when it did, it was without warning: a searing crack of thunder suddenly breaking out from the angry skies, heralding the flashing blaze of light that then snaked down to the turbulent sea, a curtain raiser for the next act: a thunderstorm of pure and unremitting terror.

There is no way of knowing how long this storm lasted but as soon as it began not one of us expected to survive. No ship could possibly weather the terrible pounding violence of the sea and the howling winds. That the *Burgaleza* would break apart and we would drown was inevitable and yet we were so exhausted, so drained, so spent and so without hope that finally even fear left us. What little energy we could still summon we reserved for keeping in one place, trying to prevent ourselves from being thrown from one side of the cabin to the other and back again. Leonor, Dona Maria—who by some miracle still carried her unborn child—her children and the orphans, and even Henrique de Sousa, were continually being violently seasick; only Diogo and I escaped unscathed for since Dom Estévao was never seen, we assumed he too was unwell. The stench was dreadful and I longed to escape and breathe fresh air but, for safety's sake, the cabin door was kept tightly closed.

Somehow two, or maybe three or four days and nights passed, each dawn igniting the small hope that the storm would abate—a hope that was instantly dashed. Then, sometime during the night of the third or perhaps the fourth day, and as I lay unable to sleep, I sensed that something had changed. Perhaps the thunder was less loud, the lightning less frequent or maybe the wind had dropped a fraction? Hope surged within me, reborn as I understood how it must have been on the Ark when the waters began to recede.

An hour later it was a certainty, the fierce intensity of the storm was lessening, the thunder was now hardly heard. Then, though lightning continued to flash, the rain dropped to a drizzle and the waves began to subside. Though I knew I would be drenched I heaved open the cabin door, desperate to feel fresh air and space.

Our ship was, of course, still battling the elements and I could do no more than look around me. Had I made a mistake in assuming the worst was over, was this, perhaps just the lull before yet another storm? I looked up at the still dark sky, perhaps hoping to see some sign that fairer weather lay ahead. And so it was that my prayers were answered for there, on the tips of the topsail's upper mast, the yardarm of the spar and on all the masts and shrouds and stays of our brave ship was a flickering light. A divine sigh that we were in God's hands. I stood watching, moved and full of wonder at its beauty, seeing how the mystery and promise of this light remained steadfast. Although once or twice, when lightning flashed, it disappeared, it instantly returned as soon as the lightning died away. It had an extraordinary beauty, a silvery glow that resembled moonlight and, despite the darkness of the sky and the still drizzling rain, it was clear to the naked eye. I knew I was soaked and that the *Burgaleza* had not ceased being buffeted by waves but I could not draw my eyes away from the light all seamen call the Holy Spirit.

Was this the first time I asked who God was? Or did I just let being aware of the divine flutter through my mind? Who had saved us? Who had given us this sign? And why was I crying? Why was my whole being filling up with emotions I could not name? I looked round to see if anyone stood near me. There was no one, except of course, in the distance, the over-worked and exhausted seamen. And I saw them waving at each other, pointing up to the light. I could feel the energy powering its way through them.

Lucas.

From nowhere he came, rising out of the deep darkness of my mind. Smiling. Standing beside me. Whispering to me, telling me tales of Zeeland and the ancient goddess Nehalaennia and her healing light. The Mother whose realm is the sea and the estuary and who protects and comforts and stills the fear of death in deep waters. Whose light fluttered on the masts? Cannot the divine be everywhere and under many names? I turned to ask him. But I was alone.

And not alone. Not anymore.

♓

It was a few days later, when we began noticeably heading north that I risked going to stand by the side of the deck. Dawn had just broken and layers of mist were hanging over the surface of the still choppy and unsettled sea. At first I looked eastwards, aware of the fitfulness of the rising sun, wondering if there was any hope of ever reaching India. Then I turned towards the west and to my surprise saw that Africa had reappeared, looming out of the mists, as if conjured up by some invisible power to remind us that we were passing a land of impenetrable mystery. I strained my eyes but could do no more than catch glimpses of deserted and forbidding shores from which rose treacherous cliffs and, beyond them, the soaring bulk of mountains wrapped in jungles. Though their beauty was discernible it was a beauty laced with unspoken threats. Diogo's relentless stoking of our fears, his all too graphic descriptions of ships broken by storms that plunged drowning men into a hungry sea made it impossible for me to forget that our chances of survival were slim, tipped heavily in favour of us hitting hidden rocks and being sucked down beneath the pounding waves.

It's still Africa, I thought, still an enigma and unknown, the only difference being that we were now so much further away from Balthazar's Africa. Surely what was out there, in the far jungles and mountains would have been as strange and impenetrable to him as they might now be to me? Yet, as the waves rolled away towards the shore, seemingly pushed aside by the *Burgaleza* as she cut through the water, I wondered just how many long days of travelling it would take to reach his home. And where was Balthazar right now and how was it possible that not knowing could hurt so much? Instinctively I wrapped my arms around myself, almost feeling his breath against my ear as I closed my eyes and readied myself for the inner journey.

'You seem lost in thought. And very far away from us all. From here.'

I swung round and, to my surprise, saw Dom Estévao standing there, looking at me. I backed away, moving just slightly along the side of the ship, aware that he had noticed my apprehension.

'Forgive me, I did not mean to frighten you,' he said, raising a hand.

There was a slight pause, a hesitation which made it seem he was uncertain about his reasons for speaking to me, even as his deepening frown suggested a caution, that he wanted to find the right words.

'I feel I must explain,' he said. 'For some time I have had the feeling that you are in some way known to me.'

I looked at him but said nothing for how could it be? I had never seen him until just after Dom Francisco's death, when Dom João de Castro had assigned him to look after the orphans. Though we had all warmed to him our hope of getting to know him had been dashed by Henrique de Sousa's marriage to Isabel and his occupation of her family's cabin.

He shrugged his shoulders, as if he too recognized the incongruity of his statement.

'Just now, just a few minutes back, as I was watching you, I knew I was right, or at least partially so. We have not met before. But I know who you are.'

My eyes widened. What he said made no sense. And yet I found I had started to sweat as if, subconsciously, I knew something of what might follow.

'It is because of how you stand, how you turn, it is in your stillness…' he began. And then stopped.

'I am, I was, a friend of Lucas van Domburg's.'

I felt the blood draining away. My body slumped and, for a moment, I thought I would faint. Instead I angled my body away from him, clasping the *Burgaleza's* sides as my mind clamped down in denial. *How could it be?*

'I last saw him in Évora, where I had gone on matters of some importance,' he began again. 'His mood was very different from the previous occasion that we'd met. This time he was full of energy and purpose. It was as if he had suddenly found something that could, in a way, save him. At one time he was a very bitter man. But not in Évora. He had changed—or rather he had become the man I originally knew. There was an openness about him, a generosity. He was as close to being happy as any man can be.'

I heard, I knew, but I could not absorb. How could this man know Lucas? And why had he come to speak to me about him?

'Soon enough I knew the source of his energy. He showed me sketches, and even some roughly coloured drawings. They were, of course, all of a young girl. Of you.'

I backed further away.

'To be very truthful I might not have guessed if young Diogo had not told me that his sister had been in a convent, the Convento Nossa Senhora da Boa Fé, the very same convent where Lucas had gone to paint. For a time I never thought beyond this being anything except an extraordinary coincidence. Then, very gradually, my memories of those sketches came back to me and I began wondering about the girl and who she was, and what might have happened to her. Even so I barely noticed you until, just after the storm, I saw you standing in the doorway. I saw how you loved the air and that it appeared to give you a sense of freedom. And then, quite suddenly, you turned round and in your grace and movement I saw what Lucas had seen and instinctively knew who you were. But, well…,' he paused, hesitating for just a moment, 'I said nothing. I have never talked of knowing Lucas to anyone. It was only when you gazed up at the heavens and at the lights on the masts that something, once again, brought back my memories of him.'

'Nehalaennia…' I whispered.

This time he was the one to show surprise, a surprise which immediately gave way to a smile, though one laced with sadness.

'So I am right?'

I barely nodded my head but it was enough.

This time, as I looked at Dom Estévao, I saw that his eyes, though kind, had a guarded quality about them. Why, I wondered, was he going to India? Though no one, as far as I knew, was sailing with him I had assumed that he was one of the fleet's investors.

Then he spoke again. 'These are dangerous times for some of us. Lucas paid both for his beliefs and for thinking he was safe. I do not wish to make the same mistake.'

'I don't understand. What beliefs?' The words were out of my mouth too soon.

I felt myself being examined. Not only examined but weighed up, this put against that, balanced, and a tally made. For a brief moment it reminded me of the Abadessa deciding whether or not I should take Lucas his lunch. Was everything now coming back to Lucas?

'I am Portuguese,' he said, 'Of course I am. I have always lived here; *there* I suppose I should learn to say. But now, since I have begun to speak, it is only fair that I continue.'

♓

In the end what he told me was not a long-drawn out tale. And yet it changed everything. His family had always lived in Lisbon and were involved in various business activities and reasonably well-off. As a child he became aware of his father's close friendship with a man called Dom Gabril Espírito Santo, a well-known physician who, though he did not treat the King, was popular with many of his courtiers. Life was good for them all it seemed. But the shadows, which Dom Estévao said had always existed, became deeper and darker when King João died in 1494. Manuel, the new king, was challenged by others, all of them claiming a greater right to the throne. In order to secure and validate his position he did what many Portuguese kings had done before him: he sought a royal Spanish bride. But securing his throne came at a price for although the Infanta, Isabella of Aragon, agreed to marry him, she, and her parents, Ferdinand of Aragon and Isabella of Castile, set a condition: all Jews were to be expelled from Portugal—and many of them were those who had, just five years earlier, been forced out of Spain. To comply with their demand Manuel was compelled to withdraw the freedom he had granted them on becoming king. This was followed, just five days after the signing of his marriage contract on 30th of November 1496, by a decree being issued stating that they must leave by the following October.

On the first day of Passover in March 1497—less than six months after the King's wedding and six months before the Jews were to leave—orders were issued that they should assemble in Lisbon with their children. There they soon discovered that their young sons and daughters were to be taken from them and given to Catholic families to be brought up as Christians. This news brought a howling surge of anger and terrible despair, resulting in chaos and hysteria as screaming children were seized from their parents, some of whom even hung onto them long enough to kill them—and then themselves—while others, defeated and in shock, handed their children over and some, to keep their families intact, agreed to be baptised.

The irony was that the Infanta whose demands had caused these tragedies died in childbirth a few months later and her infant son was dead before he was two years old. Yet by then the second act of the tragedy had taken place—a further extension of Manuel's attempts to keep the Jews in Portugal since he was deeply conscious of the contributions they had made to society, trade and culture. Therefore, to make it almost impossible for them to leave, a further order declared that they could only sail on certain ships. As a result when the Jews again gathered in Lisbon they found themselves assaulted on all sides by rough soldiers and sermonizing priests, all attempting to convert or forcibly baptise them, so that by making them Christians they could be allowed to stay.

♓

When Dom Estévao got this far he suddenly stopped. 'I fear,' he said, 'that I may have confused you, filling you with tales of a long drawn-out tragedy—and one which, nine years later, would, for the third time, place Lisbon at the centre of unimaginable terror: the brutal massacre of around five thousand Jews.

'However there is now not that much left to tell, but it is the hardest for those involved are no longer anonymous and unknown. You will recall me saying that my father had a friend, a noted physician called Dom Gabril Espírito Santo? What I did not tell you was that he was Jewish—and a cultured man of great learning. I was about four or five when I first became consciously aware of him coming regularly to our house and sitting with my father and discussing all manner of subjects: medicine, astronomy, music, calligraphy, painting. At first they also laughed a lot but, with hindsight, I now realize that this eventually not only became a rarity but that they began to sit much closer together—and I can still recall the afternoon when I startled them by dropping something and how they both jumped and looked round with expressions I understood to be of naked fear.

'And, very clearly, I remember how a few days later, and just as Dom Gabril was leaving our house, he turned to my father and that, as they stretched out their hands, they both suddenly moved closer and embraced each other. And neither of them were demonstrative men. That evening, and for the next few days, my father's expression was one of great strain and my mother warned me to stay quiet. Dom Gabril never came to the house again and my father never mentioned him again. Somehow—at least this is what I later supposed—he had managed to leave Portugal; perhaps my father had helped him. I just don't know.

'Twenty years passed. My father died and, soon after, my mother. By then I was married and settled into the business, doing well by investing in the India run, trading the cargo brought back to various cities in Europe—even as I watched and saw how life changes, how fear grips and suspicion grows.

'But then, and when I was over forty my wife died. I decided to put the business in the capable hands of my nephew—I have no children and he will eventually inherit everything anyway. Our biggest market was in the Low Countries and it had occurred to me that if I went there and understood their ways I would know more about them and we could increase our profits.

'A fateful decision,' Dom Estévao said. For a moment it appeared that he was undecided about whether or not to continue, that however much, or little, he still had to tell would be hard on him.

'Bear with me. I am nearly done,' he said, his eyes meeting mine and revealing the strain he was under.

'Soon after I arrived in Amsterdam I fell ill. A doctor was called, an old white-haired man and, although thirty years had passed, I recognized him at once: Dom Gabril Espírito Santo. For a moment I was speechless—something he initially attributed to my fever for while he had merely aged, the small boy he had last seen so many years ago had become a middle-aged man. Yet tears coursed down his lined cheeks when I told him who I was. I was soon well again, and being taken to meet his family. He had married but though he had a son I did not immediately meet him.'

It was here that Dom Estévao paused. The muscles in his face were pulled tight and, somewhere in the recesses of my mind, I knew that sooner or later he would say something that would profoundly affect me. I also knew that much of what he was talking about were things he had long ago tried to forget.

'At that time, though many merchants and traders from Portugal had settled in Amsterdam they were all Christians. Yet since either their parents or grandparents had been Jewish—and most had left when the Inquisition was established—they were always marked as being New Christians, converted Jews who were constantly suspected of secretly practising the old faith. And, it must be said, with considerable justification.

'Dom Gabril had been traumatized by leaving Lisbon but his good fortune was to have met a woman from Antwerp, also of Jewish blood but perhaps more settled into Christian ways and whose father, I suspect, was from an old Flemish Christian family. Somehow they had migrated to Zeeland.'

And then it came, quietly but with deadly effect.

'I will tell you now: Dom Gabril Espírito Santo's son was Lucas van Domburg.'

All I could do was clutch the side of the ship and let waves of different emotions ripple through me. Suddenly, and from nowhere, too many reactions struggled for recognition, too many knots demanded to be unpicked and too many facts screamed to be faced. And yet my only clear and discernible thought was the irrational observation: *so that is why his Portuguese was so fluent but with an accent.*

I looked at Dom Estévao, blind but seeing. I had so many questions. I had none. My whole being was raw and bleeding.

'Of course it wasn't long before we met,' he continued, as if it was now necessary to have done with it all, before his energy was exhausted, 'I was at his father's house and he came in from a storm, soaked through, with water streaming off him, laughing and exuding a love of life I'd never seen before, or since. There were fifteen years between us and—apparently—we had little in common. But we were soon friends. I was well aware of my life's perpetual precision and occasionally regretted my lack of adventure, of being so cautious. Lucas was the exact opposite. His dream and passion was to paint. He had no interest in medicine, none in being a doctor or even a merchant except, he said, that merchants travel. He was an enquiring man; he made me see things, feel them. I listened to him. Remarkably, he listened to me. I would say that my father was a cultured man—Dom Gabril certainly was—yet I was not, at least not in the same way. Perhaps the dark shadows were by then too close, perhaps I didn't dare.

'I hardly know how to continue other than to tell you that I stayed on longer than I'd planned. Lucas and I used to sit together in a way that reminded me of my father and his father. And I began to see the breadth of his interests and vision. And, soon enough, I began to see the dangers—though he brushed them aside. At the time he was still apprenticed to an Amsterdam painter, later he was to move to Haarlem. "I'm safe here," he said. "I know the forbidden subjects. Naturally it would be different in Spain or Portugal." Yes, he knew then, even then I should say.

'Finally I left, but not before we had made arrangements to remain in touch. Careful arrangements, through my agents, men I could trust. In this way I later travelled to meet him in Siena and later still in Toledo. And I saw that in between something had happened. He was less open, somewhat prone to sarcasm, even bitter. It distressed me and I feared for him. I had no idea that he was in Portugal until, by chance, I met him in Évora—the last place I would have expected to see him. Actually he was the one who saw me—something I will always thank God for since we would otherwise have never met again.

'He had been in Portugal for just under a year and had already begun making his preparations for the work at the convent…'

He stopped abruptly, his features suddenly old and gaunt.

'The worst has been having no one to speak to about him. Yet,' and I saw the bleakest of smiles, 'because of him I can speak to you. And about him, yes. Of course. But more because I can express my gratitude for what you gave him. I was never able to see his work in the convent. And I never will. What happened to him alerted me.'

I frowned. Despite what he had just said it was as if something was being left out, avoided and kept unspoken. Was it possible that he somehow knew what I had done, the role I had played, that I had betrayed Lucas?

'He thought he was safe, that they knew nothing of his Jewish ancestry, that the name he had taken masked everything. But, somewhere, somehow, careless words had reached their ears. His openness and respect for the universality of the divine, the sacred, his love of beauty, of learning. Perhaps it happened in Spain; perhaps it was there that he began to feel the oppression, to know what it is like to feel forever unsafe. He once mentioned that he sometimes felt watched in Évora. Yet when I begged him to be careful he dismissed my fears. "What," he had said—and with a laugh, "could be safer than painting in a convent?" A later rumour—and how are such things ever really known?—whispered of Lucas being in Évora one evening and knowing he was being followed and so beginning to realize that he was suspected by the Holy Office, that they considered him a crypto-Jew, a *converso* still secretly following Jewish ways. All this was carried by insubstantial whispers, and I heard it much later. I had to be careful with my enquiries, showing interest in a man found guilty and punished by the Inquisition is not advisable…'

Suddenly my whole world lurched and shifted and, even as Dom Estévao was carefully choosing his words, a great howl began careening through my mind, shouting and spitting out words, ideas and possibilities. Was I really grasping what Dom Estévao appeared to be saying: that Lucas was arrested and executed because of the *Inquisition*, that *they* were anyway watching him, that *they* were anyway suspicious of him, that my spiteful words had therefore had nothing to do with it?

'I now believe,' Dom Estévao continued, by then almost whispering, 'that some sense of wanting to finish the convent work stopped him from leaving at once. A delay that, even though he did finally flee, proved fatal. They were waiting for him and he was arrested. Of course there was no public announcement of what his crimes might have been but since all those who died on that terrible day were condemned as crypto-Jews there is probably no need for further speculation.'

I looked out across the sea and, though the mist had lifted, I knew in my heart that it had merely shifted and was now wrapping itself around my thoughts.

My question came of its own volition: 'So no one betrayed him?'

'No; or rather not in the way that you mean. And certainly not by anyone in the convent.'

There are no words to describe the weight that lifted from my heart, or the sadness that took its place.

♓

As we sailed up towards Moçambique and the halt to overhaul and re-provision the fleet my thoughts constantly returned to all that Dom Estévao had told me. Whether I went about my work and helped Leonor or looked out towards Africa or eastwards across the sea made no difference since all I saw was Lucas either drawing, painting or preparing colours—and, just once, adjusting the fold of a gown—while, even as the wind snapped and cracked in the sails, and the working seamen shouted, all I heard was the sound of his voice. Inevitably I recalled the last time I saw him and how he had held my face in both hands and gently kissed my forehead. Then, one morning, there was, for no discernible reason, a change and I found my thoughts had shifted to Balthazar, and how he moved and held himself, his withdrawn and concealing stillness. For a while my exhaustion was such that I could do no more than just let my thoughts drift in and out of my consciousness as they wished until, very gently, almost kindly, a moment came when though my inner eye continued to see Balthazar, it was Lucas who whispered in my ear. It was as if they had become one and the same, that together they were with me, protecting me. And then, still without any conscious effort, I heard Lucas telling me again of the lover who had knocked at the door of the Beloved and how the Beloved had asked 'Who is there?' and that when the man had answered 'It is I' the reply had been 'This house will not hold Me and thee.' The lover, Lucas now told me again, had then left to weep and pray in solitude until, many long seasons later, he returned and knocked again. And again the Voice had asked, 'Who is there?' 'It is Thou' was the reply and the door immediately opened and the lover and the Beloved stood face to face.

Did I then understand? I cannot say for it was not a question I ever asked. It is more accurate to say that I wept—and as true to add that the cause of those tears was new. The pain did not disappear, the longing and regret did not vanish; it was more that something else joined them, something that could hold and sustain me. I could not explain or define it, and did not seek to do so; but it was there. And it stayed; and was constant.

♓

By then the *Burgaleza* was well away from the ship-devouring seas of the Cape and approaching the entrance to the Moçambique Channel, taking the inner route. We knew that though she would be set to take a course through the channel's centre—in order to benefit from a less vicious wind—there was a very real danger of the pilot miscalculating and bringing us dangerously close to the coast where the winds could, almost wantonly, change both direction and force to become whirlwinds, throwing ships against the rocks, to break up as easily as eggs are cracked.

♓

In many ways the voyage up Africa's eastern coast was as frightening as the storm that nearly engulfed us when rounding the Cabo da Boa Esperança. There were often moments when the *Burgaleza* shuddered and groaned so deeply that she seemed about to break apart. A sudden high wave, a change of wind, shouts from the sailors, all these would, at times, bring us to the point of believing we were truly doomed. But then, and very gradually, it became apparent that there was a shift within the *Burgaleza*, a lifting of spirits, of laughter being occasionally heard. It was as if, deep within us, we suddenly, and instinctively, sensed that we were nearing Ilha Moçambique and that the worst was behind us. It was also when we began to hope that we might soon see the rest of the fleet and reassure ourselves that they too had safely rounded the Cape.

Lack of sleep was by then something we silently endured, taking for granted that, at best, we could only ever snatch moments of occasional half-sleep, that even then it was merely a time for demons to invade our dreams. Yet it was on one such night, as everyone fitfully tossed and turned and I lay wishing it was safe to sleep on the deck that I heard a shout. At first it seemed to be part of the ship's continuous cacophony of sounds. But then Diogo sat up, and then Leonor. Then, even as we wondered what was happening, another shout was heard and Diogo was gone.

We crowded around the door, peering out. The moon was no more than a slim crescent—which meant that we immediately saw why the men were shouting: out on the otherwise dark horizon, were blazing fires, seemingly burning on the ocean itself. Perhaps this was another of the terrors we would have to face, that we must now sail through fire and into hell? Had our hopes and instincts been so misplaced I wondered? Finally, just as despair was engulfing us Diogo returned, almost out of breath.

'Premeira Ilhas!' he shouted as if that was sufficient explanation, before stumbling excitedly over his words to tell us that they were a small group of low-lying islands. Diogo went on to further describe the islands but I hardly heard him, my whole being was fixed on the blaze of light glowing out towards the east. In the darkness that surrounded us it was truly a beacon, its flames soaring into the night sky. Was this not a sign that there was light ahead that, somehow, we would soon be safe? How quickly a mood can change.

The *Burgaleza* sailed cautiously onwards as we all huddled together, watching the fires growing closer, anxious to know what they would eventually reveal. Yet in the end it was what we heard that brought relief: the banging of drums and shouts, the shouts of sailors, Portuguese sailors, calling to us, followed, moments later, by the eerie, shifting silhouette of a ship appearing, moving like a ghost against the backdrop of the soaring flames. Then, just as we suddenly caught sight of the small figures running and waving at us, there was a great roar of voices from within the *Burgaleza*: 'The *São Pedro*! It's the *São Pedro*!' Within minutes we were close enough for everyone to see that it *was* the *São Pedro* and that she was already, very slowly, beginning to move, edging away and freeing herself from a mooring still concealed by the darkness surrounding the fires.

'They must have been waiting for us, to guide us safely onwards.' It was Dom Estévao who spoke, his observation obviously shared by our pilot who was already bringing the *Burgaleza* back on course, slipping us past the now dimming fires. 'It seems we may be the last of our fleet to have come through safely and that, in answer to all our prayers, the others should now be safe in Moçambique.'

♓

Long before daylight crept over the sea the *Burgaleza* had become a hive of frenzied activity, a sure sign that we were about to enter the bay that enclosed and protected our destination: the Ilha Moçambique. And, even as we began moving slowly forward, we saw small boats were already rowing out towards us: the pilots who would guide us to a safe berth. Diogo, apparently undaunted by an imminent lack of catastrophes at sea, was happily listing the dangers a ship could encounter when entering a harbour, telling us that, whatever we might suppose, the entire manoeuvre was laced with the need for extreme caution.

But, by late afternoon, at the time of Vespers—and though finding it strange to be on land again, to no longer feel the rolling sway of a deck beneath our feet—we were stumbling towards a small chapel perched at the very edge of the island. Inside we found ourselves surrounded and enveloped by the comfort of the familiar; the last remnants of the day's light almost gone yet the darkness held at bay by flickering oil lamps. For a moment all that suspended the sense of being in Portugal was the dull but unremitting sound outside, the relentlessly pounding waves. We crowded before the simple image of Nossa Senhora do Baluarte, the Lady of the Ramparts, like moths to a flame, suddenly overwhelmed with emotion and relief: the whole fleet *had* arrived safely. We all knew this was a true miracle, that without Our Lady's compassion, Her blessings and protection we could never have been brought safely across the seas and through the storms. Standing beside Leonor, and with Diogo just behind us, I caught the glisten of tears making their way down her bowed and haggard face. I sensed both her relief at having reached Moçambique and the nourishment she found in the words of the *São Thome*'s chaplain and that they took her, however briefly, to a world she loved and had once expected to sustain her.

♓

In the three weeks that followed, we sought to recoup our health, to garner what strength and energy we could in time for the final stretch of our voyage. Leonor, Diogo and I had fared better than most, the relative isolation of our cabin having perhaps protected us from the diseases that afflicted almost everyone who travelled in the lower decks. Although Henrique de Sousa seemed to have flourished, the family he had married into looked weak and sickly while Dona Maria, his mother-in-law, was gaunt and worn, burdened by now being more obviously pregnant in circumstances no woman could envy. The many sick seamen, along with the seriously unwell passengers were taken to the island's small and overcrowded hospital. Every day there were deaths caused as much by sheer exhaustion and despair as fevers and tremors, sores and infestations of lice. Yet beyond the most rudimentary care there was little that could be done since almost no medicines were available. Dom João de Castro, who was constantly on the move, checking the *naus*, his men and their progress, overseeing, advising and encouraging, also came to the hospital and made a list of the basic necessities so they could be sent from India. He also, having assessed the situation, sent his two young sons to the hospital, with orders that they were to help with the nursing. Diogo longed to go too but, since this would have left Leonor alone with me, he dutifully, but fretfully, stayed back.

♓

Even now, when so many memories have faded, I recognize how little I ever knew about life on Ilha Moçambique other than that the fleet's arrival doubled the population. What I do recall, and clearly, is an intangible sense of something that was ultimately indefinable: a small taste of the world Balthazar had known. Of course, by then I knew that to reach his land would take many months and bring me to somewhere very different, but what I saw in Moçambique was a melting pot of many Africas, a place where wealthy merchants came to trade, where cultures met and vastly different people connected. There were, in addition to the Swahili people of the region, not only Africans from distant port cities but traders from the depths of the interior as well as men they called Parsees from India and the Arabic-speaking Muslims who claimed their forebears came from Persia. Although Portugal had been a presence on the small island for almost fifty years it had not erased this atmosphere, indeed in many ways the Portuguese had merely added to it. New buildings had a Portuguese look but they did not dominate, there was still a village of Muslims and though the ruling families no longer lived on the island their presence was strong.

One morning Dom Estévao appeared and, after giving us his precise greetings, informed us that since Henrique de Sousa was with Isabel's family he was, at least for the day, a free man. A smile hovered between us all before he suggested that, accompanied by Diogo, we might take a stroll and see something of the island. Even Leonor was overjoyed at the prospect of fresh air and we were soon setting out. We went first to Nossa Senhora do Baluarte to offer our prayers and this time I clearly saw how it affected Leonor, the calmness she radiated as she attended to her devotions. The sun had already slanted its way in through the cross-shaped openings, giving the otherwise plain interior a luminous quality and heightening its aura of serenity—despite the waves still beating against the rocks. Diogo, as expected, was perfunctory with his prayers but I was surprised when Dom Estévao did little more than stand quietly with his head lowered. Then, perhaps because he reminded me of Lucas, I remembered how he had poured his feelings for the divine into his paintings, and knew such men make no show of praying—and lowered my own head, remorsefully conscious of my shortcomings.

From the chapel we went to see the men working on the *naus*, curious to discover how the *Burgaleza* was faring. While we knew how battered she had been it deeply shocked us to see how pitiful she looked, how much had been stripped off her and how many men were busily hammering away at her hull and, as Diogo had explained, how precariously she was balanced in the water, one miscalculation and our *Burgaleza* would sink. We shivered and fell silent, wondering how we had survived. Then, quite suddenly, our mood was sharply broken by shouts and drums and horns and we saw that boats were approaching from the mainland. The drums were being beaten to announce that the Sheikh—whom some called the Sultan—was arriving with a large entourage, almost certainly to see Dom João de Castro according to Dom Estévao. We watched in fascination as another world came steadily closer: three or four boats, each one carrying several richly dressed men—all magnificent but paling before the Sheikh. He was a tall man, wearing an open robe of velvet over a garment of fine white cotton around which shone a girdle of gold and precious stones. A multi-coloured turban interwoven with gold threads was wrapped around his head and a parasol of velvet, trimmed with yet more gold, shielded his proud, dark face. Was this, I wondered, how Balthazar had once looked?

♓

Finally, in early August, and four days after the full moon, our fleet, minus the *Santo Espírito*, which was forced to stay back for extensive repairs, we once again set sail. This time our mood was very different for, though the memories of leaving Lisbon so many months ago were still clear in all our minds, we also knew that the hardships we had encountered were well behind us. We therefore boarded the *Burgaleza*—refurbished but still far from restored—with a sense of relief and anticipation, anxious to be on our way, to be finally nearing our destination. No one appeared to concern themselves with what might happen once we arrived in Goa or stop to consider the course our lives might then take. Even Leonor, on the one occasion she briefly mentioned Goa, never displayed any apprehension about finally meeting the man she was to marry. Later it occurred to me this was deliberate since the only time I began to wonder what effect her marriage would have on my life I immediately veered away from all conjecture, realizing, as perhaps Leonor had done, that I would be powerless to change what lay in store. The difference was that when I saw Leonor praying I instinctively understood that faith and prayer gave her both solace and a refuge, pushing away the unknown, perhaps even protecting her from it.

♓

The voyage was uneventful and throughout its duration the other *naus* were generally visible—giving Diogo no chance to enumerate potential disasters—or at least not until the morning, a few days before sighting the Indian coastline, when he bounded in to announce 'something terrible'. A seaman, he declared, had told him how the seas ahead swarmed with masses of hissing snakes and that on no account should we go near the side of the *Burgaleza* since they would leap up, seize us with their poisonous fangs and pull us overboard—and devour us. We all shivered in fear; Leonor even screamed and wanted to immediately lock our cabin and stay inside until the time came to disembark. Luckily Dom Estévao had arrived just behind Diogo and, having heard his announcement, held up a restraining hand.

'Young Diogo,' he said with a smile, 'I fear you are frightening us all unnecessarily. Admittedly I too have heard such rumours but they are no more than one of the many tall tales told by sailors. A careful examination of the truth would, I am certain, reveal these snakes to be swarming fish, or maybe even sea eels.

In any case let me assure you that whatever the explanation, whether snakes, eels or fish, none of them could ever jump high enough to seize any of us, not would they even attempt such an impossible feat.'

We all smiled nervously while Dom Estévao, seeing that Diogo's reaction was laced with a certain sheepishness, quickly continued so as to leave his self-esteem intact.

'I have come at this time,' he said, 'because in a day or so we will reach our destination and I fear it may be hard for any of us to meet and talk once we have disembarked. I will have to settle the orphans before attending to my own future. And you,' he swept a hand around our cabin, 'you will have your own arrangements to make. I trust that we will meet but,' and here he shrugged, 'perhaps we will soon be scattered like the wind and never meet again.'

It was as if a sword had suddenly been plunged into my heart. I felt that a part, and an important and tangible part, of Lucas was about to leave me, was being cut away.

'Will you...' I hesitated, aware that no one knew I had ever had any conversation with Dom Estévao and not wanting to now make it known. It was the swelling ache that forced me to continue.

'Are you, are you not staying in Goa?'

His answer was evasive, imprecise.

'My plans are at present uncertain. I will have to wait and decide.'

I knew I could not press him for further details, and that I had to find some way of meeting him.

♓

It was easier than I thought and by nightfall my plan was clear. I would rise early and wait by the *Burgaleza's* side, the place where we had first met and talked.

My instinct was right. He was there, his face as drawn as always but with a slight, though strained, smile flickering across it when he saw me approach.

'I knew you would come. I knew we would have to make our farewells and acknowledge the secret, and the pain, we share.'

I nodded. No words came to mind.

'There is something more I have to tell you. If nothing else it will explain the distance I will put between myself and Goa once I can relinquish my responsibilities to the orphans.'

For a moment he fell silent, turning his head to look due east, towards India, to where another life awaited us both.

'What I have to tell you is clear enough—were it not for the fact that I have spent most of my life concealing it. And these are dangerous times to now be open, to reveal such matters.'

Again he hesitated.

'I will just say this: I have left Portugal for the same reason that Lucas tried to flee. His father and mine were more than friends, they shared a common faith, a faith I ostensibly denied. Doing so has tainted my life and in the little time I have left I want to remove this stain. I have relatives, cousins, in Gujarat and I will join them there as soon as possible, to help them with their trading concerns and, most of all, to make peace with myself.'

He looked at me.

'I fear that in telling you this I have placed a heavy burden on one so young but in some curious way I feel you have the right to know. Uncertainty, suspicion is a terrible thing. And I fear I will never quite shed its shadow, perhaps none of us will. Already there is talk that the Holy Office will extend its reach to Goa. I am not the only one to have left Portugal due to its activities.'

I had no words. How could I even begin to express myself? Yet I understood and when he looked at me I knew all there was to know.

'In many ways we are small and insignificant and will one day be forgotten. My life, and all signs of it, will vanish. Your name will never be known and Lucas is already being deliberately erased. Only if his work in the convent remains will justice be done, if anonymously.'

My head jerked up. 'If they remain...?'

'Lucas was judged to be a heretic. A Jew. In such circumstances the convent could be forced to have his work destroyed.'

I gasped.

'It will, I suspect, depend on your Abadessa and her ability to convince the authorities of the truth and beauty of what he created, that there are no secret messages embedded within it, no denials. By all accounts she is a powerful woman, and well-connected but she will have to make her moves with extreme caution.'

Suddenly I remembered standing before her, hearing her sharply asking if I was honest, if I could be trusted and then reaching out to hold my face, turning it first one way and then the other.

'She will do it,' I said, with utter certainty. 'She will succeed. I know her. I have no doubts.'

Dom Estévao smiled. 'I believe you.'

♓

A few days later land was finally sighted, bringing everyone on deck to look and cheer, and some to cry as, very gradually, we sailed closer to India. Could it be that by nightfall we would be in Goa? Not according to Diogo who had rushed to glean information. He returned, delighted to have discovered that approaching land required considerable caution and would inevitably slow down our progress. The *Burgaleza* and the rest of the fleet he explained—trying to appear as knowledgeable as possible—would be sailing upwind, a laborious process that would force them to keep tacking to catch the shifting wind. Another problem was that while our pilots were all experienced men they, like every sailor in this situation, would be wary of approaching land at night. Each pilot would therefore take his ship to as near the mouth of the wide Mandovi River as he deemed safe and there heave to for the night, remaining as motionless as possible, alert and ready not only for the dawn but, more specifically, for an incoming tide so that in the event of touching the bottom as we made our way upriver the rising waters would free us.

It was a strange night. We barely spoke, everyone retreating into themselves, listening for the last time to the *Burgaleza,* hearing her creaks and groans, feeling her gentle but unceasing movement as we considered the miracle of having survived and reflected on what arriving in India would really mean. I still avoided examining my own future by wondering again about Leonor and what marriage would bring her, and, it suddenly occurred to me, the influence it might have on Diogo's future. What would happen to him? Would his dream be fulfilled, would he be able to attend to Dom João de Castro? And would Dom Estévao find a safe haven? Would all of us find safe havens?

♓

Even before first light our brave ship was a hive of activity with sailors shouting to each other, scurrying to their stations, eagerly awaiting the signal that the tide had turned and was running in our favour, freeing the *Burgaleza* to begin her careful way up the river, assisted by a local pilot who, we now learnt, had come on board during the night. Out in the darkness we saw dancing lights and heard voices. We were not alone, the rest of our fleet, the ships judged sufficiently seaworthy to reach India were still all around us. We would travel up the river together led, as was fitting, by Dom João de Castro aboard the *São Thome.*

At last, and while still cloaked in darkness, the *São Thome* began imperceptibly easing herself forward. As she headed into the river's mouth almost all that could be heard were the calls marking every step of her progress, assurance that the depths ahead were being continually sounded. Behind her, and moving as cautiously, came the *São Pedro*—even as a slight shudder of movement beneath the *Burgaleza* revealed that we were next in line. Moments later, when we were truly under way, we saw that the *Zambuca* was already poised to follow us and that the *Urca* must therefore be waiting to bring up the rear.

As we sailed into the vastness of the river's mouth, like Jonah into the whale, we knew that on each high headland forts looked down on us. While there was a sensation that our progress was a straight line forward it was soon apparent that our pilot was favouring the river's southern bank, sailing near land in deference to the deep channel Diogo immediately declared would bring us safely to our destination.

For the passengers it was a beautiful, gentle journey. At first we were more impressed by the great river's span and it was only very gradually, soon after the open sea was behind us and the crescent moon had faded, and the sky lightened, that the surrounding mist lifted to reveal a new world. It was a world of water, of green, of trees, of a thick, dense lushness, of fish surfacing, of birds singing and sudden flashes of colour as squawking parrots flew between the banks. And then people appeared, moving about beside the river where small huts could be seen and families went about their daily life: fishing, washing, chasing a child. Sometimes a voice could be heard singing or a dog barking and once we even caught the sound of distant drums. Of course while everyone at least paused to look up, the vast majority gathered on the banks to watch us pass by, a sight they would all have seen before with the coming and going of the annual fleets. This time however there was greater splendour and pageantry since the flagship was bringing Goa a new Governor.

It took just under two hours to reach Goa. By then boats, large and small, had come out to greet the fleet and the last stretch was accompanied by the beating of drums on board all our ships while, on land, church bells began ringing out their joyous thanksgiving for our safe arrival. As we finally edged into the harbour, dutifully in line well behind the *São Thome*, we saw before us a city bedecked with palm leaves, with flags flying, people cheering and music playing, of dignitaries and great men waiting to greet our Admiral-*mor*, Dom João de Castro, the new Governor, with all the pomp and circumstance they could muster. The wide wharf, though crowded, gave the impression of bordering a large open space that stretched away to a line of impressive houses, while in the distance and framing the scene were two hills topped by buildings, chapels perhaps, that looked down on a succession of streets and the towering presence of a great church, all of which suggested that Goa's wealth and prosperity was such that it rivalled Lisbon.

♓

It was many hours later, long after we had finally disembarked, that we passed our first night in India. In the hours between the City Council had welcomed Dom João de Castro with a round of formal speeches, after which there had been entertainments, official and otherwise, with dancing and banquets. Diogo had sought out Dom Alvaro, one of Dom João de Castro's two sons, and received the assurance that we were indeed expected in the residence—all newly whitewashed, he observed with a smile—of the outgoing Governor, Dom Martim Afonso de Sousa, Henrique de Sousa's cousin.

Of course, although neither Leonor, Diogo nor myself ever brought up the subject we were all aware that we had reached our journey's end and that Diogo would soon be approached by Duarte da Cunha and that after a very short span of time—perhaps just a matter of a few days—we would start planning Leonor's marriage. While I still had no inkling of what Leonor's thoughts might be I imagined that Diogo undoubtedly hoped that, in some capacity, he would serve Dom João de Castro and eventually return to Portugal with him at the completion of his three-year term. For myself I simply accepted, with almost no introspection, that once Leonor was married I would go with her to her husband's house and continue to serve her. However, deep within me was a thought I gave great attention to: the hope, even the belief, that, after a year or so, Duarte da Cunha would himself return to Portugal and life would continue as it had always done. Though it took time for our beliefs and hopes to change, for the reality of another order to dawn, our eyes were initially veiled by all that had to be done as we settled into the quarters assigned to us within the Governor's residence.

While it was a busy time we noticed that, however Portuguese our immediate surroundings appeared, there was little doubt that we were in another country. As had happened at Moçambique, but now on a much larger and grander scale, we saw much that was alien. There were numerous Indians who came and went within the house, often it is true dressed in Portuguese clothes but there were others, men wearing turbans, who draped their bodies in fine cottons, marked their foreheads with red and white pastes and had gold ornaments gleaming in their ears and around their necks, while there were women who dressed in a confection of bright colours. And there were slaves, men—and women too—whose bodies were barely covered by cloth. Sometimes one of the city dignitaries, or a rich hidalgo or a proud soldier of some standing would pass by on a horse, surrounded by a retinue of colourfully dressed men, Indian and Portuguese, carrying silken parasols. Yet though they sometimes reminded me of the proud Sultan I had seen in Moçambique, there was a crucial difference: the Sultan had been accompanied by his courtiers and they, like those who served him were his fellow countrymen.

In truth we saw little of Goa. I was curious but contented myself with the thought that we would be living here and have ample time to explore once Leonor was married and we were properly settled. Meanwhile snippets of news came to us, such as Diogo informing us that Henrique de Sousa had managed to install himself and his new family in a house nearby, no doubt by exploiting his relationship with Dom Martim Afonso de Sousa. An unexpected surprise came at the end of our first week in Goa when Dom Estévao called upon us with the news that the orphans had all been settled with suitable, and respectable, families who would see to their future and that he was now departing, on the morrow, for faraway Gujarat. I felt the constriction within my heart and managed to follow him out of the room in which Leonor had received him. Yet, the very nature and purpose of the Governor's house meant that people were perpetually coming and going, and there could be no hope of discussing private matters. In truth I accepted that nothing remained to be said; we had had our time on the *Burgaleza.* That was the rational thought, the emotional one was that I was losing him.

I looked up and knew his thoughts were similar, even as he bowed his head and, with the suggestion of a smile, said: 'I pray for your well-being, that your life here is gentle and brings peace.' There was then a slight pause before he added: 'I will not forget you, as I can never forget the man we both knew.'

In seconds he was making his way down the staircase and was soon out of sight and gone. Forever.

♓

Almost nothing of what was taking place either inside or outside the Governor's house ever came to us directly. Instead information would be filtered in piecemeal, perhaps because of something Diogo had been told or that I might have heard on the staircase or when I fetched something for Leonor or when we made our way into church and caught snatches of the conversations taking place around us. Yet though it was almost impossible to form a complete picture we began to sense that the initial cordiality between Dom João de Castro and Dom Martim Afonso de Sousa had soured. Furthermore it seemed that Dom Martim had started to denigrate his successor—even as eddying rumours began circulating about the wealth he had acquired, that he had annually sent vast sums back to Portugal, that he struck deals with powerful Indian rulers. Certainly—at least according to Diogo—it was true that Goa's councillors had pleaded with Dom João to reverse the crippling measures instigated by Dom Martim, measures that had ruined small traders, forced food prices up and caused great hardship.

Of course what began to concern us, a small worry at first,

was that we had not received, directly or otherwise, any news about Dom Duarte da Cunha. At a certain level we were unconcerned: we were safe and comfortable where we were, there was no question of us being unwelcome under Dom João's roof. Then, on one of those mornings when whispers and innuendoes were floating about, Diogo suddenly heard someone mention Duarte da Cunha. 'It was strange,' he later told us, 'but as soon as the speaker uttered his name, he almost vanished.' Yet he ran after him, out into the large and busy street, determined to question him, eventually catching up with him when he hesitated at a corner. Diogo never exactly put anything into words but the impression he gave was that the man did not want to speak with him. Yet, somehow, he gained the further impression that Duarte da Cunha had certainly been in Goa until a very short time ago and that, maybe, who knows, he might still be around. 'He was very anxious to be gone,' Diogo told us, looking at Leonor before continuing, 'Yet surely it is now not unreasonable to assume that someone in Goa has to know his whereabouts?'

Two days later something happened that was soon common knowledge: Dom Martim and Dom João had apparently publicly traded insults and, as if it was something he had quietly planned and engineered, Dom Martim almost immediately set sail for Cochin. With him went Henrique de Sousa—who, according to rumour, had used influence to secure the post of captain of Cochin. Travelling with him were his wife and heavily pregnant mother-in-law and her children. The next day, as all of Goa busied itself discussing their sudden departure, Diogo went out, expecting to return a few hours later. Instead no more than an hour had passed when he suddenly burst back into our rooms.

'News at last,' he almost shouted. 'It was so strange, that man who had mentioned Duarte da Cunha and who had been, well, evasive, saw me and beckoned to me that he wanted to speak with me.' He looked from Leonor to me, as if making sure he had our attention. I felt Leonor tense. Was she at last going to meet her bridegroom?

'I really don't quite know why he told me. Because initially all he said was that Duarte da Cunha was not in Goa.' I felt a slight movement from Leonor and knew that though she was extending a hand towards me, she had quickly withdrawn it.

'Then he just stood there, as if deciding, making his mind up about something. But finally, and with a shrug, he almost casually assured me that, without any doubt at all, Duarte da Cunha was now in Cannanore, at Fort St Angelo on the Malabar coast; that he is stationed there. For some time, at least a year or so,' he paused, 'Then he rushed away. I've never seen anyone come and go so quickly.'

A silence fell. A question jumped into my mind and then kept rising and falling; but I kept quiet, waiting for Leonor to ask it. As she must.

'So what do we do now?'

♓

After much discussion we saw that, at best, there were three choices: all of us now went to Cannanore or Diogo went to there to investigate while we remained in Goa or a letter was sent and we waited to receive a reply giving reliable confirmation of Duarte da Cunha's whereabouts. Leonor was adamant that under no circumstances should Diogo go alone, or rather leave us alone. Eventually, between them, it was accepted that to set out without clear information was foolhardy. Leonor however was still uncertain, even murmuring the wish that her father's advice could be sought, words that were hardly out of her mouth before Diogo was gently explaining that though a letter could be sent when the returning fleet left Goa, which it usually did in December, there was no guarantee that it would arrive before the next fleet left Lisbon and that even if this did not happen there was no hope of a reply for a year or more. Here he paused, perhaps, for once, to restrain himself from mentioning the dangers and uncertainties that accompanied every voyage. Then he reached out to Leonor and took her hands, assuring her that not only was he here to take care of her but that, in a larger sense, we were safe under Dom João's protection.

♓

Yet it was then that fate played a cruel hand. Generally it is seen that though kings and generals rule and fight, changing dynasties and maps with the sword or the pen, ordinary people are left to struggle with their individual lives and problems. Yet it was as Diogo and Leonor reached their decision in one of the smallest rooms of Goa's most important building that, in the grandest official room, Dom João de Castro took the decision that irrevocably changed our lives. In his short time as Governor he had discovered numerous financial irregularities, many apparently carried out by relatives of Dom Martim Afonso de Sousa. One such place was Cannanore's Fort St Angelo where the present captain, appointed six months previously was known to be honest. Dom João's decision was therefore to send Dr Simão Martins, Goa's new, and equally honest, chief magistrate to investigate, hoping the combination would bring the perpetrators to book. It was knowing that we could all travel together, that Dom João de Castro would, undoubtedly inform the captain of Leonor's predicament, and that we could travel under the protection of Dr Simão Martins that persuaded us to change our minds. Even now I wonder what so possessed us, what drove Diogo to suggest, or Leonor to agree or even Dom João to allow. What blinded us? Why indeed did I not speak up?

♓

And so, barely six weeks after arriving in Goa we once more set sail, this time on a much smaller ship that took only three days to reach its destination and during which we neither lost sight of the coastline nor mercifully were aware of the enormity of our decision. Dr Simão Martins turned out to be a tall, lean man of few words, a man whose attention often appeared to be elsewhere and whose almost expressionless face probably served him well in court. He was unfailingly polite to Leonor, said next to nothing to Diogo and almost ignored me. It surprised none of us that he was unmarried for he gave no sign of being interested in other people or of ever indulging in polite small talk. Yet, negative as these qualities might seem, it was equally obvious that he was both a stickler for the truth and unforgiving of any deviation from the straight and narrow. We knew therefore that he would not only fulfil his brief from Dom João de Castro to uncover all financial discrepancies and name their perpetrators but ensure that the captain of the fort took us under his protection and followed the Governor's requests to the letter. Any lingering doubts we may have kept, slipped away.

♓

It is now impossible to reach back through the years and recall our precise emotions as we entered the imposing gates of Fort St Angelo to stand behind Dr Simão Martins as he was formally greeted by Manuel de Vasconcelos and a small retinue of the fort's functionaries. Which one of them, I wondered, was Duarte da Cunha, aware that Leonor was clasping my hand and was like me, and Diogo, certain that he was present. Then, as the captain turned and approached us, a fear gripped me, his slight hesitation alerting me. I saw what a tall man he was, how tanned his face was and how the large scar on one cheek broke the symmetry of his otherwise open good looks. He bowed to Leonor, extended the gesture to Diogo and indicated that he had registered my presence.

'I bid you welcome to Fort St Angelo,' he said, 'you must be tired from your journey so may I suggest that you go to the rooms I have set aside for you, refresh yourselves and then join us for a meal? Your luggage is being taken there now.'

It was then that Diogo stepped forward, politely thanking the captain for so generously welcoming us before, almost visibly, tightening his resolve and asking: 'Is Dom Duarte da Cunha here?'

Manuel de Vasconcelos was far too seasoned at fielding awkward questions to show any unease though his slight smile never reached his eyes.

'I fear that though, at present, Dom Duarte is not here I don't doubt that he soon will be.'

♓

Later that evening, just as night was falling, Diogo went to see the captain privately, aware that once Dr Simão Martins began the hearings there would be no immediate chance of extracting any further information. He returned less than half an hour later, his expression far from its usual liveliness.

'The news is not good,' he declared, 'yes, he is based here but hasn't actually been here, in the fort, for about a month. All that is known, or is at least supposed, is that he is 'somewhere in Malabar', and that he will, no doubt, eventually, show up.'

His words were greeted with silence for though several questions could have been asked neither Leonor nor I chose to voice them. Mutely we just accepted that we had now had no alternative but to wait and hold onto the belief that the man Leonor was to marry would come. Yet Diogo's words, though designed to calm Leonor served, by their very utterance, to reveal his fears. 'We must remember,' he said, 'that he is related to both us and Dom João's wife. We should not worry.'

♓

In an unexpected way Fort St Angelo reminded me of the Convento da Nossa Senhora da Boa Fé. Of course people could move in and out of the fort at will, whether men or women and, despite the presence of two chapels, it is doubtful that much attention was given to religious or spiritual matters. The common factor was that both the fort and the convent stood within enclosing walls. The fort being rimmed by protective walls designed to withstand an enemy force, to keep unwanted intruders at bay, unlike the convent whose equally protective walls were to ensure the seclusion of its inmates, to keep them from the outside world. Both had their hierarchy, responsible individuals who saw to the functioning of their establishments: those who guarded entrances, ran the hospital, the kitchens, the stores and so on. The major difference was the constant stream of people coming in and out of the fort, some on business, many to work, among them the Franciscan fathers who came to hear confessions and attend to those anxious to erase their perpetually recurring sins.

There were several families living within the fort, Portuguese men married to local women, their social order determined by the amount of Portuguese blood flowing in their veins, those with a Portuguese wife, of whom only two existed, considering themselves superior to all others. The legality of other unions was debatable, even the captain was said to have an Indian woman living with him. Otherwise women came and went to sell produce, to cook and clean. Though it was not long before I knew many of those living within the fort: the soldiers stationed there, the women they lived with, the children that ran about and all those with purpose and intent who came and went, there was one particular woman whose position I never fathomed.

She was different from all the others. Indian of course and, though I never saw her except from a distance, I sensed her beauty, and that she possessed an innate reserve and dignity, a particular grace. Once, when I was with Diogo, I saw her at the far end of the fort and asked if he knew anything about her. He shook his head.

♓

Meanwhile, the days went by and, though troubled by the uncertain reality of our situation, we sought to juggle our relief at having arrived safely and being well received by Manuel de Vasconcelos against the continuing mystery of Duarte da Cunha's whereabouts. In this strange uncertain limbo of endlessly waiting Leonor and I became increasingly grateful that we had Diogo with us, aware that without him, we would be lost. While his presence shielded us from the rougher elements of those living and working within the fort he was also responsible and unfailingly sensitive to Leonor's precarious position, qualities that did not go unnoticed by Manuel de Vasconcelos. Although, almost immediately, this resulted in Diogo being assigned to various duties—making his position somewhat more official—it also caused Leonor considerable distress whenever she was deprived of his protective presence.

Later I wondered what she sensed for in the end we had Diogo for no more than twenty-one days. Twenty-one all too brief days during which he diligently saw to our needs even as he consistently amused us with his descriptions of life within the fort, of those he met and talked to, of his growing admiration for Manuel de Vasconcelos and, because he enjoyed frightening us, of the various disasters and dangers that lurked all around us.

♓

I was braiding Leonor's hair when they came, banging open the door without announcing themselves, four of them, awkwardly holding something limp and wrapped in cloth. Startled by the noise, Leonor looked round, her expression changing so fast it was as if a mask of terror had suddenly been branded onto her face. Although motionless for the briefest instant, she then hurled herself forward, scattering combs and pins, knocking over the stool, shoving me aside, tumbling towards the hand protruding from the cloth. Even as my own emotions welled up, driven by the terrible fear suddenly engulfing me, I reached for Leonor. Despite some gut instinct telling me her fight to deny was already lost, she was sobbing as she threw herself against the men, trying to tear her brother's body away from them. 'Diogo! Diogo! Diogo!' she cried, ''Diogo! Diogo! Diogo!' I swung my arms around her, holding her back just long enough for them to lay his body on the bed, the cloth falling away to show his strangely ashen face. Somehow, even as Leonor broke away from me to kneel down and pull her lifeless brother towards her she outwardly calmed, her endless calling of his name becoming a nearly inaudible whispering, a prayer perhaps. I knelt beside her, placing one arm across her back as I half turned to look up at the men, conscious that, though nothing would change, there was that strange need to know what had happened. It was the oldest of the four who spoke. 'We were all in the storeroom,' he said. 'He was upstairs; he'd gone to check something... then...then, suddenly there was a noise, a kind of thunk and the cry of someone falling.' He stopped, as if for confirmation from the other three that what he was saying was true. 'We rushed to the ladder and saw—saw at once—that a rung had broken and knew he must have slipped,' he paused. 'He was just lying there. His neck at a...' Then his words failed him and he shrugged as if he still wanted to deny. It was one of the younger men who closed the matter. 'We just brought him here,' he said.

♓

Even now, so many years later, I am unable to think of Leonor without seeing again how deeply Diogo's death affected her. It was like being with someone perpetually falling off a cliff, forever plummeting into an abyss. It made me wonder what other feelings were locked up inside her when I recalled how completely she had usually concealed the depths of her emotions. I had only ever seen her visibly distressed when she left the convent and on the *Burgaleza*, when Diogo had comforted her; otherwise she had done little more than occasionally express anxiety. It was hard to know how much of her explosive grief came not only from losing her brother but from the welling up of all that had been suppressed for so long, of so much else that had brought her suffering and unhappiness. I also sensed that she must, despite my presence, have keenly felt the vastness of her isolation and the distance from her family. At one point she turned her tearful face up at me and asked how we could let them know, and how could the words be found that would not break their hearts? That the future terrified her was clear when, in a barely audible voice, she wondered if we would ever hear back from them or see Portugal again. In my heart I too felt the ache and pain of Diogo's death, the shock of losing his cheerful presence and youthful enthusiasm and, more practically, the barrier he provided between us and the uncertainty now closing in on us. In other circumstances I would have mourned more openly but the wildness of Leonor's condition and her distracted anguish made me conceal my feelings in order to give her a sense of calm normality. Yet inside I too was fearful. Not only were we now entirely alone but there was not even the slightest whisper to suggest Duarte da Cunha might soon appear.

♓

Though much worse was soon to come we were at least well protected by Manuel de Vasconcelos who, on receiving the news about Diogo, had immediately come to see Leonor. After offering his condolences he assured her that he had already sent a letter to Dom João requesting him to inform Leonor's family of Diogo's death. He then added that he had given strict orders that, within the fort, she was to be respected. Although I was standing just behind Leonor I was surprised when he shifted his gaze to me and said that since I was now the only one close to her, I should not hesitate to ask for anything she required, that we were both under his personal care and protection and that—despite it not being strictly true—he would not let anyone forget she was a close relative of Dom João de Castro. After a brief pause he added that he would do all he could to track down Duarte da Cunha.

Throughout the captain's visit Leonor kept her head down, almost imperceptibly rocking backwards and forwards, giving no sign of hearing, or even listening to him. Aware that he was the only one who could protect us I followed him out of our room, making a slight noise to attract his attention. As he turned I saw the scar on his left cheek, its depth catching the light.

'Forgive me,' I began, frightened that if he ignored me there would be nothing I could do, but knowing I had to seize this chance.

He paused, waiting for me to continue.

The question I put to him appeared of its own volition for it was not the one I had originally planned to ask.

'Do you,' I asked, 'do you actually know Dom Duarte?'

He looked at me, either as if seeing me for the first time, or because he was taking time to consider what answer to give.

'I know him,' he said at last, 'well in so far as, over the last few years and from time to time, I've met and spoken with him…I doubt that constitutes knowing him.'

'Do…does…I mean,' I struggled, conscious of not in any way being his equal, and therefore not entitled to ask such questions. 'Do you think…I mean does he know Leonor is here?'

The pause was almost unbearable.

'I believe I must be honest with you since I doubt anyone else will be. Duarte da Cunha may well know she is here, that I cannot vouch for either way. I cannot in all truth vouch for much about him. Though recently assigned to duty here he lives entirely by his own rules and, so far, has never been present long enough for me to even attempt disciplining him. He pays little heed to the few conventions of our life, coming and going as he sees fit, attending solely, as far as I can judge, to the filling of his personal coffers.'

There was another long pause before he again looked directly at me.

'But I am a realist: what options does Leonor have? Her brother is dead, she has no real protector—though I give you my solemn word I will do everything I can—and that will include forcing Duarte da Cunha to marry her if he appears.'

As he walked away I felt as if all breath had been removed from my body. Either way, with or without Duarte da Cunha, Leonor's future looked grim. As, by association, did mine.

♓

It is now that I see how casually I have treated Leonor, barely speaking about her except when she played some role in my life—thereby ignoring the fact that though my life followed the path others laid out for her, our lives always ran side by side. It is as if, because I knew her so well, I have failed to give her proper flesh, that there was no point in describing her for the same reason that there was no point in describing myself. Yet it is more than that: Leonor and I were different sides of the same coin and by the time we reached Cannanore we were as close as anyone can be because, to all intents and purposes, our social differences had been erased. Circumstances had bound us together on the day we were first suckled by the same woman, *our* Joaquina. I had followed her to the convent and back to the *quinta*, only to leave again and sail with her from Lisbon to Goa and then down to this fort on the Malabar coast where, it now seemed, all we had left was each other. Except for the strange twist that, as I alone now knew, we were waiting for a man who, whether he came or not, would destroy us.

Although I tried desperately to hide from the fact, I somehow knew that the moment Diogo died I would soon lose Leonor. It was as if the hysteria that had burst from her when they brought his body to us took all her energy, making her little more than an empty shell. While at the beginning it was just possible to sidestep the inevitable, my resolve began to waver ten days later, when she woke with a slight fever. The captain sent a doctor who assured me it was nothing serious and while I feel that in other circumstances, and with another patient, he would have been right, in Leonor's case he overlooked the crucial fact that she had no will to live. Two more days passed and by then all I could do was sit beside her, dampening her lips, wiping the beads of sweat off her forehead and talking to her. I knew I was wasting my time and, in the end, I simply tried to make her comfortable, holding her hand while praying and praying for her to get better, even as I accepted that she had begun to slip away. Once or twice she turned her face towards me and, as a tear rolled down her face, I felt the tender pressure of her fingers on my hand.

It was on the morning of the fourth day after the doctor's visit that, no doubt from despair and sheer exhaustion, I momentarily fell asleep. Probably for no more than fifteen or twenty minutes, but enough for my awakening consciousness to catch me somewhere between a dream and reality, not knowing where I was but gradually sensing that someone was comforting *me*, that a gentle hand was wiping *my* brow. And then the full impact hit me and I jerked up, seeing that beside me was the enigmatic and beautiful woman I had occasionally seen at the far end of the fort. What, all my senses screamed, was she doing here? Of course even as I asked I knew and turned to the bed to confirm my fears. Leonor lay still. Absolutely still. For a moment I froze but then, even as a tidal wave of grief surged through me, I absorbed how peaceful she looked, that she lay as if calmly asleep, the sheet folded, her hair smoothed. I looked from Leonor to the woman, seeing her dark eyes and wondering not only how she had known to come but why she had chosen to do so.

♓

Many years later, when my life was so very different, I often thought about this woman who, as I slept, came to be with Leonor at the moment of her dying, and how her presence had soothed and comforted her while keeping me from having to live with the terrible guilt that would otherwise have haunted me: of sleeping as she died. And how, so gently and wordlessly, she had then comforted me.

♓

I have no memories of the days immediately after Leonor's death since, for most of the time, I slept, cared for by this woman. She came and went like a dream. One morning when, though my eyes were open, I was still enveloped by the drowsiness of sleep, I thought she must be a benevolent ghost. Later I realized that the bitter tasting liquids she made me drink were to make me sleep and dull the waking pain of losing Leonor. While nothing ever truly removed this pain I accept that she restored my strength and that, by the fifth morning, when I woke to find her gone, I was less consumed by grief.

Yet it surrounded me and I understood how Diogo's death had affected Leonor. I even wondered if I too would fall sick and die but, though I deeply mourned Leonor, and was increasingly conscious of being alone and frightened of the future, I already knew that the will to live still beat within me. I thought of Dona Briolanga and Dom Martim in faraway Portugal, unaware that they had lost two of their children, that the prestigious marriage had never taken place. Yet, even as I requested Manuel de Vasconcelos to ask Dom João de Castro to inform Leonor's family of her death, I was aware of my own isolation and precarious future, that there was now no hope of me ever returning to Portugal. However Manuel de Vasconcelos not only offered me sympathy for Leonor's death, assuring me that I would still be under his protection but that I should now move to share a room with another servant. 'It will be safer,' he said.

The next afternoon I gathered together the few things I owned, separating them from Leonor's dresses and more expensive possessions in order that, as the captain had suggested, they could be sold to give me a dowry, for 'of course,' he had added, 'we must find you a husband.' I was horrified but forced myself to see the wisdom of his words. I was now vulnerable to the unwelcome attentions of soldiers and all those who eddied in and out of the fort. Perhaps I might be lucky with a husband but that would not be the case with a rough soldier.

♓

And so the last act began. Everything belonging to Leonor had been put aside and, for the last time, as I was carefully folding her wedding dress, I wondered who might one day wear it, unaware that it had originally belonged to a young woman who died unmarried, her only reason for coming to India unfulfilled. With my thoughts centered on Leonor and her wedding dress what was it that suddenly made me think of the letter that ammavan, Thayathu Chandu, had given me? What brought back his words 'in case you can find some way of it reaching my family'? How had I forgotten about it, especially since I was now in Malabar? Whatever the reason I dropped everything to look for it, almost in a frenzy, suddenly terrified that it might be lost. Yet in a moment it was found, still as well-wrapped in cloth as when it was handed to me.

But now what, I thought. Who do I take it…? The answer came even before the question was formed: The woman who had appeared to comfort Leonor as she lay dying. She was obviously a local woman, she may even know ammavan's family—for had he not said, 'We are known people'? And so, driven by an extraordinary energy and as if pursued by demons, I fled from the room I had shared with Leonor and Diogo, clutching the packet, running the full length of the fort, down to where the land ran out and everything was enclosed by the high parapet and the rooms beneath. This I knew, or so I assumed, was where my guardian angel lived, having once seen her enter a room.

♓

Could things have ever been different or was it all pre-ordained? Was it written that I would carry the letter to India, and down to Malabar? Was it inevitable that I would suddenly remember it and thoughtlessly run with it and, as recklessly, enter the woman's room without knocking? Could there ever have been other possibilities? Yet, though there has never been an answer, that final moment is still as fresh and startling as it was when I burst in. And saw, and at once, that the woman was being passionately embraced by a tall Portuguese man I had never seen before but knew, without any doubt at all, was Dom Duarte da Cunha.

♓

My mouth opened in a long and silent howl, a soundless scream of terror as the ghost of Lucas van Domburg reared up before me. For a brief moment I stood in petrified stillness, rooted by the terror of pain and the remembering of an overwhelming fear that obliterated Dom Estévao's assertion of my innocence. Was I again to play the role of a betrayer? Would I again bring death to an innocent?

And yet did I even have these thoughts? Was I not simply frozen by fear, by the resurgence of guilt? Was I not, in that split second, simply re-living the endlessly reverberating consequences of a vicious word, knowing once more the eternal scorching of fire?

My questions were never answered for, like a man trapped in a collapsing house, my only need was to get out, to leave and free myself. I swung round and ran, driven by a terrible energy; blind, distraught and sobbing with grief. Into a world darkening towards night. Propelled by a single thought: to flee the demons already snapping at my heels.

I ran and ran, out beyond the fort, down lanes and roads that wound through the deepening darkness. Until, as suddenly as I had begun to run, I stopped, exhausted and terrified. Where was I? Who watched from the shadows? Who might suddenly appear? What had I done? Already I knew my reaction had been irrational, unwarranted. I knew I was not guilty of betraying Lucas. Or Leonor. How could I go back? I spun round and round, turning this way and that—but could see nothing. I strained my ears to listen—but all that could be heard was my rasping breath. I was lost in an awful and impenetrable darkness, surrounded by an unknown world. Until—did I hear something? Were my ears deceiving me? But no, something—but what?—was out there, though how near or far away I had no way of knowing. I forced myself to be still and listen. Drums. Was it drums I could hear? But where? I strained my ears to hear, frantically looking this way and that. Until I saw the light. Moving flickers of light. Of flames. Of fire. Moving towards me and igniting a terrible fear that, even as I began spiralling into oblivion, forced out the words already erupting from the deepest core of my being.

'Holy Mother of God save me!'

♓

When consciousness returned I found myself lying on the ground, my head throbbing as I slowly opened my eyes and looked up. I appeared to be in another world, one in which I was surrounded by the blazing flames of great fire-torches. Cautiously I lifted my head—and gasped. I was in another world. Bending towards me was an extraordinary, otherworldly being—and whether male or female I could not tell—robed in red and crowned with a great headdress from which dripped streams of red flowers, a vision with a painted face, with eyes hidden behind silver masks and a mouth framed by silver canines. From where had such a magnificent and powerful apparition emerged—and how was it that I suddenly felt so safe? How indeed did I feel an extraordinary urge to seek this being's protection?

But even as I wondered a red-painted hand gently beckoned for me to rise. And it was as I did so, and despite keeping my eyes fixed on the figure before me, that I knew there were drummers and the men with fire-torches in the surrounding darkness. But I felt strangely fearless, suddenly so certain of being benevolently protected that I had no hesitation in following my extraordinary guide who, without any further gesture, turned and began walking into the night, accompanied by the drummers and torch-holders.

It was like being in a trance-like dream, in a separate world through which I floated effortlessly without any thought of an eventual destination. The distance and time of this journey simply existed and I had no desire to measure either. All I knew was that as we walked my guide swayed regally before me, both hands holding fire-torches whose hissing flames danced and glittered on the reds and golds of the magnificent costume.

Somehow dream and reality were one and, as I walked through the darkness, I felt myself increasingly, almost umbilically, linked to the mysterious being that moved before me. This unknown figure possessed an enormous and powerful energy, an energy that streamed towards me, protecting and enfolding me, surrounding me with an immense benevolence even as it revealed the sacredness of the universe.

In this strange limbo, a time of an unknown making we walked until the enclosing trees, barely discernible in the darkness, retreated and we entered a clearing and, as we kept moving forwards, the fire-torches revealed that we were approaching a large and imposing house.

As soon as we stopped, though not as close to the great doors as I would have expected, my guide turned and gestured for me to come closer. There was then a moment of total silence before, without warning, the drums broke into a thundering, pounding beat, a sound that spoke of a tremendous and almost terrible power. Perhaps if I had not felt myself so securely protected by the presence bèside me, I would have trembled. Instead, without any questioning thoughts, I waited calmly, watching to see what would happen when the doors opened. My lips, of their own volition, murmuring a silent prayer.

The doors seemed to open so gradually that I only knew they were moving when the drums fell sharply silent and the only sound was the wooden creak of them yawning slowly wider.

What happened next played out in its own time and under its own rules. First a handful of men emerged and, though it was obvious they knew all those with whom I now stood, it was equally obvious that their arrival was unexpected. One man, the eldest, shouted a question which, like the answer that followed it, was lost to me, not only because of language but because by then my eyes had fallen on the young woman standing in the doorway. As soon as I saw her I felt a frown forming, suddenly uneasily aware that, despite her distance there was something about her that sent an extraordinary tremor shivering through my body. I stiffened and then, as she stepped forward and the light of a fire-torch fell on her face, I gasped.

I was looking at a mirror image of myself.

There was no doubt about this, no sense of hesitation: our features were almost identical. It was a certainty, an absolute truth, and one instantly reflected in the woman's stunned expression as she turned towards me—and as quickly confirmed when the men looked round to see what was happening and disbelief sprang up on every face.

And yet, as I fainted for the second time that night a distant voice whispered that I was safe, that no trust had been violated, that I had come home. And that Thayathu Chandu, ammavan, was my father.

♓

My moment of stunned euphoria was brief, already slipping away as I fell unconscious and gone by the time I recovered. By then an ill-assorted host of tangled thoughts were already ricocheting wildly through my mind, releasing emotions that cascaded and tumbled like unruly acrobats, running from this side to that, rolling in confusion, whirling and struggling to be noticed. Yet, however hard I tried, I not only failed to still even one of these emotions but to understand, absorb or identify anything of what they tried to tell me. Instead I lay in a frozen stillness, inwardly in chaos, silently gasping and crying, wanting to dance with frenzied joy one moment, desperate to run away and be alone the next. One moment I exulted in the miracle of finding my father, the next I was overwhelmed by the terrible knowledge that I would never see him again, that he was almost as lost to me as he had always been. All that comforted me, even as pain and confusion tore at the heels of my elation, was that my other-worldly guide still stood nearby, still watching over me. *Who are you,* I thought? *Why, in all this, are you the only one I trust?*

I was finally brought to a gentler level by the woman whose features I shared. Although, like everyone else, she had seen me fall she was the only one who reacted, immediately hurrying to kneel down beside me, to draw me into the sanctuary of her enfolding body. Only then did she look up and call to the men. As she did so, and despite my semi-conscious state, I sensed the surrounding vibrations and knew that though the men moved closer, something was making them hesitate. It was a doubt that reverberated as the woman tightened her hold on me, almost as if to collect her energy and assert her resolve before she shouted and lifted one arm to point at my protecting guide.

For a moment there was a tense and unnatural silence. A silence out of which there suddenly came the sound of an almost inconceivable power and majesty: a harsh voice that soared into the night, speaking with an authority that could not be denied, leaving no doubt that the speaker was to be obeyed. And so it was that as the words echoed through the darkness two men came and quickly carried me into the house.

♓

Now, over six decades later, I cast my mind back for the last time, knowing I must hurry, that what little time is left will soon be gone. First I remember how it was confirmed, beyond a doubt, that ammavan was my father. How could he not have been? I had run from the fort with his letter tucked into my dress—the one he asked me to send to his family. And, though the letter alone was enough to corroborate my story, there was also my uncanny resemblance to the woman I soon understood to be his much younger sister. Yet none of this was, finally, of any consequence. What mattered to the family, to all those who are now my family, was *how* I had come to them and, most of all, *who* had brought me. And in this everyone was finally of the same opinion: I had been saved by a Goddess, a powerful and benevolent deity, a Bhagavathi who, after reminding them of the ancient role She had played in their family's history, and how they had once betrayed Her, had now returned to grant them an extraordinary blessing. And it was for this reason—and this reason alone—that they took me into their house and family.

It was many years before I completely understood the deeper implications of their acceptance since I had first to grasp the nuances of their customs. I had to realize that no woman born of an unknown mother can ever be taken into a family whose system of inheritance and descent is matrilineal, and that in other circumstances, despite the conviction that Thayathu Chandu was my father, I could never have become a member of the family.

And yet.

And yet, because the Bhagavathi had spoken, had brought me to them, they made me theirs and, in so doing gave me a home and a family. Much later, after I learnt their language and could finally tell my story, they offered me a rebirth, giving me my own identity by naming me Seetha, after a Goddess who, like me, had been born of the earth. In time, and according to their custom, they arranged my marriage, to a good man who was always, until his death a few years ago, kind to me. I am the mother of three children. It is easy to count the blessings I have received.

Over the years I have occasionally thought back to the Alentejo, sometimes remembering when I asked Lucas if he ever missed Zeeland and sensing the pause before he replied. 'It is not,' he had said, 'that there aren't moments, the sudden little betrayals of memory, of longing. It can happen without warning—a moment that suddenly reminds me of my homeland. The crying of a seabird. Even a particular gesture or smell or sound. Then the ache can be deep. And yet I now know that if I went back the memories would then be of this place.'

I have thought of the mother I never knew and the father I found too late and felt the sorrow of never having spoken to him as a daughter, or knowing when and how he died. Perhaps if his sister had been older when he left Malabar he would have seen our similarities. Perhaps, perhaps...but what is now the point of such thoughts?

And I think again of Joaquina and her warmth, of Diogo's bravado and sweet Leonor. And, of course, of Balthazar. For how many years have I found comfort in his words and been able to travel vast inner distances to meet him? Is he now at peace in his Paradise? Will we soon meet, as I pray he has now met his family?

And, for the last time I acknowledge a pain that has never truly left me, that is always there whenever Lucas comes to my mind. And I pray that his spirit is at peace.

And I think of the Bhagavathi who blessed me, who gave me more than I ever dreamt of receiving, and before whom I bow in gratitude, remembering, and still feeling, the benevolence of Her protection. I think also of the morning when the family, bearing in mind the circumstances that had brought me to this place, summoned an astrologer and how he divined Her presence within the house. A presence that is now worshipped with devotion, installed and enshrined as the Thayathu tharavad's powerful and presiding deity.

Then, for no reason at all, I catch a glimpse of the last time I saw ammavan—despite everything, I never managed to call him achan. I am at the Cromeleque and he has just given me a small ivory figure carved from a piece of Kesavan's tusks. 'I have fashioned it,' he is explaining, 'to be like your Madonna and my Bhagavathi—for are they not one and the same—both of them our divine Mother?' Now, in my mind's eye, I see the figure again and recall my distress when I returned to the *quinta* and found I had lost it. Perhaps one day, someone, the right person, will find it and bring it back home, here, to where it really belongs...

♓

The moment has come.

The night is almost finished. Stillness is settling within me. The sky is beginning to lighten, the stars to dim, the moon to fade. It is time to be silent and wait, to be without thought or desire.

I stand up. My body is now weightless and falling away like a discarded cloth. I am surrounded by darkness yet enveloped in light. I listen to the silence, knowing the benediction of the gentle whisper breathing softly in my ear and drawing my attention to the figure now emerging from the shadows. Without thought or consciousness I see the fire-torches and how their light dances on the silver of Her hidden eyes. And how, like the inevitability of a river flowing to the waiting ocean, I feel Her compassion stream towards me, surrounding me, benevolently folding my soul into Her keeping. And I see that She is lifting the flames still higher and revealing the figure of that regal and gentle Mother whose love bestows the blessing of eternal bliss. And so it is that at last, guided by the purity of light, of fire, I go closer, drawn by the certainties She offers, knowing that Her hands are already parting the enveloping folds of Her sky-blue cloak and that the door to the Beloved is opening.

Book Three

THATTAKKUTTY

If I sit as close to the great doors of our illam as I can get without being reprimanded it is just possible to see what lies beyond. It is a restricted view on which to base my knowledge of the outside world but I dare not go closer. Even now, when it will soon be dark, I cannot risk such boldness. Rather I count my blessings, grateful for the seclusion that allows me to catch glimpses of life outside these doors. Not that much can still be seen at this hour. The day's light is already being drained out of the sky and pushing our visible world into the night. The distant hills, the furthest horizon of my universe, are now a deep indigo-black, their trees and rocks blurred into a solid mass, their blended density silhouetted against the darkening sky. It is like watching a recurring struggle, an endlessly repeating battle between night and day with the day now so accepting of inevitable defeat that it merely fades away, retiring from the fray to lick its wounds and rest. All that remains are a few looming clouds, scattered fitfully across the heavens, gently wrapping the land beneath them in a pale, diaphanous mist.

It is a beautiful moment, the time when the sun finally sinks into the west and Mahadeva, pale with ash from the cremation ground, comes forth, gently leading His sacred bull while His three eyes watch over the world. The divine texts tell us that as He moves His matted locks glow with the redness of the dust stirred up by the breeze and that this is therefore a hallowed time. Yet it is also a dangerous one. It is when all Mankind hovers, breath held, on an uneasy threshold, conscious of the surrounding vastness and mystery. It is when the Lord is accompanied by His bhuta gana whose wayward and unruly ways encourage strange spirits and shadows, wraiths and demons to emerge and boldly flaunt their malevolence. It is the moment that finally compels us to withdraw into the safety and comfort of our illam. And it is when I too finally turn away from the now near total darkness and look inwards to where the oil lamps flutter, their tender, fragile flames glowing like tiny beacons, illuminating the security within. And, as always at this time, nothing is heard but the low murmuring of prayers, the chanting of the Lord's name, a muttering drone that barely registers. Yet tonight, even as I absorb this comforting, almost monotonous familiarity, I am conscious that outside in the night a low rumble of thunder has begun growling surreptitiously around the hills.

Soon, very soon, a gentle patter of rain will begin, an evening shower that will be in sharp contrast to the downpours of the last few weeks. This year the monsoon broke with unusual fury, venting itself on our parched fields with such force that we all trembled at the wildness of its outburst. Only in the last week has the rain subsided into a calmer and seemingly more benevolent mood. But I am not deceived. I sense that its true self, its latent, dangerous violence, still lurks within the relentless grumbling of the distant thunder.

Tomorrow it will, at last, be the end of Karkadakam, that most strange and powerful of months. Tomorrow, just before the evening lamp is lit, Nanikutty, our Nambiar maidservant, will leave our illam carrying with her all that is broken and damaged, all that has been soiled or ruined or spoilt in the past year. We will chase her out, shouting and hurling abuse at her, seeing her as the temporary embodiment of Jyestha, that terrifying divinity who carries a broom, who presides over all that is evil and inauspicious. Jyestha, the awful Goddess who accompanies Yama, the dark Lord of the Underworld, the Goddess whose emblem is the ill-omened crow, the Goddess who brings disease and destruction. We will not permit Nanikutty to return until the new month has dawned and we have safely entered the peaceful and propitious days of Chingam, the dangers of Karkadakam behind us. Only then—and after Nanikutty has bathed and divested herself of all that the hideous Jyestha represents—can we allow her back inside.

Karkadakam is a month when we can take no chances, when we cautiously avoid all new ventures, when we rest, replenishing and conserving our energies for the strenuous months that lie ahead. Yet though the days are fresh and cool and this is the season of rejuvenation, it is also an uneasy time and this year the unease has been more marked. I feel that there is a threatening quality in the very air we breathe, I sense the tightness of hidden tensions and catch the warning hints of vague, unspecified uncertainties. It is as if we are no more than tiny, helpless microbes clinging to the body of a great sleeping giant. Occasionally I can almost hear the beating pulse of his heart and catch the soft rhythms of his gentle breath as it sighs in and out through the trees. Though the land is now dormant, refreshed by the rain and waiting to create new life, I am unable to shake off my awareness of this giant, his presence constantly reminding me of the unseen powers all around us; powers none of us will ever fully comprehend. Too often I wonder what would happen if he should suddenly awaken and stir in anger.

This year Karkadakam's strange unease has affected my whole being, hanging in the air, bearing down with a pressure I long to deny. For almost three months, ever since Vishu, I have been trying to ignore this building tension. I have tried to sidestep the significance of what is happening. I have been, I am, afraid. I see the enormity of all these latent threats and the changes that lie ahead but am unable to discover how to withdraw from their coming onslaught. I ask no questions. I seek no help or assistance. I accept that none can be given. It is karma and though still ignorant, still uncertain, still unaware of the precise danger that awaits, I accept that it cannot be avoided, that it will eventually engulf us. All I can do is pray for the necessary strength to withstand the pain that will, inevitably, accompany it.

It is silent.

I am running. I am alone. The light is thick and grey. My eyes are open. I am not blind but before me there is only nothingness. I am enveloped in a vast, billowing cloud of rising dust.

I am frightened.

I run faster, hurtling through the enclosing mists. Not knowing where I am going. Not knowing how closely I am pursued. Running towards something that will soon loom out of the silence and reveal itself. Something I can never hide from. Something that even now is swelling into loudness. Something that knows my name and is calling me.

It is a sound that terrifies. It beats and thunders and echoes. It howls its horrors. It reverberates through the universe. And it is like the air around me, the nothingness I cannot see. It is everywhere.

It is fire.

And then all was silent.

Silent as, once more, I began my struggle, as I will always begin it, as I have always begun it, by straining to overcome the panic invading my being, seeping into my veins like a serpent's venom. Choking with fear and almost paralyzed by leaden limbs I heard the terrible laughter surround me as I hurtled into total darkness. My desperate eyes searched longingly for some sign, some glimmer of hope. Searched and searched until, quite suddenly, there, there was the piercing brightness of a single flame flickering so faintly the clouding dust should have destroyed it. It drew me closer, pulling me into its truth, showing me the steadfast sureness of its purity, lifting me out of the awful horrors of the darkness, dragging me from my nightmare's grip.

Slowly my heart stilled its thudding beat and, as slowly, dulled my terror. My hands made contact with reality, knowing the tangible, bringing me from my dream. But not without a struggle since, for a time, these indistinct horrors were more real than the known and familiar. I hovered in a no man's land, still hearing the roaring flames, still waiting for a scorching blaze to engulf me. It was only when I cried out that calmness finally enfolded me. Only then did I acknowledge that within all terrors, within all fires there is coolness, balm and sanctuary. And, in absolute majesty in that sanctuary is my Goddess. It is here, it is there, as it is everywhere, that She awaits me, endlessly patient, ready, if I reach out, if I trust enough, to gather me safely into Her arms and succour me. As Her child.

The comfort and certainty of these thoughts pushed the nightmare's last roar of fire out into a distant oblivion. It was a quick retreat, one that left me in the calm of tranquil silence and allowed the final residue of my troubled sleep to evaporate. Only then, as the veil separating me from my surroundings slipped from my eyes, was it clear that I had fallen asleep before the sanctum of our household shrine, the shrine of our Bhagavathi. And then, as reality completely reasserted itself I saw again the flame that had so bravely pierced my nightmare. A flame that was only one amongst those honouring and illuminating Her image, the air around them so still they appeared to be motionless. I looked closer, seeing how they seamlessly tapered into the inner darkness of the shrine, endlessly blurring and blending their colours. And caught something of the inner mystery of their motionless light and the delicacy with which they repulsed the dark.

For a moment, as these fragile flames held my mind, I thought of the terrible Lord whose fiery tongue devours our sacrificial offerings, whose seven arms enfold the seven worlds. I whispered his name: Agni, the Lord of the sacred, eternal flame, the god who must preside over all our rituals. The God without whom our pujas are meaningless. The God who must witness our marriages and, after the last breath has left our bodies, consume us. The God who, should he desert our kitchen fires, will leave only destruction in His wake. *Agni.* I said His name once more, softly, so that I did not disturb or offend His spirit.

Finally my fear of fire dimmed and I looked into the sanctum with calmer, less troubled eyes, seeing the depths within its central glow. I saw how the oil lamps illuminated the sacred space. And, as clearly, how they concealed its secrets, never fully revealing the source of its power or disclosing its nature. For a moment this saddened me for it made me see—and accept—

that there was still no real peace within me, that I was failing to distance myself from a lingering, restless sense of unease. I knew then that the nightmare would return, and that I could neither fight its nocturnal horrors nor prevent them from continuing to haunt me.

Though this dream first swept me into its engulfing terrors just after Vishu's morning and the month of Karkadakam is now almost over the pattern has been unchanging. And, as always since the nightmare's first unwelcome visitation, I take my mind back to Vishu, the fateful day when so much happened.

♓

Vishu. It is early morning and I am seated in my secluded corner, near my Goddess. The day is still young but already the fates have spoken, its nature is known to me and its portents revealed. And yet so much is hidden, so much beyond my understanding. It is as if I am standing alone. On an edge. Confused. A child and yet a woman. Knowing but ignorant. Between two worlds. Divided. Pulled this way and that. Offered knowledge and then denied it. Elusive knowledge. Kept forever beyond my reach. Only briefly are there moments of total knowing. Like water touching parched throats. Gushing freely, illuminating my clouded mind. Making my whole being soar, lifting my spirit high above all obscuring mists. Moments of such luminous clarity that I feel I have broken free, have lost my doubts. But then I hesitate, allowing uncertainty to, once more, insinuate its poison and send the mockery of doubt to echo unchallenged through my mind.

If only, if only I could understand why my Goddess, virgin and undefiled, is silent.

'Thattakkutty!'

Who knows how long I would have remained before Her, pondering on these matters and lost in contemplation of the light around Her, had my name not been called?

'Thattakkutty!'

I heard Amma's voice. And its sharpness. Quite clearly. Of course I did. But I kept silent. I still had the feeling that I needed to be alone. And I still had the feeling that if I went and joined the others I would have to pretend that all was well. And that was not possible. Not now. Not yet.

'*Thattakkutty!*'

This time my mother's voice was much louder. And more insistent. Commanding. This time I would have to answer. But I wanted one more moment, just one more, to myself.

'Savitri, why do you let her be like this?'

Now it was my grandmother speaking. I sighed with relief. No one, least of all my mother, would dare to interrupt her. I could steal a few more precious moments.

'That child is never to be found. And when she is seen she is always with her nose in some manuscript...or listening to some discourse and having her own opinion. She is diligent with her studies no doubt but neglects her duties. Cleverness in Sanskrit will be of little use. She is too solemn. I cannot say that she is a bad or disobedient child...She attends to her devotions but...'

'That may be so. But where is she *now*?' Amma was using agreement as an argument. 'She must be more responsible. She should be here. Now! *Thattakkutty*!'

I looked around the shadowy interior of our illam. Now that the dawn was releasing her light into the shaded well I was suddenly conscious of the enclosing walls and the security they offered, the coolness they provided. How could any of this change? How could all this disappear? It wasn't possible. I *had* to believe that. I had to ignore the omens. I had to put aside my fears and apprehensions. I had to concentrate on the promises, the assurances, of my horoscope. I had to remember—and believe—in its powerful certainty: that I would be eternal. And I had to realize that, even now, I was being called to assist in preparing our Vishu feast. Like everyone in Malabar were we not about to rejoice and celebrate? And my family, were they not well satisfied that the year had begun auspiciously? Were they not certain that the months ahead would be bountiful ones?

'Thattakkutty!'

'Coming, Amma!'

I took a brief, sweeping look around the illam's central interior, glancing to where the banana leaves were piled in readiness for the feast. Everything was in order. As it should be. Normal. Or so it appeared and so I must now believe. I took a deep breath and emerged from my corner, hurrying towards the kitchen, slipping along the side of the wall, intending to keep a distance between my mother and myself. I hoped her preoccupation with the feast's preparations would, once she had seen and heard me, keep her occupied and too busy to punish me. But I was wrong. She moved fast, cuffing my ear and inflicting a sharp pinch on one cheek as she propelled me into the kitchen.

Despite my intention to hide all pain I was unable to stop a cry from escaping my lips. Or to completely ignore the reactions of the other women, their satisfaction and enjoyment of my chastisement. All that kept their smiles suppressed was Amma's commanding voice telling everyone to get on with their work. It was a sign that I was now almost out of her mind, that I had ceased to be her major concern. If I went quickly about my duties her attention would transfer its energies elsewhere and I could let my pent-up breath sigh away. I turned to my assigned tasks, inhaling the rich fragrances around me, the delicate flavourings rising from the vast charakkus, the distinctiveness of grated coconut and the heaviness of its oil.

Why had I been so nervous, so worried? All around me there was excitement, anticipation. Even Amma was smiling now, my misdemeanours forgotten, aware only of the day's auspicious significance. Like everyone else on this special day she was wearing new clothes. The fine off-white cotton was draped gracefully around her slender body, its golden border occasionally catching the light from an oil lamp or the kitchen fires. Her flat bronze bangles jingled the familiar, soothing sound I have known all my life. From time to time she would unconsciously tuck a loose strand of hair back into the mass it had escaped from, gathered, as is our custom, on one side of her head.

Yes, all was as it should be. Even Achan's three unmarried sisters, my aunts, seemed happy enough; for them. I could just hear, outside the kitchen, over on the far side, the men's voices—but could detect nothing in their tone to suggest disquiet. I peeped out of the kitchen and looked across the distance to where my father and his two younger brothers were standing. I could find no evidence of care or concern on any of their faces. I studied Achan carefully, knowing the extent and depth of his knowledge, his understanding of omens and signs. But no, he stood, as he so often did, with his weight on one leg, talking with his head held back to prevent the paan he habitually chewed from slipping out of his mouth. And, in his usual, unconscious way, he ran one thumb slowly up and down his sacred thread. He was a man at peace with the world.

I wanted to study every face, to see what, if anything, their expressions might tell me. But it was time to eat, for the first sitting to be called and my father, my uncles, my brother, all the men of our family—and their male guests—to enjoy the blessings and plenty of our Vishu feast. Unseen and unnoticed I watched them sit. I saw how each one of them prepared himself, made his delicate obeisance to the divine, washed his banana leaf and then swept away the droplets of water. I saw the anticipation on their faces as generous helpings of steaming rice, of thorans, of curries, of uperis, of pickles, of jackfruit chips and of freshly fried pappadoms were placed on every leaf. I looked into every face, searching for some giveaway, some clue. But not one face betrayed concern. There was nothing. No hidden worries, no hesitation. I examined everyone, searched every line and fold. But found nothing. Instead I saw only contentment, satisfaction, well-being.

And then the men were finished. The soiled leaves were taken away, the ground cleaned and new lines of fresh leaves laid out. It was the women's turn to eat, to partake in the bounty provided by a generous Nature. I sat down last, in keeping with my youth, trying to be invisible at the end of the line whilst watching the activity and sensing the anticipation around me. But all the while I was aware of being apart from everything. Even as I lowered my head towards the first, small handful of food I realized the depths of my fears. The food, the food I knew to be delicious, was tasteless. True I went on eating, mechanically chewing and swallowing. But I tasted nothing. I savoured nothing. I inhaled no flavours. Instead my mind began to churn over the possibility that I was the only one with terror in her heart—even as yet again I reminded myself that this was an auspicious day. That there was no need for concern. I tried to suppress my fears, to control them. I tried too hard. I almost choked on my food. I looked up and along the line, at other faces. I looked at Achamma, wondering if her stern, wise face might reveal something. Nothing. I looked at Parvathy-edathi-amma, my brother's new wife. Nothing. I looked at all the other women of my family. I looked at my sisters, all older than me, and the daughters of my elder-mothers, my father's other wives. They ate without an apparent care in the world. I looked at my three aunts. But found nothing untoward. Every face spoke only of contentment. Even the tension between Amma and her co-wives seemed to have slackened. Then my heart jumped. Where was Arya-edathi, my sister and, like my brother Narayanan-ettan, my mother's child? Where was she? What had…? But then, though I turned and saw her standing near the kitchen I could not relax. I needed to examine *her* expression and see what it might show me. She, after all, had followed me this morning. She had come to the puja room just after me. Perhaps she had seen something. Perhaps she would display some of the disquiet I could now barely suppress. The disquiet that had filled my mind since the early hours of the morning.

But how could her face, any face reveal anything? Deep in my heart I knew that whatever I found on another face would be meaningless. *I* was the only one who could ever answer the question that now endlessly danced in my head.

Why had I opened my eyes?

It had been long before dawn and I had known, known as we all do, that I should have waited. I should have waited until I could be certain of what I would see. I should have waited. Like everyone else.

But now it was too late. I knew that. And I knew the penalties. I accepted. I knew there would be a price to pay. And yet it was not that I had been unaware of what I was doing. I knew the traditions of Vishu morning. I knew the promise it offered. After all had I not helped gather all that was needed to fill the uruli, the shallow vessel in which, every year, we place all that is necessary to ensure that promise is fulfilled? Had I not, only the evening before, helped place the measure of paddy, the newly washed cloth, the bell-metal mirror, the gold ornament and the coins, the jackfruit, the mango and the halved coconut in the uruli? Had I not been the one to run and fetch the old palm-leaf book, its sacred text already so familiar to me? And had I not been the one to place it in the uruli, to arrange it near the final embellishment of the yellow konna flower? So why had I opened my eyes too soon?

After all I had waited—and with patience—all through the evening as everything was prepared. I had watched as the two standing lamps were positioned, one on either side of the uruli. I had seen how their polished metal gleamed, reflecting the glow of their burning wicks. And I had known they would burn throughout the night, constant and alert in the surrounding darkness, guarding the uruli's auspicious contents. And I had known their faithful vigilance would remain until we needed their light to illuminate all the hopes and promises they protected. So why, why had I not waited? Why had I opened my eyes too soon?

I had, after all, been content, only the evening before, to let time pass in its own way. I had waited for the night puja to be over. I had waited for everything to be arranged so that when our Bhagavathi opened Her eyes She too would have an auspicious Vishu-kani. I knew, full well, the significance of making sure these sacred objects were the first things seen by Her, by us all, on Vishu morning. I knew this was why Achamma spent the night before the kani—not one of us believed she slept—so that we would all be so blessed. And why, long before dawn, she came to gently rouse us from our sleep and guide us, one by one, her hands over our eyes, to sit before the uruli. And then, and only then, allow us to open our eyes and gaze upon the beauty that glowed before us, knowing it would grant us good fortune in the year ahead.

And yet, knowing all this, I had opened my eyes before Achamma brought me to the kani. I had not waited until she seated me. I had not waited. *I had not waited.* Instead I had peeped out through the gaps between her boney fingers. And so I had seen, or believed I had, the ill-omened shape of a malevolent cat watching me from the shadows. Dark and still. Menacing. Malicious. The shock had been so great I had stumbled and nearly fallen, blind again—but with terror. Achamma quickly caught me and, no doubt believing I had tripped in the darkness carefully held me as I took the last few steps and panic gripped my heart. And so it was that I began losing my battle with denial. Even after Achamma had seated me and urged me to look upon the kani I had kept my eyes tightly closed, only relenting when she repeated her entreaty. And when I opened them I understood, as never before, the glory and wonder of what I saw. Too late I drank in the pool of light. Too late I sank my entire being in its aura. Too late I tried to immerse myself in the surrounding glow, to absorb the beauty of our Vishu-kani, to soak in its magic and be aware of the assurances it offered. Even as I acknowledged the little tremor telling me I had broken faith with all it had promised. For, of course, it was too late. There could be no rewriting of the slate. It was no longer a question of what I had, or had not, seen but of the visions and hopes I had denied myself.

♓

The day is now well advanced. The feast is over and I am sitting in my secluded corner, thinking of all that has happened in this last year. It is a year in which we have celebrated Narayanan-ettan's marriage and welcomed his bride into our illam. And it is a year in which I have become old enough to understand why my brother has stopped shaving and why his wife, Parvathy-edathi-amma, has a gently swelling belly. I know, full well, that before too long, I will no longer be the youngest member in our household. There is nearly a decade between my brother and myself, a decade he uses to keep us apart, to treat me with indifference. I accept my youth but sometimes find his ridiculing of my love of knowledge and learning less easy to bear. But it is too late to now expect his understanding or, indeed, affection. Like all our women I am unseen by men, almost invisible. And in any case he has now put aside childish pleasures and turned to men's ways: the performance of rituals and the upholding of our traditions.

But I have not been the only one affected by his marriage. Indeed it seems that my sister, Arya-edathi, has been almost completely altered by its celebration. Though she is six years my senior, and we have quite different tastes, her beauty and generous nature have made us close. She takes more pleasure in worldly matters than I do, delighting in the feel of fine cloth and the glitter of costly ornaments. I enjoyed seeing her happiness during the wedding. She openly enjoyed its finery, its rituals and the excitement it brought into our lives. Her dark eyes sparkled and her rippling laughter was a constant sound bubbling through the illam. Which now makes her present state so unsettling. It is as if the ending of the celebrations was a signal for her entire mood to change. I can understand that she might be missing the excitement but cannot convince myself that this is why she is so different. Occasionally she appears to be losing her balance. Sometimes she resembles a lotus, radiant and with a luminous beauty that glows before us all. And then, at other times, there is almost an air of decay about her, as if something is destroying her from within. She is not at peace. Yet though I sense the tension within her I have failed to fathom the source of its energy, its inner charge. But I see how often this current surges through her. And I see how often Amma and Achamma watch her with frowns hovering perpetually between their brows. Everything Arya-edathi does is under their scrutiny. They are often heard chiding her, warning her to stay in our northern quarters, the women's area. She must always, they insist, remain secluded and remember that we are all Namboodiris, that she is a decent Brahmin woman and, as such, never permit herself to be seen by any casual eye, by any passing stranger. Not even by chance should any man outside our family catch even a glimpse of her. Or, indeed, of me.

It is as I sit thinking these thoughts that I feel the texture of the palm-leaf manuscript lying in my hands. Just for a moment I look down and run a finger over its neat letters, feeling how finely the words are incised into the dried leaves. Then, as I look up again, I see Achan coming into the house. He has been out to receive the traditional Vishu offerings from our field workers—and to distribute paddy and new clothes in return. I wonder, as I should not, what it is *really* like to go outside and wander freely, to feel the sun on one's skin. Our men may go in and out as it pleases them but we, for the protection of our chastity and the good name of our family, must remain gosha, secluded within the illam. Sometimes I long to run out through the doors, out into the world, to roam far afield and see what it is like. But then a shudder skims through me. I know how afraid I would be, how mysterious and terrifying the unknown must be, and how terrible it would be to have strangers see one's face. Yes, I wonder about what lies beyond the doors of our illam but I know, full well, that I will never venture forth. Or ever be allowed to.

Perhaps it is in an effort to still these foolish, forbidden, outward looking thoughts that I turn my gaze back into the house, to the nadu mittam, the illam's small, sunken, central courtyard that is open to the sky above. And then, though I see the enclosing cloister off which rooms are situated, and my eyes register all that passes before them, I know my whole being is being drawn towards the sanctum of our Bhagavathi. *My* Bhagavathi. Yet though I turn towards Her I feel no need to see Her face, to know Her beauty, to understand Her omnipotence. I am young in years but I have known Her, and been close to Her, and felt Her power, all my life. Though I know She has Her mysteries there are aspects of Her I know as I know myself. She is the centre in which my prayers dissolve, the One whose benevolence I seek. I acknowledge the fire that simmers within Her. I respect Her as I respect fire, for light and brilliance. I see Her duality, Her power to consume and destroy, Her boundless capacity to protect and nurture. And the certainty of Her compassion.

For a long moment, as I centre my mind on my Bhagavathi, my emotions shift like scudding clouds. Then, as if bathed in a soothing balm, everything seems to still within me. Suddenly I am above and beyond any awareness of time or space or thought. It is a moment that hovers, unmeasured, until an involuntary shiver whispers its distant foreboding. It is faint, like a far-off echo. I catch its tension, its uncertain unease. But then I sense a far more distant comfort: the promise of sanctuary. Something tells me that if I risk taking the journey into the deepest core of my fears I will discover a great and total peace. I pause, drawing sustenance from this sensation, then offer a brief prayer to my Bhagavathi. Only then do I push my mind—and my eyes—back to my more immediate surroundings. And so come, as I must, to the dark corner where, only a few short hours ago I saw, or thought I saw, the strange feline.

Even now, though the noonday sun shines brightly overhead, this corner is still shadow-filled. I have to strain my eyes to pierce its gloom. But nothing is there. Not even an innocent shape that could have deceived me. And so I finally accept what I had hoped to deny. I *had* seen a cat. It had not been an illusion—though I cannot explain its appearance; or know from where it came. All I now understand is the impossibility of doubting my eyes. It *was* there. I stare again into the corner and, once more, this time in my mind's eye, in my imagination, I see its dark presence. I see its watching, knowing eyes and I am forced to ponder on the warning this harbinger of ill fortune has given. And what, if any, are the precautions I can take to protect myself.

It is then, as I stare into this corner, that I notice the thin line of ants. They are moving in a column of urgency, emerging from high up, trickling down the wall and, in frantic procession, making their way along the floor. My eyes follow their direction, observing how the single, seemingly unbroken line is actually made up of hundreds, if not thousands, of tiny insects, packed together and hurrying in unison. They scuttle across the floor, close to the wall, driven by some need, heeding some call I will never hear. It is just as I marvel at their single-mindedness that I see one of their number detach himself from the column and set off on his own. I track his movements, wondering how long it will be before he realizes his mistake and returns to his companions. But this ant, though no different in size or colour to the others, keeps going, drawing further and further away, moving with steadfast determination. Before long he is out in the centre of the cloister around the nadu mittam, caught in the beam of light that filters in through the doors.

Suddenly I realize where he is going. And hold my breath, waiting to see if he will really leave, if he will actually go out through a doorway, out into the world beyond. He scurries along, moving fast, with purpose, without any of the side-to-side jerking movements of the main column from which he is, by now, so far away. It is as he comes up to the doorway used by our servants that the tenseness in my body grows. I strain my eyes, not wanting to turn away and so lose sight of him when he passes out through the doorway and disappears from view.

But it is not to be. Coming towards the door I suddenly see Nanikutty, her body still wet from her bath. There is ample room for her to enter the illam and the tiny ant to pass unheeded on his journey. I do not know how Nanikutty even sees him or what makes her take her wet cloth and strike it at him. Or how she aims so precisely that he has no hope of survival. I only know that this casual, unprovoked act of violence ends his journey. His single moment of independence is short. And paid for with his life.

♓

In the midst of this time of perplexity and change there is one joyful constant: the hours of learning spent with my guru. He comes here regularly, from a nearby illam, to give instructions on devotional matters, on philosophy and Sanskrit. When we, my sisters and myself, assemble before him I am almost overcome with the excitement of anticipation and the longing to visit the uncharted realms he leads us through. For a few short hours all care is put aside and I am free to roam through wonderful lands. I can let my mind race and swell, opening it to absorb, to receive wisdom and penetrate mysteries. I can indulge in the purity of language, the delicacy and nuance of a poetic line and the satisfaction of grasping new concepts. The only disappointment is that the time passes with unnatural haste and soon, too soon, my journey of discovery is over. Yet each journey takes me further and deeper into newer territories, into lands where, once I am familiar with the main highways I can later return alone and make my own discoveries. I go willingly with my guru, following him closely as he guides me through a vast universe of discovery—and later find even greater joy in using his teachings to reach my own understanding of the realms he has revealed to me.

Questions frequently bubble up to my lips and I long to

extend the time, to discuss and investigate. But in this I am alone. Arya-edathi hardly listens, her attention wanders, her mind apparently absorbed elsewhere. Often all that shields her from our guru's irritation is her natural intelligence and, no doubt, her beauty. With my other sisters he is less indulgent; they fidget and shift uncomfortably, their concentration rarely settling. All this would normally be of no personal account at all were it not that they all resent the pleasure I take in being taught. They so actively dislike their schooling that they sometimes seek to destroy my enjoyment of it, their pleasure lying in seeing the distress their actions cause me.

I try and hide my distress, believing, hoping, that if their barbs fail to move me they will soon desist. But either I am unsuccessful or their senses are too finely tuned. 'Ask the scholar,' they sometimes say, 'ask know-it-all.' I am now, as a result, reluctant to speak, to answer a question or express an idea. And now, added to this hesitation there is a new apprehension: I have begun to feel that my guru is also amused by my distress. It is as if he has now sided with my sisters, as if he too is mocking me. At first I wondered at this feeling, believing I was becoming too sensitive. But then, only a few days ago, I made a mistake, something that is surely quite natural in any pupil's journey of learning. I flinched, steeling myself for the titter of laughter that I knew would rise up from my sisters. But finally what actually disturbed me was the faint look of satisfaction that crept subtly across my guru's face.

♓

Time is passing, following its pre-ordained order, finding its own rhythm. Nothing is ever static; nothing remains forever still or the same. Within the walls of our illam life is governed and marked by rituals and ceremonies, by the rites of passage and our daily pujas. There can be no laxness in these matters. Only by fulfilling our sacred duties and honouring our gods and ancestors can we have the satisfaction of knowing their benevolence will protect us. Only by performing these rituals and pujas can we maintain our equilibrium within the universe and so ensure our survival.

But outside the illam matters are less predictable. There shadowy forms and forces haunt the hills and ponds and trees and streams; even the air is filled with their veiled presence. They slither through the land, hover at dusk, flutter through the trees, glide down the rivers, hissing and muttering as they go. These spirits, wraiths, ghosts and demons are restless, vengeful and dangerous. They are easily offended and too often take spiteful revenge, causing death and disease if not satisfied and placated with constant worship and propitiation. Maintaining a delicate balance in the outside world can only be achieved by understanding the demands of these dangerous and unruly forces and by honouring the greater power and benevolence of Nature. It is Nature who possesses the true, and divine, energy, the force that moves the seasons inexorably forward. She is the one who sets rhythms, orders patterns, controls cycles. Outside the illam time moves in an hourglass of *her* making and is beyond our control. We are no more than helpless pawns in her game, mere observers of her powers. And yet if we are cautious and respectful there is a point where our two worlds can meet and we may benefit from her energy, even harness it. As the seasons change we can exist in tandem with Nature. Provided we perform the appropriate rituals, remain always sensitive to her needs and honour her power. For instance though we cannot order the rains to stop we can, through our offerings to the Lord of Chamravattam, move Him to intercede on our behalf. We are the ones who must defer to the moods of the changing seasons; we are the ones who must alter our rituals to suit Nature's demands. We must mark and observe, watching Nature's effect on our lives, understanding that this is the cycle of life. That it has always been this way. That it will be this way forever. That this rhythm will never change. That there will be no surprises.

It is now over six weeks since we celebrated Vishu and started acclimatizing ourselves to the growing humidity and sultriness within the illam. We watched with awe as heavy clouds began thronging in the skies above us. It was a sign that the great water-gathering monsters were already hard at work. All through the dry season, unseen and unheard, they had been relentlessly sucking water up from the earth below them, drawing it into the vast caverns of their mouths. Day by day we had seen the heaviness of their swelling burdens and known that the time was fast approaching when they would no longer be able to contain themselves. We speak of them as monsters, frightening ourselves with tales of their bulk, the thickness of their horns and the flashing intensity of their eyes but we also venerate them for their annual, life-giving gifts. This year it was with a kind of violent desperation that they finally opened their mouths and released the fury of their stored water. It was as if they had lost all self-control and were unable to restrain themselves. For days on end the rain fell in torrents, cascading into our nadu mittam with such intensity that the central well was separated from its surrounding cloister by sheets of moving water. At times it seemed that this raging, naked power would overwhelm us. We became quiet and fearful, cowed by this relentless display of the monsoon's energy. With awe we listened to the endless rage of the downpours, hearing the thunder rumble and shudder through the skies as the great monsters collided with each other in their haste to empty their mouths. We often trembled in fright when the friction of their horns sent violent flashes of lightening down from the heavens.

As always the earliest rains were the heaviest, their fury the most frightening. For days on end we endured the rush of constant downpours, watching and listening with trepidation as the monsters fulfilled their duties. The sky was permanently dull and overcast. The sun was never seen, skulking instead moodily behind dark and angry looking clouds. Then, one morning, there was a change. We woke to find the rain's character had altered, its initial fury had subsided, its rage abated. The dullness of the daytime was lightened, occasionally interspersed with sunshine. Some activity could begin again, the rain's gentler aspect allowing the cycle to move forward and the planting of paddy to begin. Yet, despite this change, the presence, the sound, the feel of water remained all around us. All we heard, all we were conscious of was the unending liquid lullaby of water draining off roofs, gushing from culverts, dripping from leaves, splashing into puddles.

The rainy season completely alters the rhythms of our lives. Many see it as a time of discomfort and inconvenience when all our movements and activities are restricted. I am one of the few who enjoys it, who even declares it to be my favourite season. Perhaps because it is then that I can most appreciate the protection offered by our illam's walls. I am no longer resentful of their restrictive barriers but grateful for their enfolding security. I even hear a soothing melody in the rain as it gushes, pounds, drips, patters and splashes all around us. I also revel in the richness of the smells that seep out of every nook and cranny, the odour of over-ripe jackfruit, the dampness of thick, woody smoke curling up from kitchen fires and, most of all, the earthy fragrance that oozes out of the land around us.

Water, rain, dampness is everywhere. Even the air is moist. The days are cooler and fresher but nothing is ever dry. Mould appears between the little cracks in stones. Buttermilk quickly sours. Smells are deep and heavy, everything is intensified by the thick, dank air. But there are also inner changes. It is a time of decay, a time when fruit is too soon over-ripe, when lushness blooms too fast. It is a time when things die, decompose and rot—even as they become fecund and generous, yielding themselves to hungry insects, birds and animals. It is when fertile renewal emerges from disintegration, when life is created from death.

And it is now, in this season of change and abundance, that Parvathy-edathi-amma, my brother's wife, edges towards the day when she will bring her son into the world.

At every stage of her pregnancy my father has performed the appropriate rituals, seeking the path that will lead Parvathy-edathi-amma to an easy delivery. My father's whole life has been centred on the performance of rituals; from his earliest childhood he has had a special understanding of their power. He knows the correct mantras, the right offerings, the auspicious times. He knows how best to please the gods and so guarantee their benevolence and protection. Yet he displays no complacency; he knows the dangers of a small mistake and how quickly an offended deity can take revenge. I see how the tightness of tension hovers around him—and know he is aware not only of the hopes but of the fears, of the dangers that eddy through our illam like drifting smoke as we await the birth of his first grandchild. Though he masks his concerns it is occasionally possible to see that beneath his practiced inscrutability there are opaque shadows of unease. Yet when he commenced the first of the long pujas that he would have to perform at every stage of Parvathy-edathi-amma's pregnancy he did so with an outward show of confidence. His first concern, once conception had been confirmed, was to seek our Bhagavathi's assurance that the child would be not only a son but one destined for greatness. Once satisfied with the portents of this puja his next task was to honour and acknowledge his future grandson's oneness with the divinity that surrounds us all.

Every day the gods are also consulted and propitiated on Parvathy-edathi-amma's behalf. I can sense that a worried expression has taken up permanent residence behind the mask my father wears to instil us all with confidence; he has an inner distance, the look of a man preparing himself for an immense struggle. As the last weeks of Parvathy-edathi-amma's pregnancy draw near all of us acknowledge that he is the only one who can guide her through the shadows and dangers that haunt *all* pregnant women. He knows that every passing day increases the threat to her well-being. He is aware of—and must battle with—the unseen, unspecified and insubstantial terrors that now edge boldly closer. He senses, as we all do, their proximity, he hears, too clearly, the hissing of their abominable whispers, the flaunting of their unspeakable hungers. He knows their deceits and desires, their power and their greed, their blood-hungry lusts and, most of all, the loathsome curses they saturate with disease, ill-fortune and even death.

♓

Meanwhile, although it is my father who either conducts or oversees all the necessary rituals and pujas, it is Amma's responsibility to take care of Parvathy-edathi-amma's physical well-being. In the seclusion and privacy of the northern quarters, away from the men of our family, she observes every minute change in Parvathy-edathi-amma's body, monitoring every sign and shift and movement within her womb. Her every gesture is watched, her moods are noted. No one relaxes or draws an easy breath. A collective awareness of her frightening vulnerability has touched us all.

Outside, beyond the immediate confines of the illam, the rite of Uccha Belli has already sought the propitiation of the evil spirits who gather at such times, who wait and watch for an unguarded moment. No word was ever spoken, no thought was fully formed but each one of us knew that these spirits were close by, hovering around our illam, hoping to satisfy their hungers and terrible lusts by devouring the blood and flesh of Parvathy-edathi-amma and her unborn child. It was to avert this awful possibility that, in the high, noonday sun, the two sons of Kelu the Malayan ended their penance. It was then, detached from all that surrounded them, tourniquets were tied around their arms and the skin slowly kneaded and stroked until the veins bulged with engorged blood. Perhaps my father had watched from a far-off distance but otherwise not one member of our family was actually present to witness the terrible moment when these seasoned practitioners of the darker arts pierced their veins. I, of course, was cloistered with all the women, confined to our northern quarters, trembling at the very thought of the sacrifices being made and hardly daring to think about the blood that had spurted up, spewing and gushing into the gaping mouths of the powers that demand such offerings.

Within the illam my father has conducted another puja with the same objective of averting the malevolent threats that hover too close to Parvathy-edathi-amma. His attention to every minute detail is, as always, punctilious but neither then, nor since, has he displayed a single moment's complacency. Instead he continues to seek the benevolence that will ensure the protection of his future grandson. He endlessly and ceaselessly devotes long hours to complex pujas, to making special offerings and the propitiation of each and every deity whose displeasure would otherwise threaten the unborn child. Not for one moment does he risk offending any deity who might place Parvathy-edathi-amma's son in jeopardy.

♓

Now time is moving forward. The day of Parvathy-edathi-amma's confinement is near. Almost everything that can be done has been done. Everything seems to be in order. Yet though my father appears to be content, Parvathy-edathi-amma, the focus of so many rituals, of so many hopes and prayers, is hardly noticed. She moves through the illam like a slow ghost, unobtrusive and overlooked, her physical presence barely acknowledged. Parvathy-edathi-amma only *appears* to be in a beam of light because of the life within her womb. She is seen and recognized merely to ensure that she becomes the mother of a healthy son. According to our customs she should not attract comment; her duty is to bear sons, adhere to our traditions and, finally, to predecease her husband. Otherwise, as now, she should remain unnoticed, invisible and obedient. Yet though she keeps her face downcast and her eyes lowered what I most sense about her is a barely suppressed fear. Her timid voice is rarely heard, and never above a whisper. She has an unassuming nature and always appears conscious of what others may say or think. She trembles and starts when addressed and often seems to be shrinking into herself. And yet, despite her inoffensive presence, I cannot help noticing how often Amma snaps at her and doubts her ability to bear a child whilst complaining about the smallness of her dowry. But, whatever the provocation, Parvathy-edathi-amma remains silent; in any case she has no choice; she must ignore these barbs for she is expected to count her blessings, to remember she is married and that her family has been saved from the burden of supporting an unmarried daughter. She is also no doubt aware that though our illam's expenses are high, and none of us are married, there is as yet no talk of Narayanan-ettan taking a second wife.

Even so it is not difficult, if you watch Parvathy-edathi-amma, to see how frequently a tear will glisten on her cheeks. Once or twice I have tried to talk to her but she shrinks away from all overtures, seemingly too terrified to speak. I wanted to draw her out and ask her about her own family, about her brothers and sisters, her parents. Most of all I had nursed the faint hope that she would describe the journey from her illam to ours, the journey she made when she came here to become my brother's wife. I was curious to know what she had seen. But, in the end, I kept quiet, never asking my questions, not only because I recognized Parvathy-edathi-amma's excessive timidity but also because, in my heart, I knew she had nothing to tell me. I knew she had kept her head down, her eyes lowered and her body well shielded from strangers with her cadjun-leaf umbrella. As both custom and decency demand.

♓

I am no longer a child. I ceased to be one just ten days ago when, for the first time, I was confined to the outside room, kept in isolation and told I was unclean. I am a woman now and, they say, polluting. I must be avoided. My body has spontaneously betrayed me and, of its own volition, commenced the monthly cycles that declare me fertile. And dangerous. I am now not only slave and servant to the moods and rhythms of the moon but bound by the strictest rules of behaviour. I must adhere to that unbending, inflexible code of conduct that governs the lives of all decent Brahmin women. From now until the day I die there will never be any degree of latitude, any indulgence, any willingness to forgive or to condone. Not even for the smallest transgression. Since undergoing my first ritual of purification—so that I could re-enter the house—I have become all too conscious of how much my life has changed.

♓

During the early days of Parvathy-edathi-amma's pregnancy talk of marriage often wafted through the illam. Sometimes there were anxious glances towards my sister Arya-edathi. At eighteen she is, of all Achan's seven daughters, too far past the age of early, decent marriage to calm his worry. Now that my maturity has occurred there is the added awareness, the pressure, that I too am eligible for marriage. I know the matter is discussed. I see my elders talking. Sometimes Achamma is present, interjecting, offering her opinion. Generally voices are kept low, barely above a whisper. Only occasionally does Achan raise his voice, usually as he paces to and fro. No doubt he wonders if any of us will ever be well settled. Ours is an ancient and well-respected family but we have no excess of wealth or land. There are far grander families than ours who must also find husbands for their daughters.

It was during one of these half-hearted conversations that Achamma suddenly raised her voice and commented on our custom that only permits the oldest son to marry. 'Just look,' she said, 'at the number of Namboodiri families with daughters who must live and die unwed. How many girls must wait until they lie on their funeral pyre to have their tali tied? Just so that they may be cremated as married women.'

My father looked at his mother in astonishment. A reaction

echoed in the wide-eyed expressions on the faces of my mother and her two co-wives. They were all amazed that Achamma, a widow, could even think such thoughts. It is decades since my grandfather died. I doubt even Achamma remembers the feel of ornaments, the jingling of her bangles or the coolness of turmeric and chanthu on her forehead. I wonder if she even recalls that day when she took her last bath as a married woman, the day she entered the Vadakkini and, in its small, claustrophobic darkness, listened to the tiny snip of her tali's black thread being cut. Yet, since that day she has, like all Namboodiri widows, turned towards Yama's southern kingdom when performing her devotions and kept her distance on all auspicious occasions. We all know that, though she was my grandfather's favourite wife, she is now, like his other two surviving widows, circumspect, doing nothing that might incur comment or displeasure. Even so she is not like her co-wives. They have almost been erased from our consciousness. They slip quietly through the illam, living their limited, ordered lives, causing no offence, making no ripples. It is Achamma we notice. It is Achamma who has retained visibility. She obeys, to the letter, the dictates of society and presents a calm exterior. Yet, beneath it, I often catch the workings of an inquiring mind. It is not difficult, if you watch her closely enough, to sense her curiosity and the presence of an iron will. Often, though no words are spoken, I feel that she is questioning, even silently challenging, or at least doubting, our customs, questioning matters that otherwise pass unexamined, thinking 'Why?' I am drawn to this side of her character and from time to time wonder how safe it would be to share some of my own doubts with her. But I stay silent, taking no chances. Just in case.

It is only as Parvathy-edathi-amma's delivery time draws near that the unresolved talk about marriage temporarily ceases. Every thought within the illam is now totally focused on the imminent birth of her child—and our longing to welcome her son into our lives. Perhaps, because of all this excitement and anticipation it seems as if I am the only one who notices the condition of my sister, Arya-edathi.

Something terrible is happening to her. She has changed. Even outwardly she is different. The quality of her beauty has altered. She has lost her serenity and there is now a wildness about her, a wildness that disturbs me, that makes me uneasy. And frightened. I sense the change in her and, too conscious of her condition, wonder what it signifies, knowing it can no longer be ignored. Not since that night, two weeks back, when I was suddenly startled out of my sleep.

At first I thought I had been disturbed by a sudden burst of thunder. Yet though rain was falling in torrential sheets the skies were silent. The room was dark. No moonlight filtered in to reveal the cause of my awakening. In the end it was instinct that told me a nearby sound had been responsible—and made me turn to face my sister, close beside me as always. But she lay still, the dark shape of her body denser and blacker than the darkness around us. She made no movement, even her breathing hardly existed. She was almost too still, too quiet and for this reason I knew she was awake. I could sense the tension around her but, unable to see her face, had no way of knowing its source. I lay down again, fixing my eyes on the outline of her body.

For a long time nothing happened. Perhaps she knew—or guessed—that I was awake and so kept still, waiting for me to fall asleep. But I remained carefully awake, conscious and curious, aware of the tension, the atmosphere of contained, frustrated energy. Had Arya-edathi not been the source of this energy she would have sensed my awareness of it and known I was awake. But, cocooned in a web of her own making and adrift in uncharted realms, she waited until she thought—or could wait no longer—that I slept. And she almost deceived me. My eyes were drooping and about to close when I suddenly detected a small movement, a slight stiffening of her body. And then, before I could question my eyes, she moaned. In the too-silent air it was a charged sound, somewhere between a sob and a cry of pain and...And what? I was confused. For a moment, in the soundless silence of the room, I even wondered if I had imagined the sound. But I had not. Within seconds she moaned again; this time more loudly. Then, very slowly, her body began to move. Backwards and forwards, almost as one with the night, hypnotizing me with the constancy of her moaning and the inevitability of her shifting, languorous movements. She was like a fish, motionless yet drifting with fluid slowness through heavy water. Until, after uncounted minutes, a strange shuddering rippled through her body and she moaned once more, sighed deeply. And slept.

For how long did I lie still and quiet before acknowledging that there was now an unfamiliar tension in my body? Why had my sister moaned and moved? Had it been a dream, an illusion? But I sought no answers. Deep within I recognized, even then, that I already knew what was happening, what had happened. Even if I could not, as yet, understand. And this almost knowing suddenly stirred within me a need to hide my face, even in the room's darkness. And to find, when I brought my hand up to my face, that it was burning hot. As if on fire.

Perhaps all this would have been forgotten had it not been for the incident at the tank two or three days later. I had gone there early, when the thin crescent of the new moon offered little light and only a few stars, those sparkling spirits of dead men, shone in the pre-dawn sky. Rain was falling in a constant stream and as I approached the tank all that could be heard was the sting of it hitting the water. Where I saw Arya-edathi. I have never questioned what it was that made me stop and slip quietly back into the shadows to keep my sister from seeing me. She was standing in waist-high water, standing where the rain could fall onto her. Her upper body was bare, her breasts just catching what little light had struggled its way into the sky. Her thick hair was hanging down her back. For a moment she stood like a statue, almost as if petrified by a strange spirit. Then, without warning, she very suddenly broke free of this enchantment and immersed herself three times in frantic, almost desperate haste until, once more erect, she stood for another charged moment, her head thrown back. And then moaned again, the same anguished sound I had heard in our room. A sound that transfixed and mesmerized me. And held me with its tension. And frightened me with its feeling of power and the aura of extraordinary heat that seemed to burn within her, somehow all coalesced with the deliberate way she moved. There was just enough light to see that her eyes were closed, her lips half parted—and that her whole body, her whole being was suffused with a strange bliss, a bliss that seemed to enclose her in a luminous glow. And then she moaned again and threw her head even further back before plunging down into the water, churning it into turbulent motion, creating waves that slapped up onto the tank's stone steps. Despite this sudden violence it was obvious, as she surfaced, that the tension had left her body. But when she lightly caressed her breasts before moving her hands down over her body, I knew and accepted that whatever force had just been exhausted would return again and again to possess and repossess every fibre of her being.

I hung back in the shadows as Arya-edathi left the tank and returned to the house. I felt drained and, for a few moments, stood quite still, caught up in the spell she had cast over my surroundings. Then I ran down the steps, barely feeling the rain hitting my body as I plunged into the still swirling water, conscious only of a desperate need to erase my mind of all I had seen. My emotions were both clear and confused. I had grasped the disturbing element of my sister's behaviour but still denied what had caused it. What frightened me was that I had begun to sense another concern, begun to be aware of the terrible, insidious thought that I too would soon become subject to such tensions. I sensed, somewhere I even knew, that the even temper of my own life was about to end. And within this strange knowing was the even more certain knowledge that once I really knew the source of all this energy, we were all going to find ourselves on the edge of something so cataclysmic that our lives would be ripped apart. Forever.

And so it was that I submerged myself again and again, sinking beneath the water, trying to drown my fears, to quell my doubts, to ignore premonitions and blot out all uneasy thoughts. Yet even though I then scrubbed and scrubbed my body, as if to erase all that I feared, nothing could set me free. I had always believed my life would be one of unruffled calm. One day had always followed the next. I obeyed my elders. I attended to my devotions. Though sometimes reprimanded for paying too much attention to reading I was not forbidden to do so. My love and knowledge of poetry, of literature and of the Puranas was dismissed—but tolerated. Nothing I did was considered unseemly and, though young in years, I always felt sure of the future—and myself. Until now.

Perhaps it was the presence of these unsettling doubts that compelled me, as I entered the house, to look into the dark corner where the cat had concealed itself on Vishu morning. But the corner was empty. Dark and shadowy but just a corner.

Or was it? Just as I passed by it seemed that for the tiniest, fleeting moment I could see two piercing, yellow eyes. I hesitated and peered closer—and saw they were no more than a trick of the light, twin reflections from a lamp. But though relief swept through me I found that as I moved towards our puja room a lingering disquiet went with me.

It was still so early that there was little light within the illam. As I walked around the nadu mittam, I could barely see the rain still streaming down into its stone-lined interior. Only as I approached our Bhagavathi's sanctum did the glow of the oil lamps give enough light to burn away the surrounding shadows and reveal Her luminous image.

Finally I stood before Her, gazing into Her sanctum, knowing again how easy it was to lose myself in the contemplation of Her beauty. She was radiant, already draped in fresh garlands, adorned with the succulent and blood-red chembarathi flowers. Channelled inwards by the light around Her I sought to reach Her heart, to find my way into the balm She radiated, to sink into Her soul-knowing eyes, to reach that region where deceit has no place. For a moment everything was so still even the flames were motionless. The air was limpid; all that could be heard was the rain's ceaseless pattering. Then a flame hissed and spluttered, jumping into movement and startling me.

A tiny trickle of water slithered down my back, dripping from my wet hair as I brought my hands together, lowered my eyes and offered myself to my Goddess. Though I knew that before Her I was no more than an infinitesimal speck I felt comforted. I understood the blessings of our endlessly recurring rituals, our acts of devotion and our pujas—even of my own offerings and prayers—and how they constantly reaffirmed our faith in the protection and benevolence of our fierce but compassionate Bhagavathi. I knew that to dispel my feelings of unease I had only to offer myself to Her. Only then would I be able to set aside the fear that something was going to disrupt the cycle of the seasons and reveal a different order.

A few days ago, as further insurance against any possible misfortune, my father sent a message requesting the Goddess Uccitta to come and bless Parvathi-edathi-amma with Her divine presence. Achan's wishes were transmitted through his intermediary, our kariasthan Achutan Nair. He, in turn, made all the necessary arrangements with Kelu Panicker, the Malayan whose right it is to incarnate the Goddess—and the man whose wife would eventually attend to Parvathy-edathi-amma at the time of her delivery.

On the morning deemed to be the most auspicious, we rose early, anxious that all should go well as we gathered in the half-light near the illam's doorway. Throughout the previous night we had been aware of the pounding beat of drums and, from time to time, we could just catch snatches of the song honouring, evoking and describing Ucchitta. For the women of our illam there was, of course, no thought of even peeping out to witness the rituals being performed in the large compound surrounding the illam; no such act could ever be countenanced. Even the men, both because of the polluting nature of the ritual's practitioners and the need to maintain their caste purity, kept their distance. Only when Ucchitta finally came to give Parvathy-edathi-amma the comforting assurances of Her blessings were all notions of caste suspended.

By then the last traces of the night had drifted away from the sky and we were huddled close to the door in a collective, almost cohesive oneness. Although it was almost frightening to be allowed to even stand near the doors and risk, however fleetingly, being seen, all we were conscious of was our overwhelming desire to see Ucchitta, to have darshan of Her. This single thought so dominated our minds that, like flowers seeking the sunlight, we strained towards Her, as if only the power of our longing would bring Her close to us. When, at last, Ucchitta halted Her slow progress towards the illam's door and began calling out to us in Her uniquely, high-pitched voice, we were filled with awe. We were overwhelmed both by Her sacred presence and by the reality of Her extraordinary proximity. Although, in the normal course of events, there was never any possibility of a Malayan ever seeing or coming close to a Namboodiri woman, not one of us transgressed this rule. Not one of us standing in that doorway ever saw the low caste Kelu; and he did not see us. At this stage there was absolutely no trace, no shadow, no hint of his existence. Ucchitta's divinity had so completely possessed his soul and being that he had temporarily ceased to be. The sacred being seated on the wooden peedham before our doorway was a divine manifestation of that same Goddess who, so many centuries ago, had incarnated Herself in one of our families. A Goddess who, after Her human death, revealed not only Her compassionate divinity and Her willingness to protect and bless us but to bestow the gift of painless childbirth on all Her pregnant devotees.

Although we were now so close to Ucchitta that we could have reached out and touched Her it was barely possible to see either Her painted face or the silver fangs that framed Her laughing mouth. Her features were completely veiled by the pale strips of tender coconut leaves hanging from Her headdress and for a moment we hesitated, suddenly over-awed by Her power and mystery as a sudden, magical shimmer of sunlight fell onto Her silver breastplate. Inwardly each one of us worried in case we offended Her or somehow unwittingly aroused that dangerous and unpredictable aspect that lies dormant within all our powerful deities. It is a potency that can be aroused without warning—to strike wrongdoers with all the deadliness of a venomous snake.

Yet as we hovered with uncertainty it was the normally timid Parvathy-edathi-amma who moved first, surging past us, shoving us aside to stand, like a victorious warrior, in the doorway. It was as if she too had been possessed, as if some inner power had claimed her so completely that her bloated and ungainly body suddenly radiated an almost primal magnificence as she genuflected before Ucchitta. All that Parvathy-edathi-amma wanted, all that she desired, all that she yearned for could be clearly seen in her expression and in the humility and passion with which she held out her offering to the Goddess. There was an unfamiliar boldness about her, even in the way she gave Ucchitta the customary gift of a white cloth and then waited to receive the Goddess's divine blessings. As she did so I noticed the roughness of Ucchitta's red-coloured hands, and how tenderly She gave Her prasadam to Parvathy-edathi-amma. And how She then pulled her so close to Her that She could whisper in her ear. A brief whisper that appeared to quite suddenly release all the pent-up tension in Parvathy-edathi-amma's face and give her an extraordinary expression of serenity. With a tinge of sadness it occurred to me that this distant deity had not only blessed Her devotee but shown her the only kindness and understanding she had known since entering our illam.

♓

Jagged flashes of lightening are leaping across the sky and down into the heart of the illam. A constant rumble of thunder rolls threateningly around us. It is a strange and troubled sound that makes us believe the gods are uneasy and growling their displeasure. There is less rain now, just a few showers and this incessant grumbling that echoes endlessly between the distant hills and us. Even when evening seeps into night and the oil lamps are lit sudden flashes of white lightening sear their way across the sky above the nadu mittam. We keep our voices muted, grateful for the comfort of our house, almost cowering within its walls, aware of the uneasy elements raging all around us. At times we hold our breath and listen for the omens hidden in Nature's terrible voice. Movements are measured. Lamps are carefully placed to prevent their metal jarring our nerves. Buckets are lowered into wells, not thrown. Doors are pushed open slowly to keep their hinges from creaking.

And so it was that in the careful, pre-dawn hush of one of these strange days a great scream rang out through the illam. Another immediately followed it and then another and another until eventually all these screams flowed into one long, agonized howl of pain. At the same time voices began calling from different rooms and bare feet were soon heard pounding urgently towards the source of these terrible sounds. The illam erupted into life, instantly conscious that, at last, Parvathy-edathi-amma had gone into labour. She was immediately carried, her great bulk writhing in pain, to the sanctuary of the outside room. Then, while she was being safely settled where her child could be born without polluting the rest of the illam, someone was dispatched to summon Cheriya, the wife of the Malayan Kelu Panicker. Meanwhile, as unexpectedly as they had begun, Parvathy-edathi-amma's screams suddenly stopped, her last terrible cry hanging for an unnatural moment in the charged silence that followed. Perhaps Parvathy-edathi-amma's pain had lessened, or perhaps she was now more able to bear or at least control it. Or perhaps Cheriya had slipped in through the small door designed for such occasions and was now closeted with the birthing mother, soothing her with expert ministrations.

But then new sounds began. Other voices cried out. People shouted. For a moment hysteria threatened. Then Amma appeared and imperiously began rattling off a stream of instructions, making precise demands, shouting orders and, finally, demanding calm before she went to stand, like a sentinel, just outside the labour room. From there, after a moment's silence, she called out for Nanikutty, our servant girl, to come and help. And then all was quiet again.

But there was no peace. It was an unnatural time. No one knew how long it would last and our anxiety had to be constantly extended to fill the space that surrounded it. Except for the drama's main players everyone was kept away from the room where Parvathy-edathi-amma was bringing her child into the world. My brother, the father-to-be, stayed closeted with the men, all of whom kept their distance and remained out of sight while all the women of the illam retreated to our northern quarters. Like all the other unmarried women I was ignorant of Parvathy-edathi-amma's precise pain but, as the hours ticked slowly by, nothing could prevent me from wondering about the suffering that seemed to accompany childbirth. Each minute and second increased my speculation as every tiny moment measured its own progress, moving so slowly that time seemed to be squeezed, almost coerced into passing. Glances were forever being cast in the direction of the outside room as if by so doing we could somehow hasten time and force it to bring us news. But none came and for two, perhaps three or even four hours little was said. For a while, as the silence gradually stretched into an almost tangible tension, we could hardly breathe. Unspecified fears seemed to flutter about us like panicking birds, filling the space with fluttery unease. Later, as the evening shadows rushed to join the darkness of the coming night, low rolls of thunder began rumbling around the sky and a terrible hissing shivered through the trees. And then we heard what we most wished to deny: the whispers of terrible voices, harsh and unnatural voices, ominous voices. Though they lurked almost silently within the gusting breezes, seeking to conceal themselves behind the thunder we were not deceived. The foulness of their whispers penetrated the thunder's deepest growls and uneasily reminded us of the dreadful and insubstantial shadows that were gathering around the illam, salivating and hungry, almost howling for their prey.

We milled in increasingly distracted groups, enclosed in a void of nameless fears. The older women began making eye contact with each other, nodding and shaking their heads. One or two began pacing to and fro. Hands were clasped and unclasped. Even Achamma looked drawn and concerned. Without a word being spoken it was recognized that something had gone—or was going—dreadfully wrong. And then as if a silent signal had been given, our behaviour changed again and, with one accord, everyone began talking. At first my elders appeared to clutch at the slender thread of hope, reminding us that this was a first child, that labour was certain to be lengthy and that Parvathy-edathi-amma was in good hands. Yet they fooled no one and, all too soon, they betrayed this hope and tacitly acknowledged everyone's growing apprehension by recalling births that had ended in tragedy. Achan's youngest sister remembered an older sibling dying in labour. Another spoke of an aunt who had burst apart, torn asunder by an impatient and misaligned fetus. One of Achamma's co-wives described how she had almost bled to death after giving birth and, in an unusually flat voice Achamma herself recalled the stillborn death of her first child. Along with the other unmarried women I kept silent, aware that as they talked Arya-edathi was holding her hands over her ears to block out these horrors.

With an uneasy shiver, I knew that we were both wondering if such a day might come for us

It was several hours into the night and long after the evening lamp had been lit and darkness had fallen that Amma finally re-appeared. Her face was set in resigned, almost bitter lines. I felt a cold sweat slide across my body, for I suddenly knew, as we all did, that our unspecified fears had been justified.

'A girl...'

Beyond silence and a few tired sighs there was no reaction. Disappointment eddied slowly around the house like the smoky wisp of a dying fire. My mother, as if exhausted by her statement, remained silent, supporting herself against a wooden column and closing her eyes. Then, into the hushed tension of this unnatural silence came the sound of a jarring voice.

'But Parvathy-edathi-amma? How is she?'

Only when my mother turned to face me did I realize that the voice had been mine. Yet though a perplexed frown puckered her forehead Amma's eyes hardly focused on me, or even appeared to register my presence. Instead she just shrugged her shoulders and answered the question.

'She may,' she said with an effort, 'she may perhaps live. But whether she will ever bear another child...'

Slowly her voice faded away into the surrounding darkness where all that could be heard was the faint rumble of distant thunder. For a moment we were all transfixed, as if held hostage by some strange enchantment, petrified into stillness by Amma's numbing disdain. Yet it was Amma who broke the spell by almost brusquely walking away and leaving us with the collective despair of our terrible disappointment.

♓

Everything is different. The entire illam has changed. The anticipation that once filled our house and so excited us as we waited for Parvathy-edathi-amma's son to be born has evaporated. It has been dashed to nothingness. A dull quietness has replaced it, a quietness that is occasionally broken by an erupting outburst of anger. People find fault with everything, simply to find a reason to release their confused emotions. And, all the while, a barely suppressed rage moves tightly through the illam. I have heard Amma muttering about painful delivery, a long labour and, to what end, another unwanted daughter.

The new mother, the cause of all this turmoil, is neither to be seen nor heard. She still lies in the outside room, exhausted by her delivery, confined there to protect us from the pollution she acquired in giving birth. It is as if an invisible wall has caged her, placing her apart from us all, hiding her, almost removing her from our lives. But not quite. Resentment towards her constantly returns her to our thoughts. I wonder at it, especially at my mother's sharp bitterness. She is, after all, the mother of two daughters—and this child is her first grandchild. Achan's reactions are less confusing. His only concern is to search out the reason for his failures, to discover how he could, so disastrously, have misread the omens. He is clear and unequivocal, seeking his answers in his own actions, searching for some small, but crucial, omission in his pujas, some slip-up in his appeasement of the gods. He finds no other explanation for the birth of a girl and so, though his face is stern and unsmiling, he has accepted. Life must now continue. It is only on Achamma's lined and patrician features that I sense softer, kinder, more understanding feelings—though, as yet, she has expressed no concern or curiosity about Parvathy-edathi-amma's condition.

Arya-edathi also appears disinterested. As soon as Parvathy-edathi-amma's delivery was over she resumed her life as if nothing had happened. Perhaps she views the newcomer as not only the arrival of one more girl in our illam but as yet another reminder of her own, increasingly poor marriage prospects. She displays no curiosity about the newborn child. And neither does my brother, the child's father. Even when, ten days after giving birth, Parvathy-edathi-amma was ritually cleansed of her pollution and rejoined life within the illam, he made no move to greet his wife. A wife who in spite of the guarantees implicit in all his pujas and rituals had presented him with a daughter.

I was the only one anxious to see Parvathy-edathi-amma and her child. I wanted to understand why her daughter's birth had cast such a pall of despondency over our lives, why there was no joy in our house, no celebrations to greet her arrival. Perhaps I was still too young to entirely grasp the despair of being female. The burden of having another mouth to feed, another marriage to eventually arrange and another dowry to be paid were still little more than abstract notions. I hovered uncertainly on that thin cusp between woman and child, between ignorance and knowledge, grasping some of the visible and practical disadvantages of being female but too unaware, too innocent and too inexperienced to sense their deeper implications.

And so, the morning after Parvathy-edathi-amma and her child came back into their quarters, I made my way to where they were closeted. As soon as I entered their room I sensed not only Parvathy-edathi-amma's immense stillness but the overwhelming aura of despair surrounding her. She lay with her face turned towards the far wall, one arm lightly, but protectively, draped across the small bundle held close within the curve of her body. As soon as she heard, or perhaps merely sensed my approach, she drew her child even closer and curled herself more tightly around it. Only then did she slowly turn over, bracing her body as if preparing herself to face whatever might have come to threaten their safety. When I saw her face I gasped, shocked at what I saw, of the shadow she had become. All her freshness, all signs of her youth had vanished. Her face was pinched and tired. Her energy had been sapped, her spirit exhausted and her responses dulled. Even the slight glisten in her dull, lifeless eyes was no more than the sadness of silent tears and, in the brief moment after she recognized me, her only reaction was to let a look of desperation flicker across her haggard face. Then, though it was obvious that she wanted to pull away, to deny and reject me, she was unable to summon enough energy. Defeated by exhaustion, she let herself sink limply back onto the bedding, staring mutely up at me with the terrified eyes of a cornered animal.

Very slowly I crouched down beside her and, as slowly, put out a hand to pull back the cover from her child. All the time I was aware of Parvathy-edathy-amma but, though she kept her eyes on me, her body very gradually relaxed. Somehow understanding that I had Parvathy-edathi-amma's permission I pulled back the last piece of cloth, inhaling the strange, fleshy, earthy smell of her baby as I did so. And then I gasped. In wonderment. Before me was a tiny, pinched, sleeping face, a small and helpless miracle lost in a fold of soft cotton. A neat and precise miracle whose every feature was clear, whose tiny fingers were curled and delicate, her mouth a small bud. Only her eyes, closed in sleep, were hidden from me. Her expression was peaceful, as if blissfully unaware of how little she was wanted. But what, I asked myself, was there to dislike? Surely she was too tiny—and too wonderful—to be considered unwelcome, a nuisance and inauspicious? It was as these thoughts entered my mind that Parvathy-edathi-amma, with a sudden surge of unexpected energy, sat up and placed her child in my lap. She moved so quickly that, for a brief moment, I thought she had disowned her child and was pushing her away, rejecting her. Yet as soon as I had settled her child into my lap I looked up and saw the pure radiance of undiluted love shining from in her eyes and grasped the extent of Parvathy-edathi-amma's tragedy. In that single moment I knew all her pain—and sensed her repressed joy. Had it not been for her aura of terrible sadness her plain features would have been transformed.

A silent smile passed between us before I looked down at the sleeping child and saw her tiny, petulant little frown and the small bubble escaping from her bud-like mouth. Though about to speak I stayed silent, suddenly catching the threat of a small sound and a too-close sensation of movement. I stiffened, tightening my arms around the baby, conscious that we were no longer alone as Parvathy-edthi-amma lowered her gaze and withdrew into her inner misery. I turned round as a shadow stretched across her bed and momentarily shut out the light. Then I looked up and saw my brother, standing just behind me, in the doorway.

'Ettan,' I said, trying not to swallow, 'isn't she pretty? Just look at how beautiful, how tiny, how perfect she is...Just look at her.'

There was no reaction. He said nothing; he gave no sign of even having heard me. Instead, completely ignoring me, he stared down at his wife, as if trying to reach a decision. Instinctively I knew he was waiting for me to leave and, as certainly, that he was about to reject them both. Aware that no words of mine would ever change his mind I pushed his newborn daughter back into Parvathy-edathi-amma's arms. Then, almost sobbing as I saw the frantic fear in her tensed body, I jumped to my feet and fled, anxious to avoid their confrontation.

♓

A few days later the monsoon finally entered its last phase and we began to feel a change in the air. A cool, rustling breeze often shimmered through the trees to surround us with a gentler and kinder atmosphere. Faint snatches of birdsong lifted our hearts. The click-clicking chirp of insects spoke of renewed activity. A lethargic heaviness was removed and splashes of brilliant sunshine surged through clearer skies.

Yet, in the end, this was merely one of the many deceptions. One of the many signs whose inner truths we overlooked. For it was on the late evening of one of these seemingly innocent, even promising, days that the final collapse began. It was then that a man, a stranger, came to our illam. Of course I never saw his face; as a woman I kept well away from strangers. But I soon heard all about him.

He was, so the gossiping servants said, a Nambiar. He was about my brother's age and I was later to remember that

Nanikutty was the one who told me how handsome he was. It was also soon known that his name was Sadasivan Nambiar and that he was, in fact, the nephew of Achutan Nambiar, my father's kariasthan. Within hours we also knew that because Achutan Nambiar was seriously ill he had sent his nephew to be his replacement. A gesture my father had accepted.

If only, if only his wisdom had not deserted him, so much would now be different. But, by then, it was only a matter of time. What was to happen was by then inevitable.

I can no longer be sure how long it took for me to become aware of this Sadasivan Nambiar's effect on Arya-edathi. At first I imagined, if I thought at all, that it was simply chance that positioned her where without being seen, she could see him. It was easy enough to believe most of this was, in fact, no more than mere coincidence as his visits to the illam were not regular or even daily ones. Furthermore his work took him to quarters we never ventured anywhere near. He could never have been visible for more than a few fleeting moments—and his attention would have been directed towards my father's needs. In truth it was not that I really saw Arya-edathi looking out for Sadasivan Nambiar but that I sensed her waiting to see him. And it was also not so much that I was conscious of her reaction when she did see him but of her sudden change of mood when she failed to do so. It was then that her pacing increased, that she walked round and round and round the nadu mittam, often looking out towards the great outer doors as she did so. Things began to affect her in other ways too and she often over-reacted. Once, when we were both in the kitchen preparing vegetables, her knife slipped and a thin sliver of blood oozed from her thumb. It was a small cut and cannot have caused her pain. Yet she gasped and stared at it in apparent shock before bursting into tears and rushing out of the kitchen

In the unreal void of her exit all that could be heard was a sudden spitting crackle from the fire. A familiar sound but for some reason it seemed vaguely ominous. Perhaps, even so, this would all have amounted to no more than a strange episode had not fate somehow made it possible for Sadasivan Nambiar to see Arya-edathi. Later, when conjecture was by then meaningless, it was impossible to wonder how this could have happened. The terrible, almost unthinkable thought is that Arya-edathi somehow engineered it. Otherwise how could a stranger, a man not of our family or caste, ever see the face of a young, unmarried Namboodiri woman? Whatever the truth, the fact is that it happened and it is sufficient to say that though I was not, of course, present I did detect a marked change in my sister that was later connected to this time. She was calmer for a start, with a more contented air about her. She often smiled, sometimes an inward, secret smile perhaps, but still a smile. Even so, even then, her expression was sometimes so unreadable and enigmatic that it reminded me of my Goddess.

Then, almost as abruptly as it had begun, this tranquil mood disappeared and was replaced with her original, distracted state. Except that where she had once contained her frustration, keeping it locked within her, she now threatened to lose all self-control. And where I had once been the only one to observe her condition others now began watching her. For a time they were deceived, at least about the true origins of her condition for, quite unexpectedly Arya-edathi came down with a fever. For days she lay in her room, moaning and tossing, sweat pouring from her body. I had no clear understanding of what was happening to her—of what was really wrong—but I sensed the presence of something dangerous. And so without knowing exactly why I insisted on being the one to sit with her, ostensibly to wipe the sweat away and care for her but, in truth, to protect her from herself. I was frightened that in her feverish state she would say something forbidden, something dangerous.

From time to time she would mutter and mumble words I could not catch. Occasionally she looked up at me in desperation, her expression of despair cutting into my heart like a sharp knife. Once she seemed on the verge of saying something, of confiding in me but then a closed look crossed her beautiful, tormented face and she turned away and sobbed into her pillow.

♓

Something terrible is happening to me. Something I cannot understand—yet know I must keep silent about. It is as if a slow fire has been lit within me and is gradually reaching a higher and greater heat. At certain times sudden flushes rush their way across my face and uneasy thoughts worm their way into my mind; thoughts I must suppress, must forbid. For the last four days I have again been confined to the outside room, paying once more the penalty for being an unclean and polluting female. It has given me time to myself, to attend to my thoughts, to try and understand the source of my predicament. But to no avail. Though I have now taken my bath and rejoined life within the illam, I feel as if I am a stranger within its walls. Of course my body has changed in the last few months. I recognize that and understand that I am now physically different, that I am no longer immature, no longer a child. It seems as if, as my childhood vanishes, that a certain natural innocence is going with it. It terrifies me for I feel I am now edging closer to an understanding of why my sister is so disturbed.

I also cannot help but observe that whereas my mother and grandmother previously used to keep a wary eye on Arya-edathi they now not only watch me as well but constantly warn me about the dangers of going too near the outside doors, of being seen by strangers. I am told to behave with decency, to move with decorum. I am no longer eligible for that special indulgence due to all children. One chapter of my life is over and, at times, it seems as if the new one is written in a script I can barely decipher. Every day brings me new doubts, new worries, new thoughts—thoughts that circle around me, fanning my strange confusion, making me question who I am and what I have now become. But at least the daytime is filled with light, duties and distractions keeping me from my thoughts and pushing my worries into the deepest recesses of my mind. It is the nights that are less compassionate for as soon as darkness descends an insidious torture begins, invading my mind with uneasy dreams, unfathomable longings and strange images. It is then that I seem to feel strange arms envelop me, enfolding me in the darkness and seeking to revenge themselves on the wasted hours of daylight. I cry out even against the idea of acknowledging the thoughts that come to me. But in vain. They laugh in easy triumph as they overwhelm me, assailing me with an unfamiliar and languorous sense of desire. My body burns and strange sensations flood through my whole being, forcing me to listen to the dangerously seductive voices that whisper all around me. Though I pray constantly to my Bhagavathi for guidance—and to rid me of all these strange sensations—I also wonder at the inner force that makes my body so betray me.

For the first time in my life I begin to wonder if I will ever be married and what marriage really means. In our illam there are, besides my sister and I, five other women of marriageable age. And this number ignores the fact that there are also women for whom there is no hope of marriage: my father's three unmarried sisters and the surviving daughter of my grandfather's second wife. They were, long ago, edged from our consciousness, their dreams of marriage pushed aside by the growing hopes of a younger generation. And yet were they not once young? Did they not also have hopes? Does anyone now think of their lost dreams? Does anyone see how life has been drained out of them, has been sapped from their bones? Does anyone see how meaningless time is for them, that their days are filled with useless chores, with empty and unending duties that have no meaning or satisfaction? I consider the differences between them and Achamma, herself alone these many years. And I see the purpose in her, the satisfaction and joy—perhaps sometimes pain as well—of seeing her children grow, of seeing her son, my father, marry and have children. Something in her has been fulfilled. And yet is she not also the mother of my three unmarried aunts? How does she feel about them, for them? And as these thoughts come to me, I think of my father's younger brothers. Both, of course, have remained unmarried in order to keep our lands and property from being divided or reduced in size. Like all younger sons they are expected to lead pious lives, devoting their energies to the scriptures and the worshipping of our deities. No doubt there are some illams where such expectations are fulfilled but my youth and innocence has never shielded me from the reality within our illam. Unless some important puja or ritual demands their presence, neither my two uncles nor the three sons of my grandfather's second wife are ever seen here after dark. None of us ever questions where they go or how they pass their nights though we all know they are enjoying sambhandam with various Nambiar and Nair women.

Nambiar and Nair women. They are the ones we secretly envy. Their lives are fulfilled without any shame ever being attached to their name. They may openly enjoy their relationships with our men or even, if they so desire, with the men of their own caste. Furthermore, should a time come when they grow tired of their nocturnal visitors they may simply bar them from their beds—and welcome others to their side. Though they may never, it is true, make any claim on our name or wealth their children can openly boast of their Namboodiri ancestry.

And so while these women may claim at least some control over their lives we Namboodiris must accept whatever comes our way. Some, like Amma, are fortunate for they marry and bear children. Others will count themselves blessed at being married at all—even though their husbands may sometimes take other wives. The less fortunate amongst us are forced into marriages where the only, all-too-brief satisfaction is wearing a tali, married off as children to men old enough to be their grandfathers, to endure a short, cruel marriage before the interminable hell of widowhood. Many wives are forced to ignore the transgressions of husbands who quite openly enjoy casual relationships elsewhere—whilst demanding that their wives live blamelessly circumspect lives without even the faintest whisper of suspicion attaching itself to their name. This ruthless and unremitting adherence to our society's visible demands, to its expectations of decency, to its sense of correct behaviour is what dominates our lives. Most especially it dominates the lives of all unmarried women who live and die in their own illams, forever vulnerable to the terrible temptations and unmentionable evils that wait to corrupt and ruin an unguarded woman.

I fear that both Arya-edathi and myself are now doomed to the emptiness of such lives. A realization that, though it now overwhelms me had not, until a few short weeks ago, ever concerned me. It is only now that I attempt to fight the inevitability of such a fate. It is only now that I try to suppress my unfocused thoughts and deny the dawning awareness of all that stretches endlessly before me. I do this in the only way I can: by submitting myself to my Goddess. I spend long hours before Her sanctum, seeking to still my fears, to trust in Her benevolence. I gaze longingly at the beauty of Her enigmatic features. I immerse myself in Her smile. I sense both Her nearness and Her compassion. Yet however often I seek some sign I am disappointed. She remains silent and unmoving and nothing ever dulls the conflicting confusions that tremble within me. And nothing ever stills the emotions now struggling against my upbringing, against the belief that I must always accept whatever fate may bestow upon me. And now, into all this inner conflict has crept a new element: the distress and confusion that wells up inside me whenever I hear Nanikutty singing. Though Nanikutty has always sung while going about her duties it is only now that I begin to understand the meaning of the lilting melodies forever on her lips. They are the songs of Thiruvathira, the annual festival celebrated by Nambiar women as they rejoice in the rebirth of Kama, the god of love. These are the songs that greet the dawn of Thiruvathira day, sung as they gather at the tank to bathe and again when they dance and adorn themselves. Thiruvathira is the day when every Nambiar woman dreams of her future husband and rejoices, certain that her observance of the festival will soon grant her a happily married life. Though this festival forms no part of our ritual calendar I have always been familiar with its songs—though unconcerned with their content. This year something has changed; behind their lyrical sweetness I have caught suggestions of a vastness, of an almost primal power I now feel I will never know. I cannot be disappointed by my ignorance for I have no real knowledge of the territory they encompass. I am guilty instead of a sense of curiosity, of an uneasy longing and, most of all, an inherent feeling that, deep within me, something is being denied. Sometimes I wonder why Nanikutty sings these songs at this time of year—softly it is true but always so that I can just hear them. But then I see that she too has changed. She moves about the illam with a fresher, lighter step than usual, her head held high and with laughter in her voice. There is a newfound air of certainty about her, a sense of sureness in her step.

And then, without knowing why, I think again of Arya-edathi's distress. And mine.

♓

And so the circle is almost formed. It is the last day of Karkadakam and I am back to where I began my recollections. All the dirt and dust and rubbish of the year has been swept up and gathered in a pile. Everything broken and unwanted has been heaped together and tied up in a huge bundle. Nanikutty has been called and, amidst the traditional cries of abuse, sent out, carrying everything unclean and inauspicious with her. With her, we believe, has gone the inauspicious Jyestha, the Goddess who brings dirt and disease, misery and strife, the very opposite of the wealth, prosperity and blessings that radiate from the benevolence of Lakshmi. In the morning Nanikutty will return, fresh and glowing and pure from her bath, having abandoned, well beyond the illam's compound, all the troubles that have haunted our lives in the last twelve months. The month of

Karkadakam is finally drawing to its close and we are now edging into the hopes and promises of Chingam. Tomorrow, when Nanikutty re-enters the illam, we will be free to begin a new year, untroubled by old worries.

♓

The second day of Chingam dawned with a pure and fresh innocence. As usual I took my bath in the tank and then hurried through the illam to reach my Bhagavathi's calming presence, anxious to offer up my prayers. I gazed into Her sanctum and, as always, soon lost myself in the contemplation of Her presence. I felt myself slip into Her compassionate arms, into Her world, into a unity with Her. For uncounted moments we were as one and I knew, with absolute certainty, the total omnipotence of Her power and blessings. I felt a strange sense of bliss, of utter peace and, for a strange moment, a knowing. Only very gradually did She release me from Her spell and restore me to an awareness of my surroundings. Her gentleness trapped me willingly and I took one more glance at Her image before moving to the nearby corner, the secluded spot I think of as mine. It was at that precise moment, as I reached up for the manuscript kept wrapped on a nearby shelf, that I heard the ominous, warning chirp of a lizard. Its high-pitched sound pierced the rain's falling splashes and alerted me to another, less expected sound: a nearby bubble of laughter. A bubble that frothed up in an involuntary, spontaneous way. And then stopped. Unfinished. Cut off. Suppressed. Yet though it was gone almost before it had existed my imagination kept it echoing through the illam's quietness and, as it finally evaporated into silence, I wondered if I had really heard it. I stiffened and listened, my ears picking through the illam's natural noises, trying to pinpoint the presence of something new. I had nearly given up and denied the laughter when suddenly I heard another sound, this time of muffled scuffling. And then again silence. But this time I knew I was not mistaken. The silence that followed was charged. Someone was holding their breath. Someone nearby. I looked out of my corner, peering towards the nadu mittam, to where the first light of day was filtering in through the rain. But I saw no one. Everything was normal. Nothing was out of the ordinary. I saw nothing and heard only the inconsequential sounds of a house coming to life.

But I was not deceived. Something was wrong, something had changed and, knowing this, I held my head up, straining to catch even the smallest sound, listening for the movements I felt someone was trying to hide. And so it was that I caught the faint squeak of a door being too carefully opened. And seconds later saw Nanikutty come quickly out of the nearby storeroom. So I had heard someone laugh. But why? And what had made her laugh? I frowned, watching her walk away, moving swiftly around the nadu mittam, stroking a hand along the pillars as she did so, caressing them, feeling their smoothly polished wood. She held her head up high, moving gracefully, effortlessly, her poise suggesting not only satisfaction and achievement but power. And then she was gone. From sight but not my mind.

A strange silence fell. And then again I wondered why she had laughed. And what had caused the scuffle. I almost stood up and almost moved to try and see more. But, before I could act, a greater force made me cower back into my corner. My face flushed. It was suddenly obvious. Someone had been with her. Someone who must still be in the storeroom. Someone who did not wish their presence to be known. The thought sank like a stone in a pond, its portents rippling out to tell me I was on the verge of dangerous knowledge.

I did not have long to wait though it seemed that as every second passed it was stretched to an unnatural length. My heart pounded, the sound swelling until it seemed to fill the house. Then I heard the tiny squeak again and knew the storeroom door was once more being cautiously opened. Crouched in my corner, where I could not see the door—and dare not look out to see—I felt the presence of someone standing there, looking to see if anyone was around. And then, unable to see me, they felt secure. And so stepped out. To where they could be seen.

It was my guru.

In an instant he was gone. Out and around the nadu mittam, out of the main doors, out and away, out of sight. He was in and out of my range of vision almost before I could register his presence. Gone, leaving nothing, no trace to confirm his passing. Gone before I could react. Before I could deny. Before I could question. Before I could ask why he had been in the storeroom. Or why Nanikutty had laughed. Or why that laugh had been cut off.

But not before he had briefly turned and seen my face. And known it was me.

I shivered. Now I was beginning to know and understand. The time had come to accept everything. No matter what might happen.

I turned and faced my Bhagavathi. I knew now that the fate of my family, and my own fate, would soon be decided. There could be no escape. No sidestepping of the inevitable. I recognized that being innocent would never protect me from mortal pain. The long months of waiting were over.

The time has come for me to understand how closely I am—and always have been—bound to my Bhagavathi. The days of denial, the reluctance, the avoidance, the refusal to see and accept what was clearly before me were over. No longer could I hover on the periphery of Her promises or ignore the vastness of Her universe. The months of gazing with intensity at Her image were over. It was no longer possible to pull back from the final leap, from going beyond, from discarding the exterior shell and plunging into the deepest inner depths, of closing my eyes and seeing. The time had arrived for me to offer myself, to enter into Her heart, into the very core of Her sacred mystery, to seamlessly unite myself with Her. The time had finally come to fulfil the prophecies that have dogged me since birth. And finally, though I can now consciously ask the question 'who am

I?' it is only now that I am disinterested in the answer. It has become meaningless. A strange power has begun welling up inside me. There will be fear and danger ahead but they will be mere ornaments on my journey. My Bhagavathi will be with me, enclosing me in Her compassion and benevolence. At last I can see the truth I have so often turned away from: that there has always been, deep within me, the absolute knowledge of the larger realm that She will soon guide me towards. This, I knew, was the moment to offer Her my entire being, to prostrate before Her. To be Her. To realize, fearlessly, that whatever was about to happen would affect my frail mortality and could not be avoided. And need not be feared.

I gazed, as if with fresh eyes, into Her sanctum and saw how the oil lamps produced their light and bathed the otherwise dark interior in a golden glow. The dullness of their metal shimmered gently and it suddenly seemed that their light was glowing, shimmering and shining all around me. Then, without surprise, I knew that I was within the aura of their golden flames and gazing outwards into the illam's darkness, conscious that the lushness of the large chembarathi garland around Her neck was cool against my skin. I knew the lightness of my fingers as they gently touched the garland's sensual succulence. I swam into the vastness it adorned, knowing I was in Her arms and that my arms were Hers. And finally, with total trust and joy, I let go of the last inner doubts and plunged fearlessly down into the embrace of a boundless ocean, hurtling towards unity with the Absolute.

♓

From that moment on there was no measuring of time. There is no way I can say if it was merely minutes or hours or even days later that the shouting began. In any case by then it no longer mattered. I only knew that, from somewhere within the illam, there was suddenly an unnatural noise that grew louder and louder until it eventually resolved itself into the hysteria of too many people all shouting at once, gathering around me, pointing fingers, screaming and accusing. I swayed, nearly fainting, gradually hearing their words, seeing individual faces, recognizing them and knowing that the last act of the drama had begun in earnest.

It is silent.

I am running. I am alone. The light is thick and grey. My eyes are open. I am not blind but there is a nothingness before me. I am enveloped in a vast, billowing cloud of dust.

I am frightened.

I run faster, hurtling through the enclosing mists. Not knowing where I am going. Not knowing how closely I am pursued. Running towards something that will soon loom out of the silence and reveal itself. Something I can never hide from. Something that even now is swelling into loudness. Something that knows my name and is calling me.

It is a sound that terrifies. It beats and thunders and echoes. It howls its horrors. It reverberates through the universe. And it is like the air around me, the nothingness I cannot see. It is everywhere.

It is fire.

And yet I was no longer frightened.

I was no longer frightened as I turned to face them. No longer frightened as I felt a great wave of a peaceful calm sweep through me and knew, at last and without doubt, that I was inviolate.

I knew them all, all their faces, all their gestures and voices. Amma, my aunts, even Achamma (so I had been right not to confide in her). No men as yet, though I knew they would soon come, drawn to the centre of this eddying gaggle of hysteria: my sister, Arya-edathi. Drawn to where they would see, as my eyes did now, her distracted wildness and the state of her loose, dishevelled hair, her crumpled clothes, her tear-streaked face and her distraught, contorted movements, the twisting of her whole body. But would they also notice, as I did, the hands that were on Arya-edathi's arms? Would they see how these hands did not so much support as restrain her? Had the women—and would the men—see that these were Nanikutty's hands and ask why they were there and then see how the tightness of their grip revealed what her carefully guarded face kept hidden? Yet even though I asked myself this question I accepted that I alone would be the one to voice it. For only I could possibly know Nanikutty was using this moment to protect herself, to generate hysteria and divert attention away from herself. Whatever was now happening—and whatever its outcome would be—was being engineered by Nanikutty.

Slowly the shouts, the screams and the cries died down into individual words, separating out, one from another, becoming clearer and less ambiguous, gradually forming complete sentences, growing into an entire statement. Then, like a ball of unravelling cotton, their shouting began again to gather momentum, to roll faster and faster, to spew out revelations, to make them plain and clear for all to see. Making them too clear—and too terrible—for any one of us to deny their meaning.

♓

Arya-edathi, they all screamed, had been found alone with Sadasivan Nambiar. A virgin high caste Namboodiri Brahmin girl had been found alone with an unmarried Nambiar man. It was unthinkable. Inconceivable. Unnatural. It was prohibited. And yet the thoughts that crossed my mind followed no such path or gave them even a moment's notice. Instead my attention was drawn up another path, lured by the hissing of the tiny inner voice that whispered in my ear, its insidious murmur telling me that Nanikutty had known about my sister and Sadasivan Nambiar for some time. She had known but was only now betraying her. Only now when she needed to protect herself, to conceal her own illicit relationship. With my guru. A relationship they both now knew I was well aware of. Nanikutty was moving fast to create distractions, seizing a God-given moment to horrify us all, to bring vengeance down on Arya-edathi, to cause righteous indignation and, by so doing slip away, undetected, from under our noses. It was a dangerous game and yet it was already obvious she was winning. No counter accusations were going to absolve my sister of her wrongdoing. All that now remained was to see how fate would deal with Arya-edathi. And then with me.

It was not a long wait. It ended with the arrival of the men. Drawn perhaps by the cacophony of the women, perhaps alerted by some messenger. Perhaps, I conjectured, by my guru himself. He was there. I saw him at once though he hung back, well behind my father and my uncles, even behind my brother. He, like Nanikutty, had masked his face, though with less success for he did not, of course, expect to be subjected to any scrutiny.

My father pushed his way through the women, shouting at them to calm down, to be quiet and explain themselves, raising a restraining hand when they all began talking at once, turning to my mother and asking her to speak. For a moment there was a terrible charged hush. Not exactly of silence but of foreboding. It was as if we all recognized that this was the last moment when things could perhaps be left untouched, when they could be ignored, and our lives continue uneventfully. But the moment passed, sighing away, taking our last hope of innocence with it. Forever.

'It is her,' my mother spoke, not even looking at Arya-edathi or giving her a name, 'she has shamed us all. She has dishonoured us all, our family, our name. She was found—and alone too—with your kariasthan's nephew.'

There was another charged pause before my mother continued.

'She is no longer my daughter.'

By now our group resembled circling flights of crows, all appearing to move as a united whole though each one of us was on a separate path, each with our own voice, our own thoughts and ways of expressing them. Amma's words released a great torrent of ill-defined words, of agreement, dissent, conjecture, rage, abuse, all shouted for maximum effect and to gain notice. Again my father raised his hand and for the first time Arya-edathi, the source of all this hysteria, was addressed.

'Is this true?'

♓

No direct answer came. Instead Arya-edathi burst out into torrents of uncontrolled weeping, struggling against Nanikutty's firm grip, trying to pull away from her as clouds of black hair cascaded over her face, heightening rather than hiding the wildness of her eyes.

'And you, Thattakkutty, what do you know of this?'

My heart plummeted and thumped hard against my chest. So this was how I would be pulled in. I looked up and at my father, knowing I would rather see his face than even glance towards my guru. Though I could sense his tension for, unlike Nanikutty, he still feared me.

'Nothing, Achan. Nothing.'

'But child this cannot be. You must know something. And,' his voice dropped to a more threatening tone,' you must tell us.'

I stayed silent. In essence I had told the truth for what did I actually know? I had never seen anything pass between Arya-edathi and this Nambiar. I had never seen them together or displaying any awareness of each other. And yet I knew. As Nanikutty knew. And as I knew about Nanikutty and my guru.

'Speak!'

But my lips stayed sealed, fear creeping across my heart, a film of sweat drifting down my body. How was this drama going to play itself out? How were they going to trap me?

And then my guru stepped forward. To play his vital role.

'These sisters are close. She knows. She must be made to speak.'

My father nodded an assent, almost peevishly accepting the obviousness of my guru's logic.

'She knows as much as the other one. Too much perhaps. How many times has she been seen gazing out of the illam? How many times has she looked out at strangers and watched them from the shadows? She is no innocent in this matter. She too must be questioned, must be made to speak. The purity of this illam must be upheld, its women must be seen to be chaste. In mind and body. Let me question her.'

There was nothing my father could say. My guru was older and a respected scholar—and the good name of the illam was now at stake. He shrugged and gestured with his hand, waving it between my sister and myself, uniting us as he gave my guru permission to proceed.

'Answer me this,' he said, 'Tell me—truthfully—which is the greatest of all the rasas and which is the greatest pain?'

Did I keep my expression a fathomless blank or did I reveal my dilemma? He had trapped me. I would not, could not lie and yet—though they would know the truth of my words—they would choose to misconstrue them. There was no escape now.

And so for the last time I turned round to face my Bhagavathi, to seek Her blessings, to beseech Her presence and, above all, to ask that She should set me free.

And then, with a feeling of utter calm and stillness, I replied, hearing my words ring out, seemingly shouting them loud enough for them to be heard throughout the illam even though, in reality, everyone strained to hear my reply.

'The greatest and most powerful rasa is sringara, the erotic emotion. And the greatest, the deepest of all pain is that of childbirth.'

The shock of my words caused a collective hissing, an inward rush of breath. Hands went to mouths as if to prevent the involuntary escape of any other such statements. Even my guru, his ambition achieved, looked shocked and gasped in disbelief, almost doubting that I had so completely fulfilled his needs even as a sly smile that barely masked his triumph edged fleetingly across his face. Arya-edathi's predicament was almost forgotten. She was no longer the quarry. I was. And, moreover, I had been hunted down without the slightest effort. The only deceit now being displayed was that of denying the truth of my words, of using them to condemn me. At least they knew that I knew what game was being played, knew that I knew the absolute truth and knew that they were liars to abuse its facts.

♓

Hours later after the hysteria had abated, after they had screamed that no unmarried virgin could give such answers and I had been confined to my room, and Arya-edathi placed elsewhere, I was still as calm as when I had given my answer. All I had to do now was wait, wait for the releasing moment that would come. And be ready for it.

Time passed but without the normal measuring of its seconds and minutes and hours. There were none of the usual markers. No one brought me food and, up in my room—the room I had always shared with Arya-edathi—its thick door remained firmly locked making it almost impossible to know what was happening downstairs. I wondered constantly where Arya-edathi was and what her fate would be. And how she would bear it. Her future was too grim to contemplate should she be made an outcaste, condemned to the hell of a living death, shunned by all Brahmins and kept beyond the protective fold she had always known, belonging nowhere and to no one. There was no worse fate for a decent Brahmin woman. And so as the shadows within the room gradually lengthened and the day grew darker and a fitful moon began rising above the trees I began to wonder how, in her present state, she would survive. I moved to the window and gazed up at the sky, just managing to see the stars but more conscious of the thicker, darker and suddenly ominous shadows of the trees and undergrowth that surrounded the illam. I shivered.

And then, without warning, a terrible scream howled through the illam, as loud and clear as if it had originated right beside me. For a moment it seemed to ring out forever, blocking out all other sounds. And then it was gone leaving nothing but an imagined echo to carry it endlessly out into an eternal silence even as its portents continued to shriek their message through my head. I did not need to wonder or conjecture or be told what it signified. I knew, with absolute and utter certainty, that my beloved sister, my doomed Arya-edathi had somehow taken her own life.

♓

I moved to the door, feeling a frantic need to go to her, to be with her broken body and console her departing spirit. To honour her. Even though I knew I would be banished and kept away, even though I knew the door was locked from the outside. I was overwhelmed by the sorrow gushing through me. I seized the door, pulling at it with all my strength but without the conviction or even the hope of it moving. But I was mistaken. The door opened easily, the shock of it throwing me backwards. In the brief moment as I recovered my balance I once again examined my position and predicament. I was in disgrace and banished to await whatever punishment my family would deem appropriate. If I left my room I would invite even greater displeasure and going to my sister would bring their full wrath down upon my head. I hesitated, briefly undecided. But then, without further thought, I walked out, moving quickly and quietly down the steep wooden stairs, drawn to where the now audible crying was welling up from somewhere beyond the nadu mittam.

What happened next I can never know—or seek to explain. I reached the bottom of the stairs and was already turning towards the noise and commotion when something caught my eye and I suddenly saw that the illam's great outer doors were open.

The moment had come. There was no further hesitation. There was no decision. No conscious thought. I felt my Goddess unite with my whole body and spirit. I felt Her arms enclose me, Her energy surge through me, guiding and supporting me.

And then I felt Her power. And heard the sound of that power. And flung back my head, laughing as I swept upwards, melting into Her form, taking Her shape, feeling with Her hands, running with Her legs, transcending all shapes and forms and space, becoming as one with Her as She, I, We ran towards the doors. And through them. And beyond them. And away.

Into the enveloping mists. Towards the swelling loudness. Towards the beating, howling calling of my name. Towards and into the fire. Uniting with the air itself, becoming like the waves with the sea and the flowers with the sun, weaving into the indivisible mystery. Becoming the absolute stillness. The breath and spirit of life. Standing in majesty. Or in simple humility. Or not at all.

ACKNOWLEDGEMENTS

Although this novel began its long gestation in 1989, during my first visit to both Portugal and Évora, I doubt much would have happened had I not met Ulisses Rolim. It was ultimately his friendship, understanding and willingness to help that drew me back to the Alentejo and made all the difference, especially after my first, and crucial, visit to the Cromeleque dos Almendres. It happened on a crowded Sunday and though I sensed its power it was very obvious that its ancient forces had withdrawn. Ulisses observed my hesitation and said: 'Come, let's go, I will bring you back at six o'clock in the morning.' After that there were many drives and walks to different parts of Évora's surrounding countryside, all of which were instrumental in bringing my vague ideas into focus. My gratitude to Ulisses, and Paula and his children, Pedro and Inês, is immense.

Through Ulisses I met the Évora historian Manuel Branco who was unfailingly patient, gradually presenting me with a detailed overview of court, convent and daily life in and around the region in the sixteenth century, thereby giving me a foundation on which to build my story; factors I deeply appreciated when I finally began to write.

It was through my friend Lotika Varadarajan in Delhi that I was introduced to people who could guide me through the labyrinth of Portugal's history and the voyages to India. While her own knowledge opened my eyes to facts and small details she also put me in touch with others who could help. I am grateful for these introductions and for the information they shared: Dr José Malhão Pereira who took time from his busy academic work to give me details of the Carreira da Índia ships and their navigational problems, checked the journey up the Mandovi River and the overhauling of ships in Moçambique. Lotika put me in touch with Vitor Rodrigues who gave me some precise and valuable information about these voyages as did the internet group—lusonautica@yahoogroups.com. I owe particular thanks to Jorge Semedo de Matos for details of the 1545 sailing and also to Alexandre Monteiro for further information.

When it came to life in Portugal's convents Lotika continued to be exceptionally generous with her contacts, most especially to Dra Maria de Jesus dos Mártires Lopes who was kind enough to take me seriously and help prevent serious errors.

Then came her introduction to Sasha Lima who, when I again returned to Portugal in yet another last attempt at unravelling the complexity of life in convents, and much else besides, not only invited me to stay but took me into a world I would never otherwise have known existed. She walked me all over Lisbon, pointing out tender evidence of the past, of where buildings had stood before the disastrous 1755 earthquake destroyed everything. She explained about food and its significance and symbolism, about birds, and the land, about Portugal's passion for the Virgin Mary and I soon understood Lotika's statement that 'Sasha knows everything.' And then there was the magical journey when we travelled from Faro in the south, winding our way north via an extraordinary assortment of convents large and small in and near small towns and villages.

And it was through Sasha's friends that I went deeper into this world, most particularly Maria José Boléo Tomé who was not only endlessly helpful but initiated the extraordinary visit to the Monastery of São Dinis at Odivelas that was organized by Maria Luisa Paiva Boléo for which I am especially grateful. As I am to Ana Mântua who helped with a visit to the Madre de Deus Convent which is now the Museu Nacional do Azulejo and who, in turn, introduced me to Ana Cristina Pais at the Alentejo department of the Ministry of Culture in Évora who, in turn, was generous with her time and contacts.

I would also like to mention Rosa Paes at the Évora tourist office who was attentive and enthusiastic about helping me on several occasions as were the staff at Évora's Town Hall where I did all my emailing. Also that on my first fact-finding visit to Portugal I met David and Lena Evans in Lisbon who were kind and understanding—and have remained so—pointing me carefully towards Évora.

I am enormously grateful to Luis Moura Rodrigues who, when he was Cultural Counsellor at the Portuguese embassy in Delhi, made the suggestion that I should apply for a research grant from the Gulbenkian Foundation in Lisbon. In turn I am grateful that they agreed, making my wanderings and first long stay in Évora possible. I am glad that the publication of this novel finally enables me to publicly thank them for their generosity since more than twelve years have passed since I seriously began work on this book.

Since these acknowledgements come at the end it may be wondered why neither Suffolk or Malabar are mentioned. I was brought up in Suffolk and have spent decades in Kerala. My debts to both are substantial since both gave me the kind of 'knowing' that is subconsciously absorbed. I am grateful to all those who made that possible.

While I have been the recipient of people's time, patience and specialized knowledge I accept total responsibility for any factual mistakes that may be present.